Make-Believe Ballrooms

Make-Believe

PETER J. SMITH

Ballrooms

THE ATLANTIC MONTHLY PRESS
NEW YORK
♦

ALSO BY PETER J. SMITH

Highlights of the Off-Season

ACKNOWLEDGMENTS

The author gratefully acknowledges the support, suggestions, and surgery of Gary Fisketjon, Amanda Urban, Cynthia Maxim, George Minot, Garth Battista, Anne Rumsey, Marie Behan, Robbin Schiff, and through the ages, Bob, Jean, Squeaky, Ginger, Mica, Smokey, Jaffee, K. James and Smith, and of course, my family.

Published simultaneously in Canada
Printed in the United States of America
FIRST EDITION

Library of Congress Cataloging-in-Publication Data

Smith, Peter J., 1959–
  Make-believe ballrooms / Peter J. Smith.—1st ed.
  ISBN 0-87113-318-0
  I. Title.
PS3569.M537912M35 1989   813'.54—dc19   88-39292

The Atlantic Monthly Press
19 Union Square West
New York, NY 10003

Design by Laura Hough

FIRST PRINTING

Wedding Blues

*A*fter Kitty fell out of the window I fell into the abyss. How could I attend a wedding feeling so hollowed out? A day before the ceremony I . . . .was still walking around in a stupor, thinking of Kitty's "passing," that big faker of a euphemism, as though she'd merely overtaken me in a low, speeding, red convertible and vanished down the ramp of a condemned highway. The rain in New York that day was warm and heavy, stunning the car top in a drumroll that might just as well have played at my own funeral—tink, tink, tink, like some pitiful, windup marching toy clapping its life away. I couldn't even remember who my brother was marrying.

That part's not entirely true. I could remember, if I had to. My brother Beck was marrying Lisa Lyman, the most heinous girl I had ever met and, in my opinion, since brothers are familiar with the cast of characters that pass through each other's lives, that my brother Beck had ever met. All the anesthesia in the world—sleep, liquor, elixirs made from little-known vegetables or from the papaya—could not dilute that unhappy June's day fact, or make my brother's name any less a synonym for folly. My sister Fishie has always maintained that Lisa Lyman was, pound for pound, the worst girl ever born of civilized man, in the history of birth, death, cribs, rattles, proud parents, et cetera. But Fishie has inherited our mother's gift for hyperbole, so how could she ever know? My sister, for all her laps around the world, surely doesn't know all the girls.

Fishie made up a standard survey on the tough, brown, crinkly side of a grocery bag, in which she concluded that Lisa Lyman, as an abomination of nature, led the "worst-girl" division in the categories of presentation, poise and congeniality—that Lisa was a kind of giantess contessa in the bitch world of the New England and Atlantic regions and should maybe consider competing on an international level. Unfortunately, in the clothes division—swimsuit, evening gown, culottes—Lisa made up most of the points she'd lost on personality, since it just so happened that she owned more clothes than fifteen normally spoiled women strung together. I could tell the final results depressed my sister, who moped for a day and a half, barely picking at her polenta. So okay, I told Fishie, so Lisa wasn't the worst girl ever born, but her score was still spectacular, thrilling—eighty-eight points out of a possible hundred.

There was a lot to do that miserable Saturday. I would go to the wedding of my unreliable and self-destructive brother and the girl he had chosen to be his hostage, and then, following the reception, Fishie and I would go bury Kitty in All Souls Cemetery, three miles outside the lackluster mill town where we all grew up. Elsewhere around the country someone would just be hearing the bad news, someone else would be giving birth to a child, someone would have just filed for divorce. It was a rotten world, and everybody, not just me, had their random sorrows. I felt even to my tasks, however, and my self-pity that day was at least specific. Kitty's death had betokened me the tearless virility that comes of sorrow, and I felt close to the Big Picture, if not dragging my feet in its mud.

Fishie had offered me a ride up to the north shore of Massachusetts, where Lisa's family had a huge house in Pride's Crossing. It was a disaster. In fact, it was one of the worst rides I believe I have ever taken, worse than any, for example, I have ever taken on a Greyhound bus—even though I have long admired the sullenness of seatmate-runaways on these buses when you ask them about their pasts or where they are going. When Fishie pulled up the morning of the wedding—in Son, a family car of sorts—I saw that she already had two passengers in the car, people to whom she had also offered rides. This annoyed me more than I can say. I had planned to stretch out in Son's backseat, my neck supported by the window on one side and my bare feet hanging out the window on the other. I had a huge deer's head I wanted to sketch on my white drawing pad. There were other things on my mind—sorrowful things, issues of mortality, mine, Kitty's and everybody else's. Instead I ended up crunched between a person I barely knew and another I didn't know at all. I would have gladly abandoned my vision of the backseat, the air rustling through my toes, and climbed into the front seat, but the front seat was completely obscured by a three-foot-high pile of clothes.

"Beck forgot to pack his things," Fishie explained once I was in the car and gasping for air. "You know, the honeymoon cruise and all."

The guy beside me put out his hand—and only then did I realize it was Dave. I'd gone to college with Dave and had naïvely assumed I would never have to see him again. How did he know my brother, for God's sake?

Dave wore a loose gold watch chain across his hip, and glasses so thick the lenses looked smeared with olive oil. Behind the lenses his eyes were white and pleading. As usual I was pleased to see people I had gone to school with already starting to go bald.

"What are you doing here?" I snarled.

"Oh, I ran into your brother a couple of weeks ago. On the street. It was an amazing coincidence. He said he was allowed to invite three hundred people on his side and he just didn't know that many people. He said he didn't think he'd met that many people during his life. So I said, How about me, can I come? And your brother—who's such a great guy, by the way, I really like him—he said, Sure, come, and bring a friend along too."

Oh, no, I thought. Knowing my brother, he had probably posted signs on the streetlights and construction sites of all the major cities in the East, announcing that he hadn't filled his wedding-guest quota yet and that there were plenty of unobstructed seats still available. Free hors d'oeuvres! Dancing! Bridesmaids! Champagne! I Dos! First Come, First Served! I could just imagine the kind of wholesome crowd this would attract. Every drug dealer and his brother would probably make an appearance.

These days, Dave told me, he worked for the Shaklee Corporation, selling vitamins and health supplements door-to-door. Before that he had been the assistant Midwestern distributor for a major brand of dental hygiene instrument. "I'm having the time of my life too. I'm not just saying that. Are you"—Dave lowered his voice dramatically—"at all acquainted with the Shaklee group of vitamins and health products?"

"Oh, yeah," I said. I wasn't really listening to him. *My poor Kitty,* I was thinking.

"Are you?"

"Yeah, I've seen the jars," I mumbled. "They're dark brown . . . they rattle. So you go door-to-door trying to force people to buy your vitamins, huh? I suppose somebody has to do that job."

"Well, Shaklee products *are* the best," Dave said primly.

How anybody could take their work so seriously was beyond me. "Well, that's good," I said, shifting my concentration to Son's cracked gray ceiling, which was peeling off in strips that resembled egg noodles. "So what makes them the best? In your professional opinion."

People love to be thought of as professionals, no matter what they do. It explains the death of mystery in their lives. Even morons like to think they're carrying out their moronic ways with some degree of polish. At that very moment Son's whole chassis shook and started making thumping sounds as if we'd suffered four flat tires simultaneously. "Ssshhh," I heard Fishie murmur, and her bitten fingers stroked the wheel. "Calm down . . . I know, let's do *rhymes*: There was a young zebra named Lou/Who set out with . . ."

Fortunately for me, Dave told me he was acting under a strict non-disclosure agreement. "The company'd kill me." Dave gave an almost self-deprecating laugh. "I can't say anything about my work. Unless you promise not to say anything to anybody."

"No, no," I said. "I can't keep secrets all that well, thanks anyhow."

"Well, you'd keep *this* secret, wouldn't you?"

I waved him away. "No, no, I'd end up telling the first person I saw, and the second and the third. The whole thing would backfire on you, Dave, please give it a rest. And please, everybody"—I took the opportunity to address the whole car—if any of you want to keep your secrets secret, *don't* tell them to me."

"Oh, and this is my cousin, Mary," Dave said, gesturing to the woman sitting on the other side of me. "She's visiting here from Munich."

Mary nodded briefly without moving her eyes from the back of my sister's head and past Fishie's ears and yellow pitbull earrings to the highway.

Mary was beautiful as a rock. Her blank green gaze was a miracle of uncomprehending vacancy. She wore her blond-brown hair Marine-style, over a smooth, white-skinned face that could handle the cut. Very few women could've worn their hair so short and gotten away with it, certainly no one I knew, but what did I know about women, anyway? When they closed their eyes, when they were dancing and a little sweaty, what was going on behind their eyes? Probably they were thinking about the same things everybody else was, but I liked to think the thoughts of women were mysteries more ancient than my own. Women knew how the dinosaurs had died out, they just weren't telling—*Ya can't make us.* What struck me first about Mary were her eyes—looking into those eyes was like gazing into the whirls and whirls and whirls of a time tunnel. One glance into those eyes and I was in Venice arguing with an elderly waiter . . . in Leningrad reading "Goodnight, Moon" to the tsar's children . . . in Beijing wishing everybody a Happy New Year, *forgetting that the Chinese New Year was actually two months down the line.*

I returned to the lowering thumps of Son. It had been a blissful trip abroad—and I believe everybody should do it before the age of thirty, go, that is, and alone, to foreign countries—but I had responsibilities in New York, and frankly I had missed America, with its perfumed magazines, military academies, cruel hazing ceremonies, Hollywood movies, choice of cable channels and evangelists, not to mention my strange, unambitious girlfriend.

I was stunned that Mary could have ended up being related to Dave. I decided to think of Dave as Mary's cousin, not the other way around.

"Mary, what do you do?" I yelled. Helpfully Son echoed my yell. Around foreign people I tend to yell, as though they were not only foreign but deaf and moronic to boot.

Mary smiled thinly, sniffed and looked out the window. Her smooth white jaw moved up and down, precisely and without sound. Mary was the whitest woman I had ever met—she looked part envelope. A moment later, when I thought she'd forgotten all about it, Mary turned her green gaze on me, tacking her gum to the back wall of her bottom teeth. "I buy the things," she said in a heavy accent, turning her cheek back to the window.

"Mary doesn't have her work papers," Dave explained. "She can't work in the U.S. yet. All she can do is window-shop, buy clothes and sneakers. At least till her papers come through. Right, Mary?"

"New York is good for the clothes," Mary said. "Uh-huh, okay, Dayffe."

"So, Hal, I talked to Beck," Fishie said before I could resume my scintillating conversation with Mary. "He told me to tell you to give him a normal wedding present. Not something recycled. He said Lisa doesn't really have a sense of humor when it comes to gifts. Beck says, I quote, Gifts are big business to Lisa."

Damn, I thought. For my brother's wedding present I had planned to do what I usually did; that is, dig up something Beck already owned and rewrap it in new paper. This is something of a tradition in our family, around Christmas time, birthdays, anniversaries. Fishie and I scavenge the basement and attic for broken lacrosse sticks, moth-eaten sweaters that don't fit, snorkel and mask combinations, warri-bead board games Beck brought back from some island and never played, then we patiently rewrap them in new paper. On Christmas morning the profusion under the tree is extraordinary—you'd think this was Christmas for a family of seventy-five.

Fishie usually pads around the room, insulting the tree ornaments. Beck squats down, feeling up the long package. "A new tennis racquet?" he says softly.

"An old tennis racquet!" I scream as Beck unwraps the blue-bordered Stan Smith autograph model he hasn't laid eyes on in fifteen years. I sit watching as Fishie unwraps the old sixty-watt light bulb that, for a year at least, faithfully lit her bathroom mirror. "Wow," she says, shaking it so you can hear the broken coil rattle delicately inside. "Terrific, Hal. I really missed this. Jeez, I wonder if you can get these fixed anyplace . . ."

"Sure you can," I chuckle.

"Thanks, Hal," my brother says, taking a few experimental swats with his old racquet. Once Beck had loved that racquet, and now he could love it again. The light in his eyes—shy, flickering, childlike—sums up to me what Christmas is all about. "I never really took advantage of this racquet the first time around, but now—"

"Now you can, swell little sport." I'm good—no, very good—at finishing my brother's sentences for him, though people tell me this is no reason to break out the mint juleps.

Next to me Dave was singing show tunes in a loud, husky voice. Since the backseat windows went down only halfway—Son was a taxi in his youth—I felt like I was trapped inside a torture box. When Dave wasn't singing, Son was shaking and thumping in protest. I kept glancing over at Mary, ignoring the half-drawn deer's head in my lap, trying to get her attention, but she was staring out Son's window at the sequence of gray telephone poles and occasionally swallowing heavily.

I tried to remember some German words, so that Mary and I could have an intelligent conversation. My mind went back to all the German movies I'd ever seen, but the only images that came to mind were eels and pickled jellyfish, men wearing shorts and black knee socks and a pack of howling German shepherds, probably my least favorite dog in the world. The only word I knew, unfortunately, was *tannenbaum*, and a series of harsh throat sounds that indicated meaty pleasure or dismay. No, I also knew *weltschmerz*, which I believed had something to do with a gigantic, staggering sorrow—the sorrow of big, strapping boys and girls, the sorrow that can infect an entire mountain village.

I held my white pad tight between my knees, with the sleeve of my jacket covering my right hand so no one could peer into my lap and see what I was doing. First I drew the deer's eyes, which were sweet and bulging, and then I moved down to the neck and jowls. I had torn the deer's face and an address label from the back of a magazine in my dentist's office. "Draw Pixie the Deer," the advertisement explained, "and you can become a famous children's book illustrator! Earn commissions, respect!" The idea was to sketch Pixie's head exactly as the head was pictured in the magazine, down to the forky brown growth under her skin. The idea of being a famous children's book illustrator didn't exactly thrill me, but I wouldn't have much money until I turned thirty and perhaps if I won, I could earn a subtle income as well as the respect of children the world over. I had no problem drawing the face, but outside Northampton I got stalled on Pixie's nose. The nose in the picture I was following had soft, dark, stiffened nostrils but I had made a couple of crucial mistakes. I had given Pixie a third nostril and an accidental scar across her cheek. Also, I had fouled up the eyes, making them so slanted that Pixie looked capable of immense cruelties, nothing at all like the smiling, idiotic beast in the advertisement.

"Isn't it rich . . ." Dave had started singing again. "Are we a pair . . ."

I gritted my teeth, and that way, for ten minutes at least, my ears melted onto my brain and I couldn't hear anything, just Son's urgent, closeted thumps. Since Son's engine is located in what's normally the trunk of most cars, the engine fumes were gumming up the backseat, a smell I hoped would make Dave shut up. But it didn't—he merely sang louder.

Finally I screamed, "It's not that we're all tippy clowns, it's *there ought to be* clowns! *Ought to be* damn clowns! Not *all tip-pee*! I can't stand listening to your version any longer!"

"No, I don't think so," Dave said doubtfully.

"No, I don't think so, Dayffe," Mary repeated in her waxen German inflections. She was sitting on the side of the car where the blue wire hanger curls around to secure the door, the result of a wreck sustained when Son once tried to outrace a Dodge Dart. The hanger bent across Mary's lap, tying on a notch inside the ashtray, enclosing her in a kind of minimum-security prison.

"So, Mary," I yelled over Dave's voice, "This Christmas your family will be together—will you all be purchasing a *tannenbaum?*"

I was immediately drowned out by Dave, who had moved along to "Get Me to the Church on Time." I was furious.

"I'm gettin' married in the morning," Dave sang. "Ding, dong . . ."

"Dink, donk. Dink, donk," Mary said. She reached behind my shoulder to shove her awful cousin. "What you saying to the people, Dayffe?"

I was more than anxious to be helpful. "It's a sound effect, Mary." I hiccuped hysterically. "Bells? Like say, on some Sunday morning back in Germany when you're walking along the street filled with *weltschmerz?* And you hear the bells coming down from the ancient steeple and maybe it's Christmas, too, and you have this little *tannenbaum* in one corner of the room all lit—"

Mary shoved Dave again. She looked confused. "Okay, what is he saying about, Dayffe?"

Dave went on singing, oblivious to all of us. Ding, dong, the bells are going to shine—hah. The bells of the world were going to go silent all at once, then they would crumble. The falling shards would strike innocent passersby and there would be more than enough lawsuits and bankruptcies and prison sentences to go around. I was so angry I bore down on my pencil too hard and the citrus slice of deer mouth I was drawing ripped through to the next page. I had to pull down another piece of paper and start all over again.

After a while Dave noticed that my mouth wasn't moving, that in fact I was glaring at everybody. "Come on, Hal," he said. "Join in for the chorus!"

"No," I snarled. "I don't sing in cars. *Ever.*"

Mary was staring straight ahead, sucking on her fingers. Whenever she finished tasting a particular finger, she would remove it from her mouth, making a puckering sound with her lips. The next thing I knew, she'd spit her gum out onto her palm and offered it to me with a thin, mocking smile. I assumed this was just Mary's way of being friendly, of bridging our two countries—or maybe it was the German way, sharing your gum with people you didn't know.

"What?" I yelled.

Mary said nothing.

"No," I bawled, "what? What do you want me to do with it?"

Mary was mute. Flustered, I picked up the gum and watched her watch me with her green, psychotic eyes as I tried to decide what to do with it. *Weimaraners have those eyes*, I told myself. *Weimaraners that kill children and other small animals.* The gum was still damp and I rolled it back and forth between my palms as though it were hot, rather than rapidly chilling. Then it occurred to me that maybe Mary wanted me to throw the gum away, but that didn't make much sense, since the ashtray and the windows were closer to her than they were to me.

Mary made a motion toward her mouth and I took that to mean she wanted her gum back, but she said, "No. You! You . . . *arschloch!* Now you eat it down!"

I put the gum in my mouth. I know that sounds disgusting, but I wanted Mary to have passion for me, and chewing her recycled gum seemed like a step in the right direction. The gum was flavorless and dry, without juice—it was thoroughly chewed out. Mary gave me her thin smile and then, grasping my chin with one hand, she reached inside my mouth with two fingers, fished around a little and plucked the gum off my tongue, replacing it inside her mouth.

"Ugghh," said Fishie, who had witnessed the whole thing in the rearview mirror.

"You are *idiot fool*, Howl!" Mary hissed.

We reached the church at around one, an hour and a half before the wedding. It was a relief to get out of Son, but show tunes were still ringing in my ears. Even when we stopped for pizza in Concord, Dave wouldn't stop singing. He had rushed through the scores to *Carousel*, *Showboat* and *A Chorus Line*, and he was starting in on *No, No, Nanette* when Son came to a rolling, thumping stop. Inside the restaurant Dave told Fishie how resentful he was that most of his favorite music was written from the woman's point of view. How could a man—a *guy* singer, for heaven's sake—ever sing "My Man" or "Bill"? I pointed out that Frank Sinatra had changed the lyrics of "The Man That Got Away" to "The Slut That Got Away," but Dave was inconsolable.

"Then there's 'The Slut I Love,'" I went on moodily, "instead of 'The Man I Love.'"

"The Slut I Love, *Jack*," added Fishie, who thought Frank Sinatra took liberties.

I was in the restaurant bathroom when the door opened and Dave loped in. As he prepared himself in front of the urinal I said casually, "So what's the story with Mary?"

At one of the tollbooths Mary had removed her shoes and begun unrolling her purple stockings. She unpeeled each one slowly, and then, when they were off, she had begun lashing my face with them like some crazy queen punishing one of her slaves. She did it in slow motion, without expression, and with each lash she muttered a series of quiet, mesmerized noises that sounded like "*Chah, Chah, Chah.*" When Mary was done lashing me, she tossed the purple stockings out the window and put on a pair of sheer black ones. "Oh, don't stop lashing me," I said mildly. "I like it when women lash me across face, cheeks, lips."

But Mary glared back at me, "*Ich pisse dir gleich ans Bein,*" she whispered—whatever that meant.

As if that wasn't enough, Mary also had some kind of sharp instrument, a pen or a knife or an ice pick, in her right-side pants pocket. I didn't know what it was, but my guess is that it was an ice pick. She kept her hand in her pocket, and at regular intervals she would jab the ice pick into my thigh. Whenever I'd move closer to Dave or shift my legs or open my mouth in pain, Mary would punish me by driving the ice pick deeper into my hip. Though the pain was unbearable, almost musical, I didn't say anything. In retrospect I believe I was in shock and beyond sensation. Now, in the bathroom, I examined my leg under the bright overhead light. The skin had broken through and there was a perfect wound on my thigh, and blood darkening my trousers just below my belt.

Dave washed his hands and held them underneath the silver blow-cone on the wall. He worked his fingers under the warm air like a miser. I had never seen anybody use a bathroom blow-cone before except for copilots in airport bathrooms. "What do you mean?"

I wrapped a damp towel three or four times around my sketch pad and then I shoved it down my pants, improvising a shield for my left thigh. "I don't mean to be insulting or anything," I said, "but is Mary *on* anything?"

Dave said, "I don't understand."

"*On anything!*" I screamed. "As in, for example, *on* methadone. *On* a major group of amphetamines."

"I don't know, but I sure wish I knew because I'd sure like to have some." Dave laughed, but it was a laugh of anxiety, rather than complicity. Then he completely lost control. "This graffiti, it's disgusting, Hal, isn't it? Don't you think? Why don't they do something about it?" Dave laughed hysterically. "I mean, I'm not offended by it, take a lot more than that to make me, whatever, but some people, I'm not shocked, but some people—"

"The drug problem, Dave! Drugs and Mary!"

Dave shook his hands miserably under the hot air. I could tell he wanted to wipe them on his pants but that his clothes were too important to him. The cone kept blowing, even though Dave's hands were now jerking wildly at the towel dispenser. He edged over to where I was standing. "Don't say anything, don't tell Mary I said anything, but I think she may be high. Dolls," he added dramatically.

"Dolls?" I whispered back.

"You know, dolls." Dave looked at me as though I were hopelessly out of touch with modern times. "Yeah, dolls," he repeated after a second. "You know, Valley of the Dolls? Dolls to get you up? Dolls to get you down? Dolls? Pills?"

"Oh, dolls. God, yes, that changes everything. Christ, yes, dolls, we're dealing with dolls here." I had never met anybody who referred to pills as dolls. Maybe the expression had come back one night while I was fast asleep or arguing with Veebka.

Dave told me that a week ago a doll had fallen out of Mary's brown bomber jacket. Dave had found it under the seat cushion of the couch in his mother's apartment, along with some loose change. It was a big red doll, Dave explained, and he grinned nervously. "I sent it to this good friend of mine who works in a drug laboratory, you know, to get the thing analyzed? And he—this good friend of mine—he said it was some kind of major animal tranquilizer—"

"*Daktari*," I murmured.

"I think actually it was a lithium Mare'd stolen from my mother. And last night I found twenty-three more of them in her suitcase. Twenty-*three*."

I was about to ask Dave what he had been doing inside Mary's suitcase, but I kept my mouth shut. If Mary had swallowed twenty-three lithiums, this could account for her dry throat and her anxious, repetitive swallowing. At the table Mary had drunk everybody's water, and then she had demanded another pitcher from the kitchen. When the waitress reminded her of the water shortage in Massachusetts, Mary had snarled something in German and upset two chairs. "Giff me vahtah not then but *now!*" Mary had howled on her feet and shaking. "Not then but *now!*"

"By the way, would you like to have lunch sometime?" Dave said. "When we get back to New York?"

"Uh, sure," I answered unhappily.

Dave took out a small black date book. "It's Saturday today. Party all night long, right? How about Monday?"

"I can't Monday," I lied.

"Tuesday's open for me too."

"I'll be going away Tuesday," I lied.

"Wednesday's good. Actually I'm having lunch with someone; but I could do it Thursday or Friday. Or any day the week after. Or else I could cancel my Wednesday lunch if you could do it on Wednesday."

Dave was the kind of guy who pushed and pushed until you broke down and were carted away and committed to a hospital for ten years. "I'll be going away on Wednesday," I lied, realizing as I said it that I'd already said I was going away on Tuesday. Where was I going? I knew then why I didn't like Dave. He made me tell lies, and afterward I felt slimy and crooked. But what could I say? I will never have lunch with you? Ever? I just didn't have the heart. Saying that would've been too barbaric—and besides, who was I?

"So where are you going?" Dave wanted to know.

"Which? Who? Him? You? Me?" I finally got it right.

Dave peered at me. "You said you were going away."

"Right," I said. "Yes. Going away. Uh, to Czechoslovakia." I couldn't stop all the lies my mind was forming, one after another, like perfect pancakes.

"How long are you going for?"

"Anywhere from a week to fourteen years," I said quickly.

"Have you been there before?"

Stop it, I begged him silently. *Stop asking me these questions.* "Myriad times," I lied grandly. "Beyond myriad. I go every year. To the springs. The healing mineral springs. The Czechoslovakian mineral springs. Myriad," I finished.

Outside in the parking lot, I asked Dave whether we could switch places for the rest of the ride. I didn't want to risk sitting next to Mary anymore, even with my drawing pad stuffed down my pants. Dave said he was willing to change places only if I called him the second I got back from Czechoslovakia.

In the rearview mirror Fishie looked at me oddly. "Planning a trip behind the Iron Curtain, fella?"

"Sure," I told Dave, "sure I will."

Sitting by the window made the rest of the trip much more pleasant and gave my poor thigh a chance to recover. It also gave me time to prepare for the strain of seeing Lisa.

My brother Beck was marrying a girl named Lisa Lyman, an heiress to money made off something profoundly ridiculous—those damp towels they tong you over on thirteen-hour airplane flights, or at certain family lobster restaurants, the ones that leave your whole face feeling sticky as a mimeograph. Family Wipes, they're called, and they come in three distinct flavors, each one smelling worse than the last: lemon-lime, Strawberry Sunrise, and the most popular fragrance, Forest O'Firs, which smells like a gymnasium whose floors have been mopped up with day-later vodka martinis.

A couple of years back, Family Wipes was bought by a huge Midwestern conglomerate, and now Lisa was so rich it was hysterical; her richness practically convulsed me; it put me on the floor—I'd rise, beg her to stop, and go right back down again. Hence the knee pads.

My sister was standing on the steps in front of the church, talking to Lisa's father. She was wearing a long blue dress, and whenever the wind blew, she trapped the fabric between her knees like a field hockey goalie.

Mr. Lyman was describing to my sister the perfect dog. "You want a broad skull, of course, with nothing rude about it," he was saying. "A benevolent expression, almost papal. Tender-mouthed, symmetrical, *clean*. Remember, these guys are gundogs. The aim here is to keep away like the plague from dogs with dishface or snipey head."

"Snipey head?" my sister said with infinite false politeness.

"A weak muzzle. The snipey-headed retriever looks something like a seal. Remember," he repeated, "these guys are *gundogs*."

Mr. Lyman was a tall man with a long, saturnine face and wide, flat hips usually enveloped by baggy khakis. He raised field-trial champions in his spare time. My Excellent Dogs, he called them, or else, These Excellent Postwar Bitches. Ever since Mr. Lyman had sold his wife's Family Wipes concern, his spare time included the mornings and afternoons of most every day. His Excellent Dogs performed precision drills across the lawns of the Northeast and, occasionally, across international grasses. All of them, according to Mr. Lyman, were descended from the great Dorcas Bruin, a glittering pup-figure in golden retriever history.

Mr. Lyman was an assimilated WASP who had been proud of his own family until his marriage to Lisa's mother thirty-five years ago. Now you couldn't really tell him apart from the rest of the Lymans. Today Mr. Lyman was wearing an old seersucker suit, wiggly pins of faded blue alternating with pins the color of dried glue. Sweat was beginning to spread across the throat of his shirt, and a limp silver whistle hung from a black shoelace around his neck.

"Of course," Mr. Lyman added sadly, "in my particular . . . unhappy circumstance, a dog with dishface or snipey head is better than no dogs at all."

Mr. Lyman had been planning for weeks to give an exhibition of raw dog talent later on, during Lisa's wedding reception, but earlier that morning his two favorite retrievers had gotten sick and then sicker. Three hours before the marriage ceremony was supposed to begin, they were rushed to the vet where it was discovered that both dogs had cystitis; they had systematically been eating the white gravel on the Lymans' driveway. The dogs had performed at the weddings of all his other children, and this would be the only Lyman wedding without Mr. Lyman's Excellent Dogs parading across the lawn. Even though it was his youngest daughter's wedding day, Mr. Lyman seemed transfixed by his loss, and this gave him a bitter, distracted, mournful air.

Lisa emerged at last from a car her sister Andy was driving, and strolled over to the church steps. "Hi, you guys! Daddy, where did you get that awful *coat?* It looks like something out of *Hanoi*. Hey, Hal, you made it, well, hello day-ah," Lisa said to Fishie, who stiffened like wheat.

"Lisa," I said, as formal as a footman. Lisa always liked to pretend she had served a tour of duty in Vietnam. Many of her analogies came from that difficult, ambiguous war. If the cut of someone's coat or a particular landscape didn't remind her of Hanoi, it was invariably Saigon, Khe Phang or her own invention, the Asian peninsula of Ix-Nay Hope.

"Proper hug," Lisa said, pulling me into her but as usual doing no kissing herself. Lisa always expected you to kiss her, and in return she just barely touched your cheek with one sixteenth of her skinny top lip. It felt like the nibble of a baby tick. Afterward you felt almost sexually embarrassed, adolescent and desperate, as though you had lost your cool and lunged when you were supposed to have bowed.

As Lisa hugged me I started humming the theme song from the State Farm Insurance TV commercial. This is not because I am in any way a slave to television—it had to do instead with a strategy I had concocted for torturing Lisa on her wedding day. What I planned to do was to plant the State Farm Insurance jingle subliminally in Lisa's mind, until she retched. The State Farm Insurance jingle had an almost satanic sticking power. Lisa wouldn't be able to hum or even think about anything else but the State Farm Insurance jingle for weeks. Soon she would suffer a terrific nervous breakdown—the Big NB, as Lisa called it—and spend the rest of her life spiking volleyballs off the roof of a mental hospital.

"Like a good neighbor," I hummed softly, "State Farm is there." Lisa didn't seem to notice, but I could tell I had done some first-rate subliminal damage, since she hummed the last two words along with me. I had planted the first seed.

"Hey, Hal." I fielded an appallingly strong handshake from Lisa's sister Andy. Also kissless, Andy always greeted me as though we were two former athletes reunited at some beery Sheraton Center team reunion. I was often surprised that she didn't whack me with a dirty towel, or string me up by my jockstrap on a locker room nail.

"How're your nerves holding, sweetie?" Mr. Lyman said to Lisa.

Lisa didn't appear to have heard him. Lisa never appeared to have heard anybody. She extended her white-gloved arms and glanced up at the steeple and the old white clock on the steeple and the clock-white sky. "Well, I'll be," Lisa crowed. "It's a Maxfield Parrish sky! How unbelievably *moving*." Lisa was always saying it was a Maxfield Parrish sky. Most of the time she didn't even bother to glance up at the sky before she said it. When it was hailing, when it was the middle of the *night*, Lisa said that it was a Maxfield Parrish sky. "So how do we think I look," she asked Fishie in a bored voice.

"You look fine," my sister answered brusquely. My sister had made a vow that morning to be nice to Lisa on her wedding day.

"God, I am *so* jealous you can wear that dress," Lisa told her, almost admiringly. "I wish I weren't so damn thin, that my shoulders went *out* more like yours, there's so many things I want to wear but I can't, they'd end up looking like Khe Phang *body bags* on me, you know?"

The legacy of the Vietnam war, the ways in which its memory intruded on all aspects of Lisa's daily life, was dully and forcibly constant. Each of us nodded sympathetically. Sometimes there was nothing to do around Lisa but purse your lips and shake your head solemnly, as though a wave had just washed away your favorite lighthouse.

"Everybody's been telling me all day that I look radiant, beautiful, yada-yada-yada," Lisa informed the group with a bored, disadvantaged expression. "That I look like a million bucks, et cetera and so forth, but I think I look like a goddamn *bag* lady. You know, someone toss me some *hot dimes* please, right now, et cetera, *thank* you. There's something wrong with this dress, it won't tie right in back."

"Let me help you," Fishie said softly. She came up behind Lisa, gathered some fabric in her fists and pulled it in tight. Lisa laughed nervously.

My sister kept pulling. Lisa's face was getting very red. A gurgle came from her throat. In retrospect I think my sister was trying to sever the bride.

"Too tight?" my sister inquired. "Now, Lisa, you be sure and tell me *when.*"

"That's fine," choked out Lisa.

"I could make it tighter—"

Lisa shook her head—by this time her larynx was completely sealed. "It's okay now," she managed to gasp.

"And how are you holding up, Sir?" Mr. Lyman said to Lisa's little brother. "Have you pressed flesh with everybody? You know Hal. Now look Hal straight in the eye, straighten your shoulders and press flesh."

Lisa's little brother was named Edward, but everybody called him Sir, since his parents wanted to get him in the habit of treating his fellowman with respect. Sir was seven and home from boarding school for the summer. He had long, prematurely gray hair that fell in bangs over his eyes and the start of his nose. His hair had aged overnight when he was four, from the strain of having Lisa as his sister. I thought of it as kind of a silent scream.

Sir went around the group, pressing the flesh. When he had shaken hands with everybody, his father frowned and said, "Now, how about the poem for all these excellent people? The one we've been going over, you and I, these past few days."

Sir looked mystified. "Me, me, me, me," he chanted softly under his breath.

"Sir? Come on, wake up, let's hear the one you and I've been working on. I'll start you off." Mr. Lyman lowered his voice. "I like—"

Sir was squeezing a green plastic grenade. At least I think it was plastic—I tensed in delight; maybe it wasn't!—but then I glimpsed the Mattel sticker and my spirits sank again.

"I like—" And then Sir stared dumbly at his father with his mouth open.

"A look of agony—"

"A look of agony—" Sir faltered.

"And why do I like a look of agony?" Mr Lyman rapped the toe of his shoe against the church step. "Sir?"

"I like a look of agony because . . . because—" Sir looked around helplessly. "Because of the fly?" he said meekly.

"Because it's *true*," his father crowed gently. "I know that's why *I* like a look of agony. I like a look of agony because it's *true*. Now, what insect, what fly?"

"Because it's true," Sir repeated. "The fly—"

"I believe you may be making reference to another poem, Sir," his father said. "The poem about the buzzing fly."

Mr. Lyman recited:

> "*I heard a fly buzz when I died.*
> *The stillness in the room was like the stillness*
> *In the air between the heaves of storm.*"

Mr. Lyman glanced around him in satisfaction. "Together we'll say it," he said. "I like a look of agony *because I know it's true.*"

Briefly I wondered whether Kitty had heard a fly buzz when she died. Probably. Veebka's apartment teemed with painfully small insect life. Sir repeated the line, and his father spoke the final two words with him. Sir, not knowing the rest, shook his head. Mr. Lyman waved him on like a third-base coach urging a runner toward home.

"*Allons*, stupid," Lisa said.

Sir recited: "Men do not sham convulsion. Or simulate a throe—"

"*Nor. Nor* simulate a throe—"

"*Nor* simulate a throe—"

"I'll simulate a throe *you*," Lisa said to her little brother, "if you don't get the lead out—"

"And how are you spelling *throe*? *Throw* as in 'throw the ball'? As in hurl, fling, toss, be rid of? *Throw* as in 'throw that javelin across the field'? Or *throe*, as in 'a violent spasm or pang'?"

Sir said, "*Throw* like in 'throw the grenade.'"

Lisa sighed loudly as above our heads bells signaled the half-hour. It had been two minutes since she had been the center of attention, and two minutes was her limit. "Bells," she murmured, turning to Andy. "Northern bells. Northern light. Maxfield Parrish painted by northern light. Oh, speaking of bells, is Timmy Bell coming to this wedding, or is he pissed off I'm marrying someone else?"

"No, Sir. *Throe* as in 'a violent spasm or pang.' This is a throe." Mr. Lyman grabbed his own throat with both hands and started making choking noises. He looked like he was having a coronary.

"Daddy," Lisa said, "*ne* die *pas* on my wedding day, *por favor.*"

"The eyes glaze once and that is death," Sir repeated after his father. "Impossible to fake—"

"Feign," his father said. "Another word for *fake* being *feign*, rhymes with *rain*. The beads upon the forehead—" With his palms out, Mr. Lyman made a gesture that in a Latin country might have been considered an insult to your wife. "And?"

"I don't know," Sir whispered.

"Yes, you do know."

"I don't—"

"*BY HOMELY ANGUISH STRUNG!*" Mr. Lyman roared.

Sir repeated these words slowly. It was obvious he had no idea what he was saying.

"Who might the author of that be, Sir? I'll start you: Emily. Emily who?"

Sir giggled. "Emily Dickbrain."

"Not on a wedding day, young man. A wedding day is sacred. That kind of talk defaces the language. That's wash-your-mouth-out-with-soap talk. You're not a trucker." Mr. Lyman bowed to the group on the steps. "I'm sorry, everybody."

Lisa whispered to me, "Sir has gotten *vachement* coarse, *peux*—you stand it?"

Mr. Lyman turned sternly back to Sir. "One of her monikers *being*—"

"Harmonica Head." Sir giggled. "Harmonica Bum-Hole Head."

"Son, I'm not whistling Dixie. One of her monikers *being*—"

"The Maid d'Orléans?" Sir's fingers were clutching the toy green grenade. He looked completely worn-out.

"The Maiden of Amherst," his father continued. "Not the Maid d'Orléans. Though both maid and maiden were, as it were, saints. In their respective roles. The Maiden of Amherst."

"The Maid of Amherst," Sir repeated.

"Maid-*en*."

"Maid-*en*."

"But that is only one of Miss Dickinson's monikers. What is another?"

"The Fly?" Sir said.

I couldn't bear another second of this pathetic interrogation. "So," I said to Lisa, "have you seen my brother?"

Lisa made a cross with her fingers that people in vampire movies make. "Hal, I'm shocked. *Il ne faut pas* see each other before your wedding. It's bad luck. It's *nasty.*"

I said, "I think it might be a good idea to find out whether my brother's at least in the same country as we are."

"Well, why should—oohhh." With her hands still extended, Lisa started scraping her middle finger with the index finger of her other hand. "Naughty boy. I can never tell when you're putting me on or not, you bad boy. You're so *nasty*, Hal, you should be put to sleep with a *dirty syringe.*"

Everybody laughed, even Sir. "Ho, ho, ho," I laughed along, feeling, not for the first time that day, a crawling and imminent dread.

Inside the church, I sat with Fishie and my parents in the second row adjacent to the bride's side. Above our heads a fat blond man in a white suit was playing a tune on a French horn, a mournful melody that seemed more appropriate for Kitty's funeral than for Beck's wedding.

Beck finally appeared, looking tremulous and rattled in a suit two sizes too large for him. Since my brother is very tall, everyone was forced to look up at him as he slouched down the aisle, whistling softly to himself. My brother is so tall that he sometimes fails to notice things of a lesser height. On popular beaches I have seen him knock little children unconscious with his knees. He doesn't do this on purpose; it's simply that he's oblivious, and if he were to glance down all the time for rocks and children, he would probably get dizzy and have to seize my arm, and then we'd never get anywhere and I'd end up wanting to hurt him. After knocking out these children, my brother is often obliged to fight the fathers and mothers, which he doesn't enjoy doing. Although Beck is very strong, he dislikes fighting. I have seen him pin these fathers and mothers to the wet sand, and afterward he strips off his shirt and swims for a long time, not only to purge his animus but also to wash the grit from the places where, during a beach rumble, most sand gets lodged—the fold where the elbow meets the forearm, the crotch, ears and navel, the winglike wrinkles on the ankle that whisper to you that you're getting older.

Triple L came forth on her father's arm. I should explain that Triple L is a nickname our family has given Lisa. It was my father's invention, since one night he referred to her, in his barely audible table conversation, as Little Lisa Lyman. A few days later he shortened this to LLL, and then to Triple L. After discovering this appellation he was, for the first time in his life, able to have a passable conversation with her. It was just the approach to the heinous Lisa that my father, with his wayfaring sense of irony, seemed to require. From then on we called her Luh-Luh-Luh, an intonation, or Triple L, or sometimes just plain Triple. Except for my brother, who was her fiancé, after all, and he called her Lease, as though he were renting her out on a short-term basis, no pets.

The only interesting moment of the ceremony occurred at the end when the minister said, "And will you who are about to witness these promises do all in your power to uphold these two persons in their marriage?"

There was some reluctance on our side. Fishie glowered at Lisa's back and flung some lint in her direction. My mother had a coughing spasm and had to be slapped on the back. Finally Fishie muttered, "Yeah, yeah, yeah, okay, okay, okay."

"We will!" the entire congregation shouted. They were hungry, I think. At the altar my brother turned and stared at them. His eyes were startled, almost cross-eyed with a confusion that in the unspecific afternoon light of the church resembled lust. It was as though he had never seen so many strange people collected under one roof in all his life. He gave a pitiful little howl.

Afterward, at the reception, I drifted around under the great yellow-and-white-striped tent, eating mindlessly. I didn't have any idea how a brother of the groom was supposed to act. The wedding manual I had consulted suggested that the brother of the groom stick close to his brother, murmuring elegy and prayer, but the wedding manual had been written in 1870, and besides, Beck was surrounded by so many people I couldn't even get close to him.

Whenever someone noticed me standing alone, I pretended to be waving at friends across the room, smiling and agreeing with them. When the person who had noticed me standing alone looked over to see who I was waving to, I altered my wave slightly, so that it became a wave of farewell. "Absolutely, Stedman, squash on Saturday, will you reserve?" I had just finished calling across the room, my hands cupping my mouth, when I saw Mary of Munich staring intently at me from one of the tables, and I turned my head away in shame before fleeing the tent.

I ended up taking an unguided tour of the Lymans' house. I was looking for a good place to disappear for a while, like a bathroom. Then, when I returned to the reception, ten more minutes would've gone by, and the reception would be that much closer to ending. This time-tested party strategy has never failed me.

I entered the Lymans' house through a back door, passing by caterers removing platefuls of stuffed mushrooms out of kitchen ovens and arranging them on monogrammed silver trays. I headed through the dining room and played a chord on the old Chickering as I passed. Instead of music lighting my soul, as I had been trained to pretend it did, the piano merely reminded me of "Kitten on the Keys," which then reminded me of Kitty, which threw me into a short-lived depression. I was on my way upstairs to wander through the bedrooms when I saw Mrs. Lyman, the mother of the bride, sitting at a writing table in the living room, staring at a drawer and tugging at its handle. I felt sorry for her, working on a drawer alone in the living room on her daughter's wedding day in her expensive lime dress, so I came forward and asked if she needed any help.

Mrs. Lyman offered me a sour smile. She was drinking her usual, Scotch mixed with Fresca. She usually began at ten in the morning, and there was no reason to believe that today she would vary her habit. "The reception's out back," she murmured. "If you go through the—"

"I know," I said. "I was just looking for the bathroom."

"Well, the bathroom is anywhere." Mrs. Lyman spread her hands and made an odd, giggling sound in the back of her throat. "You *are* an adult male, after all."

"Right," I said, rocking boyishly on my heels.

Mrs. Lyman thought of something else. "Do I know you?"

"Hal," I said. "Beck's brother." I gave a little wave.

"Oh, yes, of course," she said, sounding disappointed. "Your brother's brother. Harlan, right? Could you help me out here? This particular drawer seems to be acting contrary."

I went over to the desk. The fallboard had toppled over and jammed, and the drawer Mrs. Lyman was gesturing toward wouldn't slide out. I positioned myself between the desk and Mrs. Lyman's stockinged knees and tried jerking the fallboard up. It wouldn't move. I think it had slipped out of its grooves. "Be very extra-special careful, Harley," Mrs. Lyman murmured. "It's an antique, you know."

I kept my fingers where they were. "How long has this drawer been stuck for?"

"Oh, let me see." Mrs. Lyman relaxed her spine. "Thirty years? Thirty-five years? I can't remember. It was a wedding present to Mr. Lyman and myself. The drawer seems to be able to come out only an inch, though. But inside I can see all kinds of wonderful things. Colorful things. I wonder what they are. Ben, I mean, Mr. Lyman, has tried, but his back is a problem and I don't like him ever lifting. I think they must be marvelous things, the colored things, whatever they are. It's tantalizing, you see, Harley, to pass by that drawer and remark on all those bright, superb colors and have one's hands tied in a way. . . ."

Thirty-five years the damn desk had been broken, and Mrs. Lyman was asking me to open it on her daughter's wedding day. I snatched at the fallboard and shoved it upward, violently. I heard a small crack.

"You didn't break it, did you?"

I feigned a coughing fit, to disguise the cracking sound. I have no idea why I thought this ruse would work. We underestimate the crafty intelligence of drunks, as they underestimate ours. I proceeded to cough for two whole minutes. I coughed so much that afterward I had to grab my throat it hurt so much. "There," I said, sliding the crippled fallboard back and yanking open the drawer.

"Ahh, now, aren't you the sorcerer?" Mrs. Lyman said. I moved out of the way and stood watching as she pulled her chair up greedily to the edge of the desk. Her fingers found the inside of the drawer, and she pulled out a small glass knob and a sheet of red-and-blue airmail stamps. "These are the colors, you see, the red and the blue colors I must've seen. I thought it might have been jewelry but—" She turned to me. "Thank you again. Now, what's your name?"

"Hal," I said. I had only been over at the Lymans' house a few hundred times before. What I mean to say is that Mrs. Lyman knew my name perfectly well.

"Hal, you must," she said finally, with dulled precision, "Hal, you must come over sometime to ride my blue horse, Clover. Now that you're family now. We'll be here, you know."

"Blue horse?" I repeated stupidly.

"My horse is blue," the bride's mother said. "Yes, Clover, she is quite . . . blue. Like the colors of these stamps except . . . paler . . . yes, much paler, especially during the afternoons here—the blue hour, you know. The Ay-rab people, you know, they call it the blue hour." Mrs. Lyman stared darkly into her Scotch and Fresca glass, and the cubes swung and drifted like chimes in a slow wind. "She's a blue roan," Mrs. Lyman murmured. "And we'll be here, you know."

Yearn, yearn, yearn, all people ever did was yearn. I was sick of it, and I was sick of the reception, even though I'd been there only for fifteen minutes. I stared out the living room window onto the lawn. This large green mass, deviously planed, served mainly as a jumping course for the Lyman's horses and a training ground for the Excellent Postwar Bitches. Thorny wild plants were strapped to the slats of the fences, and young trees, miraculous as green in the middle of the desert, popped up occasionally on the lawn and at the edges of the driveway, wet by sprinklers that played and twirled plumply like baby ballerinas.

The Lymans had more money than we did, but our family was consoled by the flashiness of their spending: two pools, one hot, one cold, sauna, Jacuzzi, a paddle-tennis court, a normal clay court, fountains, topiary hedges sculpted into the shapes of giraffes, lionesses, and large ugly birds, and a gargantuan black L stamped on their chimney, which my sister insisted stood for the third letter in vulgar.

I suppose there could have been a blue horse somewhere in the vicinity, but I'd never seen it and I thought I knew all the Lymans' horses.

"Were you the best man today?" Mrs. Lyman asked. "I can't remember what with"—she made a brief, helpless gesture with her hand—"all that's going on these two weeks . . . it's been just frantic here."

"Uh, no. I'm just the brother," I said. "We thought it would be nepotistic if Beck made me best man. We wanted to pick someone outside the family."

In fact, my brother hadn't even asked me. "Don't you see, Hal," Beck had said to me a month ago, almost incredulously, "that for me to name you best man would imply that you're leading a moral and artistic life that I somehow approve of?" Later he put on his oracle voice, and tried another tack. "To be 'best' at anything, Hal," he said soothingly, "is to be consigned to a life of loneliness and isolation. Let me tell you, Hal, when you've taken out all the competition, even the non-entrants, life is a bitter piñata indeed. Take a look at Fishie—the throat of Fishie's phone is completely parched. Webs over those little holes, Hal, webs. Everyone assumes Fishie's out having fun, but what she's actually doing is sitting at home, staring at the dial, hoping someone will call her up, ask her out. To sum up, Hal, if I made you best man—well, I see no difference between naming you best man and handing you a loaded rifle."

"Would you be a lamb chop," Mrs. Lyman said, holding out the sheet of colored stamps, "and go put these in the large green bowl in the hallway? As you're going out? Perhaps these will encourage me to become a better correspondent. Thank you, Yang," she said as I took them from her.

Outside on the terrace steps, I squatted down next to Ted. Ted was the youngest son of Lisa's sister Andy, who was the only one of the Lyman offspring to be doing anything remotely interesting or controversial with her life. A potter and a hippie, Andy also read people's tea leaves. She lived year-round in Camden, Maine, with her husband, who sold Bibles. They drove a black pickup truck and listened to country music on the radio all day and drank thick, eggy, stomach-turning health potions out of an antique blender. Their five children all were christened with the names of either herbal teas or stars: Riga, Blue Rider, Windsong and Lemon Mist. Ted was originally named Betelgeuse, but for several years he has refused to answer again to that name, so his mother had allowed him the choice of what to call himself. He had chosen Theodore, after one of the chipmunks in Alvin's band of cartoon rodents. His parents, oddly competitive for hippies, called him Ted.

Ted was wearing corduroy shorts and one of his mother's oversize Brooks Brothers shirts. It was monogrammed, a big, fat red *L* in the middle, with the other two initials, smaller, slimmer versions of the giant *L*, flanking it like underweight bodyguards. Practically everything the Lymans owned was monogrammed: ashtrays, shirts, towels, letter openers, coasters, pencils, pens. It was like visiting Adult Camp.

Since my life has no children in it, I had to rely on television fathers and their sons, and I ended up saying something like, "Hey, sport."

Ted's huge white shirttails were hanging out from the back of his pants, and he was concentrating hard on an enormous knot of black ants pouring out from a fissure in the brick steps. As soon as the ants came out into the sun, Ted brushed them over to one side with a silver cake knife, so all the ants smashed into one another. Their black-bead torsos moved quickly and erratically, like lost cars trying to find a main highway.

"Look," Ted said, looking up at me briefly, "she's carrying something on her back."

"She?" I said. "Who is?"

"Pam." He pointed out a large ant jerking around on the step, balancing a bread crumb on its back.

"Pam?" I said. "Who's she?"

"She's Steve's wife. Pam is married to Steve. Steve's a millionaire." Ted pointed to an ant lying quite still on the step, brushed too hard, probably, with the cake knife. "That's Steve."

I didn't know whether Steve was dead or just resting. I don't think about ants all that much. Whatever the case, Steve wasn't moving.

"I didn't know ants had names," I said in a voice I detested for its artfulness. Don't talk down to children, I remembered suddenly from a book, so I repeated what I'd said, this time in the deep, respectful voice of an old river.

"Of course they do, Stupidface," Ted said. "Where's Helen? I just saw Helen. She *was* here. I just saw Helen."

He searched around him, then crawled over to a gleaming black Weber grill at the edge of the terrace.

"Ah," Ted said. "Helen." He picked up a blue-and-white can of charcoal fluid, which had fallen over into the grass. "Whew! Here's Helen."

"Which one's Helen?" I said, now confused.

"This is Helen." Ted patted the can. "Now I have to find George." He searched his jacket pockets and finally produced a carton of matches. "This is George," he said proudly, holding up the matches.

"Where's George?" I said. "Is George the whole thing? The cover? The cover of the carton? Is George all the matches or only one of them?" I realized immediately that this was a dumb thing to have asked the lunatic tot. It simply got him started. What I should've done, of course, had I been at all responsible, was to have said something cautionary about playing with matches. I should've evoked the great fires of San Francisco and Chicago, and the occasional news items about careless tots who torch entire city blocks. Instead, for the next five minutes I had to listen to Ted list off every single one of the matches, one after another: Bob, Ralph, Skeeter, Hank, Lorrie, Sam, Maureen, Lou, Frankie. All of the matches were slim little redheads. I soon got bored and I rose up from my crouch and started walking across the lawn.

"Don't step on Judy!" Ted howled.

"What?" I said.

"You're stepping on Judy!" Ted howled again.

"Who the hell is Judy?" I snapped at him.

It turned out that the ground I was standing on was Judy. It hadn't occurred to me that the lawn would have a woman's name, or any name at all.

"Well," I said sensibly, "somehow I'll have to get back to where I was. And at some point I'll *have* to step on Judy."

Ted started humming an old Johnny Cash song. He had a tuneless voice but so does Johnny Cash, so it didn't really matter all that much. "I fell into a burning ring of fyah," Ted sang. "And I went down, down, down . . ." As Ted sang, he stared at me as though he were making up his mind about something.

Suddenly he stopped singing. "You can step on the triplets." The triplets, Ted explained, were three dandelions standing halfway between the steps and Judy the grass. Their names, I learned, were Candy, Mandy and Pandy. Ted assured me that the triplets could withstand my weight. After leaving the triplets, Ted told me, I could cross over to Charlotte, who was a patch of weeds and like Steve, drop-dead rich.

I began warming to the idea of everything in nature having a proper name. Why shouldn't your bed be called April or Amanda? Your lamp Calvin, your ceiling Diane?

While I stood lightly over Charlotte, Ted was busy pouring a circle of charcoal fluid around the ants. Several of the ants touched the kerosene and instantly keeled over. Ted was still humming the Johnny Cash song, then he broke back into words. "They go burn, burn, burn . . ."

I stood watching him, confused, as Ted touched a match to the still silver kerosene circle. The ants scrambled for cover.

"The Ring of Fyah!" Ted screamed happily as the ants started bursting into tiny flames.

Afterward I wandered around the Lyman's property, trying to think good thoughts about Triple L. Little Lisa Lyman was actually not little at all but normal-sized, practically standard. I wanted to give the girl a break since, after all, she was my brother's new wife.

Fishie couldn't stand Lisa and neither could I, but we were hard-pressed to explain why. We found her disingenuous in a very specific and subtle way. Most of the things Lisa said sounded, at least on the surface, innocent and unobjectionable. You nodded your head in agreement—what a nice, pretty girl, you thought, and what, rich too?—but then, about a day later, you woke up suddenly in the middle of the night with a scream in your throat and sweat pouring out all over your body and you realized that what you had taken for Lisa's surface ingenuousness was in fact an utter deceit. You realized that Lisa was, in her manipulation of words and ideas, the most brilliantly malignant person you had ever met. You would have stood up in your bed to applaud her if you were not overcome at this point by a certain bottomless shame for not having realized this earlier.

Here is Lisa on the subject of her future: "So this friend of mine, Ginger, she goes, Lisa, you could do whatever you want in your career. With your family, et cetera, yada-yada-yada, using all your family's great connections and money . . . you don't even *have* to work, et cetera and so on. I mean, I think it tells you a lot about *Ginger* that *she* would be the one to suggest I would use whatever great influence I have and, you know, ever take advantage of it. I mean, I started thinking a lot about her motives, raison d'êtres, whatever."

Fishie's and my analysis: While this anecdote is ostensibly about Lisa's friend, the point of it is to tell us several things about Lisa—that she's rich, that her social and job connections are stainless, that she has no incentive to work, then at the same time she has high morals. Note the brilliant employment of the words *et cetera* and *yada-yada-yada* to reduce the effect of her boasting. The tone of voice Lisa has used to tell this story—breezy and throwaway—suggests that these attributes are so well known to everybody that they are not even worth mentioning.

Lisa on the looks of a friend sitting by her: Both girls sit on stools, their hair just washed, combing out the tough hairs. Lisa has taken off the small, lightly tinkling silver bell she always wear around her neck to attract attention (Lisa does not like it when her bell gets wet in the shower). "No, listen, really, I think you have *lots* going for you. And you are so *funny*, that is such a *gift!* And that haircut doesn't look dykey on you at *all*, not a bit. I wish that *my* face had so much character in it, but here I am stuck with these everyday so-called conventional great looks and this skin everybody says is like this flawless thing, et cetera, you know, that never needs any junk on it to glow like a goddamn *crop goddess's*. It just makes me so *mad*, looking so-called '*gorgeous*' all the time." The hairbrush keeps stroking. Time passes. More time. The friend says, softly, not meaning it, since Lisa hasn't really meant it, "Lisa, you couldn't look bad if you tried."

Fishie's and my analysis: Now, before we say anything, it has to be understood that nobody, not even the friend, has suggested that the friend's new haircut is "dykey" or in any way ill-suited to her face. This is the first time the friend has heard the word *dykey* applied to her hair. That morning she liked her new haircut! She thought it was flattering! She thought she looked pretty! Here, Lisa uses *self-deprecation* brilliantly, complaining first about the things that most people covet—natural good looks, a moist complexion—and then pretending to give a rigid self-analysis of what she claims really counts in life—character, a sense of humor, "interesting" looks—all the while subtly criticizing the superficiality of those who see in her face only beauty and worth.

What could anybody do with these analyses? Nothing. We found some satisfaction that someday Lisa would end up in Disingenuous Hell. DH is a small, reddish quarry buried deep in the molten core of the earth, filled with hundreds of thousands of people who have made a bad impression on earth.

These sorry people are put to work demolishing a rugged rock pile. Across each rock are written disingenuous mantras ranging from "I'm so *sick* of being controversial" to "I envy you for being able to gain weight; I stuff myself with butter, lard and grease all day long but I can't manage to gain a single *ounce*" to "Since your boobs are so nonexistent, Cynthia, that blouse'll look *amazing* on you." The entrance exam to get into DH is brief and rather simple, and you take the test gradually, during your lifetime. Lisa was certain to score a perfect eight hundred.

I crossed the tent to the Lymans' table, where Mr. Lyman was sitting with Sir and Andy. Mr. and Mrs. Lyman had conceived Sir very late in their lives and had no idea what to do with him. Mr. Lyman hastily made a whooping contribution to a third-rate Vermont prep school, which a few years later accepted Sir as the youngest boarder in American history. Since the headmaster thought Sir was too young to live in the dorms, he lived off-campus with a goody-goody minister and his wife.

Sir was wearing a T-shirt that his father had printed up for him on his fourth birthday. It read: "I Am a Merrye and Well-Aspected Lad." I felt embarrassed beyond belief for him.

"Kin I have a beer?" Sir said to his father.

"No, Sir, you may not have a beer. Beer is for college boys."

Sir brought an empty green beer bottle up to his lips and licked the snail-curl glass top. "Look, everyone!" Sir crowed. "I'm drinkin' beer! I'm drinkin' the whole thing!"

"Sir, shape up or ship out!" his father commanded.

"I'm drunk!" Sir screamed. "I gotta throw up somewhere now!"

"Son, I'm not whistling Dixie . . ."

Sir staggered in a circle around the table, staring up at the top of the tent with the empty bottle stuck on his lips. "Oh, I'm so drunk I gotta throw up somewhere now!"

Nobody even looked at him. Even when Sir pretended to retch softly under the table, Mr. Lyman merely adjusted the ancient cloth over his fly.

Sir bobbed up from under the table and glared at his father. "Shiva's gonna kill you!" he yelled. "It'll be a piece a *cake!*"

"How nice for Shiva," his father remarked mildly.

"Shiva's gonna kill everybody at this goddamn stupid wedding!" Sir screamed. He sank down to his knees and clasped his small hands together in prayer. "When's this goddamn stupid wedding gonna be over, anyway?" he muttered. "A hundred thousand more goddamn stupid minutes?"

"Shiva's the Hindu god of destruction, Hal," Mr. Lyman pointed out. "It's Sir's current . . . infatuation, flavor of the month, what have you."

Presently Sir came over to where I was standing and opened his mouth very wide. "Look," he said.

I gazed into his feverish mouth. Mouths are strange: I didn't know whether to be repulsed or amazed. Past the wetness and the heartlike, purplish underside of Sir's tongue, three prongs stuck down from the roof of his mouth: a miniature trident. I watched Sir's tongue slide in and out between the prongs like an exotic fish trying to escape through the bars of a cage.

"Hal, that's to keep Sir from sucking his thumb. It's known as a Tongue Thrust. We don't want him looking like a beaver when he grows up, do we, Sir?"

"We-don't-want-to-look-like-beaver," Sir said in a robot's parched, jerky voice.

"How long does he have to wear that thing?" I said.

"How long, Sir, did we agree on?"

"Until-my-grades-shape-up," Sir beeped.

Poor Sir—it must have been amazingly difficult for him to eat. All solid foods would defeat him. Apples, steaks, baked potatoes, these were out of the question. They would end up harpooned, struck through the heart. No wonder Sir was so thin and pathetic. He could only eat mush, gruel, paste, broth and water-based products.

As I watched, Sir took out a miniature tape recorder from his jacket pocket and snapped it on. The soft, high-pitched voice of a folk singer blurted through the cheap speaker.

"Oh, Sir, no, not that damn Raffi again—"

"I like Raffi," Sir said.

"This is not the time for Raffi, Sir. Why don't we reserve Raffi for—"

"Who's Raffi?" I said.

Mr. Lyman took something out from between his teeth. He blinked once, heavily. "A lower-class singer Sir likes," he replied finally.

Across the crowded tent I finally caught sight of my brother. He was standing next to Lisa, posing for a photographer, and making faces at the camera. I saw him grab two stuffed mushrooms off a tray and place them over his eyes and tip his head back. Lisa looked furious. "Oh, *très* funny," I heard her exclaim. "So funny I forgot to laugh, et cetera. I'll stuffed-mushroom *you*, buddy boy. I'm *married* to this guy?" she said to one of her bridesmaids, conking herself on the head, too softly to incur much in the way of a concussion.

Lisa's voice could carry across vast stretches of land and water. Once Beck and she had taken our Sunfish and sailed across the bay to an island five miles away from our house. They were planning to spend the night on the island in sleeping bags. That night, five miles away, I could hear Lisa's voice clearly, across the water, saying, "But I don't *want* to rough it! If you have a choice, what's the bloody goddamn point of roughing it?" Naturally Lisa won, and they sailed back that same night. When my brother walked in the door, he said, "I suppose you're wondering what we're doing back here," and I didn't have the heart to tell him I'd heard every word of their argument. Every word, that is, except for his side, which the wind had made quick work of, dispersing it to the sharks.

I hadn't seen Beck, or talked to him, since I had flown into town a week earlier for his stag party, which took place at a pathetic sex club located off Interstate 41, in the southeastern corner of Vermont.

Fishie had wanted to come along that night, as a chaperone, but I refused.

"Why *can't* I come? I know why: it's because there'll be chicks and babes on the premises—it'll be self-consciously, preppily 'outrageous,' 'rude' and so forth. You boys are terrified what I'll think. That I'll notice how divorced you are from the verities of life and tell the local papers about it. I *know* what goes on at your stupid stag parties, Hal. It's latent homosexuality disguised as sport—you use the poor women as an excuse to act thirteen years old again. Climbing flagpoles—"

"Flagpoles?"

"Yeah. You get drunk and climb up somebody's flagpole and call down to all your friends. Drunkenly. Then the police arrest you. Trespassing on a farmer's land, breathing on a human flag and whatever else they can think of. Except these aren't flagpoles to you surreal prepsters, they're 'flagpoles.' And it's not getting arrested, it's getting 'arrested.' By 'cops.' Carrying 'nightsticks.' It's unreal time. You boys need some protection from unreality—I'm coming."

"Stay away," I rasped. "It could get dangerous."

Fishie tossed her blond hair. "You mean 'dangerous'? You wish, buddy boy. Quotation-mark danger really petrifies me, Hal; I *think* I can take care of myself. Remember, I *train* with men, I race with them. I share second-rate foreign bathrooms with them. You think you boys can pull something new I don't know about?

"Wouldn't just a regular, normal party be a lot nicer? Like in somebody's greenhouse? A party that bridges the past and the present? I mean, why are you guys going to Ye Lustbarne, of all places? Maybe instead we could invite Beck's old teachers to a greenhouse somewhere—all the ones who were once duped into thinking he showed some kind of *promise*. It could be a This-Is-Your-Life kind of thing. Miss Pitt could come—Beck's third-grade homeroom teacher. Remember her? The one who used to attach Popsicle-stick carts to gerbils' shoulders and make them carry out her dirty work? What'll I do that night while you surrealists are off frolicking and false-bonding? Sew? Hem? Rock in a rocking chair?"

"You could," I said gravely, "always reconsider Lisa's invitation."

Lisa had rented the seventh floor of the Ritz-Carlton Hotel in Boston and invited her cruel friends to an all-night bridal shower. Guests were urged not to economize on gifts lest Lisa lose her temper. There would be several cases of ouzo—"club soda for the bores," the invitation added—a blind harpist and a whole barbecued pig. "Lots of frank girl talk about the male anatomy (or lack of it)," the invitation went on to say, and this promise was followed by a hysterical picket fence of exclamation marks. Fishie sent her regrets.

My brother's stag party took place the very same night as Lisa's bridal shower. I told Beck he could hold his party wherever he wanted, and perversely he'd chosen Ye Lustbarne—perhaps the most downtrodden sex club ever granted a liquor license. Located in a municipality of seventy-eight people, Ye Lustbarne comprised Merry, Vermont's only extant industry. As you rounded the corner of the Interstate, hugging a steep, plunging incline, past bitten railings where cars less agile than Son had met with garish, improbable rock-star deaths, you could see the soft pink neon winking and cooing from a mile away, throwing cool, naked shadows onto the empty road. Crickets, horseflies, cicadas, oily black crows on telephone wires: it was hard to imagine the good times rolling in Merry, Vermont, but Ye Lustbarne—the Ye part implied Yankee antiquity and traditions—had been in business for as long as I could remember.

I'd rented a car and driver for the night, and stocked the backseat with beer and tequila. By the time we arrived at Ye Lustbarne, I had succeeded in thoroughly inebriating my brother and his college friends. Beck was at a point in his drunkenness where he was unable to make even the most heavy-handed connections between things: In Burlington, for example, we stopped for more beer, and walking back to the car, Beck noticed a home-made poster taped to the side of a building that read, LOST: BROWN-AND-WHITE FOX TERRIER. VERY FRIENDLY, COMES WHEN CALLED. ANSWERS TO RICK. REWARD.

"Poor li'l puppy," he said, stumbling a little.

A block later we passed by another poster that read, FOUND, FOX TERRIER, EXTREMELY AMIABLE DISPOSITION, PLAYFUL. COLLAR SAYS RICK, and it gave a phone number to call.

"Imagine that, Hal," Beck exclaimed. "Two fox terriers on one block! Too bad these people can't get together with those other people and race their puppies! Fox terriers faster than the wind! First one to the corner wins! And both named Rick! What a race that would be! A bettor's delight! I put my money on Rick. Whichever dog wins, I win too! Whoa!"

Outside Ye Lustbarne he caught his loafer on a rock and fell heavily onto the gravel. He lay there, blinking, breathing hard, while armies of exotic insects—slender, athletic green bugs as well as moths, mosquitoes, beetles, red ants—crawled across his face. "I fall upon the thorns of life!" Beck moaned. "I bleed!" Assisting him to his feet, I brushed the insects off his cheeks and fingers. "Hal, I did that on purpose," my brother said. "Falling. It was a . . . marketing experiment. It was one of those mosquito tests, actually. To see if they could land. I was trying out a product."

Ye Lustbarne was actually a private barn, owned by a good-natured and entrepreneurial farmer who ten years ago decided he needed some extra income. During the day, at least, it functioned as a working barn. Cows were milked, cats tore mice in two, owls stood watch. At six every night the animals were gently expelled, tables and chairs were brought indoors by Vermont farmboys, a makeshift stage was dragged into place, and lights and colored scrims were arrayed over the stage. The only way you would know it was an actual barn was that strands of hay adhered to your shoes, but this seemed to me natural and thus forgivable.

"Snap out of it, Beck," I said once we were seated. "Let the *bon temps rouler, Cher.* Have a BLT or something. And another beer."

I was beginning to get concerned that Ye Lustbarne was a clip joint, one of those places where the waitress brings you over a small mug of flat beer and then, with a sweet smile, says, "That'll be two hundred and forty dollars please, that's with the tax . . ." But I was reassured by the sight of Ye Lustbarne's clientele, mostly professors and deans from the university fifty miles away. I reasoned that on their salaries, college professors wouldn't be able to afford two-hundred-and-forty-dollar beers, and it turned out I was right: Drinks were thirty-five, two for fifty.

Beck's shoulders froze. "BLT," he mumbled. "Beck . . . Lisa . . . Torture. Beck, Lisa, Terror. Beck, Lisa, Trauma. Beck, Lisa—"

He was right. "Hold off on the BLT if it's too evocative," I said kindly.

The waiter came over, and my brother ordered a slice of chocolate cake. He turned his stool so it was facing the wall and started reading aloud the graffiti that rural hooligans had scribbled on the walls. Most of it was tame and not particularly ingenious. "Mary had a little lamb," Beck recited softly. "A little lamb had Mary/Nine months passed extremely fast/And Mary had a little lamb. . ."

My brother eats a lot of chocolate for several reasons, one of which has to do with all the disappointing Halloweens he suffered as a child. When he was about four, Beck was already so tall that when he went around trick-or-treating, the mothers at all the houses said things like: "Aren't you a little large still to be doing this, son?" Or: "Do you think this is quite fair to the younger children?" My brother, in his tiny devil's mask, never knew what to say; he just stood there at the door with his mouth open under his mask, inhaling plastic. When he tried to explain that he was big for his age, the mothers usually uttered a version of the same crazy, sarcastic words: "Yeah, and I'm Eldridge Cleaver/Malcolm X/The Chicago Seven." Sometimes it was the less controversial "Yeah, and I'm Sarah 'Sassy' Vaughn," but no matter how they phrased it, the message—Go Home, Giant—was clear. Then they slammed the doors.

It always worked. My brother was no dope. The neighborhood was white as the thickest, whitest cotton collar. He knew the mothers weren't black militants, or operatic jazz singers, and this realization, which occurred every year, crushed him every time he heard it.

The lights over the stage dimmed, and the floor show began. To the strains of "Little Red Corvette," six women wearing wedding dresses came onstage and began dancing and disrobing at the same time. Since this was a New England floor show, the women's wedding dresses were sexless and baggy, and they unbuttoned easily. A sheet of crimped tin stretched across the back of the stage, and before I knew it, the six had turned their naked backsides to the audience and were gyrating their pelvises inches away from the tin.

I glanced over at Beck, but the floor show wasn't having the desired effect on him. Instead he was keeping up an inane, whispered commentary. "Look at those women's little squinched-up knees, Hal . . . they look like Unicef orphans' faces. Look at that woman to the left, her eyeballs are perfectly rectangular. Wow, you suppose that woman with the long face up front's ever really, *really* fallen in love?"

I lost patience. This stag party was costing me a bundle, and I wanted results. "Snap out of it!" I yelled. "Can't you respond to stimuli like a normal man?"

One of the naked women leaned down over our table and said, "Which one here's the gentleman getting married?"

Beck's craven, drunken friends gestured at my brother and began hooting. "You're the gentleman getting married?"

Beck nodded timidly. Someone shoved a shot glass of tequila in front of him.

The woman licked her lips. She was a natural redhead, big and playful. "For your eyes only," she murmured, and without pausing, she lowered herself down onto the hay-specked stage using only the muscles in the insides of her thighs.

"Leg bend," Beck called out approvingly. "'stremely difficult."

The woman rose, and holding her hands arclike over her head, she tilted her torso to one side in tiny, half-inch motions. Then she did ten on the other side.

"Side stretch." Beck applauded weakly. "'stremely difficult. Feel the burn," he added lamely.

"Why are we paying money to watch this woman exercise?" I yelled.

At one point my brother turned to me. "Hey, Hal, y'ever seen girls?"

"What do you think?" I yelled again, calculating how much money I'd wasted aleady that evening.

"No, no, wait. Hold on, Hal, I'm not finished. Girls about sixteen, seventeen years old? They're clinging on to each other? Like they're in love with each other? Like they all have these physical crushes on each other? Holding each other's hands, they're hugging, they don't seem to want to let go of each other?"

"Sure." I didn't know what he was driving at.

"Well, I finally figured out why they do that. They're holdin' on to each other because they know that pretty soon along the line they're gonna hafta divide. They're gonna hafta get married and they'll hafta divide. Never see each other again. They'll all get married and then they'll disappear into the suburbs or into the exurbs or into the country or into the city. Aw, hell, sure, they'll come to each other's weddings, they'll be good about that, but when the bouquet's all thrown, they'll just go divide up again and drive away. Cars. Trains. Airplanes back. Farewells. Keep in touch, stop for food on the way home, discuss the wedding, how beautiful their friend looked, take different highways home. Disappear. No wonder they hold hands back when they're sixteen, seventeen, see what I'm sayin'?" Beck stared helplessly past me. "The end is near and all of 'em know it—"

"Well, what about the men?"

"Doesn't matter about the men. Men stay the same. Men'll meet you whenever you want 'em to. Wherever. Oh, and Hal?"

I blinked to show consciousness.

"You think I oughta get married?"

I thought this was a little late in the game, since the wedding was a week away, a honeymoon boat had already been leased and Lisa's squinty-eyed, laughing face had already appeared in the *Times*. "Well, yeah, Beck," I said. "Yeah, I think you should."

"They say if you have any doubts, then don't do it. Marry, I mean. Never marry a man with charm, is what Mrs. Lyman told Lisa. Never marry a good-looking man with charm. They're selfish, passive, they'll manipulate you. Lisa says people who have charm don't know it, that that's *part* of their charm—"

"Well, Lisa's wrong again," I said, adding, "I think people who have charm are acutely aware of it."

"But I have these doubts, Hal. I have about two hundred of 'em." My brother laughed anxiously. "But you'll always have doubts, right?"

I cleared my throat. "Sure. Five doubts, though. Not two hundred. Five."

"You like Lisa all right, don't you?"

"Ahh, Lisa. Like. Do? I? Her? Um," I said finally, "both Fishie and I have a few personality problems with old Lisa. But I'm sure they'll get ironed out when she becomes"—I hesitated as terror and futility passed through me—"a part of the family. Then again, Fishie probably would hate anybody you married."

An hour later I watched as my brother's friends dragged him into the Fantasy Room of Ye Lustbarne and tied him to an armchair with silk scarves. Beck protested loudly and ironically as both his hands were cuffed behind him. The manager of Ye Lustbarne tied Beck's feet to the chair rungs, lifting his socks so the rope wouldn't slide upward. Beck's friends left the room, in search of a flagpole, but I lingered by the door. This was the ace up my sleeve, and I wanted to make sure it went according to plan.

"This is depressing, Hal," Beck kept complaining. "Having to shell out for your fantasies. Do I *have* to go through with this?"

I had a quotation all prepared. It was actually my wedding toast, if the chance came to give one, one I'd found in a paperback copy of *Jim Thorpe: All-American.*

"The essence of sports," I began, "is not winning but taking part. The essential thing in life is not conquering but fighting well."

"What does that have to do with anything?" my brother demanded. "Do you really believe in that shit?"

The Fantasy Room of Ye Lustbarne was dark, its walls plastered with phosphorescent posters showing muscular black couples, naked from the waist up, stirring from hostile afterglows. The floor was blond and black twisted hay: the back room must have been where goats and pigs found solace. Low, irritating music, such as the kind you hear in condemned Indian restaurants, squeaked and hummed from speakers hidden somewhere over our heads.

I'd hired one of the floor show dancers to come out and impersonate a falconer. The management had presented me with a list of other male fantasies, but for the most part they'd seemed to me banal and common—a French milkmaid, a schoolgirl, a dominatrix, a stewardess, a woman cop, a dirty-mouthed stevedore. And Beck had always liked birds. He liked their elegance and their independence. In profile he sometimes even resembled a beaked predator. "Ah, yes, the falconer fantasy," Ye Lustbarne's manager had said, winking horribly at me. "Very popular act. Very hypnotic. The combination of bondage and falconry is a winner. Your brother, he'll go crazy for the falconer."

I'd paid for an hour of the falconer's time. Our contract called for her to dance suggestively around the radius of Beck's chair, while Beck, bound tight, nipped at her limbs or occasionally brought a paw out from under the ropes and took a swipe at her.

"Hey, there, Hal," Beck said when the falconer stomped into the room. "Hey, Hal, you didn't tell me there would be birds."

The falconer wore nothing but a skimpy white smock, a heavy leather glove and black patent leather shoes. Over her face she wore what looked like a hockey goalie's mask, so it was impossible to tell what she really looked like. Two falcons, huge, unblinking, ash-colored birds, sat unmoving on each of her shoulders. In one hand the falconer carried a crook with a razor-sharp tip, and in the other a plateful of brown, mouse-shaped falcon snacks. As I sank into a chair by the door the falconer began a slow striptease. Whenever she removed an article of clothing, she handed it over to a falcon, who, seizing the garment in its mouth, flew up toward the ceiling and, hovering directly over Beck's chair, dropped it onto my brother's head. Returning to its shoulder perch, the falcon immediately sank its teeth into a falcon snack.

Beck, staring straight ahead of him, looked bored as a horse.

"Come on," I whined. "Nip at her. She's stimuli! Nip! This evening cost me an arm and a leg—nip, Beck! Let the *bon temps rouler, Cher!*"

"Hal," he said patiently, "what do you think I am, hopelessly insane? I'm not going anywhere near those birds—I'd sooner blow my brains out."

A terrible thing happened. I was watching one of the falcons lift off into the air, gripping the falconer's red underpants, when I heard a loud voice coming from the hallway: "I remember Beck as an overanxious young boy who kept to himself in the back of my classroom. But his cheerfulness and good nature earned him seven gold stars, the most of any child in third grade that year."

The voice was shaky but powerfully amplified. It was followed by a familiar voice bawling, "Beck Andrews, to start the journey over your life, please welcome your third-grade homeroom teacher, the former Lucille Pitt, now Mrs. James Cochran of Louisville, Kentucky!"

The door opened and a frail old woman, beaming, shot into the room, as though she'd been sucked from the door of an airplane. Petrified, the falcon dropped the red underpants onto the floor, while its mate charged the old woman's head, its wings streched out wide. Blinded by falcon wings, the old woman let out a scream and fled the room.

Outside, my sister sounded annoyed. "What do you mean? I paid your way up here, lady, now get the hell back in there and reminisce with him!"

I ran out into the hallway and nearly collided with three strangers. Behind them, obviously functioning as head cheerleader, was Fishie.

"What the hell are you doing here?" I shouted at her. "I told you you weren't invited! And why are you dressed like such a sleazebag?"

Fishie winced. She was wearing a beaded silver dress and holding in one hand what looked like a giant scrapbook. The other hand, dangling, held an enormous megaphone. "Oh, shush. And don't talk to me about sleazebag. We're holding a little life retrospective here." She waved her hand in front of her face. "Incredibly buggy outside. I was just using the pay phone outside." Fishie beamed. "I phoned in a bomb scare to the Ritz. It's my wedding-shower gift to Lisa. In lieu of lingerie. That should scatter the room, huh?"

"Who *are* these people?"

"Well, you must remember Miss Pitt—"

"Mrs. James Cochran," muttered the trembling old woman I had just seen in the Fantasy Room.

"Cochran, Pitt, what's the difference," snarled Fishie, annoyed, I think, that even someone named Pitt would sacrifice her name to a man.

"You can't be here!" I shouted.

Fishie ignored me. "You remember Joanie, Hal? Beck's first sad attempt at loving someone?"

I stared anxiously at the girlfriend my brother went out with when he was thirteen. Joanie had been two hundred pounds then, with a mouthful of braces. Now, having lost most of the weight, she looked like every other ice skater on the rink. I shook my head wildly at her.

Fishie raised the megaphone to Joanie's mouth. "Hey, Joanie, repeat after me: 'Beck, your winning smile and captivating sense of play ennobled—'"

"No!" I shouted. "You can't have Joanie say that! And you can't have people go into that room!"

"Oooh, Hal, is that room haunted?"

"Noo," I crooned. "Falcons, Fishie. There's falcons in there."

"I told you I saw crazy birds," Mrs. Pitt/Cochran said.

Fishie snorted. "Falcons, huh? What's that unreal prep-school boy code for? C'mon, Hal, do you all have the D.T.'s or something? Face the goddamn verities of life for once. Is Beck in there drunk? Is that it? Is he sodden? Are there chicks and babes in there with him? It's okay, Hal, it's not as though I've never seen the guy plastered before, or surrounded by floozies. Come on, Joanie, don't *you* be a bust too." The megaphone rose again. "Come on, honey, I'll start you off. 'Beck, I remember—'"

Now, under the yellow-and-white tent, Beck stared oddly at me. "Hal, do you remember," he began earnestly, "the time we all went to that old water mill?"

He named the town where the water mill had stood and waited for my answer. I shook my head.

"Let me see, now hold your horses a minute, let me get this one right. Let me see, it was you, me, Fishie, I don't think anybody else. No, beg your pardon, Liv was there."

Liv was our au pair girl, which immediately dated the excursion. She was from Norway originally. Taking care of us couldn't have been all that much fun, but Liv lasted three years. We taught her English for "Shut up" and "*Make* me," and "Get out of my face," and in return she taught us the Norwegian words for "Where is the pencil, Uncle Per?" and "This herring is delicious and satisfying; may I have seconds?" We became gentle, polite and interrogative people, at least when we were speaking Norwegian, while Liv ended up alienating everybody within a mile of her.

My brother said, practically in one breath, "It was a water mill. At the end of a skinny road near a cranberry bog. You took the right fork because the left led nowhere. We were in a clearing of some kind. We had a picnic lunch. Fishie sang Christmas carols even though it was the middle of the summer. You lit a raspberry-colored smoke bomb. There were earwigs in the trees, right where the two halves of the branches met. Liv almost drowned. Something was brown about the day. The water was brown, or the rocks were brown, someone was dressed in brown. Somehow there was brown."

"Nope," I said. I didn't remember at all. "Not a single water mill in my memory."

"You don't remember?" my brother yelled. "Why don't you remember? Why don't people remember the same things I remember?"

He continued in this vein, frantically. "On the way back I got mauled by red thorns. They looked like pistachio nuts. Three scratches. Like the ones precision airplanes make against the sky. You had poison ivy. Cream all over your face like a mummy and no eyes because they had pulled back so far into your huge, swelled face—"

I kept shaking my head. This was a very lyrical memory, to be sure, but I didn't remember any of it ever having happened.

My brother was rambling now. "And there were jellyfish! And we had the red station wagon then! The one that looked like tomato soup! And Fishie's top flew off! And I pretended I hadn't seen anything, but I did see!" Finally Beck yelled, "Don't you screw around with my childhood memories, Hal, if you know what's good for you!" and he stalked off under a slit in the tent, probably to annoy Fishie.

Across the room I saw him reenter the tent through another slit and take my sister aside.

Soon I heard my sister say, "Of course I do, honey. Of course I remember."

Beck said, "You do?" Beck glanced over at me as if to say, You see?

"Sure, sure I do," Fishie said, "this was your life, remember?" and taking him by the arm over to the bar and ignoring the bartender, she fixed my brother the largest Scotch and water I had ever seen.

Across the tent, Lisa was chatting with a group of her bridesmaids, and gesturing ecstatically about something. She had put on a pair of Ray-Bans with walnut frames, and whenever there was a lull in the conversation, Lisa snapped her fingers and began crooning the State Farm Insurance jingle. She looked hopelessly confused. It was a reflex with her now—Lisa was a helpless pawn. By now the State Farm Insurance jingle was second nature to her, and soon her voice would grow deep and raspy and her whole head would turn green and start spinning around and around her neck.

Lisa's attendants fell into two distinct groups. The first consisted of beautiful, slightly sulky girls who knew Lisa from Dartmouth and Miss Porter's School, who took turns appearing at each other's weddings. Like Lisa, many of them also wore silver bells loosely nestled around their throats, to attract attention. The mothers of most of the beautiful girls were Du Ponts. It was never the fathers who were Du Ponts, only the mothers. The fathers had florid last names and unconvincing or not very demanding jobs that hid the mothers' Du Pont connection like a natural body crease.

The other group was Lisa's second string: the many plain bridesmaids she had chosen for her retinue. Like many beautiful girls of a certain age, Lisa surrounded herself with plain, heavy, witty girls, whom she introduced to single men as "interesting." They were *riots*, Lisa always said, and publicly she was always announcing that she wished she were more like them.

She was doing it now. "Carrie is *great*," Lisa crowed, pushing the blinking, confused, heavy girl toward my brother's best man, who was a complete stranger to me.

Lisa did just the opposite thing with the tall, shy boys who clustered admiringly around Lisa's more beautiful women friends. Earlier she had gone up to one of them, a tall, awkward-looking boy with glasses, and said, "Why is it like this *rule* that you tall, shy, gangling-type people always get crushes on the really pretty girls? It doesn't make any sense, I mean, *entre nous*. Awkward people belong with *other* awkward people. I'm sorry to have to say that, but it's true." Here Lisa smiles radiantly. "Now, there are plenty of shy *little* girls around here more your own speed, they wear glasses, too, so you can go be awkward around each other, whatever, to your heart's content, go on, go get yourself one, quit wasting my time—*shoo*, you're making my friends uncomfortable."

Behind Lisa a small Dixieland quintet played the anthems of another generation on a stage elevated by cement blocks. Dick Dickerson and the Gang of Six, the band was called. The Gang of Six consisted of four red-faced men in their early sixties, sweating, joyless and obese. The other two Gang-members were nowhere to be seen. Sweat beads trembled on the clarinetist's horn, and the pianist had a mirror behind him so you could watch his plump, ringed hands as he played "Gone With the Wind" and "Let's Have Another Cup of Coffee." Dick Dickerson stood in front of the stage crooning into a microphone that looked like a buzzard's head. Dick Dickerson looked like he'd been performing too long. His vibrato had slowed down to a distant, retarded echo in faraway canyons. All four of the musicians were sipping what must've been bourbon, disguised in coffee cups.

As I left, I heard Lisa whisper to someone, "Carrie's more like a *dirigible* than a girl, but those two *fleurs de la* wall should hit it off perfectly."

At a certain point in the afternoon I decided to make the downstairs bathroom my official wedding-reception headquarters. With the bathroom door locked, I felt free to play with things: magazines, dental floss, old razors. I put my hair under a stream of cold water and combed it back like a roué's. I rehearsed politeness and small talk in front of the mirror—I have to, or else I'll just stand there gulping, perishing in my shoes. "Wouldn't it now, ha ha ha," I said to the mirror, and "Of course, I'd love to, but the question is, would *she*—don't forget, it takes two to make a house a home." I opened up drawers. I checked for drugs in the cabinet over the sink, but I didn't find anything more interesting than a bottle of prednisone for Sir's asthma.

But inside the cabinet I did find a note: "We know how you guests like to peer! We caught you! But don't ever change, you guys! *Ciao!* Lisa."

I couldn't bear it. I ripped up the note into little pieces and then flushed it down the toilet. Just to be immature, I tore off a piece of toilet paper and wrote, "There's nothing in this medicine cabinet of any interest, anyway, you stupid bitch," and left it propped up against a Band-Aid box.

A couple of times people banged on the bathroom door, but I gave no ground. "Upstairs, to the right, down the hallway," I shouted, or, "Kitchen, take a left, near the ironing board." I knew the layout of the Lymans' house well enough to describe it in shorthand, or at least I knew where the best bathrooms were, since I'd auditioned all of them already. I much preferred my hideout on the ground floor—it was roomy, with a soft white rug, and filled with such interesting and self-conscious reading material as a stack of old *P.M.* magazines and a copy of the New Testament.

I stayed in the bathroom for about an hour, and then I decided to try the reception again. When I opened the door, I saw Mary of Munich in the hallway outside the bathroom. Leaning against the wall, she stared at me with her thin smile. For some reason Mary seemed to be sweating heavily. Since she'd seen me, I couldn't very well slam the door in her face. "Mary," I said, doing the slight dance-in-place I do when I meet someone who puts me on edge. "Having a nice time?"

She slipped into the bathroom, then shut and bolted the door behind her. "*Ich muss schiffen,*" she muttered, setting her glass of champagne on the edge of the sink and positioning herself in front of the mirror. She took a mascara out of her pocket and without saying a word suddenly grasped the back of my head and began smearing mascara onto my lashes. Most of it went into my eyes. "Hold still," Mary hissed. "I think you look okay in mascara, no? Most of the men are looking okay in the mascara."

I squirmed but Mary was very strong. "Sexy," she murmured. "I like it when men are the wearers of the mascara."

Mary finally let go of my head and I gouged my eyes out with a washcloth. "Do not wipe," Mary ordered, and she tried to grab the washcloth away from my face. "It's sexy, no? It changes the way the men they smell. Every man, he smells a different way, you know? No man makes a different smell to him."

Behind me, Mary sank down on the toilet seat and pulled up her skirt. She pushed her black tights down to her knees and stared mockingly at me.

"Wouldn't it now?" I said, backing out of the room. "But the question is, would *she*—remember, it takes two to make a house a home," I added, shutting the door behind me. What was wrong with Mary of Munich? I wondered. I couldn't understand this woman at all. Part of it had to do with the fact that she was German and I wasn't, but even if we'd both been from the same country, I still would've been at a complete loss; and since I don't like feeling that way, I was determined to avoid her for the rest of the reception. If I ever needed a reminder, my pants seemed welded to the wound she'd inflicted in my thigh.

Under the tent, women dressed like nurses were now passing around baby shrimps stabbed in the heart with toothpicks, and cheese mysteries braided like twigs. The shallow glass lanterns on the tables shuddered with light.

Lisa's sister Andy was sitting on the porch, staring across the darkening lawn. She told me that when she was out sailing that afternoon, she'd seen a team of mother sharks. "I almost had a heart attack," Andy said, clutching her chest as though her heart were still being chased around her body. "The female shark, she's supposedly much more powerful. Than the male. The male sharks don't do anything aggressive, they just float around. Idlers. Typical male behavior. Or maybe I'm thinking of pot." Andy shrugged. "Maybe I'm thinking of pot. Female plants. I think maybe I'm thinking of pot."

Andy twisted her legs so they were crossed on the other side as she picked up her Diet Pepsi as though to drink from it. Instead she squeezed it around the middle. "You don't have a pen, do you, Hal?"

I made a cursory search through my pocket, though I knew I didn't have one. The only thing I had was a baby yellow pencil, which I handed over. Andy shook her head. "Pen. I need a *pen*. Excuse me, do you have a pen?" she called out to Senator Willem, who was passing by at that moment.

"Why, certainly, Andrea, for you I always have a pen," the senator said, reaching into his pocket. "Make it payable to The Committee to Re-elect Neal Willem," he joked, before moving on.

With his cheap ballpoint Andy punched a hole in the tin circle of her Diet Pepsi. Like many devoted pot smokers, she wasn't much of a drinker. Reaching into her pocket, she produced a chunk of gold-gray hash from a blanket of foil and laid it down tenderly over the pen hole. Placing her lips down on the triangle spout and holding the can loosely in her right hand, her red, scratchy eyes looked up softly into mine, searching my face.

"Light?" she rasped.

Outside the tent, the lawn had been set up for the raw-dog exhibition that wasn't going to take place. A lime-colored clothesline lay coiled on the ground, and the caterers had to step over it as though dodging an eddy made of rope. Every now and again I saw Mr. Lyman dialing the phone next to the screen door, trying the hospital number, checking on his dogs' condition. I felt very sorry for him. Without his dogs in attendance, Mr. Lyman was unable to enjoy his daughter's wedding day. The bulletin board behind the telephone was crowded with whistles, kite string, paper towel rolls, leashes and a diagram tacked to the middle of the cork that showed the figure of a dog and its various parts: skull, occiput, withers, loin, croup, stifle, pastern, brisket, hock. The diagram made the dog look highly edible, and below it was a scroll entitled, "Lord Tweedmouth's Guide to the Happy Puppy." Among the things it listed were: "Repetition, Repetition, Repetition, Repetition, Repetition" and "No animal, including Man, Woman or Infant, does not require a certain amount of sorrow and hard work to make a believer out of him."

I had to squint to make out the bottom line. I felt like I was reading an eye chart, but I finally got it. "Approval means a lot to a little puppy." For some reason I thought of Sir, and this made me fabulously depressed.

Under the tent, my sister was dancing with Senator Willem, a gray form with flushed cheeks on a face so soft and pale it looked deboned. Behind them, crouched by the stage, Sir was staring at them both with enormous black X-ray glasses. "I can see you naked!" Sir screamed at Senator Willem.

The senator looked up and smiled tightly, not wanting to lose any votes, even if the person he was smiling at couldn't vote. "Can you, young fellow?

"I can see your thingie!" Sir screamed hysterically. "And I can see your booberamas!" he screamed at my sister. "They're humongous!"

Senator Willem actually stopped dancing. "Uh, which in particular is humongous?" he asked uncertainly. "Were you talking to her or to—".

"Me! Me! Me! Me!" Sir howled, before collapsing on the ground in a fetal position.

Behind Senator Willem's back, Fishie gave me the help signal. This gesture resides in every woman's hand. The small, bright palm folds in and out, as though it has an independent heartbeat, then tense fingers clutch at nothing. I could hear the senator telling Fishie how much he enjoyed dancing with athletic women. "They're so much tighter. Their skin is, I mean," he added, with a giggle.

Outside the tent, Andy was blowing up colored balloons on a helium machine and stuffing popcorn into her face at the same time. Each balloon had my brother's and Lisa's initials and the date on it. The six initials and that day's date flew high over the dogless lawn, light and warm as spume. I watched a blue balloon escape, its soft string trailing underneath. It looked like a single runaway sperm.

The sliding glass doors that opened out onto the lawn had been polished so thoroughly for the reception that people kept walking into the glass and breaking their noses. The wedding was turning into a bloodfest. People's best features were going to pieces. Several guests were walking around clutching their nostrils, their heads tipped backward to stanch the blood. A navy blue medi-van was parked in the Lymans' driveway, under a maple tree, and a pair of bored paramedics were sitting on the hood, shuffling bandages and juggling splints. On the porch steps, Ted was touching tongues with a little girl.

Lisa was leading a small group of people around. "I'd give you *the tour*," I heard her say, "but *the tour* will just have to wait." Lisa made a big deal about displaying the family property, as though it were something most people would travel across state lines in order to experience just once before they died.

By her side, my brother was conducting a sight-seeing trip of his own. "Now, over there," he mumbled, "is a group of heterosexuals. See how unfastidious they are? See how sloppy and puffballlike? They're slobs! You gotta love 'em for their imprecision! Their carelessness!"

"Sshhh!" Lisa hissed.

"Kah!" Beck exclaimed as another guest ambled naïvely into the sliding glass doors. "Zikha! Che! Kluge! Zipkin! Ahmet! Mica! Another accidental nose job!"

"She's already *had* one," Lisa confided as the indolent paramedics sprang into action. "In fact, Peggy has one of the worst assembly-line nose jobs *dans l'histoire de* cartilage. . . . She looks like Huckleberry Hound. In fact, if she shatters the damn thing again, it'd only be an improvement. I mean, talk about the rhino in rhinoplasty, right? That's my Pegeen. Oh, look! Everybody, look up! It's a Maxfield Parrish sky!"

"What's that?" one of the people with her wanted to know.

"Maxfield Parrish," Lisa said carefully. It was a hard name to say after you'd had a lot of champagne.

"What did he paint, exactly?"

Lisa hesitated, and then I heard her say, "Lots of sky . . . scene things. I forget what else he did. But mostly sky scenes. Clouds, et cetera."

It was a close call. "And over there's my brother," Lisa said, recovering like the pro that she was. I hadn't realized Sir was part of the tour. "He's at that disgusting age where he likes girls for the first time, right? It's like he comes down every morning and *sprays* me, uggh, *quel* creature double-feature, right?"

Back inside the house I saw that my sister had taken a seat next to Mrs. Lyman, who had set to work on her ninetieth Scotch and Fresca. "My horse is blue," Mrs. Lyman was insisting. "A blue roan. My magnificent horse grew up by the ocean. Inside the hollow of a golden dune. And this is how she has absorbed the azures of vast oceans into her coat. My horse is blue."

"*Votre cheval est bleu,*" Fishie said absently, attempting to make this concept sound more interesting than it was. "Su horse-o es bluego. Eins horsiepoo blaudeich—"

"My horse is blue," Mrs. Lyman repeatedly numbly. She touched Fishie on the shoulder, leaving a wet mark. "You must—all of you must—come over absolutely anytime and ride my blue horse. Remember, we're always here."

"I'd love to return to Fiji," I could hear Mrs. Lyman say a moment later. "The Fijians were such big, beautiful specimens of men. Their bodies . . . their bodies actually seemed to have *working pistons* under the skin. *Bula Binaca*—that means good morning in Fijian. Did you know that?" Mrs. Lyman stared into her drink. "But I do not believe I shall ever return to the beautiful, azure land of Fiji. *Bula Binaca,*" she repeated sadly.

I fixed myself a strong drink and worked my way back under the tent. A parquet floor had been set up in back, and a few people were dancing. To get to the dance floor you first had to go through a small gate strung with black velvet movie-theater ropes. I think it might actually have been a metal detector, to prevent people from bringing weapons onto the dance floor: knives to stab Lisa, garrotes to strangle her, little Ninja stars to lodge in her scalp. Triple L was twirling around the dance floor alone, with her hands held high in the air like a bouquet and her dark glasses pushed back over her veil. When she saw me staring at her, she suddenly stopped.

"*Ça va, nouveau* brother-in-law?" Lisa screamed. When she came over, I could smell the mist of champagne on her lips. Lisa always spoke French when she was about to say something heartless or perverse. She knew about fourteen words in every language, and she repeated them over and over again. She was a whole international crowd in one—you got the sophistication and the false titles without ever having to deal with hired cars or a large, noisy group. "Can I call you 'Bro-in-law' now?"

"Go right ahead," I said. I didn't think I'd be seeing much of Lisa after the wedding, so it didn't make much difference what she called me.

"Bro-in-law," Lisa said. "Broinlaw. Bruin-lau. Like you used to play for the Boston Bruins. Or the UCLA Bruins."

"Yuh-huh." I felt like a complete fake, helping to maintain this nowhere conversation.

"Law-in-bro," Lisa went on. "Löwenbrau. Hey, Löwenbrau beer! Don't you think that's funny? I know, I'll call you Löwenbrau from now on. Like my old beau Tommy Widener over there, have you met Tommy yet? His father's like *the* beer-bottling person slash king slash owner slash major big-bucks person in Minnesota, but Tommy hates beer, he says it gives him migraines, can you bear it?" Lisa screamed. Then she lowered her voice. "Not that there's much point in being rich west of New York, right? I mean, what are you going to spend it on? A shitload of wild rice?"

I didn't have the faintest idea what she was talking about, but I manfully choked out a couple of noises. It was obvious that she was smashed.

"Listen, Hal." Lisa grabbed my wrist and peered into my face in a way I knew she thought was intimate. "Mummy's terribly worried that SUG isn't having any fun. *Peux*—you assist?"

"SUG?" I repeated.

"My grandmother. Dad's mother. SUG. It's short for Shut Up, Granny. 'Cause she talks so fucking much, right? But we call her SUG for short. We kids gave her that name when we were like *two seconds* old. Anyway, SUG doesn't know a soul here. She's this really wonderful person, et cetera, but I think she feels a teensy bit out of place."

Lisa hesitated. My wrist was gradually losing blood under her anaconda grip. Sometimes drunk people believe they're in danger of sliding off the side of the earth, and they suck onto your skin and try to take you along with them. "This is not really SUG's *thing*, Hal, if you know what I mean. She's not really a *social* person, if you see what I'm saying. She's not used to this kind of *do*, if you get my point. And Mummy's worried she isn't having a good time."

"Is your mother all right?" I said.

"Oh, Mummy's just tired. She's been under a lot of stress this week, that's all. She's tired."

"Mummy's tired," I repeated with the weariness that comes from practice. Unfortunately Lisa and I knew the same New England euphemisims. *Tired* here meant drunk on your feet. It referred to the physical state of someone prior to the time the requisite forty drinks were consumed. The idea was that if the person hadn't been so exhausted—by his long plane flight, by his restless sleep the night before—then he wouldn't be urinating into your ice trays. This was a code I wished I didn't share with Lisa.

"Mummy is *très fatiguée*," Lisa agreed. "Sleepy time *doit être* her next move if she's smart." She pointed to an old woman in black taking in the whole scene. "That's her. That's SUG. My father's mother. That sweet dear little old crow over there in the sensible shoes. It breaks my heart to think of her putting on her best dress just for me, just so she could come here and end up feeling out of place. She's really a sweetheart, Hal, and if you could fit her into your dance card, which I'm sure is *jammed* with names, I'd be like your *life slave*."

Lisa finally let go of my wrist but then grabbed me by my jacket collar. "SUG's one of those people who can't say a bad word about *anybody*. I think she may be *biologically incapable* of negativity or something. It's so incredible rare when you think about it, isn't it? She's so positive about everything, she puts us all to shame. I mean, she doesn't have much *money* or anything, but she keeps up this *spirit*, which I think is so—so, what's the word I'm looking for, admirable? No, indomitable. I think that's the greatest thing in a person. It is such a *gift*. The funny thing is, it's something—spirit, I mean—you would think came from good breeding, *mucho* bucks *sur les* premises, et cetera, but I don't think her background is, well, whatever her background is, et cetera." Lisa smiled at me almost pleadingly.

"Like a good neighbor," I hummed under my breath, "State Farm is there."

Lisa didn't seem to hear, but the jingle burrowed further into her mind. "Okay? Okay, *mon ami?* And promise you won't be put off by her mournful little tunic. Oh, Hal, I can just imagine her now in Filene's basement with her sad little purselet in her grimy little hand, being knocked about by all the pushies and the meanies, then going home to her pathetic little flat—oh, it makes me so depressed I want to blow my *brains* out, you know? She lives in this *dustbowl* flat you wouldn't believe. Like some old *Okie*, Steinbeck city, depression-era, breadlines, et cetera. It's like some Saigon *slum*, her little grub-worm flat."

For the first time I realized that Lisa was making a mature, clearheaded attempt to put her Vietnam experiences behind her, and that by evoking the cities that still haunted her—Saigon, Hanoi, Khe Phang—she was, in effect, saying, "Yes, I served a tour of duty in Vietnam, and that experience marked me; but that time is over, and now I'm getting on with my life, a day at a time." I found myself oddly moved.

"Apartment," I said, snapping out of my reverie.

"Again?" Lisa's little silver bell tinkled as she leaned even closer into my face.

"Apartment," I repeated dully. "We're in the Colonies now. We made the formal split. We say *apartment* over here, we don't say *flat*. That's why we cut so-called English muffins in two with a fork. To remind them."

"Oh, right." Lisa laughed and conked herself on the side of the head. "I get confused. That's the trouble with spending too much time in London, right? Anyhoo." Lisa looked over at her grandmother again and wrinkled her face. "Oh, now I'm so sad thinking about SUG. Now I'm all sad and blue. Give me a hug, Hal, and I won't be so sad and blue anymore." Lisa kissed me, this time on the lips, then she let go of my jacket with a laugh. Her lips were so thin and dry—I don't know how my brother managed to kiss her without feeling diminished afterward.

"I've always wanted to do that to you, Hal," Lisa said. She was standing back, still laughing. "Just to see what you'd do. Try to get you to drop your guard. You're such an intriguing guy, Hal, you know that? Maybe I shouldn't tell you, you'll get so vain you'll be impossible to be around. But really, you remind me of this house with all the windows shut. And all the doors sealed. And maybe one porch light on, but then the rest of the house is dark, you know?"

What is it about weddings that makes people try to sum up your life for you? It's kind of a misplaced deathbed instinct or something. "I don't like to waste electricity," I said slowly.

"Oh, Hal, it's only money, right? Anyway, I think your New Year's resolution should be to let someone *inside*. *Dedans*. We're all on this crazy planet together, right?"

"Right," I mumbled.

Lisa squeezed my arm again. "Anyhoo, *scusi, cheri*, my public calls," and Lisa's shoulders seemed to drop ten inches before she delivered her best ersatz smile of the afternoon.

I went over and introduced myself to Lisa's grandmother, then asked if she wanted to dance. She was a delicate-looking woman, with high, thin shoulders, and her black dress came down past her knees. Her hair was short, gray and wispy, like the feathers of a dandelion.

I led her over to the dance floor.

"Are you having fun, Mrs. Lyman?"

Lisa's grandmother glared at me. "I'm having a lousy time, if you want to know the truth, and I assume like most people you don't. I've never seen so many disreputable fakers under one tent in my life, and this isn't my first time under the tent, either, so don't—"

"The Lymans have certainly outdone themselves today," I said, thinking I hadn't heard her right. "All the flowers, the helium balloons, the hors d'—"

"It's all *shit*," Lisa's grandmother snarled. "All of it's *shit*. It's ludicrous. It's a circus nightmare. Whoever catered this circus nightmare should be burned alive at the stake. Those mushrooms they're passing around taste like rubber crutch ends. The caviar's turned. The eggs are sulfur. And the whole family's shot to shit. The little boy's a disaster, the older boy's a complete mess, one sister breeds like a rat, my son is completely out of touch with everything in the world but his smelly dogs, the mother's a lush and don't get me started in on Lisa."

"Hey, we like you," I said, and I took the wonderful old woman in my arms and we commenced a primitive fox-trot. I had learned the box step when I was seven years old and a member of Mrs. Cash's Dancing School, and was unnerved to discover that those boxes were still fresh in my mind. Oh, I stubbed Mrs. Lyman's toes a few times, but I managed to keep pace and the boxes I engineered were actually rectangular. Everything about Mrs. Cash matched, I remembered: dress, shoes, purse, stockings. I should've known that this was the sign of a troubled and compulsive older woman, but I was young, I wanted to dance in a rectangle, not analyze people. Later Mrs. Cash jumped out of a hotel room in Atlantic City after losing her shirt at keno.

I had my hands on Lisa's grandmother's spine, which I could feel shifting like beads under my fingers.

"Lisa tells me that—"

"I don't wish to discuss Lisa," she snapped. "Don't let's spoil the occasion.

Lisa was a selfish, spoiled, demonic child, and I've seen her grow up into a selfish, spoiled, demonic woman. End of subject."

"Okay, okay," I said, "you're barking up the right dogwood here."

"I'd rather listen to the great music," Lisa's grandmother said. In a minute she was moving her small, white, gentle head in time to the song. "I'd be a beggar or a slave for you," she sang in a high, tremulous voice. "And if that isn't love, it'll have to do, until the real thing comes along."

SUG fixed me with brown, acute eyes. "And do you love someone?"

I thought of Beck, Fishie, Kitty, Veebka, parents and, again, Kitty. "Sure," I said. "My family."

"Family doesn't count. I like to say God gave us our relatives, thank God we can make our own friends."

"There's this girl I like," I said almost dopily.

"Ah. Then why are you dancing with me and not with her?"

I explained that Veebka hadn't wanted to come to the wedding. Veebka said it was because of the lamb and the duck, but I knew it had more to do with the fact that we'd recently been at each other's throats.

"And is it the real thing?" SUG wanted to know. "Or will it have to do until the real thing comes along? Will you marry this girl?"

"Oh, it's real," I said uncertainly. "Real enough. And I don't know if I'll marry her. We live together," I went on. "In New York. I moved there because she was there."

"That was unwise of you, if I may say so," Lisa's grandmother said. "Rule Number One: Never, ever move to a city to be near someone. A man did that once to me and I left him in a matter of weeks. It destroyed our friendship and it was boring, besides. Rule Number Two: Never live with a man, though I should be saying this to your girl. Why should a man who's accustomed to getting something for free suddenly be levied with a tax? Remember what happened in Boston two hundred years ago, the business with the tea. The men wouldn't stand for it."

Several of Lisa's Farmington friends were dancing with each other. I stared at them: there is something gripping about girls dancing with each other. For the first time I began noticing that Lisa's friends, at twenty-eight, were at an age where their small, bewitched faces had less in common with their eighteen-year-old selves than with what, at age fifty, their faces unsmilingly would become. Already I could imagine these girls' chins set in middle-aged worry, the faint lines curling under their noses later framing stubborn and bigoted mouths. My face, however, looked the same, and that's what scared me.

Other than the girls, no one else was on the dance floor except for a woman dancing alone with her baby. The baby was a boy baby that looked like a newborn chick. The mother was swaying around one corner of the dance floor, swinging her hips softly, hypnotized, staring into her baby's soft blue eyes. Sometimes she held him up so his head was even with hers, at other times she held his head loosely to her chest. During the most romantic part of the song she draped the baby's sausage-link arms around her neck.

I watched as Triple L dragged my brother onto the dance floor and deposited him right in the middle. She hung Beck's long sloppy arms around her neck, as though she were arranging the leaves of a plant. In a little while I heard her say, "Hold me tighter, Beck. Quit stomping on my shoes. *Quit* it!" Lisa still used many whiny expressions from her childhood, among them "*Quit* it!" "You and what army?" and "A *doi, doi,*" this last expression uttered in a deep, echoing voice.

"No, put your fingers *here*. On my back, stupid—lower." Lisa smiled and shook her head when she called him stupid, and then she pinched Beck's fingers and placed them over the points on her shoulder where she wanted them to go. "God, I have to treat you like this *enfant,*" she said in a bright, declaiming voice, so everybody could hear. "This little piggy goes here, this little piggy goes here, I'll little piggy *you*, buster, if you don't *watch* it."

My sister and I stood on the sidelines watching as Lisa hauled Beck around the dance floor. "I'm going to have to cut in," my sister said after a while. "This is too demeaning for words."

This meant I would have to dance with Lisa, which I couldn't and wouldn't. I would rather have touched a burning ember to my forehead. "How about you go dance with Lisa?" I suggested. "I'll dance with Beck."

Fishie's refusal came quickly. "If I have to dance with Lisa, I won't be responsible for myself."

"Don't go hidin' from me, Mister Moon," Dick Dickerson sang, and pointed up at the top of the tent, where there was no moon, only sagging canvas.

I watched my sister go over to Beck and Lisa. Fishie pulled Lisa aside and drew my brother away. "*Scusi,*" my sister said in a high disgusted voice. Such was the level at which my sister and I found ourselves at this point of the afternoon. Lisa made us both feel so helpless and impotent that we were reduced to doing vocal imitations of her.

I had no choice but to dance with Lisa, who threw her arms around my neck. "I'm seeing a lot of you today, aren't I, Löwenbrau?"

"You are indeed," I said weakly.

Unfortunately the song ended, and a slower number began as Dick Dickerson smiled to the polite applause from people over sixty.

"Just a gigolah," Lisa sang vaguely. "Everywhere I gah." She laughed. "That's the girl version, right? This old music is *great*, isn't it? Don't you just *love* old music, Hal? The whole nostalgia thingie? It's *molto bene,* no?"

I pushed into Lisa hard, to silence her.

"So my friend Wicky really likes you," she said at one point. I was trying to push Lisa over to the band's microphone cords so she'd electrocute herself, but it wasn't working. She seemed to know that I was trying to kill her, and stepped safely out of reach of the black wires. "Wicky Huntington. She went, Who *is* that guy? I'm not supposed to be telling you any of this, by the way, Wicky would disembowel me, so don't you dare say I've talked to you. I went to Farmington with her. During that year with the baby and all. *Uggh*, that was *vachement* foul, the business with the baby. Anyhow, Wicky's from Ohio. She was born in New York but she moved to Ohio when she was about two seconds old. Her mom's a Du Pont. Shaker Heights," Lisa added, as though trying to be helpful. "I used to go skiing at her family's place in Wisconsin. Lake Geneva," Lisa added, the bright, watery stars of falseness appearing almost romantically in her eyes. "We used to go to Nevis together during break. Her parents had—well, they still do have—a—"

"I'm sure glad Wicky's not from, oh, say, Columbus, or, say, Madison, Wisconsin," I said sarcastically.

"No," Lisa said, sounding worried. "No, not those places. I said Shaker—"

"I was just kidding," I said. "It was a hilarious joke."

"Right," Lisa said, glancing at me oddly as though someday, she hoped, I would develop a feeling for what was appropriate and what wasn't. Then, without warning, she seized my arm. "So Beck tells me you're still in New York, Hal. I think that's *so exciting*. I *love* the city. I think the city's *great*. I don't think there's anyplace like it anywhere else in the *world*."

"Well," I said, "I kinda like Madison, Wisconsin."

"Madison? I've never been to Madison. I've been to Lake Geneva, though. Skiing. Wait, didn't I just tell you that?" Lisa laughed and said, "A *doi, doi*. But I think New York is like *it*. New York and Paris and London, those are the big three. And maybe Bombay, that is if you get off on fabrics, though I just *don't*. Except the poverty in India is *sooo* depressing. I went around Bombay feeling like I had a ten-thousand-pound weight on my shoulders. It was like *Khe Phang* or someplace."

"Put 'Nam behind you," I mumbled inaudibly. "Get on with your half-life . . ."

"Wait, what was I just saying? Oh, yeah, Bombay. Fabric. I love saris, though. Except the idiot woman with no chin at the Intercontinental didn't know how to tie one right and it kept falling to the floor. Imagine living in Bombay, you know goddamn sari *central*, all your life and not knowing how to tie one? I mean, what *good* are you, right? But you have to admire everyone's *spirit* there. It's so, whatever, indomitable. In the face of all that grime and shit and horror twenty-four hours a day, I'd probably just keel over and die, you know, could you please pass me that revolver so I can kill myself, *thank* you, you know? Except they do have this *amazing* orange juice." Lisa laughed. "For some reason. In India. For some reason it doesn't have that much pulp at the bottom. The great orange juice sort of halfway salvaged the place for me. But otherwise, Ix-Nay to Bombay."

I gave in. I was beaten down. I couldn't take it any longer. I had to join in or else implode. "I know *exactement* what you mean, Lease," I heard myself saying sympathetically.

"Can I tell you why I'm so distracted today? Can I tell you?"

"*Dis moi,*" I begged.

"This friend of mine, Steve, he was supposed to come today and never showed up. He has Hodgkin's disease, lymphoma, whatever, and he claimed he couldn't come today because he was *tired*. No, *tired* wasn't the word he used, he used the word *exhausted*. Can you believe that? I go, Steve, you're in *remission*, what *is* the fucking problem here? I mean, if it were anyone else getting married here but *me*. This guy and I have done everything together except the dirty deed, right? But I thought that was so self-whatever of him. Steve: self-righteous, self-serving. What's the word"—Lisa looked at me apologetically—"self-whatever. Don't you think? This is the only wedding I'll ever have, after all."

Don't count on it, sister, I thought. "I *hate* it when other people get sick," I whined. "It's *rude* is what it is. Sometimes they're just lying there in the hospital and they can't even speak, they have all these *wires* sticking out of them. And you go, Hello in there! Hello! Anybody home? And you realize they haven't heard a goddamn word you've said because they're so-called *unconscious* or *in a coma*. You've wasted your *breath*, breath you might otherwise have used to *breathe*. It's *infuriating!*"

"Exack-a-tack-ally," Lisa screamed, clutching me tighter. "The sick are such *shits!*"

My sister airlifted me out of Disingenuous Hell by tapping Lisa on the shoulder. "Gimme this dance," she snarled.

We clumsily switched partners. "Lisa, you come over here with me," Fishie said, firmly steering Triple L over to the other side of the dance floor. I was left dancing with my brother to "Just One More Chance." Behind us, Lisa's wretched older brother Chris was slam-dancing with his local floozy even though everybody else around him was waltzing. Finally Beck said, "Why are we dancing together, Hal?"

"I don't know," I said, feeling suddenly and desperately nostalgic. "Because after you leave on your honeymoon I won't see you for—well, I just don't know when I'll see you next."

"Ah, that's sad and somehow final," my brother said blankly.

"Yes," I said, "it is."

He stared at me. "Hal, are you wearing mascara?"

"A little. I was wearing a lot more before," I chattered, "but I wiped most of it off. Have you ever worn mascara? They claim that it's waterproof, but if it is, why when women cry does it leave streaks? And why—"

My brother pushed me away. "I don't want to dance with you anymore, Hal. I have many more important things to do, interesting corners of this room to visit, interesting people to start up conversations with. You're too weird to dance with—"

" 'I know the meaning of repentence,' " Dick Dickerson sobbed into his oversize microphone, " 'now you're the jury at my trial.' "

"I'm too weird?" I snapped. "You *invented* weird, buddy."

"Hey, not as weird as you are," my not-at-all juvenile brother said, wandering away as Dick Dickerson began to whistle to the chorus.

I looked around for the girl Lisa called Wicky and someone finally pointed her out to me. Wicky wore a silver cowbell around her neck, too, but it wasn't a subtle bell like the other girls were wearing. Wicky's bell was the largest I'd ever seen in my life, so heavy that her neck was bent over, and whenever she took a few steps foward, he looked as though she were being propelled downhill. I decided against introducing myself and then, later on, marrying this cow. I could tell her bell was bound to cause major problems.

I drank a gin and tonic. Gin would grant me the perspective I needed. While I was squeezing the lime over the ice I suddenly felt the tails of my jacket being lifted up into the air, and at first, before I turned around, I thought the Lymans had hired a team of bouncers to throw me out.

But it was Mary of Munich and she was leering. This time around her green eyes looked even wilder. I suspected she'd just done a few more dolls in a filthy crawlspace somewhere. "Just wanted to check on your bottoms," Mary said.

"Mary," I said humbly.

She fixed me with her steel-green look. "I leave soon," she said slowly. "You come with me?"

"Where are we going?"

Mary shrugged. Her finger gently flicked my tie, then she shrugged again. "Who gives the goddammit. . . .?"

"Where's old Dave?" I said, to change the subject.

"Dayffe, *il est même plus solide que l'ennui.*"

There was a silence, then Mary said, half closing her eyes, "You not so good, you know?"

I cupped one ear. "Say what?"

"You not so good to look at. You the best one here and not so good still. That's just for this night. No one more good here this night, okay?"

"Let me get this straight," I said. "You're saying that there's a crummy selection of men here at this reception, but that out of this pathetic, second-rate group of has-beens or never-beens, I'm the one you find the least unappealing. Is that a fair summing-up?"

Mary laughed soundlessly. "Yeah, Howl."

"That means a lot, Mary," I said slowly, "coming from you."

"So then you come? I make you come, right?"

"No," I said. "No, I can't go anywhere. I live with someone. I have a girlfriend."

"So, big deal." Mary laughed. "Big deal. I have girlfriend also. In Tübingen."

"Do you really?" I said. But I didn't move.

"*Das Ich Mir schneissegal.*" Mary shrugged. "I find someone else then. But don't you think you are any good to look at, because you are not." She shrugged a final time and vanished across the lawn.

Later an obscene and blaring torpor overtook everyone under the tent. There were some thirty people left, all sagged into chairs, around tables, sipping their final drinks. The tent sat still under a light rain, and the few mosquito flares left lit—tribal wood sticks with kerosene-doused cloth wrapped around their tops—sputtered, their final flames on the verge of quitting. Bits of shredded balloon clung to the grass. The Gang of Six was staggering around the stage, packing up their instruments.

At one of the tables Mr. Lyman was putting Sir through his paces. Sir was crumpled on a chair, in tears, holding a dirty paper plate in his lap. "Was Miss Dickinson a tall woman?"

"No," Sir whispered. Then, more loudly, "No."

"Then she was—"

"She was small."

"Like?"

"Like?" Sir repeated.

His father waved his hand, an impatient flag. "Like what?"

"Like me?" Sir said meekly.

"Remember Dickinson's words of keen self-appraisal," Mr. Lyman said " 'I am small like the wren. My hair is bold like the chestnut burr. And my eyes—' Sir, what were her eyes like?"

Sir's long white hair whipped around as he shook his head wearily.

Mr. Lyman gazed at me. "Hal, can you shed any light on this nomenclatural dilemma?"

"Eyes like a filthy groveling garden pest?" I said. (I had made that up. I still didn't know the answer.)

Smoothly, with a sense of deliciousness, Mr. Lyman said, "My eyes, like the sherry in the glass that the guest leaves."

I took this as a hint that the reception was over and that Mr. Lyman wanted everybody to clear out. Two things usually signal the end of the long party. The first is that the leftover fathers turn on a television set and watch the last inning or period of whatever game happens to be on. The second is that a Motown record is put on the record player, either an early Jackson Five album, or something by the Temptations or the Four Tops. When a Motown record comes on, it is usually time to leave large gatherings of whites.

Mrs. Lyman had long since disappeared into her bedroom. After the cake was cut, she developed an allergic reaction to her lipstick, which made her red mouth swell, as though someone had punched her repeatedly in the lips. Outside, the rain was coming down softly onto the lawn, and patches of ground were turning to brown paste. Mr. Lyman kept ordering up Scotches for the diehard guests. He told the actor-waiters he'd brought in from New York to take off their white coats and have a drink on the house. At one point I saw him talking on the telephone to the vet. "I want to hear how those dogs *are*," he said, furious. *Let me speak to one of them*, I half expected him to say. *Put those dogs on the phone right this minute.* "This is Ben Lyman, who is this? What is your name? Miss Diamond? And what is your so-called title, Miss Diamond? I'm writing that down," he roared, and proceeded not to. "I'm writing that down, D-I-A—" He roared again.

My parents had returned to their hotel, Lisa's bridesmaids had slunk back to the shores and town houses of Boston, Connecticut and New York, Senator Willem had passed out on the floor of the Lymans' greenhouse, surrounded by children, led by Ted, who were busy placing sunflower seeds and driveway pebbles in his open mouth and under his tongue. Sir was in tears. I didn't know what Fishie and I were doing sticking around; habit, I guess. Beck was our brother, after all, and his getting married made us both feel a little bit like children again, helpless. Plus, I have to admit that I've always wanted to know what happens to people right after they've been married. What do the new man and wife say to each other? Do they eat, or argue? Do they fall asleep? Unfortunately no one seemed to know where my brother was. A search was made of the house, and nothing resembling my brother turned up. My sister and I volunteered to go look for him.

It hadn't grown any cooler outside, and there were crickets and midges buzzing around our heads and ears, trying to escape the sucking drizzle. Fishie and I crossed over the Lymans' white gravel driveway and slid underneath the top bar of a split-rail fence. I took my shoes off and walked barefoot on the grass, and then I took off my coat and borrowed tie. I can only stand to be in a coat and tie for so long, then I feel like beating somebody up.

From our vantage point we could see Triple L wandering around the lawn, still in her wedding dress but with her arms crossed over a fishermen's sweater that I recognized as belonging to my brother. She had changed into sneakers too—a pair of fluorescent orange Converse All-Star High-Tops. I could hear her bell tinkling, even from that distance; I suppose that was the point of Lisa's bell in the first place.

"Now, I gave Beck that sweater as I remember," Fishie said thoughtfully, staring at Lisa. "I didn't give *her* that sweater . . ."

We tromped into the orchard on the other side of the driveway, squashing apples under our feet. The ones on the ground had small black holes in them, as though from BBs. The dangling apples were red stars on the dripping trees. The rain gave them a new coat, a shine, that made them look like young apples, even though they weren't. Behind us, Lisa was saying good-bye to her horses. She reached through the high hinged windows of the stable and hugged their necks.

Beck seemed surprised to see us, and slightly embarrassed, while Fishie and I felt the same way for having stumbled across him. He was sitting in the rear of the orchard, under a dead, scrawny apple tree, with his back facing the Lymans' property. When he saw us, he got up and started walking toward us, then he stopped. His cummerbund was twisted around three times and his glasses were fogged up with humidity and rain. There was sweat on the stripe of his shirt where his tie had been, and his fly was half down. All Beck lacked was a drunken grin. I noticed that he'd taken off his black tie and bound it tightly around one forearm, as though he were in mourning. While we were standing there he lit one yellow-tipped match after another from one of the boxes of commemorative matches that the Lymans had had made up for the wedding. The boxes said LKL and BLA in red letters and, below the initials, the date.

Fishie said, "Aren't you going to join your new wife?"

The wedding match flared, then he rubbed it out between his fingers. We all stood there in the orchard, watching as Triple L trod tipsily through the wet, unmown grass in front of the stables. When Lisa reached the fence that separated the lawn from the road, she put both hands down on the wood and rested her head on her fists. My brother stared in her general direction.

"What are you looking at?" I said after two minutes of tedious silence had gone by.

"My lash," my brother said dully, dreamily.

"Your lash?" Fishie said.

"It's reflected. In my glasses. A row of my lashes. They look kind of neat, yup. I wish you could see 'em, but then you'd have to be me to see 'em. They look so . . . so expert."

I knew what Beck was doing: He was withholding expression from us, the way he had done as a child. My brother used to like to walk around with his eyes as dead and soulless as he could make them, saying nonsensical things in a blank, passive voice until he got his way. It was as though his pilot light had been disconnected.

"What's the matter, honey?" Fishie said.

Beck was having trouble talking. "I can't. Uh, uh. You see, the thing is . . ."

We waited around for my brother to say something. I couldn't see his eyes behind the fog blurring his glasses and I found myself getting impatient. It was already dark out and I wanted to bury Kitty sometime before, say, midnight.

"I've been a bachelor for too long," Beck said in a low voice. "You can't ask a guy to do an about-face on the, uh, the cusp of a guy's second trimester on earth. I just can't go through with it, you guys. I'm not a Marine, after all, uh, right?"

"Wait, what do you mean *you can't go through with it?*" Fishie said. "You just *did* go through with it. Unless"—she gestured over toward the Lymans' soggy lawn—"I've just been watching a movie."

"Yeah," he said. "I think it was a movie. Yeah, it was a long, extraordinary movie. That's right. The filmmakers really got it down, the whole thing. I'd give that movie, uh, two thumbs up . . ."

"Are you feeling sick?" my sister wanted to know.

"Sick, I'm sick, yes."

"So what do you have?"

We waited around for Beck's answer, but all he did was to start kicking apples and playing with his feet. I noticed that what I had thought were his formal wedding shoes were actually black Reeboks.

"Maybe he ate too much popcorn at the movie," I chirped.

"Beck, it's not all that bad." (Fishie lies staring straight into your eyes.) "Lisa's a very, very nice girl. You'll be happy if you just give it a chance."

"I don't even like Lisa," my brother moaned.

"Lisa?" I said disbelievingly, almost swearing her name. "What do you mean, you don't like Lisa? What's the matter with the Excellent Postwar Bitch?"

"Beck," Fishie said, "you can't turn back now. It's not in the rules. The Lymans spent a fortune on this wedding. Plus, wasn't there something in the ceremony about us upholding your marriage; trying to keep it from crashing and burning? We all said yes, we would uphold it. Or aye, whatever it was we were forced to say." She gazed evenly at my brother. "You can't welch at this point and turn us all into liars. We've got reputations to think about, at least I do."

"Why don't *you* marry Lisa?" Beck said to me.

"Because," I said for about the ninetieth time that day, "I have a girlfriend."

"Who, *Veebka?*"

"Veebka the idiot duck-and-lamb walker?" Fishie added. I could tell both of them wanted to say something mean about my girlfriend but didn't have the energy.

"Because," I said, finally giving in, "I don't like Lisa, either. I think Lisa should get the electric chair." I was annoyed that the reverential mood that should have preceded Kitty's burial was being destroyed. "You want to know how much I *really* can't stand Lisa?"

"No, I don't know, how much?" my brother screamed delightedly.

"I think Lisa's a blackhead on the face of the earth!" I screamed back. "I've never liked her, and Fishie can't stand her, either!"

"Hal," my sister said, "let me speak for myself, please." She turned to Beck with great seriousness. "Beck, I hate Lisa. I hate her more than I've ever hated anyone, including my diving coach and Marlene Bauke. She's pond scum. She's a disaster area. She's heinous. I can't say enough bad things about her—I could but I don't have a year. Pretending to be interested in me just because I can cadge her tickets to the Olympics . . ." Fishie stared at me. "Hal, please, *never* put words in my mouth."

Beck was nodding his head stupidly. "Jeepers," he finally said. "Jeepers, you guys. I'm glad you guys finally told me how you really feel. You know, I don't know if I've ever told you this, but your opinions are very important to—"

At the mention of Lisa's name I looked up across the lawn. Lisa was walking past the striped industrial cans that balanced the jumping bars. Her thin white arms were crossed and she was calling out my brother's name. She was also, I realized, headed in our direction. Her wedding dress was catching on the high, wet grass, the train trailing behind her solemn as a plow, especially when she ducked under the horse jump with its heavy crimson iron rod. I was suddenly reminded of other parties of Lisa's that I'd been on, all of which ended at four in the morning with a game of limbo. After a certain point of the evening Lisa would be so smashed that you would ask her something and her only response would be to roll her eyes back until they looked like garlic cloves, then she'd drawl, "Leem-bo, leem-bo." Even if you told Lisa that her house was on fire and her parents had just gone down over the Virginia countryside in a single-engine Cessna, the only thing Lisa could manage was "Leem-bo, leem-bo," and then she'd call you "Mahhnn," in an accent that made you feel acute embarrassment for her.

"*Capitano*," Lisa now called across the field. "Time to go for a sail, Meester *Capitano*."

"Quick," Beck said. "Let's get out of here."

Fishie didn't budge. "Beck," she said sternly, "that's your wife. You can't do this. You're supposed to go on a cruise now. And you can't involve *us* in it. You're someone's *husband*, for goodness' sakes."

Beck had disappeared into the trees. He's very agile and we hardly saw him go, just the branches rustling in his wake, and when we started following him across the fields, crouched low so Lisa wouldn't see us, he quickly lost us. Fishie and I followed in the approximate direction where he'd run, past a blackberry bramble, until I finally glimpsed him hidden in a wild square of woods, his knees squashed in the dirt beside a knobby gray tree stump.

Beck may be quick, but because of his size it's difficult for him to hide; he would make a terrible spy, for example. Mosquitoes had gathered in his stubble and on his arms, but he wasn't hitting them for fear of being detected. Instead he blew at them, uselessly.

We came up softly behind him. "Beck!" Fishie whispered. "You're a grown man. This is not acceptable."

"All aboard, sweetie," I heard Lisa calling from the orchard. "Ready about hard-a-lee."

Fishie and I hunkered down next to our brother. "Don't give me away," he begged. I had never heard his voice sound quite so pathetic before. "Please don't give me away."

"Beck," we heard Lisa bawling. "Beckie."

We hid out in a shack in the woods for a couple of hours, just the three of us. Fishie discovered a box of stale Triscuits and we ate them greedily.

I sat in the cubbylike kitchen, staring out the windows at the rain, while my brother played with an old ham radio he had found in one of the closets. Later on we heard the snorting of a horse, and hooves against the gravel of the Lymans' driveway, and when I looked through the trees outside the window, I spotted Mrs. Lyman astride a giant blue horse. She was wearing high brown boots and a blue felt helmet that fit her like a walnut, and she yelled out my brother's name again and again through her swollen lips.

"Agghh," my brother moaned softly. "This is it, Sundance."

I wasn't sure whether Lisa was following behind her mother so I volunteered to creep outside and investigate. I ducked through the bushes and stood concealed at the edge of the orchard. There was only one equestrian that I could see, and as far as I knew, Mr. Lyman's golden retrievers were trained only to sniff out birds. The blue horse paused in the orchard and Mrs. Lyman dug the heels of her boots into its withers. "Come out of there, you son of a bitch! Come out of there!"

I went back to the cabin and was debriefed. I told my brother that Mrs. Lyman had his number, and that it was probably only a matter of time before we were discovered and brought to justice. The Lymans probably had us surrounded, I said. "And they're going to hang you high, laddie."

"I told you we shouldn't have holed up," my sister told Beck. "*Of course* the Lymans would check out this dreary place. It's probably a guest house for the B or C lists."

"Look," I said, "we should probably bury Kitty before it gets any later."

"Bury Kitty?" my brother said. "What's the matter with her?"

"She kicked the bucket, Beck." Now Fishie was fiddling with the knobs of the ham radio. "She lost her mew and then she died. She jumped out of Hal's apartment window. WonderKitty. I told you on the phone—"

"Kitty?" Beck was staring at me. "Your kitty? Hal's kitty? The kitty that looked like a pig?"

"Yes, my kitty," I said. "The same. The one you and"—I gestured at Fishie—"that one used to dress up and torture."

Kitty had been through a lot during her life. Ever since we'd rescued her from the gas chamber we never ceased to remind her that she owed us prompt, uncomplaining service for the duration of her life, no matter what. Fishie, for example, used to dress her up in discarded clothing. Small steel-rimmed glasses sat balanced on Kitty's nose, and a fluorescent green T-shirt covered her body and trailed after her as she walked. At times she even "consented" to wear a Marilyn Monroe wig, and mew an approximation of "Happy Birthday" to Beck, who played the president. On several occasions Fishie and Beck would haul this hapless cat down to the beach, lifting her up over the puddles so that her T-shirt wouldn't get soiled. On the beach, Beck would squeeze Kitty between his knees and Fishie would take Polaroids of her. Once they slid out of the camera, Fishie would force Kitty to look at them. In most photos Kitty's eyes were a shocking, otherworldly red.

"This is you," Fishie would say meanly. "This is what you look like—a blond sixties burnout. An aging hippie. Why, I've seen people like you lingering in your college towns *forever.* Drinking bottomless cups of coffee, running a yellowed finger through your filthy beard. Reading Nietzsche!"

Now Kitty was gone.

Fishie steers Son with just the tips of her fingers—pale white nails like moons and very well-chewed skin. The nervousness before swimming races is permanently signaled in my sister's nails. Son is panting air, pumping hot, sweet mist into our laps, a smell that is fruity, fermenting, non-automotive. Fishie likes to remind us that Son could explode at any second. Other VW Fastbacks of the same vintage were recalled, hysterically, ten years ago, but Fishie refuses to return Son to Detroit even though Aretha Franklin lives there, so there might be parties. All of Son's faults just make her heart grow fonder, just as they used to charm Beck, since Son is a family car and each of us gets him for five years. Son is a classic, Fishie keeps saying—fucking car doesn't even *work* most of the time it's such a classic.

About two miles from the graveyard, Fishie turns on the high beam on Son's lone headlight—the other one's still stuck on a telephone pole somewhere in Scranton, Pennsylvania, courtesy of the time Beck wanted to show us he could drive Son using only his breath. He wanted to prove that his lung capacity was greater than Fishie's, which was, of course, a no-win situation, and as he attempted to blow the steering wheel over to the right with a series of deep, mournful sighs, Son smacked into the pole. The leftover light is small and weak, like the glow of a night-light behind a bedroom bureau, and the drivers on the road that night, trying to be helpful, flashed their lights at us, but Fishie only muttered, "I know, goddammit, I know."

Nobody mentions Lisa, or the wedding, or the institution of marriage, or much of anything. My brother sits off to one side of the backseat, in another world. At the start of the trip he kept glancing backward to see if anyone was following us, but he doesn't bother to anymore. He rubs his long, tired fingers against Son's clouded window. Since you cannot turn the heat off, the interior temperature is always about ninety-one degrees. Riding in Son is like living in a small, hot tropical republic. "Well, shove another rag in the vent," Fishie snaps. My sister doesn't take kindly any such criticisms, especially since her time with Son is limited. She has him only for another three weeks, and then he's mine.

We park at the entrance to the graveyard. The sign reads, VISITORS WEL-COME, and my brother gets a laugh out of that, until I tell him that his humor is both inappropriate and obvious, that he's pointed out the same sign before, when we were burying Great-aunt Loreen, and he laughed the same way then. I've heard it all before.

I open the trunk to get Kitty's ashes. Son's engine is in the rear of the car, the trunk up front. The lock's broken and I have to pry it open with a huge screwdriver. Son requires several minutes to stop after you turn him off; he sits on the curb, small, uncertain, chugging. My brother produces a silver spoon, fork and knife from his pocket, the utensils with which he was supposed to eat his tournedos at the reception, and he hands them over to me with a little sigh. Beck suffers from the most innocent, instinctive form of kleptomania. It has more to do with bad nerves than with bad character, though his character is certainly suspect as well. If you offer him a light, he will pocket your lighter. If you lend him your newspaper, you will get it back in strips, with all the interesting articles torn out. The monogrammed champagne glass from the reception bulges out of his jacket pocket, along with a pale linen napkin. He slumps against the empty guardhouse with his hands in his pockets, frowning, saying he'll stand watch for us.

Fishie and I set off toward the plots of ground devoted to the old whalers and suicides in our family. I'm carrying the box of ashes, and Fishie has the spoon, the fork and the knife. It is risky, of course, burying a cat in a human graveyard, but last week both of us agreed it was worth the risk.

"Where do you want to do it?" my sister says when we stumble onto our family plots.

I point to the left of a grave marked Ezekiel, a great-uncle who suffered from hysterical blindness off and on during his life and who died, like most of my relatives, from self-amusement. Fishie squats, rubs her fingers in the curling tracks of the capital letters. The graves of both Ezekiel and his wife Loreen are right next to a smoke bush, whose blossoms exactly resemble Loreen's hair when she was alive, and this, added to the darkness and fog of the graveyard, makes me want to get the ceremony over with as soon as possible.

"Right here," I tell my sister, pointing to a small patch of ground four feet to Ezekiel's left.

Fishie begins digging with the monogrammed Lyman spoon. The earth is so wet after the rain that the root-beer-colored dirt comes up easily. A late mist is coming off the pond, grazing in and out of the graveyard like the ghost of a sheep. I clutch Kitty's remains and watch as Fishie paws out the dirt. After a while I pitch in, using the Lymans' yellowing silver fork. Soon enough my brother turns up, whistling a mournful teenybopper hit, his hands still deep in his pockets.

"May I do anything?" Beck says, sounding like a houseguest who feels he's overstayed his welcome.

Neither my sister nor I say a word. Beck stands there, idle as ever. "Jeepers, I feel bad about that silverware. Maybe I should take them back after we're done."

"I don't think that would be so brilliant an idea," Fishie tells him.

"Anything, uh, you want me to do?" he says again.

"You may set the table," I say. "You can peel onions until you weep." I cannot get this brother-as-houseguest-on-earth idea out of my mind. Actually there is not much anybody can do at this point. I have prepared a script for the burial that I wrote in honor of the occasion. It borrows heavily from the Episcopalian Book of Common Prayer and one of the Bangles' videos. Kitty loved the Bangles, especially their lead singer, Susanna Hoffs. *Jeez, can those Bangles ever move,* I often observed Kitty thinking as we sat watching MTV together on the couch.

Fishie strikes rock with the spoon head. She now has a six-inch-deep hole, brick-shaped, and she rocks back on her heels, tossing the spoon aside.

I lower the box into the ground. For a second I wish Veebka were there, and then I think, Naahhh, Veebka hated Kitty too. She even divided up the rent so I had to pay Kitty's share. Veebka once told me that she thought Kitty belonged in an ancient, crumbling barn somewhere, that cats ought to live in straw. I told her that if there was any more talk like that, she'd end up in the barn. Kitty could live with me, up at the main house, in splendor.

I hand Fishie and Beck a script. "Okay," I say. "I go first, then you. The first section's all mine."

"Wait," my brother says. "Where's my glasses? I can't see anything without my glasses."

"You probably left them back at the cabin," I say. There he was, waiting in the darkness of his bad day, reading cabin literature—a battered 1963 Farmer's Almanac, which is about as forward-thinking as my brother gets: confirming old rainy weather rather than forecasting it. Both Beck and I wear glasses from time to time. To see us together you would think that glasses are a secondary physical characteristic of our family, like our eyes, or our stooped shoulders, or the fact that we're always broke.

"You won't need them, anyway," I tell him. "Your part is simplicity itself." Your part is nonexistent, I felt like saying. You shouldn't even be here. But I'd decided to let Beck read Fishie's part, along with her. They could read it together, like an abominable little chorus.

"Oh, Kitty," I begin, staring down at the dim type and making a petting motion with my hand.

"What?" Fishie says.

"Pay attention to the script," I say. "The part in red ink. The red is your part. And his. I'm blue."

Fishie says, "This script says, Ohhh Kitty, then exclamation point. Then Damn Kitty, exclamation point."

"Right. When I come to a pause in the text, I want you and him to come in with your voices. Clear, strong. Hale."

Beck tells me he thought he'd have actual whole sacred paragraphs to read. He looks disappointed. I wish my brother would remove his black tie from his forearm, since he's starting to remind me of a student protester.

"This isn't really much of a *role*, Hal . . ." he starts to complain.

"Well, what are you going to do?" I say. "Whine to the union? Complain to your agent?"

"What does 'Egyptian Hand Movements' mean?" my sister says.

I am forced to demonstrate. First you touch your fingers to your thumb, as though you're casting the shadow of an aardvark's head against a white wall. Both hands should be at shoulder level. Then you bend slightly at the knees and open and close your hands, smiling insanely all the while. "Pretend you're a couple of belly dancers," I say. "But keep your tongue in your mouth at all times. Tongue should play no part here."

"This is pretty strange, Hal." My brother coughs a nervous sort of laugh.

"You've just jilted your bride and *this* is a little strange? What the hell are you talking about?" I scream. "Get real, weirdo!"

My brother offers his usual forlorn adolescent response. "*You* get real, weirdo," he mutters.

This is the first time any of us has made reference to the wedding or to the J-word, and my brother's shoulders start to droop. "Oh, cheer up, you weirdo," my sister rasps at him. "Lisa'll find another husband in about two seconds. She can go off and marry that scuzzy beer-and-ale heir and they can be heirs together."

"*I* want to be an heir," Beck says softly.

"Oh, Kitty," I begin again.

"Ohhh! Kitty! Damn! Kitty!" Fishie and Beck chant loudly. Then Beck starts snickering.

"This is not a joking occasion," I say coldly. "Please wait until I give you the hand signal before you read your parts. And don't scream. Give me some piety. Ohhh, Kitty, Kitty. Murmur it. Like you find the mere thought of it unbearably exciting. Try to sound a little pro-life. Pro-Kitty."

"I didn't like Kitty," my brother says. "Kitty always—"

"I don't want to hear about it," I snap. "Kitty never liked you, either, weirdo—"

"Hey, simmer down, you two," Fishie says, still blushed with champagne and holding one of her small, special-occasions purses to her hip.

I have to start all over again. My brother tries to look pious by shoving his hands under his cummerbund, shuffling his feet and making his lower lip quiver. Instead of looking pious, he looks like a shepherd who's just been told all his sheep have fallen to wolves.

"Oh, Kitty, now we enter thee—"

"Hey," my brother says suddenly. "Hey, Hal, if all Kitty is is ashes, wouldn't she be happier spread out all over someplace? Like over the Atlantic Ocean? Hey, Hal, we could drop her from a *chopper*—"

"No," I yell. "She wouldn't. Kitty wants to be buried here with everybody else in the family!"

"But Kitty was such a lumpen thing, don't you think she'd opt for extreme *lightness* now that she's dead? I mean, if you want my opinion, I think we should drop her from a *chopper*—"

"I am fully aware of Kitty's wants!" I scream. "And Kitty wanted to be buried here in the fucking family plot! In the fucking family pie! And if there was going to be any sprinkling, I would sprinkle the fucking ocean over Kitty, not vice versa!"

"Hal," Beck mutters, "it was only a suggestion."

"Stick to the goddamn script!" Then I calm down. I think of the ocean and the sky. I think of the serenity of cows, and how they're able to sleep on their feet. I think of Veebka's stomach and how peaceful it is, resting my head there. Part of my irritation has to do with the fact that I'm not wearing my glasses, either. I left them in one of the Lymans' bathrooms. Nothing has a definite edge or a keen point. Everything looks mushy.

"I know you didn't mean to be thoughtless or malign," I tell my brother. "Drop her from a chopper. *Drop Kitty from a chopper*, now that's very amusing. I know you only said it because it sort of rhymes, and so yes, it was amusing. But I didn't spend a week writing this script for you to start deviating and improvising—"

"I'm hungry," he says suddenly, turning to my sister. "All I had to eat at that reception were those mushrooms. And a little bit of smoked salmon, which I think had turned . . ."

"The food wasn't very good," my sister says. "Those cheesy things . . . those wafting cheesy things . . ."

"Cheese Wafts," my brother says immediately.

"Those Cheese Wafts, they tasted like ammonia. What kind of cheese was that, anyway?"

It is obviously open season on the Lymans now. How can my brother and sister be so insensitive? But I don't dare say much, since I can't see anything. Without my glasses I feel extremely vulnerable, fair game myself. The lone streetlight in the graveyard parking lot shimmers ahead in the dark like a giant gold-spangled snowflake.

I forge ahead. "Now, dust thou art and unto dust shalt thou return . . ."

My brother stares down at his three-dollar Korean watch. The dial is cloudy and he licks the glass. When he does, his arms flap out like wings and I see him suddenly as white meat. It is a terrible thing, to see your brother as chicken meat, an oven stuffer. I realize I must be starving too.

"We go down to the dust," I continue. "Yet even at the grave we make our song." I gave them the signal.

"Ohhh! Kitty!" my sister and my brother cry, their hands and bodies swaying. "Damn! Kitty!"

Our lives will have nothing in them like the beginning, I think. I can't see anybody now. I'm reciting words into a fog. Without my glasses I can't even make out the faces of my brother and sister. They look as dark, greased and pudgy as old mittens thrown down in the mud. All I can make out is the dusty echo of their chorus through the dark, silvery graveyard. *Ohhh Kitty . . . Damn Kitty . . .*

"Oh, let's just shove the box into the hole," I say crossly.

"May I?" my brother says.

"I don't think that was cheese at all in those Wafts," my sister says, standing there watching my brother. "I think it was a cheese scent of some sort. A new product in the Family Wipes tradition of excellence."

"The bacon-and-olive things were good, except the bacon never cooks when you do that . . . it just swells up all fatty . . . so repulsive."

I watch as my brother lays the tiny butter box into the earth and stands back. "Don't you want to put a flower on it, Hal?"

In my blindness I can't see any flowers, so I shake my head sadly. "Dirt back in," I command softly.

My brother sets to work with the spoon. With that in one hand and the fork in the other, he looks as if he's about to make a meal of the earth.

"Use your hands," I say suddenly.

Both my brother and sister crouch down to shovel dirt into the hole with the sides of their hard palms. They are obedient undertakers. When the hole is filled, they pinch the folds of dirt, as a cook crimps a piecrust.

"In the midst of life," I tell my fog, "we are in death."

Drag

*T*his was not the first time that Beck ran away from Little Lisa Lyman. He would do it again and again, until he got it right, but at the time . . . both my sister and I, knowing nothing of this emerging pattern, were serenely ignorant, and in our ignorance we could concentrate upon the sad, enduring image of Triple L wandering around drunk and pre-cruise on her parents' sodden, expensive lawn, bawling out my brother's name, and upon the consequences of what my brother had done.

After sealing Kitty underground, Fishie took me aside into the disordered darkness of the graveyard gates.

"Now," she inquired, "don't you think this is bad?"

I like it when things are either good or bad, when Fishie doesn't need to get all that specific and detailed. There is a mythic simplicity to her definitions of bad and good: murder and forest fires are bad, sunlight and gold medals are good. The in-betweens—dusk, fistfights, small arsons, bronze anything—she doesn't even care enough about to mention.

But I assumed Fishie was referring to Kitty's funeral, so at first my pleasure at my sister's mythic simplicity was stiff—I thought we'd done a whale of a job. "I am under the impression," I said, "that we've just come out of a stupendously moving event."

"Shut up about Kitty, Hal. *Beck*, he's the subject here. His choosing *us*, his family, over a *girl*."

"But the girl is Lisa," I whined. "You know, Lisa? Triple L? The girl none of us can stand? I mean, *I* like us better than Lisa . . ."

"I know it's Lisa. And Lisa's an abomination, et cetera. And her score was still spectacular, et cetera, I'm not forgetting that. But it's not only Lisa, it's us over *any* girl. It could be anybody. And that's not good, that's *bad*. There is something to be said," Fishie concluded nobly, "about marrying outside your immediate family. Extending your circle of intimates. Learning to rely on someone who, odds would have it, wasn't in attendance at your birth. I mean, back there in the woods it was like we were all *nine* again, nine and ten, trying to play music with spoons on pans."

"Isn't this anti your usual philosophy?"

"Wait, what is?"

"I thought you didn't want Beck to marry anybody. Or for me to marry anybody."

Fishie is the self-appointed family protector, stenographer and smoother-overer, since she makes the most money and, if she wanted to, could buy us all off. In the past, for example, Fishie has offered my brother and me generous sums of money to leave whatever girlfriend Fishie didn't like at the time, or whom she found unsuitable—sums ranging from fifteen hundred (a low price only for when she sensed the girl in question was on her way out, anyway) to ten thousand, which she offered to me three years ago in exchange for ditching a certain Ramona.

I forgot: Fishie had anted up in a big way when it came to Lisa: Thirty thousand dollars, half on Premediated Argument Leading Up to Lisa's Dismissal, the other half payable when Beck could provide my sister with documented evidence that Triple L had permanently dropped out of his life. Unfortunately Fishie soon withdrew her offer after realizing that Lisa could match her offer gagged, and with her hands tied behind her back, and my sister didn't want to get into an uncomfortable bidding situation with the Lymans. Fishie, for all her bravura, is financially conservative, and she always goes out of her way to avoid an auction. "Put a price on my own brother's head?" she ended up saying indignantly. "As though he were a painting, or a duck decoy I liked?"

One thing I'll say about Fishie, though. After completing one of her little deals, Fishie never fails to send a valentine. If we break up with the girl on a Friday, the valentine is invariably in our mailbox by Monday morning. I think Fishie buys valentines by the thousands, then hides them in a bottom drawer. They always have little messages on them, too, things like, "Welcome back to the meat market," followed by a huge question mark. But you always know who sent it, that it's from her.

"You misunderstand me, Hal," my sister said after a moment of silence.

"I'm a friend to my brothers, not an enemy or a fiend. There's a difference here I think you're failing to see. In the past, I admit, I wanted to prevent both of you from wasting your time on the wrong girls. But Lisa *is* suitable, in her way. Which is not to say she's bearable, but she's not unsuitable."

"So what do we do?" I said glumly. "Turn him in? Isn't it a little late in the day for that?"

"It is a little *late*," Fishie said, "for Beck to turn around and decide he can't stand Lisa, either. Don't you see that all we're doing is encouraging him to evade responsibility again? And that this reflects a certain lack of spontaneity on our parts?"

I looked over at my brother then, who was squatting before the smoke-bush hair of Loreen and muttering something under his breath to the hazy sprigs. He was gesturing with his hands a lot, as though involved in a lively dialogue with the bush. My Great-aunt Loreen had actually liked my brother the best of all of us, and I'm not saying that just to be dramatic or self-pitying. Loreen thought Beck was quite brilliant, and that he had talent on the piano, so when she died, she left him all thirteen of her little black-and-white TV sets. Between us, Fishie and I had to share a roll of perfumed tissues and a bunch of padded pink satin hangers. Just thinking about it still burns me up.

"What's Beck doing back there?" I said in a low voice.

"Oh, I don't know." Fishie turned away. "Thanking Loreen for all those millions of channels, complaining about his rotten reception, how the hell should I know, Hal? I've had it up to here, anyway . . . don't you see his problem, that he's suffering from drag?"

"Drag?"

"It's like swimming, Hal, you know. It's a hydrodynamic principle. Like for airplanes. Bernoulli's principle, it's called. You know, that the faster a fluid travels, the less pressure it's able to exert perpendicular to its direction? Right? To its direction of motion?"

My sister thinks everything—love, life, death, accomplishment—is exactly like swimming, and she's wrong. Swimming is like swimming, I tell her again and again, and swimming is boring. Life is like *hockey*, played against a dirty, wild-eyed, high-sticking team of unshaven barbarians.

"Mew, mew, mew, mew," I said loudly, tuning Fishie right out. This is a trick that I learned from Kitty herself. Whenever she was experiencing an emotion, in particular, boredom, Kitty always said, "Mew, mew, mew, mew"—four in a row just like darts, very fast, superb clarity, good head voice.

"So what did I just say?"

"Perpendicular. Thing. Fluid. Drag. The airlines . . ." I hadn't been listening to human voices: an airborne cat was in my head.

Fishie frowned. "Drag's the opposite of Bernoulli's principle, Hal. Drag goes to explain whatever forces there are that make a person go backward. Toward childhood and eventually the womb."

"Agghh, the Pink House," I moaned.

"Precisely. The Pink House. And drag's what holds a person back. Drag is what makes a person sail headfirst backward toward the Pink House. And your brother, if you want my opinion, is suffering from a hideously advanced and probably incurable case of drag. See, that's why people like Marlene Bauke prefer to shave their skulls. To reduce their drag."

Marlene Bauke is my sister's main competitor in the Seniors Swim Tournaments. She is originally from the Black Forest of Germany, and the villainous sound of her hometown has added to her reputation as the "bad" swimmer and to Fishie's as the "good" swimmer, a distinction that delights my sister, since she thinks of herself, entirely without reason, as the embodiment of a swaying American cornfield. When you think of swimmers these days, you think of Marlene and my sister; nobody else trains as compulsively or wins as often. I remember a year ago I was sitting with my parents watching the Senior Swim Classic in Edinburgh on television when Marlene pulled ahead of my sister in the final few yards and won the race. In the living room, the Great William cupped his hands around his mouth and began softly booing. Beck, who was lying on the couch, got up and poured a carton of milk into the back of the television until the set hissed, but not to the point where we lost our picture.

"That was the budgies' milk, son . . ." the Great William murmured.

"Of course Marlene won," my mother said presently, in her best tired voice. "She has no breasts and she's bald."

My mother wasn't only being a bitch—it was true. Marlene doesn't have a single hair on her entire body. Her head is smooth and still as a tide pool, and she has the torso of a very thin batboy. Begoggled, standing with her arms crossed at the starting block, she is a sight that makes your eyes sore.

Back on the couch, my brother yawned. "Marlene may have won this race," he said, "but I daresay she lacks some of the social opportunities that Fishie enjoys. What I mean is, Marlene may have won, but what kind of social life do you suppose she has? What kind of fun? Does she have anything resembling an after-hours life? Sex and such? Recreational pellets? No, none, I think." My brother, who had recently met Lisa and was then being hauled to three or four parties a night, had begun using this line of thinking about people who were accomplishing anything at all with their lives. My brother's point was that the gene scientists and brain surgeons of the world may have agile, talented minds but that at parties you'll always find them in the unpopular rooms, pressed up against the wall, volunteering every few minutes to go out on ice runs. "Breasts are the minimum nubs requisite for tour-de-force social success in major cities," Beck went on in his dreamy, phlegmatic voice. "Without those nubs a-standin', a girl, victorious or not, is dead meat socially. And Fishie has nice breasts, *great* breasts."

"Yes," I said as Fishie strode up to the platform to accept a nice plate from a dissolute Scottish lord with a five-inch chin. Fishie's arms gleamed with the petroleum jelly she had rubbed over herself before the race, and little bubbles of water winked and died on her shoulder. Ten minutes later Fishie was smiling painfully at the TV sportscaster, Jim Johnson, a former swimmer himself and now a color commentator and low-grade alcoholic.

"Didn't Fishie name her breasts once?" Beck said as my father's rare pink canaries began screaming in unison for their milk.

"I hope not," I said. "Nope. I don't remember that."

"Then who are Maggie and Christina? Where did I get those two names? Why are they running around in my head? I mean, do you know anybody called that? If they're not Fishie's breasts, do you think maybe I could've gotten those names from anywhere else you can think of?"

"Oh, shut up," I said crossly.

"What happened out there, Fishie?" Jim wanted to know.

Fishie has the postrace insincerities down cold. Her eyes ice over, she goes into an automatic pilot that manages to disguise her essential hostility, and unless you knew her well, you'd think she was for real, a sportswoman of rare character. Fishie had staged a concerted effort to be kind ever since Beck, Kitty and I confronted her about what a general bully she was when we were growing up: throwing heavy cans of soup at our heads; ignoring us for days on end; and, when she wasn't busy ignoring us, applying the sleeper hold to our necks until we sank, barely breathing, onto our childhood lawn with its single bush in the middle, clogged with balls. Her other tactics included body slams, full nelsons or, her favorite method of torture, foreign substances—sea salt, turnbuckles, jalapeños—rubbed into our eyeballs while our parents weren't watching. Later, once we were out cold, Fishie occasionally Super-Glued small household objects onto our faces and necks before lashing our nude, ornamented bodies to the trunks of young pines.

"Marlene was the better swimmer out there today," Fishie said to Jim. "I went out too hard, and the final two hundred yards my arms and legs were on fire. Marlene simply paced herself better today."

"Well, second place is nothing to be ashamed of," Jim said, laughing slightly.

"Hmmm." Fishie was staring at her wrists, flapping them. Carefully she added, "Less hardware for my mantelpiece, maybe."

"Do you think the altitude might've had anything to do with your poor showing today?"

"If so, Jim, Marlene faced the same obstacle and overcame it. No excuses, Jim. Marlene was simply the better swimmer out there today," Fishie went droning on, as if she were under the influence of an acclaimed hypnotist. "Certainly Marlene's a tremendous competitor. She always gives a hundred and ten percent, you know? And she did the same out there today. She's a great champion and a great example, not only to the youth of Germany but to children and amateur sportsmen all over the world. Her swim today was both brilliant and measured, a dazzling display of aquatic motion and a privilege to watch."

"Why is Fishie being so amazingly boring," Beck asked me. "Doesn't she know she's on a major TV network?"

"Yes," I said, "and that's why. She doesn't want to seem the depraved bad sport we know she actually is."

"Oh, your sister's not boring in the least," my mother told the both of us. "She's a good sport. You're just not listening to her."

"Fishie," Jim was saying, "do you think Marlene's shaved head had anything to do with her performance out there today? That it might have contributed to her tremendous time out there at all?"

"You know, Jim, that's a very good question. All I can say is, whatever strategy works for a particular swimmer is right on the money as far as I'm concerned. As I've always maintained, any given swimmer can give another given swimmer a run for her money on any given day. That's what makes competitive swimming the great sport it is."

"Oh, God," Beck said, "my respect is ticking away. Tick, tick, tick." He made his entire right arm a minute hand, his chest became a clock face.

"You've never considered shaving your own head?" Jim wanted to know.

"Me? Shave my head? No, why should I? No, never. My . . . I don't think my boyfriend would go for it."

"Fishie's boyfriend," I said, "is so slow on the uptake he probably wouldn't even notice."

"Fishie's boyfriend is not slow on the uptake," my mother said.

"Our viewers, Fishie," Jim went on, "are probably interested in how you got your name. There have been many stories but none of them confirmed. Certainly it's a highly unusual first name . . ."

"Yes, Jim, it is," Fishie said.

"And I'm sure our viewers would be interested in finding out from you what exactly the origin—"

"Well, that's very flattering. Thank you, Jim. But I'm sure the viewers are hardly interested in my personal life, don't you agree? And after all, a girl has to keep a few secrets to herself, doesn't she?"

The truth is, Fishie can't even remember how she got her nickname. It's one of those nicknames lost to family history. She got it, now no one remembers how. No one kept track, although we do faintly recall her real name, which is Lily. That she's a Pisces could be one reason. Another is the obvious one, that she is far more comfortable and contented in the water than floundering around in the demented, less liquid air.

"Fishie Andrews," Jim said. "Second-place winner here today, losing for only the second time in her life to Marlene Bauke."

"Piss off, Jim," Fishie said suddenly, her mask of composure falling away.

"Why don't *you* strip and get your butt out there and try swimming the sixteen-fifty freestyle in *one second* yourself? It would probably take you an *hour*, that's why . . ."

What happened after that still embarrasses me to remember it, and to this day it remains something of a black mark against our country. As Marlene was escorted out in front of the cameras, my sister began screaming at Jim Johnson. "So I come in second for once in my life! Big fucking deal! I've won every other goddamn dreary meet this year! I won the Masters Games, the relays, all three individual medleys—"

"Oh, Fishie's gotten so *vain*," my brother exclaimed.

"—and I knock my *butt* off swimming in front of thirteen million people! In Scotland of all places! Isn't that enough?"

"No flies on you, baby," Beck whispered from the couch.

"Oh, no, your sister's not at all vain," my mother said.

"Fishie Andrews, the runner-up," Jim said, by way of summary and dismissal.

"Easy for you to say, Jim! Easy for you to say! Standing here . . . in your hideous madras jacket . . . calling a race you don't know anything about! Have another bourbon, Jim! You with your perverted desire to see bald women parading around the sides of pools! What the hell's wrong with you, anyway?"

"Definitely no flies on this baby!" my brother screamed joyfully.

"Fishie Andrews, runner-up today," Jim said again. He turned to Marlene Bauke, who was standing uncertainly to the left of the starting blocks. "You must be thrilled with your victory today, Marlene—"

"Yes, I pleased to be will win today." Marlene, looking embarrassed, smiled at Jim, who was trying his best to push Fishie out of sight. "See, I push, and I push, and sometimes I no longer push can—"

"Oohh, sometimes I no longer push can! I pleased to be will win today!" Fishie mimicked in a high voice. "Good English! Do you today will win be pleased? Push can no longer sometimes I no?"

"Fishie Andrews," Jim kept saying as my sister leapt up behind his shoulders, making snarling faces behind Marlene's shaved head. Above my head, the pink canaries screamed for their daily lactose and my brother responded by turning the volume to full blast.

"Your sister's . . . not . . . doing this . . ." my mother said.

"Son, you shouldn't have disposed of the budgies' milk in that particular way," the Great William murmured.

"Bald horror! Hairless amoeba!" Fishie shrieked at Marlene, before finally stalking off to her dressing room and her usual post-race concoction: two ounces of Calvados, lime, no ice.

* * *

My brother shuffled over to the cemetery gate.

"Honey," Fishie said, "Hal and I have something to tell you. We've been thinking—Hal and I have been thinking, that is—so brace your little shoulders and breathe out from your stomach." She hesitated. "We think—Hal and I think, that is—you should go back to Lisa and try to make a go of it."

"We do, do we?" my brother said.

"Yes. Don't we, Hal?" Fishie glanced over at me for support.

"Yes, we do think that." Actually I hadn't been listening. I was recalling Kitty, how sometimes her white legs, stretched out, resembled a rabbit's, how other times her dry, pink, sticky lips parted and Kitty became a salmon, and how during those times I wanted to smoke her.

Fishie spoke rapidly. "Hal and I, here, we feel you haven't given it your best shot, Beck. We think you should go ahead, go off on that damn cruise. Remember: We're only a phone call away. You can reach out and touch us anytime, any hour of the day, ship-to-shore or the regular way, whatever you like. And collect too. Hal, in particular, would be pleased to accept your collect calls—"

"Oh, no, I don't think I want to do that, really," my brother said in a rush. "No, really. I don't really think I want to do that."

"We'll drive you back in Son," my sister went on, ignoring him. "Right now we'll drive you back, and you can return the silverware and make up some very good story that doesn't stagger the imagination *too* much."

"Or else you can make up a series of elaborate lies." I added, since I am by nature sneakier than my sister.

"And you should apologize to her, of course."

"But her mother—"

"We'll handle the mummy," Fishie said warmly. "You see, Mummy lives in a cocoon of sherry, Beck, not unlike you sometimes. We'll bring Mummy some Grand Marnier as a so-called family house gift, but it'll have Mummy's name scribbled all over its label in ink only she can read. We'll say it's from you, and you watch if amity doesn't reign in the Lyman household in a matter of minutes."

"I like Mrs. Lyman," Beck said thoughtfully.

I said, "I thought you said she was spoiled and overbearing."

"I've altered my opinion somewhat," my brother said. "She's an excellent horsewoman, for example."

I said, "It would be nice, I think, and less confusing for all of us, if you stuck to one opinion."

The day had been long and we were all getting testy. As we walked toward the car, with Fishie on one side of my brother and me on the other, we passed under the blurred streetlight, the same one that combined earlier with my blindness to resemble a huge snowflake. When my brother passed underneath, the thick, straited bulb dimmed, then went silent. I tripped lightly over something just then—the sudden darkness tilting the ground under me. Fishie, not noticing the quieted light, didn't stop walking, she plowed on ahead.

I paused to stare up at the light, stretching the ends of my eyes out so each eye must have looked like five stitches sealed over a cut; sometimes you can see better that way. Flush against the trees, the bulb was now a dim, dull shadow.

"Hey," my brother said, "I did it again. Now, what do you make of that?"

"What do we make of what?" Fishie said.

"The streetlight thing," my brother said earnestly. "It went off again, all by itself. I didn't do anything." He shook his head. "I swear."

"Listen," Fishie said, "if I've told you once, I've told you a billion times: You'll find out when you're dead. There could be a lot of answers here. Remember, when there's more than one answer to a question, there's no answer at all. So wait until you're dead and you'll get the answer in the answer book then."

I have been at my brother's side many times when this has happened. At first I thought there was a hump underneath the road that activated the streetlights, but then I was confronted with a series of doomed streetlights that were nowhere near traffic centers but instead on forlorn back roads in various towns and cities. When these streetlights observed my brother coming, they gasped and then shut off. They knew the party was over, that with my brother around all good times would start to deteriorate. Perhaps it was coincidental, that my brother's approach always coincided with the bulb's decline and fall, but this had happened way too many times for luck. None of us knew what it meant, Beck's ability to turn off streetlights without using his hands or throwing rocks, but we all agreed it was definitely a talent of some kind, though not one that was likely to bring him much by way of income.

Beck went so far as to consult a psychic, an enormously fat woman who lived in a ground-floor apartment in Hell's Kitchen. My brother, she suggested, was a reincarnated lesser god who in another life had probably been able to control weak solar eclipses but who now, in these reprehensible modern times, was reduced to shutting down streetlights. Most people are imperfect, the psychic explained as her husband and brothers snored on the couch behind her. Beck had nodded, impressed—*imperfect* is his middle name. People were reincarnated, the story went, if they didn't manage to overcome the frailties and addictions and weaknesses they suffered in their past life. It happened all the time. The fat psychic added that for two thousand dollars she would be glad to light a candle for my brother's soul, five thousand if he wanted her to keep constant vigil at that flame and wave away the moths and little flies that came, falsely, to worship.

"And what if this isn't it, Hal?" he asked afterward.

"What if what isn't what?"

"What if this is as good as it ever gets? What if we're dealing here with a spirit that's still on a practice run? Mine, I mean? What if my spirit is the one that the next person in line will have to overcome? I mean, what if I'm not the final entrant?"

Beck is always looking for a way out, an excuse to act badly, and I realized that this rip-off psychic had just handed him another. Now he could carry on acting badly and blame it on the fact that his imperfect soul was merely on a ragged test run through time, and that the real work would come later, when the next victim, screaming, was handed his Swiss-cheese spirit.

In front of Son, my brother turned to me. "What if Lisa won't take me back?"

I gazed at him sadly. "She will. It'll be your first married argument, but I think she'll probably fall for it." *Jesus wept,* I thought.

During Kitty's burial I'd been thinking delightedly of *not* having Lisa in our family, of never having to attend a family reunion with her, of calling my brother and never having to hear Lisa pick up the phone and say, in her zesty, salad-dressing voice, *"Pronto."* My spirits collapsed like a roof, then rose up again. Maybe she wouldn't take my brother back, maybe she'd already eloped with the beer-and-ale heir. Then I thought, No way. The truth was, Lisa was probably going crazy with worry.

We dropped him off at the head of the Lymans' dark driveway. He slammed Son's door and stood there, blinking in the cool nighttime air, the fog still in clusters over the vast lawn, the house set far back, with its lights on, the sheds beyond it darkly stuffed with bales and bales of hay.

"So much has happened today," Beck said, leaning on his elbows against the roof of the car. "I don't know what to—"

"What you do is this," Fishie said. "You go up to Lisa and you take her in your arms"—despite herself, Fishie shivered—"and you say something inane like, Hello, Mrs. Andrews, just like they do in the movies. And *she'll* counter with, Hello, Mr. Andrews, and that'll be a nice moment. In fact, it'll be the first moving and significant use of your married name."

"Lisa's keeping her maiden name," Beck said stupidly.

"Oh, yes, so sorry," Fishie said. "How *ignorant* of me to have thought for an instant that Lisa would ever take another's name. Terribly sorry."

"I just wish Lisa wore glasses," Beck blurted out.

"Why's that?" I said.

"So I could tear them off her face and say, you know, Lisa, you're a beautiful woman without your glasses. You're not a librarian type at all. And then I'd reach behind her head and unclasp her bun, and her hair would pour down, since her glasses and her hair would be . . . connected somehow. And she'd be grateful to me for revealing to her the woman she really *is.*"

"Lisa doesn't wear a bun," Fishie pointed out.

"Oh, this is a fantasy. In this fantasy, you see, Lisa's a librarian at the university checkout desk. And I'm a student, sort of a sleek-looking student. And at the end I tear her glasses off her head and her hair drops down about eight feet and she's revealed before me . . . luminous. You know, a merry fluffball. No?" As always, my brother finished weakly.

"Hah. Good luck with that one, pig," Fishie said, starting up Son again.

"So I can call you guys up, right? Just to check in?" Beck said in a casual voice, as though he didn't care if he ever got through.

"Sure," Fishie said softly. "Maybe not tonight but . . . very soon. In New York. Hal has my number. I'm house-sitting, remember? At Bob's place?"

Bob was Fishie's boyfriend, a professional bowler and moron who this summer was plying his trade in Australia. None of us knew why Fishie liked him. When I asked her, she was sullen, uncommunicative and plain unhelpful. "Well, what else do you want me to do, Hal? Marry some stiff from the suburbs? Some lifeless lawyer? Have a thousand children all named Amy or Jennifer? Pack 'em into a Volvo station wagon and die a vigorous death in some mall parking lot? Besides, I like non-WASPs—they have more energy and less sexual shame to 'em. Fewer crossed arms to that gang. And their wakes—ah, Hal, have you ever been to one of their wakes? They're transcendent! All that keening and unashamed boozing . . ." Wakes? What does Fishie know about wakes, about the notion of the open coffin? Fishie has maybe been to one wake in her whole life, and she probably crashed it, for the Calvados.

This summer, though, she had agreed to live in Bob's apartment while he was away losing one frame after another to the Australians, and also to walk his dog, BB, which was short for Bowling Ball, which was Bob's idea of hilarious.

Beck leaned inside Son's window. "There is much grist here for the annual Christmas card. Much grist indeed."

Fishie gave a little strangled laugh. "Just remember to leave us out this time, honey, okay?"

"Have no fear." Beck had said the same thing last year.

"Go," Fishie said. She seemed sad. Despite her tough-girl act she really loves Beck, but she usually expresses that love like a cigarette girl in a gangster movie. "Go on, get outa here, ya big galonga. . ."

"Well, I suppose. . ." My brother didn't move.

"You look a little rattled."

"If you're not a little rattled," my brother said, "then you're not paying attention. You're not fully alive, right?"

"You got your story down?"

"Oh, yes."

"Okay, what is it?"

In the car we had rehearsed the story Beck was about to tell the Lymans.

"I was abducted by Mick and the Rolling Stones."

"Just say the Rolling Stones," Fishie said, "since of course that would include Mick. Hey, where did those Stones take you?"

"Onto their tour bus."

"And what did their tour bus look like? Nice-looking? Good rugs? Taste factor?"

"I cannot remember."

"I *can't* remember," I corrected him gently.

"I *can't* remember."

"Oh? Say, why's that?" Fishie already knew the answer to all these questions—she was merely preparing my brother for a rough interrogation.

"Mick placed a hood over my face and forehead, rendering normal vision impossible."

"Excellent. Except it was Keith. Keith's in charge of hoods."

"Fishie, what does it matter who—" Beck mumbled.

"It just does. Mick would *never* put a hood on you. Keith would. It's a difference of sensibility. And I would add just two things here. Two words, qualifying words. *Heavy* and *cotton*. So now it's, Keith placed a heavy cotton hood over my face and forehead, rendering normal vision impossible." Fishie stared at me. "That's in case Lisa says something about always being able to see through *her* damn hoods."

"Got it," my brother said, but I knew he would foul it up, turn it into "sheer white hood" or even "totally transparent hood."

"And be nice to that pathetic child, Sir. He needs a male influence, even if it's you. So pat the kid sometimes."

Still my brother didn't move. "Okay," he said lightly, then he brought out his petting hand from behind his back. "Farewell, my brother," he said to me.

"Farewell, my brother," I said, just that once. I still didn't understand why the Rolling Stones would have any interest in kidnapping my brother and holding him hostage on their tour bus. But sometimes it was better not to question these things, even in the interests of verisimilitude—besides, I knew the Rolling Stones enjoyed playing by their own rules.

"Go!" Fishie yelled. "Have a good marriage! Breed." Then, as we were speeding off under the roof of thumps, she said, "No doubt Lisa won't stand for a mimeographed Christmas card. She'll have a picture of them both squinting on some glazed beach in Mustique, surrounded by pansexual royals." Fishie shook her head tiredly. "He'll probably never work a day in his life again."

Last year my brother's Christmas card, his final installment as a bachelor, was sent off, before anybody could do anything about it, to about a hundred people, including childhood friends of my parents, old teachers and girlfriends, cousins, aunts and uncles, just about everybody he knew. One copy went to his prep-school alumni magazine, and Fishie and I each received two apiece. The letter came in the format of one of those mimeographed family newsletters you get around Christmastime, the ones that go on forever about prestigious awards and prodigious accomplishments the family has been blessed with during the year.

My brother's letters, on the other hand, were a depressing litany of all the complaints and injustices he had suffered since the beginning of the calendar year. It was a dark gray afternoon, six days before last Christmas, when I received it.

> Dear ————— (Beck wrote Hal in red ink, so it looked like a small whip.)
>
> Greetings from the Northeast, to all those who have ever eschewed me, and a Merry Christmas to you all, during this friendless holiday season. I am presently living in Concord, Massachusetts, where suicidal stems of sunlight slant across the bare trees and my back lawn, and there is a frost on the eager seedlings I planted with such hope and prudence last spring and they are all dead now as most everything I touch dies, withers, dries to a powder that then joins the dusky atmosphere, imperiling the unborn, probably sons of bitches anyway, further darkening the oppressive boards that plank the December sky. As Thoreau wrote, "the Concord Nights are like the Arabian Nights. . ." but Thoreau had a pond, and steps leading to that pond, and I have nothing but a glass of gin, smooth surely but swimmable at one's own risk, and furthermore, Thoreau was a liar, a hypocrite and a bore.
>
> It has been another miserable year for me, and the vulgarity of the Christmas lights beribboning the trim, godless houses, the heaving, alcoholic Santas on city corners shaking their heavy, corny bells—all this asks nothing of my spirit but that it spiral downward. Tonight, as ever, I am alone, drinking a pitcher of Manhattans, the phone is severed from the wall. I ask you: What greater pleasure is there than to hear the *tambours* of a snapped-off beer top as alone I gaze out onto the lawn from the brick porch, alone in the freezing salty air, then turn a solitary figure-eight back into my cheap, pathetic and poorly decorated house?
>
> My hobbies include racquetball, squash, travel, movies, books, foreign languages, baseball, gourmet cooking, triathlon "Iron Man" competition, singing with a quintet, fiberglassing boats and sailing them alone around the world, elective surgery, law, arbitrage and amateur gynecology. Busy! Am translating the *Inferno* back into Latin . . . am town councilman and zoning supervisor for the state, also single-handedly run year-end

cancan show at the Militia Club, great fun for all hands—say!
you're never too old to kick your legs and then, as gravity takes
over, bring them back down, shattering the precious little bones,
later dying alone, without friends or colleagues, in a VA hospital
on the side of some hill. . . "Welcome Home, Men" carved by
some insane lawn mower into the long grass.

Discard that last paragraph—it was all a lie. I have no
hobbies. Only hobby I can think of is living in past and
extracting baby-tooth messages from it . . . find myself in a dark
forest, the direct way lost . . . am losing hair, too . . . it tears
out in mashy, maddening chunks . . . ceiling drips too . . . this
pitiful house sinking into marsh, me with it . . . only trip this
year to visit Hopie *Williams* Santo and big brute of husband in
Florida, even though find Sunshine State cheap and depressing.
Loathed him, didn't even like her, kept wondering whether he
knew anything of Hopie's trollop rep in school. Hopie losing her
looks . . . sad, her looks peaked at eighteen, now she looks like
an old girl, her features mashed like a reflection, as though she's
bending down too close to a pond mirror surface . . . I got
drunk at edge of swimming pool, insulted them both, was
"asked to leave," later "did."

In family news both siblings doing much better than I, that's
for sure. Hal in NYC, unsuccessful artist doing so-called
"constructions," living with drip and mess of a girlfriend . . .
don't know why Hal likes this one, has privately admitted to me
there are things about her than mightily annoy, so this one may
not be long for the world. Thank God for things said in utter
confidence which I can now share with you all! Fishie swims on
. . . is slowing, though, meet times a shadow shy recently,
suggested to her she shave head for mobility-plus. However,
commercial endorsements for products she wouldn't be caught
dead using bring Fishie a sweet half mil a year. Fishie putting a
big one over on public, i.e., she does not drink Coke! Hates it!
Doesn't wear Little Harriet swimwear, either! What she does is
put on Speedo suits and then, artful seamstress that she is,
switches around the tags at midnight before race. Artificer!
Clever, Mr. Bond, I say, stroking made-up long-haired cat, very
clever! And no longer her secret!

Am seeing venal shrink three times a week. As I walked into
shrink's office for the first time, wall artwork paid for by troubles,
I said to myself, Now, my boy, you will never become president
of United States. This was more traumatic than I'd ever
imagined . . . every little boy grows up, mitt in hand, grease in

his curls, with possibility he might someday take that huge office
. . . but there I was, talking to myself, eliminating all my
chances . . . for if it ever came to light that I had sought the
help of licensed therapist, the controversy would certainly
destroy my chances of ever grabbing that trophy . . . I would
become laughingstock of entire nation . . . an emotional stut-
terer! . . . in this nation that still loathes scandal. Me . . . never
to be president, the Boss, the Chief of them all . . . the
unwashed . . . the glowering . . . I am quite destroyed. . .

And on and on, for another three pages. These Christmas letters came in
the mail regularly, even though every year my brother promised he would end
this inglorious tradition and start sending out normal cards featuring reindeer
or snowflakes. When Fishie received last year's epistle with her name penciled
in after the "Dear," she screamed for days. "Doesn't he have any sense of
propriety at all? Any pride? Did you notice that dig about my meet times?
What if somebody from Coke, or Little Harriet, sees this fucking letter?"

Afterwards Fishie and I made a pact not to have much to do with my
brother anymore, since he obviously had a talent for spilling confidences. But
pacts like this, of course, are desperately hard to keep when it's all in the
family.

We had to move, Veebka and I. Now that Kitty was dead, we didn't need
such a big place anymore, since Kitty had taken up the space a warm, giant
pig would normally occupy. We were also running out of room, which was
mostly my fault: the warehouse in the Bowery where I usually kept my
constructions and paintings had gone bankrupt, so I had to store everything in
Veebka's apartment. I stacked my constructions around the sides of the bed
and up against the living room walls. I crammed four boxes under the kitchen
table and three more in the hallway. There was a box to sit on when you were
taking a shower and six more in front of the black swinging window gate that
had served, when Kitty was alive, as a kind of Kitty Prison. It was there,
between the black bars and the windowpane, that I used to trap Kitty for hours
on end. "One year," I would announce, clapping the gate shut and sliding the
black thick cylinder over. "There are laws in this state, in case you didn't
know. . . ." Kitty would pace along the windowsill for a while and then I'd
pretend to be the governor, and that I'd just had a quiet change of heart, Kitty
was free to go, wasn't she lucky.

The presence of my boxes made life extremely difficult. For one thing,
neither Veebka nor I was able to move around very easily. At night I had to
decide exactly where I wanted to be for the next thirteen hours or so, since it
took me about an hour to get to the bedroom or kitchen without knocking
down about forty things along the way.

I had one place where I loved to sit, an overstuffed green armchair in one corner of the room, near the radiator, where I kept supplies of food and drink, a toothbrush, toothpaste, a clock and newspapers. Veebka sat in another corner of the room, barely visible, surrounded by plays and other theatrical paraphernalia. Veebka is an actress-waitress, and when she wasn't spilling food onto people's laps, she was sprawled out on the living room floor, preparing audition pieces that she hoped would show off her range. We had to shout across the room at each other, which hurt both our voices, particularly during Z nights. On Tuesday nights all our words had to begin with Z. It was a thing we did.

"Zal," Veebka would yell across the room. "Z'I'm zonely zover zere."

"Zoh, zou zoor zirl," I would say. "Zy zon't zou zome zover zere zif zou're zo zonely?"

"Z'I zant. Z'I'm zapped zover zere." I knew the answer to that question but I always asked, anyway; just trying to be a friend, I guess; just trying to keep our rotten love affair alive, I suppose. Veebka had a point—she couldn't move an inch either way. She was pinned in the corner like a rat in a lab experiment. At least my place was close to the door and, hence, nearer the natural world and its potential for pleasure, but Veebka lived in one of my boxes, she rested her boots and her elbows on a box, boxes were suspended over her head, dangling, and if our life had been a movie about a killer loose under the big top, that rope would have been dangerously frayed, unraveling. But I am no Killer Clown—I made certain all the ropes were durable and double-tied. Some nights I couldn't even see Veebka at all because of all the boxes that stood between us. All I could make out was the bounce of her hyena earrings, yellow and spotted, with the standard hyena jaws grasping her earlobes and, here and there, patches of her kind, plump, tired face, which I enjoyed squeezing and making infantile sounds come out of, particularly the sounds of a dolphin. "F-a-a-a-h-h-h-h," Veebka went with her lips, while I held them out in a whistle formation. This superlative dolphin imitation practically made me start sweating. "F-a-a-a-h-h-h-h."

I had made Veebka those hyena earrings myself, for her birthday. She had wanted cross-country skis, but I told her that gifts you bought in stores had no meaning, since everybody could buy the same thing. I always say that when I'm low on cash.

"But I wanted to go skiing with you this winter," Veebka complained.

"Ssshhh," I said, stroking the Veebka doll I had constructed, since I couldn't get remotely close to the genuine article. "Homemade gifts are priceless. You don't want what half the world already has, do you? Where's the exclusivity in that?"

Sometimes Veebka's apartment looked like a construction itself—dark-haired boy; blond, unhappy girl; plant, bed, radiator, window and a thousand boxes—but I found its architectural harmony greatly pleasing. I would look up and catch glimpses of Veebka sitting across the room and wave at her through forests of Popsicle sticks and cotton balls and bits of muskrat fur that I had rescued from the garbage cans around town. I suppose I should've realized that I was slowly losing Veebka, but I was so involved with my constructions that I couldn't see anything else. I hadn't kissed Veebka in nearly two months, since it took so much effort to cross the room to her spot. I blew her a lot of kisses from my green armchair, though, if long-distance kissing counts for anything. I guess, however, in retrospect, that kiss blowing is really no substitute for physical closeness.

Veebka was hardly ever at the apartment anymore. A couple of months earlier she'd taken a job with a pre-Broadway production of something called *America, Sing Out, Sing Strong!*—some idiotic musical about a woman general and her singing, dancing troupe. Veebka's job was walking the animals in the cast, specifically a lamb and a duck. She walked them to the theater at six every night and then, after the show ended, she had to haul them back to a special air-conditioned trailer, sort of a stable on wheels, where they spent their nights. The lamb and the duck were living the good life, I'd say, certainly better than the pathetic life I was leading. Their stable was equipped with a television, a VCR, a top-of-the-line compact disc player and a re-frigerator with an ice machine that produced not the gray sickle-moon cubes but the clear, solid rectangular ones. Veebka had landed the job through her grandfather, who was an ex–big-shot producer out in California; and since she hadn't gotten any acting work for a long time, she took it, hoping it would lead to better things, such as understudying one of the leads.

Veebka seemed to get along well with the lamb and the duck at first. Most afternoons she even left for the theater an hour early so she could get down on the black rubber mat and roughhouse with them, throw them up into the air and catch them, toss them whiffleballs, teach them new commands. She brought them toys and exotic foods she thought they might enjoy. "They're really exceptional animals," Veebka told me one night, sounding almost envious. "Their concentration, I mean. I wish I had that kind of con-centration onstage. The lamb . . . it even gained some weight for this show."

This much was true. The lamb had added an additional twenty-five pounds to its stocky seventy-pound frame, adding credence to its role as a turn-of-the-century lamb.

"Who would know?" I said to Veebka. It seemed to me that anyone who might possibly have ever crossed paths with a lamb at the turn of the century would hardly remember what it looked like.

"It's not for those people, Hal. It's for the actor."

"Mew, mew, mew, mew," I said, bored blue.

Veebka was initially so enamored of the lamb and the duck that she hung up glossy pictures of the three of them in our bathroom. Veebka squatting with her arms wrapped amorously around the lamb's neck. . . Veebka and the duck backstage (an "art photograph," since both of them were reflected in the makeup mirror) . . . Veebka in a cowboy hat pretending to "ride" the lamb, but I could see the toes of Veebka's boots balancing gently on the ground. Photography might be a celebration of tricks, but this particular trick didn't work. If Veebka had put her full weight down on that lamb, it's back would've snapped like a cheap toothpick. I'm not saying that Veebka was overweight, only that she had a certain fullness to her, and that this lamb was getting on in years, and that the combination of Veebka's full weight and the lamb's ripe age would surely have spelled L-A-W-S-U-I-T.

They were good-looking and festive animals, I thought, the lamb and the duck. They each wore matching red leather collars with silver bells along the fringe, and you could probably hear them coming at you a mile away.

But sometime during the run Veebka turned against both animals. After one of the shows someone told her what a good job she was doing with the lamb and the duck, and Veebka had burst into tears. She didn't want to be a good lamb and duck walker. She wanted to be an actress. At home that night she told me the lamb and the duck were coconspirators, systematically attempting to destroy her confidence. The duck wanted her soul, she said, the lamb was trying to maim her, both of them were ganging up on her.

"Jo, jome jon," I shouted across the room. "Jow jould ja jamb jill ja jerson? (It was Saturday, J night.)

"Jut jis jis jay, Jal. JI jon't jink je jamb jould je jexactly jrief-jicken jif jI jied."

"Jou're jaranoid!" I shouted. "Jazy! Jou're joe jout jof jouch jith jeality. J'I jon't joe jif jou jan jever juccessfully je jought jack, jor jured!"

As Veebka grew to despise the animals, the amount of time she spent at the theater became noticeably shorter. The director complained that the lamb and the duck were no longer responding onstage; whatever serenity they once had radiated now seemed to have been shattered, and were there any problems or incidents that Veebka was aware of? At night Veebka would sit in the corner of the apartment, barely visible inside her box, and harangue against the lamb and the duck for what seemed like hours and probably was. "I can't stand this any longer!" Veebka would yell across the room at me. "The lamb is *crazy*. It spits at you and then it eats and throws up. The duck is vindictive. This is not show business, Hal, this is insanity."

One night I went into the bathroom and discovered that Veebka had airbrushed herself out of all the photographs and marked up the lamb's face with a crude black pencil, drawing heavy exes over its eyes and bubbles coming out of its blubbery lips, filled with writing. I think Veebka would have me believe that these were comments the lamb had uttered about itself, presumably during moments of candid self-appraisal. "I am worthless." "I cause more pain than my life is worth"—coarse, unnecessary graffiti. Also Veebka, who couldn't prepare eggs without smashing them all over the floor, suddenly began showing an interest in gourmet cooking, legs of lamb a specialty. Her favorite recipe, Navarin d'Agneau, called for the lamb to be pulverized repeatedly with a heavy mallet. Then you added:

> *3 tablespoons best-quality olive oil*
> *25 medium-sized pearl onions*
> *1 cup Cognac (Armagnac, if possible)*
> *4 huge carrots, peeled and cut into thirds*
> *1½ teaspoons black pepper*
> *3 cloves garlic, slivered*
> *Thyme, rosemary, bay leaf, salt to taste*

Veebka garnished with parsley and we consumed it at once, with a bottle of Burgundy, Châteauneuf du Pape or else a decent Bordeaux.

The lamb and the duck had their star turns in the show, one in the first act, the next during the harvest festival, another in the interminable ballad and again for the finale—milking applause each time like a couple of children. At the curtain calls they even did a torchy bow. The lamb took a tiny half step backward, its stubby tail dropped down, then it placed its small, stocky woolen forearms out and laid its head down between them like a girl mooning on the windowsill in a yearbook picture. Several feet to the right, the duck spinned in place, twirling rapidly on its Band-Aid-colored feet. The audience, of course, went mad for these cheap lamb and duck theatrics. They were charmed, violently. Sometimes they even stood up on their chairs, chanting, "Lamb, duck, lamb, duck, lamb, duck"—you know how audiences can get turned on by nothing at all.

The Sunday after Beck's disastrous wedding, once he was finally on his cruise, I had nothing else to do, so I accompanied Veebka along on one of her daily duck-and-lamb walks. The first thing I noticed was that neither animal seemed all that happy around her, a dissatisfaction that appeared to be mutual. It was the lamb's eyes, though, that unnerved me the most. I was routinely beaten up in high school by boys with eyes like these, and after a while I couldn't even bear to look—the lamb reminded me too much of sand and pebbles filling my mouth, of compresses across my forehead and the leaden sympathy of women wearing white.

All four of us—Veebka, me, the lamb and the duck—strolled along the seedy streets, heading in the direction of Central Park. Veebka walked slightly ahead of me, with the lamb and the duck trotting obediently behind her.

"Oh, they aren't that bad," I called, trying to keep pace.

"Come on, goddammit," Veebka snarled, looping the lamb's red leash once around her wrist and yanking hard. "Move your butt."

The duck, on the other hand, gave Veebka no trouble at all. It was a good-natured bird—quite old, I think—and I actually liked it.

We were passing through the danger district of town. Since it was a rainy Sunday afternoon in June, there was no one on the streets but an occasional straggler. Everybody else was away at their other houses. Some blocks were completely empty. I saw a flock of school tots, their waists roped together like baby convicts, each a knot in a white, squirming line. Other people limped along in the raucous rain, holding black umbrellas over their heads. I passed the mute tick of neon, circulating like zigs of yellow blood. In the trucking district I saw whores, shocking as wolves' tongues in their red one-piece bathing suits. They strode through the rain, sticking their heads into truck windows so high they had to stand on warped platform tiptoes to do it. One of the girls spat out her filter butt like a tooth. The other ground out something under her high heels.

"Does the lamb really curtsy?" I said, hoping to lure Veebka from her hostile silence.

"The goddamn lamb doesn't do anything but *simper.*" Veebka jerked the lamb back in step with her and they charged off down the street. I had to race to keep up with them. Veebka walked rapidly past double-parked cars while I stayed on the sidewalks, dodging pedestrians. I could still see the back of Veebka's head as she marched along, and occasionally the duck's gray back feathers, its sodden, flirtatious walk. The lamb's tail stuck up white, hard and rubbery as a shuttlecock.

I caught up with them at the entrance to the park. The duck was wrapping its leash around a mailbox, but I grabbed a coil before it could strangle itself. As we passed a park bench a small boy in a New York Knicks sweatshirt leaned over to pat the lamb on its head. "Get your hand away from that goddamn lamb," Veebka snapped.

I was astonished by this. For someone who kept saying how much she wanted children, Veebka certainly had a brutal way with them. The boy began to cry, which infuriated Veebka even more. "How'd you like to have a stump instead of a hand, huh? All you have to do is reach down and pat the damn lamb. Go on, kid, take a chance."

"Veebka," I said as we walked away, "you used to be so nice. Your world view used to be pearly—"

"Yeah, the old days. Back then I had things to be nice about."

The lamb sat down heavily in the gutter, twisting so that one of its forearms slanted oddly behind its neck, exposing the yellow gravel of its stomach.

"I'm so fed up with this," Veebka yelled.

I offered to walk the lamb for a little while, but Veebka said she'd get into trouble with the union.

"Aw, come on, what union?" *Union* is one of those words that loses me entirely.

"The animal handlers' union. Membership mandatory. Come on," she shrieked at the lamb. "Okay." Veebka dropped both leashes onto the pavement. "Have it your way."

Veebka was always in a bad mood those days, a regular career crisis. She wanted to be an actress but was spending all her time during the day with the lamb and the duck and four nights a week as a waitress at an East Village café. One of Veebka's small revenges annoyed me endlessly: She deliberately ruined her customers' meals in order to place some distance between what she wanted to be doing—acting—and what she had ended up doing—serving food to a bunch of look-alike downtown jerks. So long as she was an inept waitress, Veebka thought she wouldn't lose sight of her first career.

If I happened to be downtown for any reason, I'd go to the restaurant and take a seat at one of her tables. "I'd like the swordfish with the little baby potatoes," I would say when Veebka came to my table after I'd waited patiently for thirty-odd minutes.

"And the vegetable?"

"Broccoli."

I like broccoli, since it reminds me of coral, which reminds me of blue, perfect water, which reminds me of Fishie paddling away, which puts me in mind of happier times, when I didn't live in New York City.

"Anything to drink?"

"White wine."

"Coming right up" was Veebka's mumbled response, part of her repertoire: mumbling, shuffling, sneezing, dropping silverware, spilling beer into customers' laps. About an hour later she would bring me a Caesar salad, or a cheeseburger, and a vodka martini, anything but the food I'd ordered. When customers complained to the management, I could see a peculiar relief cross Veebka's face.

In the park the lamb and the duck sat in front of us like irate little slaves. The lamb shivered, then jerked its leash along the stone. I think it wanted to go for a swim in the boat pond.

"So why didn't they get a younger lamb?" I said.

"They started off with one, but it squirmed too much onstage. Old lambs are quieter."

"I thought you said this one was only ten."

"Times seven. Lamb mathematics is times seven. This one's at least seventy."

"The lamb and I are going for a spin," I said, taking the leash in my hand. Behind me, the duck was thrashing around under the park bench, trying to nip dirt off its tail feathers.

"Hal," Veebka called after me, "the union."

What was she talking about? A minute earlier that she-lunatic had tried to set both animals free! This was inconstant and I shook my head. At age twenty-seven one should know at least the meaning of responsibility. And it wasn't as though the union were following us around wherever we went, inside an unmarked Buick. This is what I mean by Veebka's paranoia.

I looped the red leash over my shoulder and started trudging toward the boat pond. The lamb followed without interest. We walked halfway around the boat pond, pausing in front of the small, crowded café. The pond smelled of rotting garbage, perfume and melons and cigarette smoke. I kept crunching peanut shells beneath my sneakers, and sometimes they stuck to the little triangles of the grid and I had to kick back like a dancer and thumb the shell off my heel. Whenever I did that, the lamb slammed into my knee. Moss hooked on to its paws as it slithered toward the edge of the water and stood there on the muddy banks, teetering.

Either the lamb was terribly thirsty or else intended to kill itself. I had fantasies of death by water, the lamb and I going down together. Or just me drowning, alone. I seemed to remember this exact scene in the movie *A Star Is Born*. The man drowns himself because his wife is getting much more famous than he is. *A Lamb is Born*, I thought. I imagined myself drowning in the boat pond, and then, two months later, the lamb would be nominated unexpectedly for an Academy Award. As the envelope was opened, an unusual tranquillity would seize the auditorium. "And the winner is . . . the Lamb!" the presenter would shout over national television. The lamb would struggle up to the stage, and when the applause had died down, it would clutch the Oscar to its chest, and after making the usual banal comments—"I didn't even have a speech prepared," "Good Heavens, it's heavier than I thought it would be!"—the lamb would say quietly, with heroic dignity, "My name is not . . . the lamb . . . It is . . . Mrs. . . . Hal . . . Andrews." The spirit of the ensuing standing ovation moved me greatly.

At the end of June, Fishie came to my rescue. "I need you," she told me over the phone, "to do me a gargantuan favor. I'll even *pay* you to do me this favor."

That afternoon I had to go downtown to the M & M Gallery, where my show was opening in a couple of weeks, so I told Fishie I'd stop by Bob's apartment later on that evening.

"Oh—and, Hal, you'll never guess who dropped by, out of the blue. Just like a dirty little raindrop. Your brother," she said, before I could guess.

I didn't ask her what Beck was doing in New York, but I immediately suspected the worst, that Beck had run away from Lisa again. I was somewhat divided on this issue, I realized. On one hand, if I was married to Triple L, I suppose I would have been in constant flight myself. Not only would Triple and I have separate bedrooms and enforced separate vacations but also separate houses, in remote corners of separate continents. The minute I heard that Triple had set foot in Antarctica, I'd arrange at once to be airlifted to Africa. If Triple boarded a steamship to Africa, I'd fly hurriedly to Australia, where I have friends, good friends who I had taken in not so long ago and who I hoped would do the same for me. I would've insisted on living in a separate epoch, too, had I not known it was impossible to bend time this way. On the other hand, I never would have married Triple in the first place.

When I arrived at the gallery, Maude was sitting at the front desk typing something. She barely looked up as she reached under the desk and buzzed the door open. In the rear of the gallery Matthieu, Maude's sleazy boyfriend, was prowling around a table, staring at a smashed television set with a broken antenna. A dark-haired woman shadowed him, her lips set tight.

"Children, I was *just* thinking of you," Maude said, rising.

For some reason Maude always called me Children. Usually she called me Children when there were other people around and the other people assumed without thinking that Maude was addressing everybody in the room, but I knew that Maude was referring only to me since on several occasions Maude had called me Children when there was no one else in the room. She was also the owner of the gallery, so whenever she said "Children," I had to spring to attention and say, "Yes—what is it?" Matthieu, on the other hand, never spoke to me except in a tone of derision. I knew for a fact that Maude had gone to battle with him to arrange my show in the first place. Unfortunately they were partners and co-owners. When Matthieu had come into her life several years ago, Maude had named him her personal manager and now Matthieu handled all the gallery's money. This was a big mistake on Maude's part, I think. It is always a great mistake to mix up a woman's money with her love.

Maude kissed me on both cheeks. "Here is the guest list for the opening." She handed me the piece of paper she had been typing. "Oh, and this is Perry, have you met? The artist who will be showing with you. Perry, Hal, Hal— well, you do it, Hal, you're old enough."

I nodded at the small, dark-haired woman who was now bent over the television set, pulling small red wires from the back of its box, and at Matthieu, still blinding himself with cigarette smoke.

"A good trail mix," Maude said. "They may not come, of course, but it's a good group. All Perry's English colony-type friends are coming—don't you love it, Hal? Isn't that hilarious? They come over here to New York and they colonize, immediately they colonize, just like red ants. They see no one else but each other, isn't that right, Perry? They all go to the same dentist to take care of their crumbling teeth. When one of you all gets a cold, you all march off to the same cold man. Colonization must be in the blood, no? Will someone please talk to me, Children?"

"It's great, I love it, I love it," I said absently as I scanned the guest list. Whatever it was, the guest list, the British Empire, I loved it, I wanted it in my life. Practically no one I knew was on the list except for Veebka and my brother and Lisa and Fishie. I had invited lots of people but it turned out that most of them were going to be out of town that night. I'd even sent an invitation to my old art-school teacher but his wife had called to tell me he had been found floating in his widgeon off Martha's Vineyard, wearing black tie, with no lenses in this glasses, an apparent victim of heart failure. "But Enrico was a *very* good sailor," she added wildly, "who hated formal events. . . ." As she babbled on I began to suspect that *I* was the one who had shoved Enrico off the dock. What could I say? "I'm sorry" is what I ended up saying, over and over, before I hung up.

"Rotate your piece," Matthieu said to Perry, squinching up his eyes against the stream of smoke pouring up from his mouth. Like everybody else in the room except me, Matthieu was wearing dark glasses. Those art people, they wore dark glasses all day and all night, as well as during meals. It drove me up the wall. I had never, for example, seen Maude or Matthieu's eyes. Sometimes I wondered if they even had any. Maybe there was nothing behind those dark glasses but twin gaping holes, or matching marbles. Not long ago I went to one of Maude's openings, and everybody in this world of cheap white wine, including the children, was wearing dark glasses. It was way past midnight too! I excused myself and ran outside in search of a drugstore, but since the gallery was on a black, bombed-out block of the Bowery, way down where the island stopped and the black water began, I wasn't happy about my prospects. Finally I found an all-night Korean grocery store on Lafayette and bought a cheap four-dollar pair of shades. Then I strolled back inside the gallery and *voilà*, before long Maude had come up to me. "Take those off, Hal," she said, "they look ridiculous." She crushed them in her fist.

"Here, this way so it gets the light," Matthieu was explaining to Perry. "See, we have those big lights on during the show, but up front here it's all in shadow."

Perry said, "I don't want light on my TVs. It's too American. The gold light, it contradicts my work. It's that TV has replaced the fireplace, the reredos—"

"How's that sweet girl you go out with, Hal," Maude asked.

"She doesn't talk to me," I said. "I hardly even see her anymore. She spends all her time in her box."

"Doesn't talk to you?" Maude patted my cheek with her pencil. "What's going on? Doesn't talk to *you* of all people? But, Hal, you're about to be *misunderstood by all*, doesn't she know what she's about to miss?"

"What do you mean?" I said.

"Fame. Who was it, was it Rilke that said, Fame is the quintessence of all the misunderstandings collecting around a new *mark*. Wasn't that Rilke?"

When Matthieu didn't answer, Maude sobered up. "That's a shame, though, Hal. That can affect the work. How's the work going, by the way? Anything you want to slip in at the last minute?"

"It's going all right," I said. "I've just finished a big piece." I told Maude a little bit about my new construction, which lately had taken up the last few inches of space left over in Veebka's bathroom. The box I used was an old portable brown wardrobe, tipped over on its side, which contained a large green basin filled with water. The basin sat in the center of the box, and I'd stuck some reeds to the back with Elmer's glue so the water would resemble a lake. I fashioned a small, unsteady pier using gray twigs braided with moss, and then I suspended the dock over the basin. I called this one "The Failure of the Buddy System."

You had to use your imagination. It was based on an early experience I had at Camp Wawami, up in Vermont. Whenever you swam at the Camp Wawami lake, the counselors made you use the buddy system, in which the various campers paired up so at least one boy always knew where the other boy was. You weren't allowed to swim off, or drown, without first informing your buddy of these plans. At Camp Wawami nobody had wanted to be my buddy. Everyone else got picked and I was always the only one left over. I had to divide myself internally in two, but I was used to that, it was no big deal. The point of my box, if it could be said to have a point, was that nobody at Camp Wawami had bothered to look out for me and I had sunk to the bottom of the lake. I think the box made this argument vengefully and well, and I was pleased that all the pieces had come from a single dumpster.

Dumpsters were about my favorite places. I liked to heave myself inside city dumpsters and spend my afternoons there, digging around, surrounded by old bottles of Lysol and Cheer and Tide, bottles and cartons I identified as makeshift buoys rather than used-up containers. I'd wade through diseased mattresses, cracked plates, stained couch cushions, I'd get coffee grounds and used dental floss all over my clothes, but I liked seeing the variety of things people threw away. In fact, the pleasures of garbage often seemed to me superior to the company of most people. Did garbage ever complain or keen? Did garbage jilt its bride or discuss life in tedious swimming metaphors?

Country dumps pleased me the most, through, the closest things to war zones I could ever imagine. It wasn't only the odor of rot that made me think this but also the vision of destroyed and bulldozed land, the rats, the shattered husks of automobiles, as well as the orphaned yellow machinery stuck here and there in the damp and muddy knots of earth, stalled with their scooping elephant noses in the air. Even the gate house, where they checked to see whether or not you had a sticker on your back window, seemed more like a government checkpoint than a banal entrance to a disposal area. It wasn't likely I'd ever see battle, and these country dumps gave me the squalor of war without any of its terror, or Spam.

I knew, though, that Maude would end up making me rename "The Failure of the Buddy System" to something totally inappropriate. "Your titles just aren't political enough," she always complained. "They're inert and they're obvious and buyers just won't go for them." The last box I'd lugged into the gallery contained a fork, a twisted spoon's head, a button off a girl's red flannel shirt, onion peels and an old boy's comb I'd found in the gutter and washed off. My working title was "Monday Afternoon Walk," since I'd gathered all the material during a walk I'd taken on a Monday, right? But Maude said, "What the hell does that mean? Sounds like Monday, Monday, can't trust that day. Bore me to death, Hal." Instead she insisted that I call it "Why Are We in El Salvador?" Buyers liked the contemporary, she explained. They liked it when the artist showed he had a conscience and made references to timely issues.

I wasn't convinced, and complained to Maude and Matthieu that I wasn't all that enthusiastic about the present tense. Too grating and noisy, the present tense. It was exhausting to have to think on your feet that much. I was much more enamored of the past tense, though the future conditional was also very attractive to me. Now that was a tense! "I would have, if you hadn't been so horrible . . . I would have, if you'd only been nicer . . . If you hadn't dropped me when I was a baby, I would've turned out happy . . ." and bitter sentiments like that. The present tense, on the other hand, made people feel guilty.

"I love it," Maude said when I finished telling her about my new box. "This new piece, what are you planning on calling it?"

"Toxic Waste: The Enemy of the Unborn," I said, just for a joke.

"Perfect!" she shrieked.

I left the gallery late in the afternoon and headed down to where my sister was staying, in Bob's apartment on Eldridge Street. Fishie had told me over the phone that she would prefer to talk to me in person, and that it was important.

I hadn't seen Beck since we had dropped him off at the Lymans' driveway and watched him walk the first few yards down the driveway, past two white driveway signs that read, DECELERATE DECISIVELY and WARNING: DOGS. Below WARNING: DOGS was a group picture of several golden retrievers, the bigger dogs in back, the smaller ones kneeling down in front, like carolers about to burst into a chorus of Adeste Fideles. Why potential thieves were thought to be frightened of a platoon of caroling golden retrievers was a mystery to me.

All I knew about my brother's sheepish return was that Lisa hadn't believed his Rolling Stones abduction story, and that she'd decided that Beck should "do a bitsy-wit" of penance," as she put it, for his vanishing act after the wedding. I can't honestly say that I blamed her, and this was a first for me— the one and only time I hadn't blamed Lisa for one thing or another. Anyway, Lisa had conked her head a few times, said, "Can you believe this . . . this *espèce de* person?" to her friends and forgiven her new husband. They had even bought an award-winning house together, in Greenwich, Connecticut, which Lisa immediately christened Egret's Nook, even though there weren't any egrets around for miles. There, my brother was able to carry out his penance in relative privacy.

"Oh, no, not Connecticut," I groaned when Fishie said that Lisa and Beck had moved within commuting distance of New York. "What a non-state." Indeed, Connecticut seemed to exist only as a state you pass through to get to other, more interesting states. It reminded me of a big simple square, like a brown paper bag that the surly girl at the supermarket stuffs your groceries into. If my brother ever invited me to visit, I planned to plead fatigue, or even sudden death.

Beck's penance was simple and unusually harsh. For a full month Lisa was making him cart her around Greenwich and its environs in a red rickshaw. If she wanted groceries, for example, or wanted to go shopping in town for a blouse or bathing suit, my brother was forced to lace his anti-mud boots, hitch up, and begin the long trip (two miles, a long way if you're hauling another person behind you in a rickshaw) to Greenwich proper.

Bob's apartment building was in a miserable part of town, along a street filled with gutted playgrounds and funeral homes constructed to look like small, dilapidated Southern plantations. I was looking for number 42, and after going up and down the block three or four times I finally stopped in front of a dingy, unmarked building whose front door seemed to be missing a lock. A man with slightly green skin was standing on the red front stoop, his dirty fingernails wrapped around a crowbar. He was slamming the crowbar into his palm, over and over again. "You didn't see two kids running down the block, did you?"

"Nope," I said.

"I'm gonna break their skulls," he said loudly. "Break their skulls in two, three pieces. My whole place. Cleaned out. I live in the basement, somehow they got around Satan—that's my dog—broke in through a window. They even took my after-shave." He shook his head. *"My after-shave!"*

"Sorry about that," I said, even though I was wondering how after-shave would smell dabbed on green skin. The fact that this man lived in the basement went a long way toward explaining his pallor. "Uh, is this 42 Eldridge?"

"Unfortunately," he said. "Unfortunately it is. And if you're here to rip off some apartments, buddy, you've got another think coming." He waved his crowbar almost delightedly.

Across the street, several nice young men lit a white Cadillac on fire. "I'm just here visiting friends," I said hurriedly.

He nodded briefly, then offered me a dirty hand. "Killer."

I was flattered. "Thanks," I said, looking down, pawing the stoop with one foot.

"No, *I'm* Killer," the green-skinned man said. "What's yours?"

"Oh," I said, thinking this was a jolly game. "My name is Luka."

Killer's eyes glanced up and down the block. "Gonna kill those guys, Luka," he said, stepping aside and waving me through the door with his crowbar. Inside the crimson lobby, on the floor next to the mailboxes, I nearly stepped into a pool of what looked like urine. The air smelled of cat litter and pot smoke. Poor Fishie, I thought as I walked up the shabby, flaking stairs. Poor Fishie, having to house-sit this dump. Did Bob the Bowler make so little money on the tour that he was condemned to live in a place like this? The apartment was on the sixth floor, and by the time I reached Bob's apartment, I had to hold on to the knob to keep from sinking to my knees.

The door was ajar, so I simply pushed it in and walked into the living room. There they were. My brother was lounging on an ancient brown couch, with a jug of red wine clenched between his knees and a long white straw running from between his lips to the bottom of the bottle. He looked deeply tanned, but his eyes were scorched and I guessed he'd been ingesting one chemical or another since early that morning. Across the room, my sister was sitting in an armchair in front of the window, a trayful of chocolates on her lap. Outside the window, the view was of dirty, relentless brick.

Fishie rose to kiss me. "Moi," she said, and "Moi," and she kissed my other cheek.

"Eurotrash," I hissed. Fishie's breath was warm with chocolate and wine, and she pretended to undo the buttons on my shirt and slobber all over my neck before I could push her away. It was clear that I had walked into a private drunkards' convention.

"Hal," my brother said grandly, tonguing the straw to one side of his mouth. "What a fair-weather surprise. I have a great joke for you, by the way, ready? It was in my bubble gum. It seems there's this man, he goes to the doctor, complaining of chest pains. The doctor says, How long as your chest been this way? The man says, Oh, two days. The doc says, We'd like to keep you here a few days, for observation."

I waited. My lips began forming a mew.

My brother smiled anxiously. "That's it, Hal. I'm afraid the rest of the joke, the punchlike part, was torn off. See, I ripped the wrapper accidentally, I was so hungry for the gum, and I lost—what would you call it?—the *essential* part of the joke. But you can just imagine what the doc must've—"

"Ha ha," I said, shaking my head admiringly. "I'd like to keep you here for a few days. For observation. And you're right, Beck, you can just imagine what the doc would have said after that—maybe something funny, even."

My sister held up a chocolate next to her ear and shook it. "Gimme your opinion, Hal, is there junk inside here or not?"

"Junk?"

"Gross nonchocolate material."

I held the chocolate, squeezed it, shook it. "I think it's okay."

Fishie took a bite, then she spat. "Uggh. There was yellow inside. I hate the yellow." She chucked the chocolate out the window. "These damn chocolates. Why don't they have the decency to label them? Practically every one has some kind of junk in the middle, something *disgusting*, cherry, lime, coconut." She glared at Beck, sipping happily again from his straw. "Of *course* they were a gift from Lisa."

"This," I said to my sister, "is the worst-looking apartment I've ever seen in New York. In fact, not just in New York but anywhere. It boggles my mind."

"It does, doesn't it? Bob thinks it's funky, though. That's the expression he uses—"

"It is not funky," I said. "It's squalid. It's depressing as hell. It's a thorough hellhole." I didn't want to tell Fishie about the green-faced man downstairs, but I managed obliquely to address the issue of security. "You might want to make sure you lock up at night," I suggested, my voice as weak as the downstairs door.

"I haven't had any trouble," my sister said. "Really. And I'm stronger than most men, anyway, Hal. Certainly I'm much more powerful than you are. I can carry Bob around on one hand."

"That's because his brain weighs less than a baby grape," I said.

"This place is quite a bargain too. Bob only pays like two hundred dollars a month."

"I'm sure it's worth every penny." It was true: seven dollars a day for Bob's apartment seemed not too high, not too low.

Above our heads, the ceiling, closing in around a battered light fixture, was painted the faintest powder blue, to suggest sky. The blue plaster was coming off in turbulent rinds, and just then something fell from the overhead light, fell deftly through the air and into the shag rug. Stunned, the rat—at least it looked like a rat—rolled over once and then sped off into the kitchen.

"Oh, God," I said. "I think I'm going to be sick."

"I planned that," my sister said quickly. "That was all planned. That was a friend of mine."

"Was that a rat?"

"That was a frisky field mouse."

"It looked like a rat," I said. "Rat eyes . . . it had rat hair, rat affect. . . ."

"Let me remind you of a little New York axiom, Hal," Fishie said. "Mice and rats do not, cannot, coexist in the same quarters. If you have one, you don't have the other, that's the rule. It's *graven*. That's because rats eat mice. And as you just saw, that was a frisky field mouse, and as I mentioned, a friend. Hence, this place has no rats."

"You should get a cat," I said, feeling a sudden pang of emotion for Kitty. Would it ever go away? Or would I still be mooning over my dead pet at the age of ninety?

"I tried." My sister crossed the room and sat down in the armchair. Behind her, the solid dirty brick climbed up and under the window shade. "Just the other day, in fact. I went down to the animal shelter and I had this one very old cat all picked out, this cat I felt extremely sorry for. I had my checkbook out and everything, but then I made the mistake of looking the cat in the eyes and saying, You're going to help me with my mice, aren't you, Kitty? And the animal-shelter woman grabbed the cat out of my hands and said, I'm very sorry, miss, but we can't turn over a cat to anybody who has mice in their partment. And I said, Why? And she said, New York City mice are so toxic, their insides are so poisoned, that they end up killing the cat instead of the other way around. Now, isn't that terrible testimony to a terrible city?"

"What are you doing in town," I asked my brother, momentarily forgetting the rat.

"Lisa's pregnant," Fishie answered at once. "We think it's the Antichrist, but we're not sure yet. That's my gut feeling, though. Lisa's actually half jackal, Hal, in case you didn't know. She's at the doctor's now, and Doc's telling her to give up all the good things she likes, like eating the contents of people's henhouses. So we're celebrating the coming of the apocalypse—oh, it won't be long now, cheers, everybody!" Fishie gestured at Beck with her wineglass. "Actually, I'll let *him* tell you. He's the Antichrist's dad, after all."

"Aagghh," my brother moaned. "I'd *hate* it if Lisa had a demon seed."

"Oh, come on." Fishie grabbed the bottle of wine out from between my brother's knees. "Think of the advantages: tickets to sold-out concerts, tables at restaurants, openings, no more waiting in line."

"Congratulations," I said to Beck. Fishie handed me a glass of wine and refilled her own glass. The idea of my brother as anybody's father was staggering. "That was very quick work."

"Well, Lisa's doctor says she's extremely fertile," Beck said brightly. "Apparently her ovaries—"

I put my hands over my ears and mewed until I felt drained and empty. I didn't want to hear about my sister-in-law's inner garden.

But Beck had already switched directions. "Yet I fear it does not augur too well."

"Why's that?"

"Don't you see, Hal, someone's trying to tell me something? Now that a new life is soon to emerge, well, the more experienced life, a greater life, has to go? And the finger of good-bye, friend, is pointing at me."

"But you're only thirty," I pointed back.

My brother stared at me. His eyes were as small as drips of batter, and reddening by the second. "Most cats are dead at seventeen."

"So is it a boy baby?" I went on. "A girl?"

"Yes," Beck said. "No, no, no, give *me* that," he called to Fishie, who was poised to pitch another chocolate out the window.

"Aren't there *any* real chocolates in here? You know, I honestly don't think there are any, they all have these *middles* I can't stand."

"I thought you didn't eat chocolate," I said. "Or drink wine, for that matter. I thought you were a healthy girl. Or at least that you were a Calvados girl exclusively."

"Well, I thought I'd splurge just for today. And as I said, the chocolates were a present from a jackal-gal pal of mine. To try and fatten me up. And I have reasons to splurge too."

"Do you know what'll be the most fun about having a kid?" Beck nosed his straw back down the neck of the wine bottle. "And that is, dressing it up. Imagine having the power to dress up another human being in the morning and make it wear whatever you want it to! No, wear this . . . no, don't wear that . . . I mean, if I got mad, I could dress it up like a horrible dwarfish clown! Or a gangster! Or an immaculate little tennis player! Or a court-martialed sailor!"

"So what's the favor you want to ask me in person since it's so important?" I said to my sister.

Fishie hesitated. "Well, I mean, I wanted to tell you about the baby first of all. Or Beck did. That was important, I think, you know, the Uncle Hal bit. And the second thing has to do with Marlene, speaking of jackals."

"Marlene Bauke?" I was actually fond of Marlene Bauke. In fact, when I was younger, I had a small crush on her, which I never dared admit to my sister. I had met Marlene several times after races and found her shy, hardly villainous at all. If Fishie had known of this infatuation, however, she would've taken the cap off her Super Glue and I'd have ended up dangling from a tree, not my favorite way to spend a weekday afternoon.

"Of course," my brother babbled on, "I could refuse to dress the baby at all. I could say to it, Hey, baby, you're not going anyplace today! You can't go out onto that street naked!

As my sister talked, she wandered around the living room, touching the peeling walls with her thumbs and pretending to bounce off. "Marlene's challenged me. To some kind of dumb competition in Europe. Three of them, actually. All distance events, the kind where they play *Rocky* music when you leave your dressing room. It's not my thing, really, but lots of bucks, lots of sponsors, all televised and so on. One's in London, second's in Amsterdam and the last in Paris. To see who's best, et cetera." Fishie faked a yawn. "Golly, I wonder who's best."

"So when does this happen," I asked.

"Couple of weeks. My manager says do it but I'm trying to decide." Fishie bit into another chocolate and then stopped chewing as disgust pinched up her mouth. "Another unlabeled loser, some kind of sick cherry crap."

Fishie wound up and hurled the chocolate out the window. It skipped off the brick and fell flat to the courtyard, and I stared down after it. A hundred feet below the window, an enormous German shepherd was roaming the alleyways between the buildings. I wondered whether this was Killer's dog, Satan, and I decided it must be. The courtyard was jammed with old, spotted sinks, toothpaste-gummed faucets and rags made from the short sleeves of shirts, whatever the super felt like dragging out there to abandon. From somewhere on the street came the surreal, tinkling song of a Mister Softee ice-cream truck.

"Hey!" I called down. The German shepherd glanced up wildly, its pointy black bat-ears twitched, and then it started dashing in crazy circles around the broken sinks, like a housewife gone mad. "Where were you?" I yelled down. "Where were you when your teeth and paws were needed?"

"What's that, Hal?" my brother asked.

"But I think I'm going to do it," my sister went on. "Don't you think I ought to do it, Hal? Beat that flat-chested little Kraut? I mean, I'm certainly in good shape these days. I've been working out six days a week, running, weights, you name it. There's only one problem, though, right? The dog. There's got to be someone here to walk the damn dog."

"What dog? Is this an invisible dog?"

"BB? She's out cold. She sleeps under that ugly card table Bob has in the kitchen. But anyway, Hal, getting back to the race thing, here's where you come in. I mean, didn't you tell me you were looking for a new place? That things were getting just a wee bit crowded where you were? At Veenie's?"

My sister hates Veebka, and she never waits until you've broken up with somebody to tell you what she thinks of them. At the beginning of the summer she'd made me an offer: five thousand dollars, plus a bonus, if I told Veebka I already had a wife and two blond, wispy children in a faraway state.

"I want that little gerbil *out*," Fishie had said, dangling the certified check in front of my face. "Out, out, out! Out of my brother's life! I don't trust that creep as far as I could hurl her! Don't you think it's a little odd, Hal, that Veebka was the only person in the apartment when Kitty jumped out the window? Am I the only one who finds that strange? Doesn't this lead you to certain uncomfortable, albeit unavoidable, conclusions vis-à-vis a certain *shove* theory I've been keeping to myself? Well, doesn't it? Say something, Hal, goddammit! I'm willing to pay you medium-range rejection money . . . and face it, you need the bucks; you could buy a hell of a lot of things with five thousand dollars. . . ."

Of course I turned her down cold, even though she was right, I could've used the money at the time. "You don't want me to go out with anybody," I told Fishie in a pathetic voice. "You don't think anybody I go out with measures up. I *love* Veebka. And she's *not* a suspect in Kitty's death, so you can stop thinking about that. You don't know her at all, and if you did, you'd be—"

"I don't want to get to know her," Fishie yelled. "She's a bore, and this is my one life, and I don't want to spend it getting bored. Living with that girl is like a little death, Hal, and I don't mean the good French kind, either. *Actress?* I mean, come on! What's she ever been in? *A Streetcar Named Desire*, period. Which nobody went to and which turned out to be one of the great bombs of the theatrical season. And she played a *man*—is that normal? When people ask you what your girlfriend does for a living, do you really want to raise your hand and say, She walks a lamb and a duck?"

Fishie had a minor point there. Veebka *had* only acted in this one play since I'd known her, and an all-girl, French language version at that. She played Stanley Kowalski and her big line was *Tigre! Tigre! Lache cette bouteille!*—shouting at the recoiling, underage girl who played Blanche Dubois.

I turned back to Fishie. "So you're asking me whether I'll agree to *live* in this building?"

"It's not so bad, Hal. You get used to it. It's a little noisy, that's all. But noise is stimulating to you artistic types, least that's what I've always heard. Nice Spanish neighbors—you learn a second language. Hal, you could be bilingual—and everybody's very family-oriented . . . nice smells of frying in the air as you come home at night. You'll be the only white boy here, so you'll get insights into expatriation you might not have had before. It'll be like Paris in the twenties, and I'll stock up on booze so it'll really be like Paris in the—"

"Hey," Beck said, "that sounds very appealing, Fishie. I'd be willing to live here if Hal—"

"But what about the neighborhood," I asked. Downstairs I had noticed that Bob's building appeared to be squeezed in by vice. On one corner of the block was a liquor store, festooned with black cords of Christmas lights that blinked chaotically, even during the day. The store was painted dark red, and a group of old men was gathered on the corner in front of the clear locked door, the chain of lights winking and glittering behind them like some holiday pageant gone horribly amiss. The bodega next door sold individual cigarettes, stale and inflated by the heat, ten cents apiece, and while I was searching for Bob's building I'd seen the old men passing around a single ten-center among themselves, even though its head looked like a hard orange lipstick. On the other corner—next to a travel agency whose sign advertised QUICKIE DIVORCES IN SANTO DOMINGO!—was a marijuana store, disguised as a back-to-school emporium. A theme tablet with thick lines, a kilt, a kilt pin, a pencil and a single record album, Kenny Rogers's *The Man and His Music*, were arranged in the window against a black cardboard background.

How dumb did they think I was? Kenny Rogers. I couldn't believe it. Just the night before I'd read an article in which Kenny was talking openly about his recent liposurgery. Kenny had had some fat sucked out of the pit of his stomach, and an inch or two taken from the back of his left knee. "Best thing

I ever did!" he was quoted as saying, as his sixteenth or so wife looked on. "The operation sucks!" he'd said, and afterward he laughed and laughed. The famous bad temper I'd heard about before was no place in evidence. Kenny kept his hand on his wife's bare knee, and maybe this explained his terrific, laughing mood.

Kenny used to be good, back in the days of "Ruby," but now, I don't know, he's changed. Those days when Ruby took her love to town were good, period, so I'm probably confusing the song with the time.

"This neighborhood's just fine, Hal," Fishie said softly.

"I don't think—" I started to say.

"Here, have some more delicious red wine." She refilled my glass. "Decisions should be made on a lot of delicious red wine. Oh, and I have another big surprise for both you guys . . ."

My brother and his brother looked up, as though joint timing were the thing both of us were best at.

"I," Fishie announced, "have decided to shave my head."

"Wow," Beck said. "I'm speechless, Fishie, that's—"

"I decided I could get around a lot faster that way. I mean a *lot* faster."

"Why in the world do you want to shave your head?" I didn't want to have a bald girl for a sister; people would laugh and point at me. "Couldn't you just train a little harder?"

"I *want* to shave my head, Hal. I train hard enough already. If I trained any harder, I'd be in a body cast somewhere."

"Maybe I can shave something, too, in sympathy," my brother mused. "You know, I've always had this . . . desire . . . this inclination . . . to shave off all my pubic hair . . ."

I was horrified. "Why would you ever want to do that?"

"To plumb the roots of childhood." my brother responded automatically. "To retrieve certain insights that have gotten smoothed over along the way."

My brother enjoys this depraved enterprise. In fact, he does little else with his time. He once came over to my apartment in the late afternoon with a stack of videotapes ranging from *Mary Poppins* to *The Sound of Music*. "Now you and I, Hal, we're about to have an experience of memory and desire," Beck announced soberly. "We're going to flick these tapes into your VCR and sit back and wait to be flooded by the thoughts and emotions we had at the time we first watched these movies. When we were kids. And happy-go-luckier than we are now. Buried emotions are going to rush through our minds at a very revealing clip. It'll be our first annual childhood film marathon, yours and mine. It'll be fun."

I sat there impassively as my brother slipped *Chitty Chitty Bang Bang* into the VCR. During the movie my brother stared at the television screen, occasionally making a sudden spasmotic movement with his chin. Five hours later, during *Old Yeller*, when I brought out a case of beer to kill the pain of having to spend an entire evening watching dumb old movies, Beck snatched the beer bottle out of my hand. "How could you, Hal?" he shrieked, sounding genuinely upset. "How could you be so corrupt and unthinking? Can't you see the immorality of watching *Old Yeller*, a notarized childhood classic, drunk?"

As we watched my brother made little hiccuping sounds in his throat, then cried when Old Yeller kicked the can and, two hours later, cried again when Bambi's mother couldn't find her way out of the burning forest. "I'm remembering!" Beck cried out occasionally. "The swings and the slides . . . the Space Trolley . . . the old chocolate factory . . . the snow . . . like a great master goose being shaken from a pitilessly high angle . . . the Muscovy ducks . . . the time Fishie set my parakeet Lou free . . . how he went veering up over the swamps . . . how I never saw my sweet little bird again."

"So what do you think, Hal?" Fishie said. "I mean, about the head-shaving business but also about you living here for a little while. It'll just be for two months, after all. And dogs are excellent props for meeting women. Especially BB, since most people are so astonished that a dog that age can even walk. See, women, they reach down and pat your dog and they say, Why, he's so *cute*, but what they actually mean is, *Please sleep with me right now, Hal*."

"Fishie," I said, "I think first of all, if you shave your head, you will live to regret it. And as for me living in this dump—"

"I want to shave my pubic hair," my brother said mildly. "I want to shave my pubic hair very, very badly now." My brother was no longer using his straw but instead drinking straight from the bottle. Beautiful damnation rose in his eyes. "You shave your head, Fishie, I'll shave my pubic hair, Hal can shave whatever he wants to shave. We'll all match, we'll be triplets."

I looked at him with pity and disgust. "Beck, don't even think about it," I said slowly. "It'll grow back and then it'll itch. You won't be able to sleep it'll itch so much. And you'll look like a freak. Lisa won't come near you. I mean, what an *infantile* idea."

"So solly," Beck said, "mine mind's made up." It was something he had always wanted to do, he explained, but also something he had been fearful of doing by himself. Now that Fishie was planning to take a razor to her head, this was the perfect opportunity! This was news to me—I couldn't recall my brother ever having mentioned shaving off his pubic hair before, and I think I might have remembered.

My brother carried on. "And it'll be a secret, you see. A secret between me and myself. People'll be talking to me at a party, they'll think, Hey, this guy looks pretty normal, what a great guy, I'd like to get to know him better! But see, *I'll* know that beneath it all I don't have any pubic hair. So it'll be a kind of conspiracy with myself, against people at parties . . ."

"Beck," I said, "your sample party conversation is a dream. Nobody would ever confuse you with a great guy or even a good guy. People will look at you and they'll *know* instinctively something's wrong with you."

He thumped the couch pillow, like a fan trying to get some excitement going in the bleachers. "Fishie, you have two razors, I hope?"

"Better than that, buddy. I have a six-pack of the things. Of the cheap little blue ones."

I turned to her. "Fishie, please don't encourage him. I mean, this is pretty deranged, don't you think? It's like getting drunk and walking into a tattoo parlor and then you wake up the next morning plastered with butterflies and hearts that say 'Alma Mia' inside. *You* go ahead if you want, shave yourself bald, but don't drag *him* into it."

"Hal, I don't want to shave alone. Beck's right. It's lonely when you do it by yourself. In fact, it's my opinion that if you were a real warrior, Hal, you'd agree to shave a little something, too, as a gesture of solidarity."

"Come on, baby," my brother said, rising from the couch. "Off with that troublesome pubic hair."

"Family," my sister said almost pleadingly. It sounded like a moan, and she liked it so much she said it again.

"I'm not shaving anything." I glared at my brother. "Particularly my pubic hair. And I don't wish to be a part of this family anymore."

"Hah." Fishie frowned. "You can't escape. We'll hunt you down and kill you like a mangy dog."

"Come on, baby," my brother said again. "Off with the hair. It won't itch at all, trust your old brother. And later on tonight, when you glance down at yourself, you'll be a kid again. You'll be flooded with the random highlights of an eight-year-old's sensibility: crickets, fishing rods, trips to the scary dentist—"

"Come on, Hal," Fishie begged. "Be a warrior."

"Off with the pubes, Hal," Beck hissed. "Hack 'em off with a rusty knife."

Fishie disappeared into the kitchen. I heard the faucets running, and when she returned, she was carrying a tin bucket filled with soapy water. Two blue razors stuck out of her mouth like a strange orthodontal experiment.

"Hey, I'm psyched," Fishie said vaguely, softly, sitting back down in the armchair.

"Don't either of you," I asked, "want to give yourself a chance to reconsider . . . like when you're not plastered on cheap hippie wine?"

"I'm hardly plastered, Hal," Fishie said briskly. "I'm just a little *relaxed*. It must be . . . why, it must be because I'm a little *tired*. I must have had a long *plane flight*, you see. Remember, I can hold my liquor better than most men can, don't forget that. You, Hal, when you get drunk, you just sit there and yell at people. At least *I* don't insult people, abase myself left and right."

It was true. I didn't hold my liquor particularly well. I made all kinds of mistakes and scenes. Usually I asked to speak to the management, even when I was drinking alone. I was always surprised to find out it was the management's night off.

"Pubic, pubic, pubic," my brother hummed. "Hair, hair, hair. Da-doo-da."

"Last chance, Hal," my sister said, pulling a pair of scissors from its light blue sheath. "Will you join us in shaving or won't you? How about just cutting your bangs? Or your chest? Girls like the smooth, nonmonkey chests, don't forget. Or what about your head? Yeah, you could be bald like me, we could be bald siblings together . . ."

"No," I said. "No fucking way."

"Last chance," Beck hummed, "doo-da-dee."

"*Solidarensk,*" Fishie wailed. "*Family . . . Lech Walesa . . .*"

"Oh, shut up, both of you," I snarled. "I told you, I've seceded. Think of me as the South."

I heaved myself into a sticky armchair and watched as Fishie began hacking off her long blond hair. She grabbed her bangs in her left-hand fist and sliced away, not bothering to cut across evenly. "The last time I was intimately involved in another person's baldness," Fishie remarked, "was when I shaved all my dolls. Do you remember, Hal? I chopped off all their hair, gave them buzz cuts? Hey, shouldn't we have some music here? Hal, go put something gay on the machine, some decent shaving music, anything but the Replacements, they throw up in concert too much . . ."

To irritate her I put on the Replacements and turned the volume up as high as it could go. Over on the couch, Beck had loosened his belt and lowered his corduroys slightly, so the belt buckle flopped between his raised knees. He wriggled his boxer shorts down several inches and, aloofly squirming, gazed down at his lap like a landowner surveying a tranquil summer lawn. "Now, just where does one begin . . ." he said softly, happily.

Fishie glanced over at him and smiled secretly. "Hal, you should get a picture of this. My camera's in the bedroom. Under the bed. There's six left in the roll."

I shut my eyes and listened to both Fishie and Beck clipping away lightly at themselves. In the courtyard, Satan was growling and barking, and the Mister Softee truck was playing yet another chorus. I opened my eyes and stared up at the blistered blue ceiling, expecting more rats to fall from the overhead light and join their leader. Bob's apartment was much bigger than Veebka's, though it was at least ten times more dilapidated. The rooms were laid out student-style, in a simple shape: a narrow hallway with three left turns: a kitchen, a study and a small, miserable bathroom. Outside the bathroom, the hallway emptied out into the cramped living room, and beyond, the diseased couch, separated by white, peeling French doors, was Bob's airless, triangular bedroom, its walls plastered with posters of famous bowlers bowling, none of whom I had ever heard of.

I could live here, I thought. *I have no standards.* Living in a hellish slum for two months was perhaps not the crowning glory of my life, but I realized that it did offer two distinct advantages. The first was that there was plenty of room for my constructions, and the second was that I could end up saving a great deal of money. The idea of living rent-free for the summer, even if the place in question was Bob's apartment, appealed to my New England frugality.

When I looked up again, Fishie had turned into a stern young Marine, and my brother was midway through his attempt to become an eight-year-old boy again. In pubic terms I'd say Beck had reached the awkward and jeered-at age of twelve and with each snip of his scissors he turned a year younger. Pieces of Fishie's hair lay in blond wings on the shag rug, and gazing at her short, authoritative scalp, I felt embarrassed about the dull patina of my civilian loafers. I almost saluted her.

My brother cast aside his nail scissors—nail scissors were all Fishie could find for him, since she was using the big pair—and dipped his blue razor into the bucket filled with plush suds. I watched at he applied a lip of shaving cream to the double blade like toothpaste. "I need a mirror, someone," Beck announced. "Can I take that mirror over there off the wall?"

"Why don't you get yourself a compact mirror?" I snapped. "It's a perfect size."

The whiteness under my sister's hair was now visible, a rich marble color. "Now, boys," Fishie said vaguely, *"like* each other . . ."

"Ow," my brother said. "I nicked myself."

"Careful," Fishie called across the room. "You break it, you buy it. You cut it off, you can't use it."

"This is scary," he mumbled.

"Hal," my sister said, "could you get me the dog clippers out of the bathroom?"

"When I first got pubic hair," Beck murmured into his knees, "I tried cutting it all off. Just like now. No one else had any but me. Then they got some of their own. And I forgot about it, having it first. See, then you get *older* and no one even notices—"

"*Stop it!*" I yelled. "This is extremely offensive, Beck! This is like the official definition of what's offensive!"

"Hal, those clippers?" Fishie flexed her scissor blades.

"God, Hal, what a giant prude you are . . ." my brother murmured.

I stormed into the bathroom to get the dog clippers—a room consisting of a green-and-purple-striped bathtub on four lion's paws, protected by a mildewed shower curtain with a hideous bowling ball motif; a gasping toilet; and a single narrow window, thickly painted an unappetizing avocado green.

Inside the tub it looked as though a miniature avalanche had taken place. The ceiling hung heavily over the two faucets, barely grazing the huge chunks of salty plaster that filled the bathtub. I found the clippers and then wandered into the kitchen to try to catch a glimpse of BB, but all I could make out was a sprawling black shape, breathing soundlessly, and a pair of soiled pink lips smeared against the cold summer floor. It was too dark under the card table to distinguish anything else.

Soon a hum filled the living room as Fishie prepared to shave the top of her head. "I'll need a mirror as well," she pointed out. "Even *I'm* not that coordinated."

"Look, okay," I said finally. "I'll do it for you."

"Cool." My brother held up his razor.

"Her, not you," I said. "You go infantilize yourself, don't get me involved."

"Thanks, Hal," Fishie said. "you're coming back to us. Maybe this means you're back North with us?"

"I am still the South," I said nobly. By then certainly I felt as battered as say, Georgia, after Sherman came to visit.

With the dog clippers in one hand I stood behind Fishie's skull and gazed into her yellow stubble. It was like looking at the back hair of a young farmboy's crew cut. Shorn, her head had a nice pleasing oval shape, without the odd bulletlike peaks and valleys I'd seen on the skulls of other bald women, namely Marlene Bauke. Marlene, in her dark glasses, looked like the punk daughter of a poached egg. A woman had to have a fairly nice-shaped head—no conical elevations, for instance—in order to have enough confidence to get bald in the first place. The greasy clippers hizzed in my hand like a furious insect as I pushed them across Fishie's few remaining hairs. Soon I got into a seasick rhythm, me, the clippers and the Replacements, and found myself shaving the same places over and over again, relishing the blackboard smoothness of her skull. Every so often I shook out the clippers and blew the yellow feathers out from between the combs.

"Ahh, Hal, that feels good," Fishie said as I drew the clippers around in back of her ears. She kept her eyes closed as I shaved her, a contented smile on her closed lips.

"What's that music I keep hearing out the window?" Beck said.

"That's the Mister Softee ice-cream truck theme song," I said.

"It's pretty."

"No, Beck," I said, suddenly very annoyed. "You're wrong. It's a nightmare recording. It's sinister. Surreal. It plays over and over again like a stuck record in a horror movie about the vengeful ghost of a little girl who's come back to her playroom in order to massacre the new tenants." I had ardent opinions about the Mister Softee theme song. "It's like what you might hear playing in ironic counterpoint to a stairwell murder or a neighborhood drug deal gone sour, or someone falling off the fire escape—"

"No. It reminds me of happy children on the merry-go-round."

As far as I was concerned, the only time the Mister Softee song would be appropriate to a merry-go-round would be if all the horses suddenly came alive, sneering and neighing obscenely, finally bucking the children onto a cement parking lot. "No, Beck," I said again.

"So, Hal," Fishie said presently, "how about it? Living here . . . just for the summer? Honestly, I wouldn't ask if it wasn't important. Don't you want me to bring a little glory home to our family for once? I mean, *you're* not doing much, Beck-boy over there certainly isn't, don't you think at least one of us should try to bring home the gold, so to speak?"

I got stiff. "I have a gallery opening in two weeks. In case you've forgotten. It's not as though I'm some kind of idler."

"Hal, I didn't mean *that*. I just meant in terms of girls . . . the little tool you go out with, you know, I say get married or cut bait. That's my philosophy. Don't you want a girl who has a little more energy? Who's doing something with *her* life too?"

"Fishie," I said, "If I found a girl with energy, you'd be complaining about her background, about her not being from some incredibly slick domicile. And if I found someone with a background you actually approved of, you'd say she was a stiff, a boring pod."

"Let me see, who do I know . . . ?" and Fishie was silent as I stood there behind her, considering whether or not to shave off her ears and drop them into the courtyard for Satan. My sister likes getting things done, using a vast catalogue of social contacts that she's accumulated since prep school. If, for example, you need to see a doctor whose schedule is booked solid for six months and Fishie finds out, she'll immediately say, "All right, who knows him?" or "Yeah, I went to school with his sister, I'll call you back in a minute." You can almost hear, in the mock-naïve rustle of Fishie's eyelashes, the riffle of a Rolodex.

"I told you, I'm perfectly happy with Veebka."

"Ah, but I'm not, Hal, and that's the most important thing," Fishie said breezily. "And don't forget, one of the classic symptoms of clinical nighthawk depression is that you don't even *realize* you're depressed. Same thing with women. If you think you're in love with someone, you're actually probably clinically depressed—"

"I'm not clinically depressed," I snapped. "And Veebka's just fine, leave her alone."

Fishie suppressed a false yawn. "So sorry," she said. "An image of Veebka just came into my mind, and I had to yawn. I had this urge to select a coffin for myself in preparation for a sixteen-year sleep . . . just entertaining the idea of her."

"Hello! This is extremely curious and rewarding," my brother called from across the room. He had finished shaving, and now he was staring down into his lap, frowning.

"May I see?" Fishie said.

"No, no," my brother said.

"I've seen it before," Fishie said crossly. "It's no big deal. Both brothers dangling in the breeze while my excellent Super Glue softens under the sun—silvery, glimmering oxides . . ."

My brother abruptly stood up. His heavy blond cords slid noiselessly down to his ankles. "Look," he said dreamily. "I glance down at myself now and it's just like I said, Hal: I'm eight years old again. It's working, you guys. I can feel it working. Anybody want to go fishing? Or let's play catch? You can use my glove."

I closed my eyes, feeling the vibration of the clippers in my fingers. Fishie was bald as a cueball.

"Nope," Fishie said, then swung around to face me. "Hal, go play catch with him. I'll pay you."

The first night in our new apartment, Veebka was in a terrible mood. I'd agreed to move into Bob's apartment before Veebka could protest, or even lay eyes on the place, and she was furious.

Three men named Moishe had transported our stuff downtown. Moving men in New York are always three Iranian cousins named Moishe, with black beepers strapped to their belts. The home office is manned by a fourth brother, also named Moishe. "You got that box, Moishe," one brother asks, and the answer's always either, "Yes, Moishe," or "No, Moishe, my grip, it is weak." The Moishes grunted and wheezed before dropping your piano or chest of drawers down twenty flights of stairs, creating instant antiques of everything you owned. The Moishes dropped three of my constructions onto the landing, and when they were finished moving, those Moishes had the nerve to charge me a hundred dollars extra! For moving me into a building with no elevator!

Fishie had left me a chart, neatly typed, stuck to the refrigerator door with four pineapple magnets. "On the Care and Feeding of BB the Dog."

1) Feed BB three times a day, morning, afternoon and night. Same with walking. BB likes the park but takes forever. Impatient, you will feel like striking her but DON'T. Bob would be very displeased and you would be unable to live with self.

2) Should BB start swelling up like a blowfish, do NOT kick or puncture her. Instead, give her a pink pill—they're over the stove in white nickel-bag-

like envelope—and jam it inside a cube of hamburger. Do NOT hurl hamburger at swollen dog. Instead, pat it down her throat but not so she CHOKES to death. *BB rejects pill, what do ya do?* Do NOT strike or SLAM HER HARD against wall. Bob would be very displeased and you would be unable, etc.

3) BB has many longtime "dog friends" that you will encounter in the park. Some of these animals she has known for years, and as with any longtime friendships, occasional problems arise. Should BB show signs of antagonism toward one of her "old friends" do NOT—repeat, do NOT— yank BB harshly toward you as this will KILL HER. Bob would be very, etc.

4) BB's vet is a certain Dr. Vincent Kennelly, a REAL SLEAZEBAG. Still, better than waking up one morning to find DOG DEAD BECAUSE YOU IGNORED SYMPTOMS, since Bob would, etc.

5) Who cares? I don't like the dog much, and nor will you. Have fun, though. Thanks for doing this. Wish me luck. XOXO, Sis.

Beneath the chart were Fishie's three phone numbers, in Amsterdam, London and Paris, the vet's New York number and fifty twenty-dollar bills.

So far all was well. The only problem was with BB herself. Never in my life had I come across a dog quite so depressed and listless. BB was seventeen years old, a mutt whose aged, gray-white coat turned to yellow shag on her stomach. She was practically blind in both eyes and spent most of her free time under Bob's card table, grunting, dreaming loudly, and I concluded after a couple of days that her dreams must be pretty horrible. Now and again I heard her lick her lips and yelp. BB reminded me a lot of my own strange, silent dog back at home, the dog who stood there watching, smiling enig-matically, as you were clubbed to death by someone you counted as a friend.

"What are you going to do with yourself, Hal?" Veebka kept saying that first night in Bob's apartment.

We were sitting out on the fire escape, and I was staring down at Satan as he nosed around among the courtyard sinks. "How's that?" I said.

Veebka was silent. "Do you think we'll ever get married?" she said carefully.

"You mean, you and me get married?"

"Yes."

"Well, gee, I don't know. I'm not a mind reader."

"The only reason I'm asking is that . . . because you know there comes a point where you have to know that—where I do, I mean—about somebody. Whether it's worth your while to wait around so long."

We had enjoyed this same conversation many times before. I always told Veebka that I planned on waiting until I was more successful, or until I was making more money, before even considering marriage. She always replied that this was an unrealistic way of thinking. Even if I did make a lot of money,

Veebka said, I'd probably still say I wasn't successful enough yet. It was a tiresome subject for me, especially since I had recently started to resent Veebka, a reaction I blamed entirely on my own sister's brilliant propaganda campaign.

"Well," Veebka said, "do you have any idea when you might *think* you'll be solvent enough?"

I knew one thing, that I would be solvent in a couple of years, since I came into a trust when I turned thirty—if I lived that long, that is. My biggest fear was that I'd die in the interim, in the middle of, say, working on a construction, and that some well-meaning friend would offer to finish it for me. This "friend" would paste a scrap of old pink hotel soap where I had intended a spatula to go, and my reputation, for what it was worth, would be ruined forever. In the meantime, though, I received dividend checks every month, each one for about seven dollars and thirty-three cents, on pink, thin-grained checks from Southern industrial companies, huge monoliths flushing industrial waste into creeks and waterfalls I had probably once canoed over innocently. "So there's that," I reminded Veebka. "Oh, and also, I'm planning to win a genius award."

I'd been reading the newspaper earlier that evening when my eye had caught sight of a headline: TWENTY-FIVE WINNERS NAMED IN GENIUS AWARD CEREMONY, and the paper ran a group photo of these so-called geniuses. The winners were of all ages, and for some reason they were clustered around the Washington Monument. Most of them stared cryptically at the camera, but I knew this was merely an act, a meager drama meant to disguise their essential emptiness. I couldn't believe who had won, either: a woman who studied the maternal instinct in rats, another woman who had taught goats how to applaud with their hooves and a Trinidadian poet who wrote haiku! Haiku! I was so offended. Haiku writing was so easy it made me laugh! I could write haiku blindfolded, gagged, bound, in my sleep, undersea, with thumbtacks stuck in my eyes, or clenched in the talons of a red hawk! All you had to do was mash together three things that had no connection with one another (starfish, anise powder, your old desk; clams, cookies, zebras) and toss in some fog at the end.

I had drafted one myself on a napkin:

> *Napkin, pencil*
> *Sister who swims, stupid brother*
> *Fog cherry blossom buoy fog*

The maternal instinct in rats? I could study the maternal instinct in rats just by spending one hour in Bob's apartment and watching rats parachute down from the ceiling! Female rats had children, they developed instincts, hence they showed the maternal instinct! What was so brilliant about that?

I showed Veebka the newspaper article, which she scanned briefly before handing it back. "So?"

"Well," I said. "Me. My boxes. Genius. I'm going to grab one of those babies. Don't you see the connection? Doesn't something reach out and hit you over the head here the way it does me?"

"You're not a genius, Hal," she said patiently.

"How the hell do you know?" I rasped.

"Because you just aren't. You lie around in bed all the time. You sleep. You read and then you do a little work and then you go back to sleep and then you read some more magazines. Geniuses are more . . . spry. I mean, aren't they?"

"I've been resting up," I said. "We're like that. We need our rest—"

"Hal, you haven't said or done anything geniuslike since I met you."

I could have pushed Veebka off the fire escape then—really, I could have. It would've been the easiest thing in the world to say, "Hey, look up there!" and while Veebka's head was turned in childlike trust I could have shoved her though the fire escape bars and then howled loudly, to camouflage the sound of her crash in the courtyard. I could picture the headline: GENIUS SHOVES BITCH TO HER DEATH: SHE DESERVED IT! CRIES HIGH-IQ KILLER. But surely Satan would clasp her in his jaws at once, leaving practically no evidence behind. Then the headlines would read: DOWNTOWN WOMAN MYSTERIOUSLY MISSING. Soon Veebka's face would be plastered on every milk carton and lamppost in the city, and eventually someone, somewhere, would trace Veebka to Bob's apartment . . . and then to the fire escape, where they would discover a fiber from her blue sweater clinging to a single metal bar. GENIUS GETS LIFE, I thought sadly, NO PAROLE.

A hundred grand a year—this would solve all my immediate problems, as well as pay off most of my debts. It would be convenient, too, to pass through life as a genius. The best tables in restaurants would be yours. Movie theater owners would wave you inside for free, and if the projector broke down midway through the film, only you would know how to fix it. Crowds of little girls playing glockenspiels would follow you around on the streets, delighted by their proximity to you. Your friends, knowing you were a genius, wouldn't be able to keep their eyes off your face, searching it for signs of incandescence. Even when you ordered a club soda in some dive, everybody at your table would sit back in awe. They wouldn't be able to believe it! Later they would say to their friends, "*Then* Hal ordered a club soda—it was the most amazing thing I've ever seen."

I stayed up late that night, watching Veebka sleep and listening through the walls to the music that issued from other people's apartments. Someone was playing a song whose bass line I recognized, but I couldn't make out the words or the tune. I decided that yes, I was a genius who throughout my life had been too modest to admit it to myself. The truth hurts! Coincidentally, this also happened to be one of the salient characteristics of genius—a humility that takes your breath away. I remembered reading an article about Einstein once, about how down-to-earth he was, so gentle with the children and stray animals of Princeton. He'd bend down and hand out Tootsie Rolls and Mars bars, he'd pat their heads and exchange a few words like "Hi!" and "Hey!" and "What a lovely blouse—is that silk?" and, to the boys, "Hi!" and "Hey!" and "I can't see your face—is it haircut time?" To stray dogs Einstein would say "Sit!" or "Sshh!" and since everybody knew Einstein was a genius, they assumed these simple commands carried triple or even quadruple meanings.

I began noticing that Veebka wasn't spending much time in our new slum. She explained that the lamb and the duck were taking up more and more of her time, but the main problem, I think, was that Veebka was petrified of the neighborhood. She wouldn't even come into the building unless I was at home, with some knives nearby. She always called from the pay phone on the street corner and I'd have to walk down and then escort her back up the several hundred stairs. On our way into the building we'd cross over the stoop, past the lounging, beer-drinking boys, and Veebka, beaming like a Thanksgiving Day float, would step gracefully over their ankles and shoulder holsters, her arms and hands extended, and then, when she reached the apartment, she would collapse on the couch.

So I guess I wasn't all that surprised when Veebka announced at the end of July that she was going on the road with the cast of *America, Sing Out, Sing Strong*. The show was going to zigzag across the country in preparation for a Broadway opening, and the job would last all through the summer, and maybe into September, at least according to plan.

"It's only two more months," Veebka told me. "Until the fall. I don't want to be here all summer, Hal. It's hot here. It's too hot already. The natives will start going crazy, too, and I hate it when they do that."

Four days later, on my birthday, I put the finishing touches on "The Failure of the Buddy System" and dragged it over to the M & M Gallery. At noon I received a letter from Fishie signed "Bald," wishing me a happy birthday. She also enclosed a check for five hundred dollars. Later that afternoon a bouquet of lilacs arrived from Baltimore, with a card paper-clipped inside one of the clusters. The card said, "Happy Birthday, Dear Hal. Missing you. Love, Veebka."

She'd left the day before, for Baltimore, the first stop on the cross-country tour. For some reason she was quite cool when we said good-bye, but I didn't think much about it at the time. I thought she was just distracted, or else trying to conceal bravely just how much she was going to miss me. "I'll tell you happy birthday now," Veebka had said. "I'll tell you it now, but I'll call you too." She seemed profoundly bored by the idea.

I was unwrapping the lilacs when I accidentally brushed them off the stove with my elbow. The flowers spilled across the kitchen floor, and some of the stems rolled under the sink. When I bent down to pick them up, I noticed a second card that had fallen out of the plastic container and was now lying facedown on the floor.

This one read: "To my Darling Veebka. Thank you for a very special evening. And no, I don't think you were *forward* at all. . . . Hope these guys bloom! Mark."

Mark? Who was Mark? I stared at this card for a long time. It was one of those cards you get from the florist, with a vine of tiny yellow cupids climbing up its borders. As I reread it my stomach emptied out. I reread the words several times. I even counted them, up to twenty-six and then back down to zero, not counting the dots. Each word was worse than the last, even if you were counting backward. The issue here, I said to myself, isn't so much that someone named Mark is in the picture but that Veebka has sent you secondhand lilacs for your birthday. A minute later I stopped thinking and realized almost immediately that this wasn't the issue at all. Then I became crazed.

I stayed in Bob's apartment all afternoon waiting for Veebka to call. I didn't know what, if anything, I planned to say to her. Maybe I'd hang up on her. Maybe I'd say that I couldn't talk then, that I'd call back later, and then I wouldn't bother. Maybe I'd repress my fury and get cancer and die. Or maybe I wouldn't answer the phone at all.

I didn't do any of those things. Instead I leashed up BB and dragged her along the wet docks beyond the highway. It was near twilight by then, and the air smelled smoky and rotten. Streams from the broken hydrants trickled through the gutters, carrying such assorted flotsam as movie ticket stubs; soft, damp butts; fragments of postcards; a cracked, snapped pencil; a bra strap; a heel of broccoli; a crushed red lid off a box of Ritz crackers. The sidewalks were screaming up at me. A few lights came on high in the shabby buildings facing the water. Beyond the docks, stretching out into the calm, dark water, the first furry malevolent violent light of dusk grew up over the flimsy coast, only a mile away but vivid like the sordid, bitten waterfront of a foreign country seen from the window of an airplane. The dirty water drifted past me. The birds were winding down. BB was frozen in a squat. Other dog walkers appeared, men with puffy faces and women with made-up eyes squinty from a hard day at the office. The fat twin brothers who owned the gyro store slid the heavy diamond-patterned gate downward. The six o'clock shuttles to Boston and Washington arced across the aching white sky. *Hang on*, I said to myself.

As I was leaving the park a balding man in a wheelchair made his way along the waterfront, shaking a metal cup. He rolled up in front of my knees, trapping me.

"I've just got out of jail, buddy," the man said. "I've been sick. I've been in the hospital. I just got back from Vietnam. My house, it just burned down. My daughter's sick now. I don't have a home. I've just been evicted from my apartment. My wife just left me. My—"

"Which sorrow is it?" I said. "Hospital or jail? Wife, eviction or hospital? Jail maybe? Jail-wife-hospital?"

"The jail hospital," the man said automatically. "But my daughter—"

I could tell he was about to launch into another explanation, so I searched my pocket for change. "All I have is fifty cents," I said, which was true. I'd left the apartment so abruptly that I'd left my wallet behind.

The man waved his hand. "Ahhh, I don't want to take your last fifty cents. I can't take a man's last fifty cents. Times are tough. Times are hard. Even the subways are in a hole . . ." The man coughed loudly, showing perfect yellow teeth.

"No, really," I said, "take it."

"Sure?"

He took the two quarters from me, then clacked them onto the gleaming arm of his wheelchair and started to roll away. "Enjoy!" he called over his shoulder. "Remember, times are tough! Even the dancing girls are kicking!"

Enjoy. Enjoy what? Bob's apartment? BB the depressed dog? The idea of Mark and Veebka in frenzied, voluntary copulation? My pathetic life? Why had this cripple said that to me? Why? Why did men in wheelchairs have to tell me stupid jokes? I was supposed to tell *them* jokes, cheer *them* up. I tried then, I really did, to think up a good joke. What had my brother told me about the man who went to see the doctor, complaining of chest pains? A moment later I remembered it wasn't worth repeating. All I could think about were the lilacs. I didn't even know what to do with the damn flowers. I didn't want to toss them into the garbage, but I didn't want to keep them around, either, so when I returned to Bob's apartment I stuffed them into an ugly trumpet-shaped vase. A few minutes later I decided I couldn't stand looking at them, so I shoved a paper bag over the vase. The lilacs smelled the way I imagined Mark smelled—sweet and stupid, like a bimbo croupier.

"Gosh," I said aloud to the dog. "Gosh, Veebka, I really *like* a forward woman. Why, it prevents me from having to do any work whatsoever. See, I can just lie on my back here and . . . oh, Veebka, gosh, gee, wow, gee, wow!"

Still, every few minutes I checked the phone receiver, to see if the dial tone was working properly. After a while I even stopped doing that, for fear that Veebka would try to call me during that one second when my receiver was off the hook.

The phone finally rang at around nine that night. I let it ring three times while I plugged my tape recorder into the wall socket next to the toaster. What I had done—and this is slightly embarrassing to admit—was to create a forty-five-minute tape of party sounds. I had clanged dishes and pans together, so that when Veebka called she would think I was being toasted, and that trays of exotic food were being passed around the room. I'd called up this old Japanese girlfriend of mine and forced her to repeat after me things like "What delicious canapés!" and "Hal, they want you in the orgy room" and "Babe, I'm going to give you a birthday present you'll *never* forget," this last incantation recited in the sleaziest voice this junior account executive could manage. I had dubbed her voice over a party scene I'd recorded off *Dallas*.

I picked up the ringing phone and switched on the player.

"Hi?" I heard.

I didn't say anything at first. Then, very coolly, I said, "Hello?"

"Hi?" the voice said again. It was a girl's voice.

"Who's this?" This didn't sound much like Veebka, but Veebka was pretty adept at disguising her voice.

"What delicious canapés!" the tape recorder breathed. "And what, they're homemade? Hal, you mean you *cook*, too?"

"Mary-Ann. Mary-Ann Beavers. Is this Bob Moore, wait a minute—"

I didn't know anybody named Mary-Ann Beavers. At first I thought it was probably some old classmate who I couldn't stand, someone who'd looked me up in order to torment me. I was almost sure it wasn't Veebka, so I turned down the volume on the tape machine. I couldn't imagine who it was.

I took the wrong-number angle. "What number are you trying to get?"

"Is this Bob Moore of—just a sec, Cat, hold on one second." I heard the phone slip and fall and strike what sounded like wood. The girl picked up the receiver again. "There. Sorry about that. Bob Moore, 42 Eldridge Street, is this him? The bowling guy?"

"Cat?" For a second I thought it was Fishie, pretending to be Kitty. My sister has a habit of calling me up late at night and pretending to be one or another of our deceased childhood pets—the hamster, the dirty black poodle, the three-legged turtle. Fishie always conducts these conversations in the voice of whichever dead animal, and at some point mentions that she's calling from hell, even though I know perfectly well that she's in New Hampshire, where she usually is, living alone—just her and her huge swimming pool, the diving board upholstered with transparent packing bubbles so that when Fishie jumps, she can hear the snap-snap-snap sound she loves.

"I have everything I need," Fishie whispers in the poodle's soft, inexplicably Middle Eastern accent, "except water. It's hot here, Hal, hot as hell!" and she then issues a crazy poodle-laugh that soon turns into an agonized scream. Usually I have to remove the receiver from my ear.

I assumed it was Fishie, calling from London. "Okay," I said, in as bored a voice as I could manage. "Sing it. Pretend you're Kitty and that you're in hell and that it's all my fault that you're there. Go ahead, start singing. Sing your heart out in a dead cat's voice. Mew away—"

"Sing *what?*"

"Happy Birthday."

The girl's voice softened. "Oh, is it your birthday?"

Something was wrong. I didn't know who this might be. It wasn't Fishie, and it certainly wasn't my brother, or Lisa. "Happy Birthday to Yew," the voice started to sing. "Happy Birthday to Yew, Happy Birthday to Bob Moore the Bowler of Eldridge Street, Happy Birthday to Yew." The accent was Southern, but I didn't know anybody Southern.

"So here's the much-in-demand host *himself,*" the tape recorder whispered. "One of the great parties, Hal; I don't quite know how, but you've managed to surpass even your*self.*"

"I know an Eldridge," the girl went on. "Eldridge knows me." She laughed. "He knows all about my *things.*" She laughed again. "But I don't know you well enough to tell you stuff about Eldridge. Eldridge and the Eldridgemobile, woo woo, right?"

"Look," I said finally, "who is this?"

"I said that. Mary-Ann Beavers. I said that to you already. And this is my dime, 'kay? And it ought to be me askin' you the same—too polite to, I guess. Must be too well brought-up, I guess. Wait," the girl said in a low voice. When she spoke again, her voice was loud and cheerful. "Yes, Amy Stardust," she said into the phone. "Sure 'nuf. I'll meet you at Meg's at eight-thirty. Would you? Swing on past here and I'll be on the stoop, so what else is new, right? And I want a Cheery Cherry Coke. Diet. Two, actually." The girl's voice whispered, "My mom's in the room, that's why I'm so weird all of a sudden."

Coolly I said, "If you have to meet someone at eight-thirty, then you're already late."

"It's six here, look at your watch, dumb-dumb brain. Six. At least the sun's gone away. Ha ha, Bob, NYC's prob'ly all in the dark, correctamundo? That's a double meaning. Havin' to wait till tomorrow to get the sun again, you. But I also mean slow, like people who're in the dark and can't help it. Ha ha. Just kiddin'. No, I had to pretend you were my friend Amy Stardust. She wants to be a model too."

"Hal, is there any more ice?" the tape recorder whispered.

"Where are you calling from?" I said as I switched off the tape recorder.

"Texas. Yippee. Bore me, I mean. Bore me. Just kiddin'. Aagh, I've just taken some poison 'cause I can't stand to be here. Oh, no, I'm commitin' suicide. Just kiddin', Bob, Texas is fine—"

"Where?" I said, as if my knowing the precise town would make the least difference in how I acted. I don't know why I kept this girl on the line—I was curious, I suppose, and feeling lonely, and I had time to kill before I had to drag BB outside again.

"Oh, you would never've heard of it. The town, I mean. It's not on maps. Actually, it's on one map, but that's like a finder's item—collector's item, I mean. Patent, Texas. It's a dump. It's a dumptown, like Dumptown, U.S.A. It's this made-up place too. This guy who made maps for a living started it. That was his whole little mini-reason to live, makin' maps. Everybody who does maps makes up a place somewhere so no one can steal his map ideas. So this map man, he puts in Patent just so his copyright or whatever'll be respected, you know, patent pending and all that. Anyway, he ended up likin' the idea of there bein' a patent so much, he dug the first pit here. Pit's what it is too. Population three-twenty, three-thirty, naked and drippin' wet and stupid. 'Cept for Eldridge, but he isn't from here per se. I mean, he was, but now he lives in Doyle, which is about four miles from here. And that doesn't include me, of course."

By now I was pretty confused. "Well, how did you get this number?"

"'Course I won't get naked for any of those gorp-faces," the girl went on, still stuck in her last thought.

"How'd you get this number?"

"Not that I haven't, right? Been naked. Woo woo, right? I've done everything twice. Just kiddin'. My mom's the one who says she's done everything there is to do, not once but two times, and it wasn't so great, either. So I like sayin' that, too, but it's not true for me, I just said it . . . ahh, I don't know why I said that. Sorry I said that—"

"You're calling from Texas? Texas is a million miles from here."

"Y'ever heard of information? Operators? Waitin' around for you to call 'em? I mean, how do you *think* I got your number? You figure I dragged it down outa thin air?"

I still didn't understand. "There are eight million people here—"

"I just asked your name, stupid. It was easy. I go to the operator, look under the name Moore and give me some Bobs and I'll wait here till you do that and then I'll decide, right? And she goes crazy all of a sudden, even though she was just waitin' around gleamin' her nails or something, waitin' for a little *action* in the operator chamber, you know? I go, How busy could you be, bitch, you answered my call, didn't you? I feel like writin' her supervisor a letter and blowin' her out of the water, wham, bam, shores of Tripoli. I could do that too."

"I'm sure you could," I said politely. I was stalling for something, I don't know what.

"I liked your name. That's all. I liked your name. It's such a borin' name, too, you know? Bob Moore? Just kiddin', Bob, it's not *that* borin', there's worse out there. And my brother, he has this bowlin' journal he gets every month, and there was your name as one of the top lowest money winners of the whole decade, and it said you made your home in NYC. So here I am callin' you. Then ol' operator-face there said there was a Bob Moore on Eldridge Street, so I knew there was some karmalike thing happenin' here.

Since I'm kinda quasi-seein' this guy Eldridge. Y'ever heard that song, 'Why Did I Choose You?'"

"No," I said.

"Well, I'll sing it to you sometime. Song stylists do that song a lot. It's sort of like, I would still choose you, you old bat, even though it's too late, anyhow, you know, neither of us has a body that even makes it anymore. Anyway, I'm sittin' around smokin' these cigarettes I stole from my mom's carton, that's another reason how I thought up your last name, Moore. 'Cause Mom smokes the Mores brand. I steal from her even though it's menthol and the tobacco's inferior as anything. I mean, they say menthol's like this fresh crazy-clean Rocky Mountains Colorado air taste, right? But it's just smoke all the way—I'm not *too* dumb, right? Anyhow, there's nothin' down here to do but steal from people, so I take my mom's Mores. Frank—that's my brother—does, too, but that's just 'cause he's cheap. I do it 'cause I'm too lazy to go to the store, so there's a difference. I hate the menthol, too, it's like rubbin' your nose down in a puddle of Ben-Gay, brushin' your teeth in it till your spit gets Ben-Gay too. But I'll take whatever, right? Mom hides 'em in the microwave so we won't take 'em. Yeah, that works a whole lot, Mom, that's not obvious, Mom, way to cover your tracks, Mom . . ."

I was standing in front of the window now, and across the courtyard I could see a plump, shirtless man, cooking a can of soup. He wasn't using a pan, he'd just stamped the can onto the burner and turned on the flames. The flames flowered up around the smoking can.

Then it occurred to me that Veebka was trying frantically to reach me but that she couldn't because the line was busy. "Look," I said, "I have to go. What is it you want?"

"Look, you don't have to get huffy." This Mary-Ann sighed loudly. "*Brother* . . ."

"What is it you want?" I repeated.

"Okay, I need a little somethin' for my hair, some hair dye. I need the blue and I need the yellow. Though you could just get me the blue and that'd be okay, actually. And I want some mascara in any color that isn't black or brown. Waterproof, too, so I won't drip. And I want you to send 'em to me here, and I'll send you the money back, 'less you want to make a present out of 'em, and then it'll be all square between us. See, I can't get any of those things down here, that's why I hadda call somebody in New York so they can do this gigantic favor. Oh, and I need these things about a month and a half ago, so step on the gas. Just kiddin'. But I do need 'em A-sap. So run, don't walk, to your local drugstore. 'Kay? Just kiddin'. Kiddin' about you runnin', that is, not about you sendin' me that dye A-sap—"

"Why do you need that garbage?" I said.

"'Cause I just do." She was silent for a second. "You'd need 'em, too, if it was just you down here bored outa your mind with another stupid, pathetic sunrise for company. I like set an extra place at the table for the pathetic sunrise, it's so stupid down here."

"Do you work?"

The girl paused before answering. "Oh, yeah, I work. But it's not what I really do, if you know what I'm sayin'. I'm kinda like this super-model, actually. That type. I'm like this actress slash model. ASM, face of the decade and all. Only it hasn't happened for me yet. But it's in the cards and all. My mom says it's in the flip of the all-magical, all-knowin' tarot card deck. I take care of my hands too. That's in case I lose my looks, I can model off my white fingers. I wear gloves so my fingers won't chop off. I have about the whitest fingers in the history of all women ever. But why'm I tellin' you all this stuff about myself? I know, it's 'cause you sound like a doctor. Like an M.D. You have this M.D.'s voice, so that's why I'm—"

"Right," I said. "Listen, and thanks for—"

"Just kiddin'. You have a regular voice. See, I'm workin' down here for my mom. She wants me to be a model, but she says she wants me to earn my own way to the top. She wanted to be a model, too, but the breaks didn't go her way, right? So she's cuttin' hair, 'kay? She cuts the hair and I sweep it up and then just sort of help out. People come in and ask for her by name. She's a star, sort of. I make the combs antiseptic, junk like that, even though I spat in the jar once 'cause Mom was about to cut the hair of my greatest enemy, this girl you would not believe—"

"Well," I said, "not to cut you short or anything, but—"

"Mostly I just sit around and drink beers, though. On the stoop. Not the main street but the one over from Main. I'm like a baby lush. I can see things goin' by, like some big nothin'. Stuff goes on, but it's so usual, it's like nothin' at all. Oh, and I put the hair in the dustpan and take it home. Mom says to throw the hair away, Mary-Ann, hair's dirty, hair's still alive. She says there's a zillion microdot bugs you can't see in human hair and your eyebrows. They stay still 'cause they don't want to let on to you they're there. Even if you wash your hair fifty times, the microdot bugs are just waitin' around in your eyebrows, ready to pounce down and get into your eyes and make you go blind. But I put all the hair I sweep up into this wood chest I have, and I label it. I think I can maybe blackmail somebody with it one of these days. Say, Here's your hair, lady, if you don't give me a million dollars or something, I'll make a movie out of it, I'll publish your hair, whatever, you'll be sorry you were ever so mean to me."

Mary-Ann sighed. "I'm talkin' too much. I can't stop it from comin' out. Just kiddin'. Brother. There, see, I *can* stop, I *can* put the brakes on if I want. It's just like you're this M.D. voice, cat. Are you some kinda M.D.?

"Yes," I said after a minute. At that point it didn't matter what I told this girl. Why not show some versatility? Why not be Bob the Bowler? Why not be a combination bowler-doctor? "Yes," I said again. "I'm a championship bowler, and also a young intern. It's a busy but satisfying . . . life."

"See? *See?* What'd I tell you? I can read people's minds. So what are you doin' for your birthday, you hunky young doctorin' bowler?"

"There's a huge party," I said. "*Huge.*" That wasn't a complete lie. There are parties going on in New York City every day, every night. The fact that I'm never invited to any of them only gives me slight pause. "At the bowling alleys. My girlfriend's giving it. She loves me *very much.* It's a kind of a bacchanal—"

"Whatever that is, right? That's like you with a hat on your head and everybody toasts you and all?"

"Right," I said, wishing she wouldn't drag it out.

"See, I did it again. The ESP thing. My friend Amy sits back, she goes, How do you do that, Mary-Ann? See, they consult me. They got no pride, they're like shamed dogs that way. I tell 'em all about their lives and loves. I shut off all the lights. We live next door to this place, Tucky's Grill, and the GR part in grill is all burned out so all you can see is *ill*. Ill-ill-ill, flickerin' all night and half the day at least. The Tucky part's burned out, too, for that matter. Ill-Ill-Ill, it goes all night. Spooky, right? It spooks my victims right out. And I'm wearin' my white gloves and I bring my white hands up real, real slow. Mom gives readouts on people too. She dresses like a Gypsy at the high school with all this makeup on her face and she tells the little kids all these good things. Nothing bad. 'Cept once she told this one hateful brat he'd be maimed in a Jeep accident if he didn't quit actin' so hateful to people in general. Mom's real good-looking, too, and nice, so they all take her word for it. She got in trouble for that, with that little boy's mother, too, afterward, so they didn't let her do it this year. Anyhow, Mom told me I'd be a real successful model, a hit in my chosen field. See, that's what she wanted to do too, model, but then the breaks didn't all go her way—"

"You told me that part," I said wearily.

"Mom says luck's got a lot to do with it but you gotta create your own luck, you can't just wait around to hear this knockin', right, here's your luck, would you like to be a famous person? Well, yes, I would, right, so here's a ticket to NYC. You gotta go after it, you gotta want it. Anyhow, what was I sayin'? Oh, yeah, Mom says I'm like this really talented *person* but that I haven't found a focus for my individual talents yet. What she said was, I'm quotin' Mom here, Mary-Ann, You'll be very successful at whatever you want to be, and I go, Like modeling? and she goes, If that's what you want, Mary-Ann, and I go, That's what I want, Mom, and I'm gonna get it too. And Mom goes, If you want it bad enough, Mary-Ann, you just hitch your wagon to a starry star and—"

"Look," I said, "hold on a minute. I have to go to the party. The birthday party. You know, the one at the bowling alley. I'm late."

"Oooh, wait, there was an unqote back there too. Endin' after Mom said if I wanted it bad enough. So it's unquote. Mom didn't say the stuff about hitchin' up the wagon, I read that on a poster once, they had a tiny ballerina all photographed in fog. Anyways, I hope they have a giant cake for you, Bob the Bowler Moore. Eat a piece for me. No icin', though. I'm on a super-diet to shed some major poundage—"

"I really have to go," I said, "uh, Mary-Ann."

" 'Kay. But wait, here's like this birthday prediction for you from Mary-Ann Beavers. You will get what you want, right? Set your sights on what you want and it shall be yours, 'kay? That's from me to you. That's my birthday present. So don't say I didn't give you any present or anything. And don't drink too much or you'll get sick and chunder all over your girlfriend's blouse, 'kay?"

"Okay, sure thing," I said, and hung up.

The phone rang three minutes later. "I forgot to wish you a good night, Cat! Sleep tight! And if the bedbugs come 'round, spray 'em till they're dead on their backs. Use Black Flag, that stuff really works. And don't worry about gettin' older or anything. People just get better. Mom says whatever age she's at's her favorite. I s'pose you have to say that, though, so you won't be this regretting person who wants to kill yourself all the time. Oh, and hold on to your seat 'cause I forgot to give you my address. . ."

Mary-Ann read me off a series of numbers that I didn't bother to take down. "Also, to remind you that if it's not too late that the time of the day you were born—what time were you born, anyhow?"

"Ten," I said.

"P.M. or A.M.?"

"P."

"Whew. *Brother.* 'Kay, here's what you do. You gotta leave your party at ten. Or make that nine forty-five. Tell 'em you got a previous appointment with history. 'Cause at ten o'clock you are gonna get a big surprise, Cat!"

"What?" I snarled. By this time I was holding the receiver two feet away from my ear.

"At ten o'clock, when that time comes and you're in a dark room, if you go into a room and turn off all the lights and concentrate real hard, you'll redo your own birth. You'll start relivin' all this junk. You could even have this urge to spank yourself and then you'll find yourself cryin'. *Cry-i-i-in* over you, right? Speakin' of which, there's this girl I know here in town, Shallala, she froze her placenta and then she *ate* it. Isn't she *disgusting?* Shallala goes, it's so nutritious, Mary-Ann, it's got all these vitamins and major minerals in it, you know, et cetera. . . . She's actin' like her gook's got all these *food groups* rolled up into one gooky puddle, but I was so busy throwin' up in the corner at the thought of that I wasn't even listenin'. And I went around afterward and told people what this girl'd said, and people acted like *I* was the crazy one, not wantin' to munch out on placenta all day. I mean, it wasn't like they'd do it them*selves,* but they thought it was generally okay. Anyhow, at nine forty-five you should go excuse yourself from your party, and then you go home into a dark room and lay your head across your knees and it'll be just like bein' a fat little baby again."

"Thanks for the tip," I said.

"Oh, there gonna be any famous people at this party?"

"I really have no idea," I said.

"Well, if there are, get their autographs for me. I'm like this star-struck person. That's why I wanna come to NYC. To hobnob with people like that. I hear you're like walkin' down the street and you look up and there's your basic celeb leanin' against the lamppost, readin' a newspaper—"

"Definitely," I said. "They all live in one big house . . . kind of a barnlike edifice, not so very far from here. Sort of a star *frat.*"

"I think that'd be so excellent," the girl said. "So unbelievably cool."

"Well, then, come on up," I said, thinking, If this girl ever comes to New York, she will never even make it out of the bus station alive.

"Oh, and tell 'em to make their autographs legible too. 'Cause when I show 'em off to people, I don't want to have to explain what the personal message says, and also who wrote it. And that's To Mary-Ann, M-A-R-Y dash A-N-N, no *E,* best wishes, thanks for everything, it's fans like you made me what I am today, and then the name. Legible. Isn't Mary-Ann Beavers a good name? Or should I change it to Stardust, like Amy wants me to, so we can be even better best friends . . .?"

I didn't answer. I was exhausted.

"I *like* Stardust. I think it's a name you remember. I mean, it's not like Betty or Sue or anything, it sticks in your ear. But I don't know if it's good, two people bein' named Stardust—"

"No," I said. "I think one Stardust in the world is plenty. In fact, one Stardust might already have . . . overloaded the delicate balance—the ecological balance—of the planet."

"Yeah, well, what do you know, Bob, right? Just kiddin'. Oh, and talk about me! So that people'll be filled with anticipation if I ever come to NYC! Now sleep tight, Cat. Don't have too much fun, 'cause I'm not, 'kay?"

After I hung up, I roamed wildly around Bob's apartment. My first thought was how lucky Mary-Ann was to have found me at home, and not to have called someone less suitable and more of a pervert. She easily could have dialed the number of some real scumbag, or else a whole troupe of scumbags. They would've passed the phone receiver around and had fun with her, insulted her, called her things, made lewd suggestions about her last name. She was extremely fortunate to have gotten hold of me instead. In fact, I felt like calling her back and telling her just how lucky she was. But I didn't have her phone number. All I had was an address somewhere in Texas that I hadn't even written down, and there wasn't all that much you could do with only an address.

While I waited around for Veebka to call, I listened to a Spanish couple arguing. This same couple kept a rooster as a pet. They chained the bird outside their window, its red claws kite-strung to the openmouthed curlicues of the security frille. "*Puta!*" the fat man yelled, as he always hailed his wife. "*Que te la mame tu madre!*" the woman yelled back. They had a terrific marriage—she was his best friend and he was hers. I watched as he leaned out the window and pulled the rooster back inside by the legs. He was wearing a white undershirt bled yellow under the fatty pinch of his shoulders, and I could see the scramble of black hair on his fingers. The rooster, too, began screaming insults. They were having a three-way-fight.

An hour later Veebka still hadn't called. And the girl who *had* called me— or rather, Bob Moore—had put me in mind of a country song I once heard; one line went, If the phone doesn't ring, you'll know that it's me. Then I started making up excuses for Veebka, wanting to give her the benefit of the doubt. She had lost or forgotten Bob's number, or else the circuits were busy. It happened sometimes: All the circuits are busy, please try again later. Perhaps she had suffered a calamity involving the duck and the lamb. Maybe these two malcontented animals had run off a flight of stairs and broken their heads open, and Veebka was now in the waiting room, or emergency room, chain-smoking, her head buried in her hands. More likely, though, she was out somewhere with Mark.

I felt terribly sorry for myself. I was also very hungry. BB was stirring in the corner of the room, groaning. "Oh, go walk yourself, shithead," I snarled. Then it occurred to me that maybe I should go downstairs to the bodega and buy myself something pathetic to eat, in honor of my birthday. Many pathetic foods produced in this country are ideal for people celebrating their birthdays alone. What did birthdays matter, anyway?

First, though, I had to go to the twenty-four-hour cash machine. In front of my bank I was greeted by a skinny black wino. "Good evening, sir," he said in a deep voice as he pushed open the door, "and how are you this evening?" Without thinking, I bowed and replied, "Fine, thank you, suh." As if I were addressing a white-coated footman from another, gentler age! An era of honorable rites, and women wearing hoopskirts! As though I were entering the lobby of Blake's with a party of seven! What was the matter with me, anyway?

The bank was empty, except for a very old woman sitting at a metal desk, resting her hands on a fishbowl that was filled with assorted change. "Cancer," she called out softly as I strode up to the cash machines, "and leukemia. Cancer and leukemia."

I twisted my head around and gazed backward at her through my elbow. The old woman stared straight ahead.

"Cancer," she intoned, "and leukemia."

I withdrew money. "Nice night outside, eh?" I said awkwardly over my shoulder, since it seemed odd that she and I were alone in the bank and not saying anything.

The old woman didn't answer.

"It's my birthday," I chattered on. "Twenty-eight, can you believe that I've made it this far? Without a scratch? Two more years, then I really have to start getting worried, huh? Gray hairs, pre-nuptial agreements, mortgages. . ."

After almost a minute of silence had passed, I heard again the familiar words: "Cancer. And leukemia. Cancer and leukemia. Cancer—"

I turned on her. "What do you want? Why are you saying those two horrible words over and over? Why can't you say something else? What the hell's the matter with you?"

The old woman said nothing. A minute later she commenced the same recitation. Shaken, I gave her some change on the way out, which she took from my fingers without breaking her powerful, absent gaze. Outside, the skinny black wino shook his coffee cup like a sleigh bell. I gave him some change, too, but this time around I didn't bow or say something inappropriate, such as, "We'll be needing the car too" or "Please remind *Mrs.* Andrews that she has my pipe." *Everybody line up,* I thought tiredly, *I'll give you each a dime. Even though it's my birthday. Pathetic,* I said to myself.

I went straight to the bodega and headed immediately for the frozen food section in the back, past the dusty yellow cans of garbanzos and tamales and enormous sacks of white rice. I passed by huge glass jars of sugary macaroons; dried, freckled sausages pig bits, knuckles, knobby claws, floating slow and aloof in a juice runny with muscle dye—but these foods were not nearly pathetic enough for what I had in mind. As far as I knew, they were probably the staples of some unfortunate diet. In a Spanish country they might've been pathetic, but here they were just strange. For a food to have authentic pathetic status, it had to be utterly marginal or suggestive of bygone youth, or else frozen, with an expiration date stamped on the bottom, slowly ticking away. Tonight I opted for something frozen.

This was going to be the Night of the Pathetic, I thought, with the first moment of genuine happiness I'd felt all night. Pathetic objects would dominate my life! In the morning I would not be the same.

I sorted through the frozen selections and finally chose a TV dinner, as a genre among the most pathetic things I knew. Bachelors took them home and ate them noisily with a fork that had busted a tine in the dishwasher; unhappy business people with no social lives ate them on the run. The one I picked out was a Thanksgiving Feast, and this made me think of people who for one reason or another couldn't go home for Thanksgiving and were stuck in New York City. This would make a virtually flawless Pathetic Dinner! This feast consisted of a couple of slabs of turkey, frozen peas hard as marbles and mashed potatoes swimming in something called Pilgrim Sauce. To one side, a pathetic climax, lay a small, soggy triangle of Mayflower Pie. Inside, the packaging promised, were paper dolls of a Pilgrim and an Indian, along with many fashion accessories. You could dress up the Pilgrim and Indian dolls in various ways, casual or formal, and then have them act out scenes on your dinner table.

I had to admit, you couldn't eat much more pathetically than with a Thanksgiving Feast. Leaving the store, I was proud of my selection, and also grateful to the bodega that it stocked such surefire sorrowful foods. To top off my Night of the Pathetic I bought myself a rotting banana on the way out. What a pathetic fruit! A popular fruit, to be sure, but a sad one—it was the bruises, I think, that mimicked the bruises that often result from a doomed and febrile love.

Back in Bob's apartment, I unpeeled the stale, squishy banana and stuffed a tiny blue candle into its hull, then set the oven at a hundred and seventy-five. The directions on the back of the TV dinner called for three twenty-five, but I thought it would be infinitely more pathetic if it cooked too slowly and the insides ended up damp and cold. The Mayflower Pie would sparkle with ice! Brrrr! Pathetic! I pulled back the foil and slipped the tray into the oven, already smoking from the spilled grease of a thousand former tenants. Ancient lives, barely lived—pathetic! While I waited for my dinner to at least partially cook, I busied myself with the Indian and Pilgrim dolls. I dressed them up in their primitive, loose-fitting clothing and I made them fly. Then I made them copulate. Afterward I made them argue about trivial issues—corn, millet, sand dollars ("You expect me to take sand dollars instead of *cash?*")—and then, begrudgingly make up.

Having grown tired of this sport, I set the table for one and, convinced that the Night of the Pathetic should somehow be immortalized, took down my old Polaroid camera, and a mirror from the wall, which I tilted so I could take photographs of myself while eating. I removed the meal from the oven, sat down at the table and, when I took a bite of the turkey, discovered to my delight that no, it hadn't cooked all the way through! It was, as I had hoped, soggy and cold! "Pathetic!" I cried, this time aloud. The room flashed as I took a picture of myself eating the lukewarm turkey. I had to cup the camera like a catcher's mit, and even though the camera appeared in the picture, the photograph that slid out was a good one. I took several more pictures of myself in various positions. Me, peeling the banana; me, alone, holding a small orange noisemaker; me, eating the corn one kernel at a time; me, holding up the Pilgrim and Indian dolls. I planned to Federal Express all these pictures to Veebka, to show her what a spectacularly miserable time I was having.

I played my phone messages. The machine said there had been seven calls, and at first I thought there was some mistake. I turned up the volume and was immediately overpowered by the sound of my brother's ancient Stratocaster guitar twanging out the Mister Softee theme song. Message two was the final few notes of the same melody, and message three resumed the opening bars. I fast-forwarded the tape, but to my dismay, all the messages were the same.

I suddenly remembered what the girl, Mary-Ann, had said, and glanced down at my watch. It was a little before ten. I didn't believe anything would happen, but just for the hell of it, I went around turning off all the lights in the apartment. Then I sat down on the living room couch and laid my head between my knees, breathing slowly, calmly, not at all hysterically. Outside, the woman and the rooster had teamed up to scream at the man, and the echoes of the courtyard pulled their wailing through my windows. Satan began to bark crazily. I tried to push my head down farther between my knees, assuming the nuclear-attack position, but already my tongue was touching the couch and the veins in my neck were popping out. I maintained this contortion for a couple of hours, until it was way past midnight and my birthday was over for yet another year, waiting for the grim, treasured contents of my childhood to be revealed in a way that would prevent me from repeating the same mistakes over and over again.

Why I Live Alone

*T*hree things happened to me the week after my birthday. The first was that Veebka told me she was in love with a man much worse than me; .... the second was that I received a letter from Mary-Ann Beavers; and the third was that I lost all interest in electric lights and descended into a moody, twilit world of obscure urban horror.

Veebka called two days after the blessed day, from Baltimore. The day before, I had Fed-Exed her lilacs back to her, along with an assortment of birthday photographs. I hated returning perfectly good flowers, but considering the circumstances, I thought this gesture was both appropriate and warranted. Veebka's lilacs deserved flattening or worse, such as manhandling by immoral, obese postal inspectors. I Scotch-taped Mark's twenty-six-word card to the stems, so this card would be the first thing Veebka saw when she opened the package.

"Hal," she said when she called, "I want to explain something."

"Really?" I said, and hung up.

The phone rang a minute later. "Hal?" she said.

"I'm sorry," I said, "Hal's dead, maybe *I* can help you," and hung up. It rang again.

"Sweetie's Dry Cleaners," I said. "Closed for Puerto Rican Independence Day." I hung up again.

The phone rang once more. "Golden Charioteer Chinese Restaurant," I said. "Closed for Hal's birthday week."

The phone rang yet again, and before I could think up another small, family-owned business and holiday, I heard Veebka say, "Hal, *don't* hang up. I think you owe it to me to at least listen to what . . . I want to *explain* something to you."

"Yeah, *what?*" I yelled. "What the hell do *you* want to explain?"

"I'm sorry . . . let me start—"

I was barely listening. *You should have pushed that girl off that fire escape when you had the opportunity,* I thought, *jail or no jail.* Occasionally a word or sentence of Veebka's penetrated my brain, which I was aware was in seizure, drifting and controlled at the same time. "Hal, he's just this *guy.* Some guy I met, he came to the show one night . . . I'm sorry about the lilacs, I just didn't have time to find a florist. And when Mark sent me an arrangement, I just thought I'd—well, I'm sorry. I did the wrong thing, obviously."

Finally, a long silence. "Well," I said almost dreamily. "What do you expect me to do? Or say?"

"I don't know. I don't know what to tell you, Hal. I just don't think I could stand the way we were living anymore. I can't live in that place, that disgusting apartment. I just wasn't brought up to live in a place like—"

"Oh, yeah?" I said. "You think I was?"

"Do you know when I realized I couldn't take it anymore? It was when I started calling our phone machine from the theater when you weren't home and then hanging up. Because I knew that if the phone machine answered, then we hadn't been robbed. Because I figured the thief would've swiped the phone machine too."

"Well," I said after another long pause, "do you like this Mark person? This cretinous piece of croupier garbage?"

"I don't know. I don't know if I'm in love with this person or not. That's one of the reasons I went away. To think it over. The situation, I mean. Probably, though . . . I don't know."

The clanging of the long-distance bells were like warning buoys on a foggy bay of water. "What does this person do?" I said, still in my dreamy voice.

"He's a commodities broker."

Now, this was about the worst thing I had ever heard—a commodities broker. A commodities broker was not better than I was. I didn't even know what commodities brokers did. I imagined a group of portly blond men living on the Upper East Side in suites of chrome, leather, and black speckled marble. I imagined commodities brokers had portable bars in their kitchens, bars that slid out on gray rubber wheels whose squeak had been exterminated. Commodities brokers tended to hang ridiculous signs in their apartments—I AM THE CAPTAIN OF THIS SHIP AND WHAT I SAY GOES in the pantry, and, over their bathroom doors, HEAD.

That's *so* boring," I said softly. "That's a boring fucking thing for someone to do with their life."

"At least he's financially secure, Hal. That does make a difference. I mean, he's someone you could imagine . . . providing for you. I mean, I wish I could tell you something else. I wish I could just say I missed you like crazy and that would be that."

"Well," I said suddenly, "I love you."

"You know what the hardest thing is? I shouldn't tell you. Maybe it's a terrible thing to say. But it's that I felt like telling *you* about it. Immediately almost. I mean, when I started seeing Mark, you were practically the first person I wanted to tell. I didn't want you to *know* about him, but then I also *did*. Just because you want to let someone who's close to you, a friend, know you're making *progress*. Romantic progress of some kind. But that's sick, though, right?"

The warning buoys started clanging again. "We're closed!" I yelled. "It's the Year of the Rat! The two-timing Female Rat!" When I hung up, the phone didn't ring again.

I didn't bother to tell Veebka about the lights. It didn't seem like the right time, and she probably wouldn't even have cared. This had happened about a week and a half before my gallery opening. I was sitting in the living room, opening up my mail, when the light next to the couch went black. This seemed appropriate, I thought, and didn't bother to replace the bulb. Instead I read by whatever yellow-gray, available light penetrated Bob's living room. Over the next few days I gradually discovered that lights were, in fact, useless to this sort of pitiful existence, and soon I boycotted the light switches altogether. A pathetic defiance, but defiant nonetheless.

Anyway, that first night, under an envelope from a singles' club, an L.L. Bean catalogue and a couple of bills for Bob, I noticed a thick pink envelope with thick, loopy writing on it—the kind of writing many high-school girls practice, heavy with childish loops, the *I*'s dotted with balloons, the *O*'s wearing sentimental faces. The return address was Patent, Texas, and a zip code no one in my family had ever even heard of. The back of the envelope was stuck shut with a squiggle of hard purple wax. The letter stank of cheap perfume. Even if it hadn't been addressed to Bob Moore, Mr. NYC Bowler, I would've known who it was from.

Printed on pink tissue paper, it ran to two pages.

Bob,

Hi! What's up, Cat? No, I'm just kiding! No, I just got finished talking to you and here I am writing you 5 min. later. I guess I am hooked on you! Don't you dare show this to your girlfriend because I'm just kiding! (again!) No, let me tell you something about myself. First, I can't wait to come to NYC someday because you will be the first person I see! (I hope!) Oh, hold on, did you have fun at your birthday party, did you pig out, did you save me some cake? Cake is an aphrodesiac, did you know that, so your girlfriend better watch out (Just kiding!) P.S. Where is my hair dye? Just kiding, no, really, I would appreciate your sending it and telling me the $ and I'll send you or maybe give you the $ in person!

Oh, I have a brother named Frank to. He's 28 years and I think he is going to make it because he's got what it takes and he wants it badly, here is a picture of him he says he is going to NYC w/me and gonna move in with you if that's alright with you! (Just kiding!) Oh, you better hold on to your seat because I am gonna call and write you every day if that's "K." And when you write yours it better be a long one! Oh, have you ever had anyone ask you for your name? I bet you have because if you're as cute as your voice is I bet you are a babe! How do I look in this snapshot, good, I hope.

Love Ya Lots!!!
Mary-Ann Beavers

In the margin she'd written, "Mary-Ann Beavers is a good name!!!" and her name was flanked by two stars. Below the stars she'd written, "Turn the Page, Cat!"

I turned to the unheard-of third page:

Oh, I forgot to tell you I love to write poems so here are some I wrote for you. Since you sound like a doctor can you tell my feelings by my poems! (I hope so!)

TIMES PRECIOUS AS GOLD

There's times precious as gold
Some of them whispered, some told
By people to each other
To sail a sea, to make friends with a Cree
Indian. Remember these moments of gold
Til you're really old

That's my favorite. Here's one I wrote after I called you. Turn
to the backside of the other page, Cat!

I flipped the other sheet over, even though the tissue suddenly felt as heavy
as twenty of Bob's bowling balls.

CALLING PEOPLE

Calling people can bring them together
Oh, yes, oh, oh, yes
Calling people can get them to meet in the
Mess Hall, if they're in the army or the navy
Phone calls go through sun and sleet
Phone calls gave me the number of Bob Moore
On Eldridge Street
Phone calls are a way of life, I reckon
Phone calls to the veterinarian can calm an animal's
Strife—and cause that animal to beckon!

I couldn't finish it because I ran out of words, so you can fix it
up for me. Do you think you could get it published for me? I
sent it to Ann Landers but she didn't print it. (Bitch!) Mom says
if Ann L. likes your poem well enough to print year after year
you're fixed for life! No, really, I want to live and visit NYC so
bad I wonder if you could do me a favor and check how much it
costs for a bus ticket and a plane ride from Texas (BORING!) to
NYC. Bye again, luv ya, Mary-Ann.

I wadded up the paper and threw it out the window. *Everybody leave me
alone,* I thought with a sudden burst of fierceness. *I don't need more trouble in
my life.* Mary-Ann's poems were the worst I'd ever read, particularly the
second one, which sounded like an anthem for the phone company. The
novelty of Mary-Ann was beginning to wear thin; just thinking about her, I
felt frayed. Why did everybody want to come to New York to be famous? This
is what I wanted to know, even though I already knew the answer would be a
rousing chorus of "New York, New York," the singer's legs spread apart, one
hand straddling one jutting hip, the other stretched taut in the air, fingers
frozen wide open. I was suddenly sorry that Mary-Ann knew where I lived—
or rather, where Bob the Bowler lived—and I wished I hadn't kept her on the
phone for so long. Most people wouldn't even talk to someone like that, I told
myself. Most people would've said, "You have the wrong number," before
hanging up.

I stared at the photographs. The first one showed a boy and a girl standing under a sign that read MEMORY MOTEL in black letters against an illuminated yellow board. The boy in the photograph reminded me of a crocodile. His face was long and his lips barely hid small, even fangs. He was wearing an orange tuxedo shirt with ruffles, and his shoes were white shiny leather. To his left, in a white crinoline dress, was, I deduced, Mary-Ann herself. She had a heavy jaw and unnatural-looking blond hair blow-dried back. She was pretty, I suppose, but nothing special. You saw a lot of people who looked like that. You saw them all over the country, in large malls, standing in line to buy blue jeans at the Gap, or on skating rinks, wearing pink puffy coats with fur collars, performing endless figure eights to string versions of "Purple Rain" and "Gimme Shelter."

On the back of the picture was written, "Me and Eldridge at the You-Are-Your-Memories Dance. Do you think I could make it in NYC as a model?"

I held my red lighter up close to the second photograph. It showed a man standing in front of a bar, sweeping the dirt around with the snub toe of his boot. I couldn't see his face very well—it was hidden by the shadow of the bar sign—but I made out the hat string looping under his chin and the long, skinny legs squeezed into new jeans. The man had acne in his stubble, and his small eyes, squinted shut against the late sun, floated above a mean, dreamy smile. There was an almost depraved confidence to his stance. He held his cigarette so close to his knuckle that it looked as if his whole arm were smoking.

The caption for this picture was: Frank Beavers, do you think he has what it takes to make it in NYC?

Oh, Christ, I thought. *No. No, no, no, no.*

This epistle caused the scales to fall from my eyes, and I resigned myself to living in the dark, without resorting, cowardly, to electrical lights. I grew to like the gray, grainy half-light of the mornings, and at night the infinite variations of black. I read by candlelight, having stocked up on cartons of beige votive candles, placing them in strategic locations around Bob's apartment. I even invested in an old-fashioned whaling lantern, which I hung in the living room, but I didn't light it all that often, since I couldn't really stand the smell of cinnamon oil.

One night, walking into Bob's apartment, I thought I saw a shadow imposed against the hallway wall. I moved slowly down the hall, but when I reached the kitchen, the shadow had disappeared. My first thought, of course, was that I had caught a burglar in the act, but when I went through the apartment, there was nothing there.

I decided that maybe what I'd seen was just an insect, magnified by the lights shining across the courtyard. Light from thirty different apartments, cast through windows painted over for generations, distorted the shadows and lines of everything in the courtyard. Of course Bob's building was very old and inhabited by the usual vermin—roaches, fleas, water bugs with and without wings. Sometimes a mosquito would fly in through the window, but they seemed out of their league in this city. I would track the mosquitoes for a while, then urge them in the strongest terms to return to the sorrows of the country. The less charismatic insects—June bugs, praying mantises—I would spray with shaving cream. I even bought a small yellow stepladder for this activity. I would set it up under the winged beast and then climb up and blast it with foam. Sometimes I would gaze up at the blue ceiling, covered with clouds of shaving cream, and think for a moment that I was not in a city but instead in a meadow somewhere, lying on my back on a blanket knitted for me by a girl I loved. This image was so powerful that often I even changed into shorts, mixed up a pitcher of margaritas and stretched out on Bob's dirty shag rug, sipping my drink and staring up into the beautiful, foam-clouded sky and thinking I knew where I stood with things.

Soon, however, I had another suspicion—that Bob's apartment had larger, more dangerous animals behind its walls. The tabloids were constantly discovering alligators, wolverines, even the occasional brown bear, prowling the streets and sewer systems. It wouldn't have surprised me one bit if such a predator lurked behind my walls. Bob's apartment building had just been named one of the worst in New York at a recent buffet luncheon honoring landlords and builders. I'd grown accustomed to seeing Bob's landlord, pains-takingly sketched by a courtroom artist, flashed across the six o'clock news after the weather and before sports. Bob's landlord was always on trial for something, if not for setting fire to one or another of his buildings, then for slaying tenants whose faces he didn't like. These courtroom drawings cap-tured his essence, and I don't say that lightly—artists are notoriously tough on other artists. It is supremely hard to draw jowls, or any other kind of fat, jiggling flesh on a man's face, but this particular artist, this contemporary Grosz, had solved the problem by using what looked like a tempera solution and brushing bruiselike swirls all over the landlord's cheeks and neck. The effects were remarkable—Bob's landlord brought to life!

By now even I was fed up with my new lodgings, so I called up my sister in Amsterday. It was all Fishie's fault. In fact, I blamed her entirely. There I was, doing her an enormous favor by house-sitting Bob the Bowler's apartment, walking a creaky, groaning dog three times a day, and in the meantime my whole life was coming apart, caving in, and who knows what sort of wildlife was enjoying free rent at my expense?

For some reason my sister's coach, Lamar, answered the phone. Now, Lamar is a strange story: he and Fishie had gone out for a couple of years, but after they broke up, he stayed on as her coach and manager, a situation I would've found extremely awkward, not to say intolerable. Lamar was the man who organized all of Fishie's commercial endorsements for products she pretended to use but actually, privately loathed and spat upon. Together they made a killing, fooling America's children.

Lamar told me that Fishie was secluded in a town about forty miles north of Amsterday, getting ready for her race, and that she didn't have a number where she could be reached.

I didn't believe this lame explanation for a second. Lamar has always been overprotective of Fishie, since he receives a giant cut of her earnings, and my distinct impression was that he simply didn't want my sister to be bothered by a family member in crisis.

"Tell her," I screamed (not because I was angry but because the connection was miserable), "tell Fishie I cannot live like this! Tell her that her brother Hal says this goddamn slum is untenable!"

"From what your sister tells me, it can't be all that bad," Lamar shouted back. Although many waters separated us, Lamar's deep, patronizing voice came through the receiver and bounced around Bob's kitchen more emphatically than anything he'd said thus far. I knew he didn't want to bother Fishie with anything that didn't have to do directly with swimming, but I couldn't stand being patronized, especially by a man as venal and self-serving as Lamar. "I'll tell your sister you called," Lamar said finally.

"Damn right you will, Lamar!" I yelled, this time not because the connection was bad—which it still was—but because I now was furious. "Tell Fishie it's her *goddamn* fault that I'm staying in this dump in the first place! And tell her she's gotten her little wish, too, that I've broken up with Veebka! And that for once she didn't have to lay out a red cent for it!"

After hanging up, I briefly considered calling Beck to ask his advice, but I knew he'd probably say gleefully that he was more than willing to take my place and move in. Rather than precipitate another encounter with him, and a second desertion on his part, and possibly even my own reunion with Triple L, I'd rather live in the dark and remain vigilant against the threat of feral ambush in Bob the Bowler's apartment.

Matthieu greeted me at the doorway of the gallery, "Hal, *ca biche?*" Then he frowned. "Why it it you are wearing what you are?"

I was dressed that night in the long, skin-sucking wading boots that clammers swear by, and a pair of striped bell-bottoms that looked like something you'd pick up at a Cowsills estate sale. As a genius, I had decided that I had responsibilities to myself, not the least of which was to invest in a disturbing wardrobe, and a day after my phone conversation with Veebka I lost myself in the cheap boutiques of Fourteenth Street, where I spent the afternoon wandering from one smoky emporium to the next, laying out money for raincoats, assorted eccentric shirts, inappropriate women's shoes, hats, purses and galoshes. I thought that if people assumed I was a genius, then it might have a beneficial effect on my sales, and I kept hoping I might bump into a genius judge on the street, in a coffee shop or at a museum. So far this hadn't happened.

Before I could answer, Maude came rushing out of the back room. "Children!" she cried.

She looked about as frightening that night as I'd ever seen her look, and I almost screamed. Her hair was braided in cornrows, and the scruffy braid ends had been dipped in yellow wax. The waxy braid ends had hardened like bullets, and I noticed red marks on Maude's throat from where they'd whipped her skin.

Maude kissed me multiple times on the cheeks as her braid ends slapped my neck, practically breaking the skin. "What a delicious jacket." She rubbed the lapel. "Is it thrush?"

"No, no," I said, "just a normal jacket. . . ." It was, in fact, another hole-filled castoff from my brother's closet. You put a quarter or a nickel into any one of the pockets and a second later you heard it hit the floor.

"Well, peek around the room, Children, see what we've done."

It was five o'clock. The reception was scheduled to start at around six, and people would probably begin coming at six-thirty, or else they'd arrive so fashionably late that they wouldn't come at all. I had decided to come a little early just so I could have time to wander around the empty gallery and worry about my future. On one side of the room my constructions were set up on black, thickly painted school desks, and all of them were labeled. Seeing all my boxes lined up together like that reminded me of Veebka, and whenever I thought about Veebka, I started thinking about Mark as well. I even had a box consisting entirely of Veebka residue—a lock of her hair, a crooked initialed dinner knife she'd used as a child, a tuft of lamb's wool and a couple of dead lilacs. I hadn't wanted to include it in the show, but I knew if I kept it around Bob's apartment, I'd develop such an unhealthy attachment that I'd probably end up sleeping in it. I stood for a long time in front of the Veebka box, trying to figure out what was wrong, and then I finally noticed the label that Maude had pasted to the frame: "An American Tragedy: The Plight of the Farmer—Is Federal Aid Forthcoming?"

That had nothing to do with anything. *Damn her,* I thought, and immediately surveyed the rest of my boxes, checking the titles for further tampering. My Kitty Memorial Box—which contained empty, sterilized cans of her favorite foods (liver, veal ranch dinner, chicken joy) and some of her leftover squeak toys (the tiny soccer ball, the gray whale)—was now entitled, "The New Russian Peasant—Marxist or Capitalist Merchant—You Decide."

Infuriating. Not only did this despoil the memory of Kitty, it despoiled me too. Kitty was neither of those things. Kitty had nothing to do with the Soviet economy. I would've torn that label off the box and ripped it into shreds with my teeth, but unfortunately all the labels were laminated, glued there for eternity.

What made me feel even sicker, though, was the sight of Perry's television sets lined up on the other side of the room. These looked like objects even my country dumps would reject. Small wires and shattered fuses protruded out of the broken glass, which was painted white and gray and ugly beige. I think Perry was trying to make the point that—oh, God, I didn't know what her point was, something to do with white, some *white* point she was trying to make, what did it matter, anyway? I made a note to myself to ask Perry what in the world her televisions meant, but then I thought she might feel insulted if I didn't understand her work. Leafing through the catalogue, I saw that the TVs went for two thousand dollars apiece, almost three times as much as my constructions were selling for. This was ludicrous. This was a clear case of price-gouging robbery. You could buy a perfectly good Zenith for two hundred dollars and drop it off the railing of a bridge and end up with the same distressed results—a savings of eighteen hundred dollars, plus you could feel like a modern master at the same time.

I was hoping Veebka might show up that night. *America, Sing Out, Sing Strong* had closed in Minneapolis, and now Veebka was back in New York, looking for a job. She'd come to collect all her stuff one morning when I wasn't there, and left behind a gratuitous note. "Good Luck, Hal. Hope you sell everything. I will try to make it to your opening, but I may be up in Maine then." Maine: Veebka and I had never gone to Maine together. As far as I knew, Veebka didn't even know anybody in Maine. I suspected that Maine was where Mark the commodities broker spent his summers. He probably had a huge "cottage" up there, complete with an armada of blistered boats and an insane mother hovering at the upstairs window in a soiled pink nightgown. I couldn't bear the thought of the two of them in Maine, so I imagined instead two black seal heads sticking out of the slick, frigid water.

"All Matthieu and I ask of you, Hal," Maude said to me, "is that you talk to people. Let them shake hands with the artist, as the expression goes. Answer all their questions pleasantly and don't be defensive. As I've told everyone that you're very active politically, you might want to say some words about *that*. And for God's sake tell them you have many more boxes at home, in the event no one goes for these but likes your . . . your whatever, your approach."

I actually didn't have a single box at home. I didn't even think I had an approach. I hadn't been working on boxes at all recently. All I'd been doing was moping around in the darkness of Bob's apartment, torturing myself with the memory of Veebka. I actually couldn't have worked even if I'd wanted to, having burned my hand a week earlier when the candle I kept next to my bed flared up suddenly in the middle of the night. I'd forgotten to blow it out before falling asleep and the wax had caught on fire. I threw a glass of water over the wax, and of course this made the flames flare up even higher, toasting my fingers and turning four of my nails brown. My hand was swaddled in an Ace bandage, and if anybody were to ask me what happened, I planned to tell a series of conflicting stories—shark, car door, mugging, lightning. One of the other of these tragedies, described in stark or haunting detail, would make people feel sorry enough for me to open their wallets.

People in dark glasses started arriving at around eight. My brother and Lisa arrived fifteen minutes later; this was almost as bad as letting Beck take take over Bob's apartment, but tonight I didn't care. I watched through the window as Beck brought the red rickshaw to a halt underneath a street lamp and began chaining it up with a bicycle lock. As he clicked the two ends together, the bulb over his head burned brightly for a second, then abruptly sizzled. My brother glanced upward with great disdain as Lisa, not noticing, daintily dismounted.

I wondered whether he had actually pulled the rickshaw all the way from Connecticut, down the Sawmill Parkway, or whether Lisa had allowed him to haul it by car to a prearranged spot somewhere in the middle of Manhattan before making Beck get out of the car and carrying her the rest of the way. How couples work out crises such as this, I thought, is one of the mysteries of married life.

I had not seen Lisa since the wedding two months earlier, and I was shocked by the change in her face. Naturally she'd put on weight—she was pregnant with the Antichrist, after all, and the Antichrist was bound to pack a certain amount of good, solid muscle—but her face seemed different as well. Her left lower lip, for example, seemed to have dropped an inch or so and frozen up. I wondered if she'd suffered a stroke, and if so, why my brother hadn't mentioned it. Beck, on the other hand, looked healthy and good-humored. A month of running another human being around in a rickshaw, sometimes two or three times a day depending on whether his wife was in the mood to shop, had given his upper arms a hard knottiness and his face a bright, alcoholic flush.

Lisa approached me inexorably. "Kiss, kiss, Hal. Hug, hug. So *congratulations*, dearie, this must be a *bit* exciting for the boy, *n'est-ce pas?* Christ, we got so lost coming here, Beck has like zero sense of direction. We practically ended up in Les Reines."

"Les Reines?" I said, when what I actually felt like saying was, *What in the world is the matter with your mouth?*

"Queens, Hal," Lisa said. "My God, where is everybody? Are we *that* early? Social suicide minute, this is not real social suicide, it is only a *test.* If it were *real* social suicide, you'd be informed what station to turn to, et cetera. Thank God it's only your bloody gallery opening, Hal, right? Now, remember, just because I'm pregnant doesn't mean you have to follow me around all night *fetching* me things. I'm perfectly capable of doing things for myself. This night's for *you*, Bud, remember that."

"Well, yes, certainly it is for me," I said with the lameness at which I seemed to have recently excelled.

Lisa dug into her large handbag and pulled out a bottle of some kind of brown liqueur with a couple of hooded monks on the label. "Here. *Presents!* Presents for all! I asked Mummy to pick this out for you. Mummy's kind of a connoisseur . . ."

"Lisa," I said, "the fact that your mother's a professional drunk doesn't really prove that she's a connoisseur of fine wines and liqueurs. In fact, usually it's the other way around—people like your mother will drink *anything.*"

As I might've mentioned, I can say hugely unpleasant things like this to Lisa because nine times out of ten she isn't even listening. "But thank you," I added, "and thank her. I'll uncork it in a little while."

"Have some now, Hal," Beck urged. *"I itch terribly!"* he whispered into my ear while Lisa was looking away. "When I'm pulling the rickshaw, it's okay because I'm in motion, right? But right now, like when I'm standing still, it's driving me up a wall. I *have* to dance, I have to move . . ."

"I told you, Beck," I whispered back. "I told you this would happen—but you didn't listen, did you? You wanted to go on this little *nostalgia* trip down Memory Lane."

"Give me that bottle," he commanded. "I'll open this sucker up for you right now. Tonight I think I'm going to have to get royally slammed. I can't take this itching much longer."

"Well, none for me right now," I said, wanting to keep vaguely sober for my opening.

"Have you sold any boxes yet?"

I explained to Beck that it was still early in the evening, that most people didn't come to openings until much later, if they bothered to come at all.

He wagged a finger at me. "You haven't sold a thing, have you, Hal? Well, there'll be other shows, don't give up hope, whatever—"

"Look," I spat, "I'm not quite ready to call it a night yet."

Beck has never been particularly crazy about my boxes. Once, when I told him I was going to make him a construction for his birthday, he replied, "Fine, Hal, I won't give *you* anything for *your* birthday, either," and stormed off.

Beck squinted at me. "Incidentally, Hal, why are you wearing those ugly clothes?"

Lisa, who had wandered off to look at one of my boxes, re-joined us, so I didn't have a chance to answer. She drew me aside. "Hal, I just shook hands with a guy over there who has a *metal hook* for a hand. Can you stand it? As though he's fresh back from *Hanoi* or someplace and still dreaming of choppers—*thwap, thwap, thwap,* you know. *Aagh,* there's elephant grass under my bed, it's NB time back on the mainland!" Lisa rubbed her hand over her stomach and bowed her head. "Did you hear that, baby?" she cooed in a cold, high falsetto that chilled my spine. "Mommy just shook hands with a man who was half lobster, half human . . ." I knew that Lisa was only trying to communicate with the baby on its own level, but to me she just sounded spooky. She looked up at me suddenly. "Oh, Hal, I shouldn't have touched my baby! Now my baby's going to be born with like this spiny *lobster* head, uggh, foulness . . ." And Lisa shook herself all over, like a hound drying off after a swim.

"Then we'll love it even more," my brother chimed in. I glanced at him oddly, since these words sounded a little stagy, as if Beck were then reciting them from the back of a cue card at a Bozo the Clown convention.

Lisa rolled her eyes. "Yeah, sure. Right. Maybe *you* will, Beck, *pas moi*. I'd be in like *Rio* in two seconds. With like a new *passport*, witness-relocation program, et cetera."

I knew that she'd probably sell a lobster-headed child into the service of a traveling circus right out of the hospital. I felt terribly sorry for her offspring, even though it wasn't going to be born for another seven months or so. *Don't do it, Bub*, I silently begged the luckless fetus. *Stay put.*

"So you're looking forward to being a father," I asked my brother.

"Yes, indeed," Beck said with a terrible artificial brightness. "Another hat for me to wear."

"Boy or girl?" I said.

"Oh, a girl, *une demoiselle*. At least it'd better be. It's all so fucking *subjective*, Hal," Lisa mused. "Eating for two is . . . I mean, having two stomachs and not being able to drink or smoke or do anything I really enjoy. But it's all for the benefit of the baby. I am so grateful, though, to be able to . . . to . . . *do without*, there's something so fucking *subjective* about it all . . . hey, I can't see that box," Lisa said suddenly, in a loud voice. She was trying to peer around the shoulders of a man standing in front of one of my constructions.

"Oh, he'll move," I said crossly. "Give him a minute." At least if it's a girl, I thought, Lisa will be able to brush the child's hair over the three sixes more easily than she would a boy, since a little boy was bound to inherit my brother's receding hairline.

"I can't see that box," Lisa said, even more loudly. "Beck, go over and offer that man some money to move off to the right so I can see . . ." She punched him hard on the shoulder. "Do it, Beck!"

I was horrified by this little display. All the Lyman children, with the exception of Andy, the hippie sister, were spoiled rotten. They were always expecting other people to wait on them hand and foot. In restaurants they sent perfectly good things back to the kitchen, or demanded that waiters kill horseflies and tiny moths buzzing over their heads even though the life span of flies and moths is certainly short enough. "But I'm a Lyman," Lisa's wretched arsonist brother complained to the cop who pulled him over for tossing cherry pits into the tollbooth hamper. "I'm a Lyman," I heard Lisa once say in a Chinese restaurant, "and you're only a goddamn waiter." The Lyman children were fluent with the language of tips, payoffs, hush money, the way other children knew a sport or a pastime. Lisa often said, in her sweetest voice, when she and Beck were in some kind of jam, "Beck, why don't you just give our 'friend' here a little oil to keep his *moto* running?"

My brother shifted uncomfortably in place. "I'm afraid I don't have all that much cash on me at the moment . . ." he said in a worried, breathy voice.

Invariably it was the other way around. Lisa, like many rich people, was constantly forgetting her wallet, leaving it in the pocket of her "other pants," and otherwise preferring to travel without much cash. Most of the time Beck had to pay off the truffle-bearing waiter, or the sommelier, or the policeman, and he had become gaily accustomed to spending his own money. He had sold the few stocks he still owned and was now faced with the prospect of crippling taxes next year. This is one of the difficulties of going out with a very rich girl—the competitive streak it engenders, which, within a short period of time, causes one's own moral and financial ruin.

Lisa pressed a bill into my brother's hand, but before he could do anything, I tapped the man on his shoulder and asked whether he wouldn't mind moving a few inches to the right. Smiling, the man obliged, and I returned to where my brother and Lisa were standing. Lisa glowered at me, even though I'd just saved her twenty bucks.

My brother grimly pocketed the dirty bill. "Anyplace to get some hooch around here?" he mumbled.

I pointed him toward the table where thimble-sized plastic glasses of white wine were assembled. "Something *nonalcoholic*," Lisa screamed after him, before turning back to me. "Hal, I can't drink the way I should with this fucking baby on the premises, you know? I mean, not that I'd even want to, right? I want to make sure the baby's born *looking* right, after all, even though it's probably already got like this foul *crustacea* aspect—"

"You told me, Lisa," I murmured, then excused myself. I wandered the room, hoping that somebody would talk to me who wasn't a member of my family or a grotesque relative by marriage. I went over to Perry's side of the room, and it was there that I discovered to my horror that practically all of the TV sets had already been sold. In fact, everybody seemed to be on Perry's side of the room and not mine. Oh, there were a few people among my boxes, but they were chatting and not really looking at my work. I stood by the door, smiling, ready to answer any questions anybody might have about the materials I used, my inspirations, my ambitions, my genius and so forth, but I guess everybody already knew the answers to these questions.

Back in the front of the room, I saw that my brother and Lisa were both talking to different people. To a woman I'd never seen before, Lisa was saying, "Pregnancy is *so* subjective, you know . . ."

"Oh, I know all too well," the woman replied. She had let her hip relax, and I realized she must've thought she was talking with a normal expectant mother! Normal woman to normal woman! It killed me! "We have two at home, a boy and a girl . . . Scott and Tanya—"

"Yeah, right," Lisa muttered, as thought these children were phantoms and the woman herself was the victim of a cruel hoax. Lisa was going around that night acting like the first pregnant woman in the history of the earth. This must be very lonely, I reflected. How does she bear the responsibility of being the first?

I was standing by the entrance, trying to get a little air into my lungs, when Beck ambled over. "Hal, there you are," he said pleasantly. "Lisa wants to know whether, if she bought all your boxes, you'd smell a rat."

"Yes," I said tiredly, "tell her yes, obviously that I'd—"

"I *told* her that," Beck said, "but she wouldn't listen!" He shook his head and skulked back over to confer with his awful wife. A minute later he barged back over. "Forget what I said, Hal. About Lisa wanting to buy all your boxes. She said she was merely musing aloud, but guess what now? Lisa's going to use a *pseudonym*." My brother beamed. "Todd Cooper is the one who'll actually be buying up all your boxes. That's so you won't know it's really Lisa. But she also wanted me to run it past you first, since she doesn't totally believe in anonymous philan—"

"She can't do that." I paused. "I reserve the right to limit quantity here." I paused again. "I still think I'd know deep down it was her."

"Hal, you want sales, don't you?" My brother looked baffled and hurt. "I think it's awfully nice on her part, especially since she's just lost so much money."

This much was true. Lisa had mentioned her stock-market *debacle* several times already, and by way of illustration she pointed at the rickshaw chained outside to the dark street lamp.

"Back when we had money," Lisa liked to begin these conversations, and I would tune right out. I didn't swallow this match-girl act for a second. It was my experience that when people you knew to be very rich complained that they no longer had any money, it meant merely that they had only recently become aware of their assets, as opposed to the past, when they went along, spending happily, oblivious to any limits. Even "poor," they were still much richer than ninety-nine percent of the population. Poverty merely implied the loss of a certain heedlessness.

At one point in the evening Lisa positioned her mouth an inch from mine and yawned deeply into my face. "I'm so bored, Löwenbrau," she moaned. "Not with you or your *stuff*, I think it's fabulous what you've done *avec les* total waste products. But the baby . . . the baby is whispering that it wants very much to go to Nell's. Do you know where that is, Hal? The club? Do you know Nell? She's a wonderful person, *très* lively, *tellement* versatile—"

"Yes," I said crossly. Nell and Fishie were friends, even though they had peculiarly little in common. "Of course I know where it is, I'm not *that* out of it."

"Of course you're not, sweetie, *Aupres de* the meat district, *très* side of beef and so forth, Flossie the Cow, Ferdinand the Bull, et cetera. No, really, Hal"—Lisa peered into my face—"really, back to this art thing, we throw garbage away, you see, assuming we'll never see it again and then here *you* come swooshing through the air like *Wonderdog* or someone. It's like this re-*merde*-ation that you're *emperor* of, and it's *wonderful to watch*, your *growth*. No, and you have grown so much since I've known you, too, Hal, zero fooling, I'm on the level here." Lisa smiled at me, as if at a dim-witted exchange student. "Anyhoo, this friend of mine, her mother's a Benedict, of the lumber-mill Benedicts, mucho bucks and so on . . . they started the Philadelphia Symphony—"

The name Benedict meant nothing to me. "Lisa," I said, "I don't care who your friend's mother was. I'm not impressed."

As usual Lisa took no offense, even though she was listening this time. "Impressed? *Ce n'est pas le* right word. It's only that I can *do* things with it."

"Yeah?" I said. "Like what?"

"Like play the name game. Like compute who knows—"

"*What* name game?"

"The game of who knows who, there are ten people in the world, et cetera, and they all know each other? I could play it all night . . . you went to Exeter, right, didn't you, Hal? Here, I'll try one: Did you know Marshall Phipps? Or my good friend Jeannie Cantrell with her giant jaw and the overbite that makes her look like this huge radioactive jackrabbit?"

I didn't like this game. Not because I couldn't play it just as well as Lisa could, but because it made my life appear to be enclosed in small white walls. After ten minutes of complacency I usually found myself panting for air and booking plane tickets for the Empty Quarter. Of *course* I'd known Marshall Phipps and Jeannie Cantrell.

"What about Christina Sanders? You know that little flirt?"

"Nope," I said, stonewalling. Every boy at Exeter knew Christina, it was hard not to.

"Did you ever hear what *I* once said about her? That every man has a girl like Christina Sanders once in his life? And that the girl usually *is* Christina Sanders? Don't you think that's funny?"

I don't approve of people who quote themselves, but I laughed, anyway. just for the sake of moving right along. And then I decided to experiment. "Shut the hell up!" I yelled. "Stop talking for one goddamn minute!"

Lisa appeared not to have heard me. It was absolutely amazing. I stared at her as she babbled on. "And of course, there's Tricia Wade. With that horible *growth* on her cheek. Which she says is a beauty mark but you know it's like this xylom-phlom tree-bark *fungus* or something, like her mother's an ex-shrub or an—"

"You're a horrible girl, Lisa!" I screamed. "Stop it! Stop it! How can you say these things?" but my words had no effect whatsoever. There she stood, three feet away, as I howled into her face, but still rattling on, blithely and insultingly. I couldn't believe it!

My brother lurched over and threw his arm around me. "Hal," he shouted. "This is a *disaster!* What a nightmare for you, buddy!"

I noticed that my brother was drinking Mrs. Lyman's liqueur straight out of the bottle. This implied that my brother was nearing the sloppy stage in his drinking, a danger sign if ever I knew one. Beck had often counseled me that a man's final drink of the evening should match the color of his shirt, since he will certainly become so drunk at some point that he'll slosh that drink all over himself. My brother's coat was a brownish tweed, Mrs. Lyman's liqueur was amber; this was another danger sign.

"So what are you doing with each other these days," I said to Lisa, "other than being pregnant?" I glanced over her shoulder—a rude thing to do, I know—to see if anybody was showing any interest in my boxes. To my dismay and annoyance, my side of the room was deserted. The Empty Quarter.

"Me?" Lisa stroked her hair. "Well, the baby takes up a lot of time. Don't you, baby?" Lisa screamed softly at her stomach. "What? You still want to go to Nell's?" Lisa gazed at me sympathetically. "*Elle veut* boogie, Hal, I'm helpless to her fetal demands, they're *ruthless*, and they also lack charm; in fact, I don't know how much longer I can disappoint . . . do you know Nell, Hal? Did I ask you that already? She's a terrific person, *très* warm, *très* with it, *très* on all the time—"

"Yes, you did ask me," I said. "And yes, I've met her a couple of times."

"Ohhh, Hal, I *envy* you so much. Being in the early stages of your relationship with Nell, there's *much* upcoming. I can promise you. It's like a book, a fabulous novel, that you read up in the attic . . . during a rainstorm . . . I almost feel like giving away the denouement, the wondrous ending to come . . . but I shan't . . . you can't make me, Hal . . . you can't, you just can't!"

I tried to look disappointed. "Awww, Lisa," I finally muttered.

"Anyway, what do I do, you wanted to know? Well *I* don't know, Hal. *Hal. Hal.* I serve on boards, I suppose that's what I do. I think it would be asinine for me to keep a regular job . . . even though I've just lost all my money, so I'll probably have to get one soon, right? I work with flowers. Posies and croci . . . the flower show . . . all volunteer . . . they don't pay you a cent. In fact, I'd probably be insulted if they so much as *tried* to pay me."

"Leese," Beck said, "tell Hal about your work with the homeless . . ."

Lisa visibly brightened. "I was about to," she murmured, grabbing me by the collar. When she finally spoke, her voice dropped seven octaves, an attempt to sound thrilling and compassionate at the same time. "Hal, I've gotten involved with a project with *homeless people.* Men, women, heartbreaking infants *sans* roof over their *têtes.* It is *le problème de* this decade, but the work is so rewarding, the work—"

I was surprised to hear this. Working with the homeless was just about the last thing I ever would have pictured Lisa doing.

My brother spoke up dully. "Lisa's spearheading the local movement to prevent the town selectmen from building a soup kitchen in Greenwich."

"Sweetie, it's not *just* me. It's me and a lot of other people too. Who *care*." Lisa looked earnestly at me. "I don't like soup, Hal, I just don't like the smell of soup. Or the texture. I mean, of course I like *some* kinds of soup, but most of it's ix-nay material, *trop* box lunch, *trop*—what's the word—*soupy*. I have nothing against the homeless, Hal, for Christ's sake, don't get that impression, I mean, I'm not some kind of *monster*. I think most homeless people are incredibly spirited. And vivid. And they're in incredible shape, too—lean, I mean. Not a spare ounce of—"

"That lean and hungry look, Lisa," I suggested.

"Exactly. *Exactly*." Lisa's voice rose back up to its terrifying falsetto. "Isn't that so, baby? Yes! Yes!" She touched my arm. "I tell my baby *everything*, Hal. Not that she'll remember a damn thing later on, though, right? Kids don't remember a single thing that happens to them before the age of five. I read that somewhere. You can ignore them, scream at them—and later they'll have like zero recollection of that time in their lives. Incredible, no? And if they give you shit, you just call up the Parents Hotline, you know, 1-800-MISTAKE, as in 'I Made a Big—' By having you in the first place, right? Hey, speaking of *les petits*, Hal, I have a joke for you. Beck's already heard it but he has to laugh, anyway. What did the Hispanic firefighter name his two children?"

I waited patiently.

"Jose and Hose B! Don't you love it? Don't you think that's funny? You're not laughing!" Lisa screamed at me.

"How's your brother doing, by the way," I asked.

"Sir? Or Chris?"

Chris was a drug-soaked arsonist thug. I didn't want to hear about Chris. Sir, on the other hand, haunted my waking dreams. "Sir."

"Oh, didn't Beckie tell you? Didn't your own brother tell you about poor Sir?"

"I try to keep my communication with Beck to a low hum," I said.

"Oh, it was *horrible*, Hal. Sir pulled a *gun* on my parents. Like this Uzi. One morning, like over his *Wheat Chex*. Daddy wrestled it out of his hand, but not before Sir got a couple of Daddy's dogs. And Mummy in the kneecap. I mean, everybody lived and all, but they had to be operated on. Mummy had to use a cane for a month. So my parents had to send Sir to like this hospital for"—Lisa put on a sad face—"a hospital for all the troubled little boys and girls of this earth." She sighed. "McLean. That's the place where you see everybody you ever went to prep school with, right? Sir's in like the McLean Romper Room division. I think that's where he's probably going to finish up his coursework . . ." Lisa shrugged. "You could do worse, I suppose. And McLean even *looks* like a prep school from the outside, so huge dif, right? And don't you *dare* tell anyone about this, my parents would die if a lot of people knew."

"Oh, I won't tell," I said hastily.

"My whole family's kind of coming apart," Lisa said glumly, almost apologetically. "It's kind of . . . kind of a bad thing. Sometimes I just wonder . . ." She hesitated. "At least Sir can play lots of Ping-Pong . . ." she finally said. "He likes Ping-Pong. And he's good at it, too, he does good spins . . ."

By now there were a lot of couples in the room. It seemed that I was made aware for the first time that most of the world was made up of pairs. *Of course,* it dawned on me, Noah's ark, my parents, Beck and Lisa, Adolph and Eva, Bob and Fishie, James and Carly, Sid and Nancy. And not just my parents, everybody's parents. Man and wife, lamb and duck, Veebka and me, the list went on and on.

I stayed by the door, smiling, feeling vaguely like an old, idling automobile—like Son, in fact. While I was pleased to have anything in common with Son, I couldn't help noticing that a lot of people seemed to be exiting by the back door of the gallery, just so they wouldn't have to walk past me on their way out the front and not know what to say. The worst part was that as far as I knew, the M & M Gallery had no back door. Someone must have shattered a window with their fists and climbed out through the fractured glass, and then others had followed. I guess it had seemed worth their while to risk being cut, to risk their good black clothing being torn to ribbons, in order to avoid having to walk past me with their heads lowered in embarrassment.

While standing there watching this vast exodus, I drank perhaps ten small plastic glasses of wine, a spoiled Riesling that Maude had bought several cases of. I kept hoping that maybe Veebka hadn't gone to Maine with Mark, after all, that she'd suddenly burst through the gallery doors and salvage this terrible night. Hell, I would have been glad if the lamb or the duck showed up; at least they knew and liked me. *Go home,* instructed a stern voice inside my head, possibly the voice of a superior court judge. *End this humiliation right now, it won't get any better.*

Across the room, Lisa was nodding earnestly to a very thin, gentle-faced woman on crutches. "Don't worry about it," Lisa said, flicking her hand dismissively. "Once the cancer *metastasizes*, once you're *riddled* with it, I mean, in your *pancreas* and all, you'll get your belief in religion back. *Trust* me, I know of what I speak. You'll turn into a holy roller . . . cancer made holy rollers out of a couple of friends of mine . . . I mean, they're all *dead* now, of course, but before they died, they became, you know, *reasonably* soulful . . ."

That did it. I grabbed my coat down off the rack.

"Beck," I said, backing away from the room until my shoulders were pressed up against the front door. "I'm taking off. I think I might've just reached my limit here. Say good-bye to your wife for me."

My brother perked up. "Hal, can I come with you?"

"No," I said. "No, Beck. You have a wife here, remember?"

My brother offered to run me back to Bob's apartment in the rickshaw. He was swallowing hard, always an indication that he was trying to be kind. "It's quite the comfortable little rickshaw, Hal, you know. A couple of days ago"— Beck paused—"when Lisa was asleep—it was late at night—I climbed inside and curled up there, just to see what it felt like to be the passenger and not the driver. It was *comfortable* . . . you'd like it, I think—"

"Naahh," I said. "I'll just take a cab."

"Aw, come on, Hal," Beck said. "This is your big night, don't you want to be waited on a little? Wave out this night in style?"

"Okay," I said after a minute. "Okay, Beck, if you want. I won't argue, as long as you don't race the thing."

We went outside into a worn, humid night, a light rain, and in the small cars parked along the Bowery, boys and girls were scrambling in the backseats, the only signs that the unlit cars were occupied and fertile. While my brother's fingers began fumbling with the rickshaw lock, I looked around for a pay phone. I needed to do one more thing. I found a phone booth several blocks away, got information and then dialed the number I wanted. "Nell," I said when she picked up the receiver. "It's Hal Andrews."

At first I don't think Nell knew who I was. For one thing, I rarely went to her club. I was too scared that her doormen wouldn't let me in, and that the huge, well-dressed crowd that formed on the sidewalk every night would begin jeering at me for psychologically obvious reasons (they couldn't get in, either) and I would be forced to turn on them and scream, "Hey, I was only *pretending* to want to go in! It was all a big joke! I'm actually a *sociologist* doing a survey on the difficulty levels of getting into New York clubs! I'm no aspirant, I'm a *researcher*! See, that's the difference between you and me, *ya big losers!*" I hadn't been to Nell's for maybe a year—fear had kept me away. "Uh, Fishie's brother?" I added.

"Oh, of course. Hullo, Hal. How is Lily?"

Nell is one of the few people Fishie allows to call her Lily, possibly because the name sounds so silken when Nell says it. "Oh," Fishie says, wincing slightly when she hears Nell's bright, inflected Lily. "Lily, is it?" but it's a baby-wince, and if you weren't one or the other of Fishie's brothers, you wouldn't even know her face had moved.

"Oh, Lily's off doing some kind of challenge match," I said dopily. "In London, Amsterdam, et cetera . . ."

We chatted about my sister for a while. I told Nell that she'd shaved her head. "Mmm," Nell said, "it must look yummy on her. Lily's face could handle such a drastic . . . reaccenting." Behind her, the sounds were extravagantly noisy—plates crashing, loud clarinet music, screams from the kitchen. Soon Nell, whose time I realized was extremely limited, said gently, "So what may I do for you, Hal?"

"Well, Nell," I said, "there's this girl who's going to try to get into the club tonight . . ."

"What club? My club?"

I had no desire to alarm her unnecessarily. "Yes, your club."

"And you want me to hold her for you, is that it? Until you arrive? Take her phone number, hold her hostage in the kitchen?"

"*No!*" I cried. "No, Nell. On the contrary! What I mean is that under no circumstances should you or anybody else allow this girl to get *in.*"

"Is she a member?"

"Unfortunately, due, I think, to some amazing slipup on the part of one of your people, I think she has one of those little key rings or whatever . . ."

"Well, if she *is* a member"—I could hear uncertainty in Nell's voice—"I don't know whether I can really prevent—"

"Dammit, Nell, listen to me!" I shouted. There were times you had to shout at people, even Nell, to get your message across. "I don't want her in there! If you had heard her tonight . . . the foreign languages are getting out of control! It used to be one French word for every, say, eight English words, but now it's one English word for every two French! The proportions are out of control! It's *manic.* Tell your goons, *please,* to refuse her entry!"

"They are not goons," Nell said quietly, with dignity. "My people at the door are trained professionals with a job to do. Just as you have a job to do, Hal, just as I have a job to do . . ."

I had said the wrong thing, and I realized it immediately. Sometimes you have to be careful with your expletives around Nell. "Sorry, Nell . . . whatever. Okay, so they're not goons, they're total pros. They get the job done. And you're right, I spoke much too quickly. I don't know what's the matter with me these days . . ."

My moody, extended abasement seemed to restore Nell's sprightly mood. "And what's the Pretty Poison's name?"

Pretty Poison—aww, you had to love the British, or the Australians, whatever Nell was. "Lyman. Little Lisa Lyman. She's the Family Wipes heiress."

I now could tell that Nell was amused by this prefix, since it was identical to her own in olden days, but she didn't say, "I know that girl very well." She merely said, "Family Wipes . . . hmmm . . . they gave me shingles once . . ."

"Lisa says she's known you for a long time. Socially. Lisa says knowing you is like curling up with a wonderful novel. In a leaky attic, I think she said."

Nell laughed icily. "Yes, well . . . the name's not familiar. But then again, I know so many people . . ." I listened to her gripe about the sheer numbers of fabulous people who came into her club and claimed friendship if not kinship. All I could think of was how busy and interesting her life sounded as compared to mine.

"Nell," I said, "it'll be a cinch to recognize this girl. She'll pull up in a red rickshaw, pulled by a very tall man who has a certain weariness to his face. And she'll be saying, 'Faster! Faster! Mush! Mush! you know, pretending the man has been groomed since birth to be a *husky!* Now ordinarily, I realize, these might be unusual enough grounds to let someone into your club, right? In the jaded search for originality and the usual eclectic mix? But *don't. Please*, Nell, just *don't.* My sister," I added, flipping out my trump card, knowing that Nell would be utterly swayed by this, "feels that same way as I do about her."

"Lily hates her too? Well, your sister hates everybody, Hal, doesn't she? So you're telling me it's not just a private grudge on your part? Honestly, though, we all have the occasional private grudge—there are people I don't even speak to . . ."

I realized two things then: that I had no clout at all with Nell, that she was my sister's friend and I was just a poor relation calling from a pay phone. The second thing I realized was that I had better hurry up before the operator broke in. Fortunately, just then Nell said, "All right, Hal, all right. Don't get hung about it. We'll tell the rickshaw girl, whatever her name is—"

The British people and their expressions continued to delight me. "Hung about," I said timidly. "Is that . . . is that from 'Strawberry Fields Forever'? The *Sergeant Pepper* Song?"

"Is what?"

Get with it, Nell. I thought angrily. "Hung about, as in Nothing to get hung about? Is this your mini-tribute to the Beatles?"

"No, dammitall, it's just an expression," Nell said. *You are wasting my time,* I thought I heard her think. "Hal, what the girl's name again?"

"Lisa Lyman." *Remember your shingles,* I prayed silently.

"Lisa. Well, why don't we do this: We'll tell Lisa the club is closed tonight for renovations. And that all the other people in line to get in are—"

"Carpenters," I interjected. "Rug men."

Suddenly Nell got into the spirit of it. "Siding supervisors! Vacuumers!"

"Go, Little Nell!" I screamed.

"Contractors! Architects! Blueprinters! Couch Upholsterers!"

"Whoa!" I had to say, finally. "Whoa, Nell! No more, girl!" Both of us were panting by this point and I wanted Nell to conserve her strength—she is not a large woman—for the festivities ahead. My own strength didn't much matter, since I was planning to go home and straight to bed. At the end I thanked Nell profusely, and also told her that if there was anything I could ever do for her, a return favor, to just let me know.

"Don't worry about it," Nell said, and hung up politely, but she did hang up. The message was clear: There were no acts that I could ever perform for Nell that another, more successful person couldn't do twenty times better, or more stylishly. I left the phone booth and climbed into the rickshaw.

"So, Hal, how is it back there?" Beck called over his shoulder.

"Very comfortable."

"Now hold on there," he said. "There are potholes in this city the size of lost continents, so hold tight. . ."

I sat back in the rickshaw seat, one hand squeezing the trembling red siderail. It was a short ride back to Eldridge Street, and my brother kept off the large roads, preferring instead to hobble down small, dark, silent streets packed with old warehouses and theatrical costume lofts. I clutched Mrs. Lyman's liqueur under my coat. Occasionally my brother, trotting ahead with the two red wooden bars pressed down upon his shoulders, would stop and ask me to pass the bottle forward to him. Then he would pass it back and resume his slow hobble. After a while I tried to get Beck into a steadier pace. I much admired the Tennesse walking horses, whose gait is supposed to be the smoothest in the world—but without a whip it's difficult to maintain this pace in a walking man.

As we approached the avenue that turned into Eldridge Street, he picked up his speed. I realized Beck had been keeping his neck down, slouched, when suddenly he raised his shoulders, slowing the rickshaw at first so that I tipped back into the hard wood seat that Lisa had softened with a black and white sweater, and started cantering. Soon we were proceeding effortlessly together. As we passed beneath the streetlights, one after another, ten yards apart, their bulbs sprayed out with an unnatural brightness and then, just as abruptly, they dimmed. As each bulb browned, my brother glanced up shyly. I counted off the streetlights: "Five!" he shouted, and "Eight!" Every now and then Beck would attempt a whinny of happiness, or a snort.

He dropped me off on the corner of Eldridge Street, in front of the blinking liquor store. He was breathing heavily. "You've put on some pounds, eh, Hal, haven't you? You've turned into quite the porker."

"I'm one sixty-five," I said absently, "same as I've ever been." As I dismounted, several of the old winos on the corner stared at the rickshaw and started laughing.

"Yeah? Try weighing yourself sometime," Beck said. "I think you'll find you've shot up a little."

Beck turned to the winos. "Any of you old guys want a ride someplace? A little spree through the downtown area?" He tried out his high-school Spanish. "*Quieren ustedes venir con migo? En este* rickshaw?"

The winos shook their heads and laughed. Perhaps they assumed my brother was a phantasm, an image borne of one too many. They stared at the bottle of liqueur he was now holding in the same fist that held one of the rickshaw yokes, its glass throat in his fist, wood rubbing up against the two monks.

"Well, I'm sorry, but I've got to keep moving," my brother remarked to me. "As I told you, if I stay still . . . if I stay still in place, I itch *so awfully.* Come on," he called over to the winos. "*Ven conmigo.* Hal, how do you say, It's free of charge, in Spanish?"

"Don't ask," I said; I'd taken French and, for that matter, the tuba. As I went into the liquor store and slid ten dollars under the bulletproof plastic sleeve, I looked out the window and saw one of the old winos tentatively approach the rickshaw and climb into the seat I had just vacated. He smiled at his friends on the street corner, then called out something that made them all laugh. Then all of them climbed aboard the rickshaw. Beck waved at me through the glass. "You don't mind if I take this with me?" he called, holding up Mrs. Lyman's liqueur bottle. I shook my head slowly, as the Christmas lights festooning the outside of the liquor store burned out. The man behind the partition swore gently. "Don't worry," I said faintly, "the bulbs are probably still good."

Beck handed the bottle to one of the winos, and then, with a burst of breath, lifted the two thick yokes to his shoulders and steadily started moving off in the rain, back downtown, until he was gone. Inside the liquor store, the man slid me back a pint of gin. I now had big, glorious plans for the evening: I was going to drink all the gin and fall asleep. While the rickshaw ride had cheered me up considerably, I began thinking, as if for the first time, that Veebka was gone, that I didn't have a girlfriend anymore. For three weeks or so, for some reason, it hadn't really sunk into my mind. On the way back to Bob's apartment we had passed a series of parked cars with signs in their windows that read, NO RADIO. Some of them read, NO ANYTHING, YOU ALREADY TOOK IT. I decided this was a good idea. Once I got upstairs, I would print a sign on my chest that read, NO GIRLFRIEND. See if anybody bothered me then! Walking up the countless steps, I told myself that I'd never meet anybody like Veebka ever again. If I did meet a woman I liked, I'd have to tell her my whole life story—which I was tired of telling to women—and introduce the girl to Fishie, have Fishie hate her and attempt to purchase her early departure, introduce the girl to Beck and have the girl say to me afterward, "Don't be offended, but is there something chronically the matter with your brother?" And then the girl and I would break up, or she would be pecked to death by terns, or depart from me in some other violent fashion, and once again I'd be cast adrift. I just wasn't in the mood.

Love was a coincidence, I decided. It was a coincidence when you fell in love with someone at the same time that they fell in love with you. It was as much a coincidence as meeting a long-lost friend accidentally on a crowded street in a large city. But you couldn't keep meeting the same person over and over on the same street, and I supposed I should be glad that Veebka and I had liked each other at the same time for as long as we had. Now, though, the coincidence was over.

When I inserted my key into Bob's lock, the apartment door swung open by itself. I waited for the police lock to clatter to the floor, as it usualy did, but nothing happened.

"Hello?" I called out nervously. I wasn't expecting anybody, as far as I knew, and only Veebka had keys and was simultaneously in the country, much less New York. Then I thought, *Of course, it's Maude and Matthieu. They've arranged a party for me, to celebrate my opening night.* No wonder they'd been ignoring me for most of the night—they were merely conserving their enthusiasm until later!

As usual, the apartment was black and stifling, smelling faintly of pastilles and candle wax. Ahead of me, on the coffee table in the living room, I could see a candle, lit and wiggling. I didn't think I had left any candles lit. Had Bob's nightmarish dog lit some candles? Was BB a private worshiper of some evil, larger dog? Satan, for example?

"Hi!" I heard a female voice call from the darkness. Another figure, not the one the voice had come from, stood up, but it was so dark I couldn't make out a face. It was a man, I think, but clearly it wasn't Matthieu. It wasn't Bob, either. *It must be Mark,* I thought bitterly, and I was suddenly incensed that Veebka would bring the croupier into my apartment and light candles around him.

"Hello?" I called again.

"Hi," the same female voice said. "That you, Bob?"

I stopped at the doorway to the living room and it was then that I saw two beer bottles reflecting goldly in the candlelight, and two people I'd never seen before. "How the hell did you get in here?" I said to the one closest to me, a small, thin man.

"Easy," the man said. He gestured with a finger to the black police lock, which was tipped against the living-room wall. He grinned suddenly. "Just gave it a push, that's the end of that."

The other figure was already up on her feet, hugging my shoulders. The girl had a sweet, sickening smell to her neck and her ears that practically made me gag. I think it was the combination of sweat and showgirl perfume, but there was a foreign substance mixed in as well, something unknown-smelling, slightly burnt, that unnerved me. You whiffed this scene on strange tropical islands on days you felt pale and unwanted—it was the odor of fruit rinds, of burning grass and tires.

She released me. "We made it! Can you stand the fact that we made it? You recognize me at all, Bob? From the photos I sent you?"

This was not an art-gallery party, I slowly realized. Similarly, the girl was not Veebka and the boy was not Mark. I stared at her. I knew that voice but I didn't recognize the face. I was looking at a white female, aproximately twenty-five, blond hair stuffed underneath floppy blue felt hat, jeans, and white boots so small they looked like pony hooves. The only fat to her was in her white cheeks, which were touched up with a red blush powder. White lace gloves covered her hands, ending at a point just before her elbows bent, where the ragged lace clumped like bubbles. She wore much too much makeup: blue swipes over her eyes and mascara on her lashes and lips that gleamed as though they'd been buttered.

Then I remembered where I'd seen this head before—in a photograph, as she'd said—and where I'd heard her voice—over a telephone—and at once my heart and stomach seemed to become the same empty, beating organ.

"Mary-Ann, right? Mary-Ann Beavers? The good name, right? We been waitin' here for you hours and hours, Bob! Where the hell were you at, anyway?" She laughed. "Well, not hours and hours, but like one hour minimum. That's plenty. I got the sense life was passin' me by, though . . ." She laughed again. "Oh, and this is my brother—my quasi twin brother Frank . . ."

The brother barely tipped his chin into his rib cage before reaching down to grasp his beer.

"Uh, how did you get up here?" I said. I made out for the first time a white calfskin purse hanging from the bulb of one of my chairs.

"Greyhound. Leave the drivin' to us, right? Hey, and Bob, you'll never guess who we saw in the Greyhound station, either."

"No," I said, "I can't."

"Take a guess." She gaped dumbly. "Hint, it's a big one."

"A big what?"

"Star! Whaddaya think, dummy?" Mary-Ann gave me a shove, which made me rock in place. She was very strong. "*Brother*," she sighed. "A big star, now, so who? Can't you even guess? Three guesses is all you get."

"Well, I guess I don't know." I was starting to lose any energy I had left over from my night.

"A star of the first magnitude. And it's a guy. I mean, it's a man. I'll give you a hint. No, I'll give you three hints. Tortoise glasses. That's hint number one. Hint two is 'Another day has ended, Jobeth, and that's what goin' on.' That's hint two. If you can't get if from hint two, then there's somethin' severely wrong with your motors. I'm totally givin' it away here . . ."

I tried guessing, even though I wasn't really in the mood. How had these people gotten into my apartment? What were they doing there? After my second guess I made my way over to the other side of the room and pressed my back up against the greasy panes of the French doors. I didn't want to sit—

sitting, I felt, would place me at a disadvantage. These people should be arrested, I thought as I jovially named names. At every suggestion Mary-Ann would say, "No-way-no-how-no-good-dogs," or else she'd just sigh and say, "*Brother,* I like *totally* gave it away before, I cannot believe you, Bob . . ." and then she would look over at Frank, who was busy playing with his gigantic Western belt buckle. His bottle stood up between his clenched thighs.

"Babe Ruth," I said, making my final guess.

"I said first magnitude, dummy brain, not second or third. Get your magnitudes or whatever straight, 'kay?"

"Montgomery Brewer," Mary-Ann finally told me, staring so as not to miss my haddock-mouthed amazement.

The name meant nothing to me. I shook my head.

"Oh, very funny, Bob," she said, as if waiting for me to drop my act. "It must be laff-riot time here in NYC, jokes, jokes, jokes . . ."

"I'm sorry," I said, more formally this time. "I don't know that particular individual."

"Montgomery Brewer. You know, the anchorman, anchorperson, whatever? He was just sittin' there in the bus station, pickin' somebody up. Prob'ly his niece or nephew or like that. Maybe his trashy girlfriend. Even though he's married, I'm sure he cheats around on his nice wife all the time. He was alone, too, no bodyguards or nothin'. He's a real little guy in person. They always are, when you see 'em up close, you know? He was wearin' dark glasses over his real ones, you know, those flippy plastic things. I almost went up to him, but then I got too intimidated."

"I don't know who Montgomery Brewer is," I said again, dazed.

"Funny, funny, funny. Funny, Bob, you're a crazy card in a short deck." I heard her deep, almost sleepy sigh again, then she took another breath. "*Brother,* Bob, y'ever watch the news at night? Six and eleven! Y'ever keep in touch with the world?" Her expression suddenly changed. "Oh, I'm sorry. You're prob'ly at the bowlin' alley or somethin'. Maybe at the hospital, doin' your rounds, right? *Sorry.* You're prob'ly not allowed to watch TV, you're too busy savin' people's lives and then bowlin' to let off steam—"

"Sometimes they allow me to watch." For several days I'd forgotten I was a dynamic bowler-intern. "Uh, there's a TV in the nurse's station . . . and at the lanes there's one over the bar, a little black-and-white set."

"Well, the newscaster, then. With Jobeth Steele who's so feeble I hate her. She's always interruptin' Montgomery with these dumb-ass updates, all this local nothin'-at-all, which is why I hate her feebleness so much. That's durin' weeknights six and eleven. They put the black anchorpeople on durin' the weekends. That's to show TV minds're fair and all, the executive people are, I mean. All the white newscasters, Montgomery and all, get to have these great weekends cookin' barbecue, flyin' down to South Padre and Port Arkansas, and the black newspeople have to sit in the studio all weekend sweatin' under those hot hog lights. Montgomery Brewer. Channel Twelve. Montgomery's like *it* where I come from."

"There is no Channel Twelve here." Television depressed me, and I was trying to keep references to it out of my life. TV made me think of my Great-aunt Loreen and the thirteen miniature sets that my brother had inherited. It was because of television that Loreen died in the first place. One day she fell down in front of one or two of her TV sets and broke her hip. She remained there, on the rug, for three days, unable to move. When the emergency medical service men knocked the door down two days later, Loreen thought they were Bill Cosby and Phil Donahue. "Bless you, Bill," my great-aunt said as they lifted her up onto the stretcher. "I think your show is quite true to life, no matter what the critics say." And "Phil, I loved the way you . . . took on men who cross-dress, and who can't give to the . . . women who hate men . . . because they love them too much . . . because they avoid intimacy, and because they love the hate that the men spread on the women who have married male strippers . . . who are virgins . . ." It was a pathetic and depressing way to go, and I blamed TV entirely.

On her deathbed, Loreen had closed her eyes briefly. Her gray eyelids flickered. Fishie and I hovered over her sheeted form, arguing petulantly about room selection and Mai-Tais, since Loreen thought we were two gallant emissaries from *The Love Boat,* and neither Fishie nor I wanted to burst her bubble. Presently Loreen, opening her eyes slightly, murmured, "Oh! I see a figure in white . . . in a long white robe . . . and holding a beautiful sparkling . . . is it a lantern that she is holding?"

I nudged Fishie, assuming that we were getting a first-rate glimpse of God.

Fishie looked disgusted. "She's . . . she's describing the goddamn Columbia Pictures lady . . . logo, Hal," she said in a withering voice. Sure enough, as I glanced through the TV guide I saw that during the time Loreen had been lying on the floor of her apartment, Channel Eight had been rerunning something called *Columbia Pictures: The Golden Years.*

"No," Mary-Ann said, "it's Jobeth who does the local. Montgomery's the big international guy, Mr. Iran-Iraq, Mr. Persian Gulf. Wherever that is, right?"

"I meant, I think he's just a local broadcaster," I said. "Meaning just your area. Not out-of-state."

"You're kiddin'."

"No," I said gloomily.

"Aw, shit. Shit, Bob. Well, Montgomery Brewer's one of the big dogs down where I come from. That boy pisses with the big pups." She laughed at that for a long time and then wiped her mouth.

"Well, this is a huge country," I said lamely.

"No shit. No shit as regards that. Oh, and Frank and I, we helped ourselves to a little somethin', hope you don't mind."

There was an open box of crackers on the coffee table, and some cheese and a bottle opener and four or five dented bottle caps lying there like obsolete Spanish coins.

"We kind of quasi-stole your beer too. And your dog was hungry, so I gave him a piece a bread. But I left a couple of bucks on the stove. That's fair, right? And I used your phone once. 'Case you see some kind of mystery charge on your monthly. To call my mom. But I reversed the charges even though Mom was practically stranglin' the receiver. She goes, Mary-Ann, the guy's a doctor, he's prob'ly loaded, Mr. Golf Club, Mr. Cadillac Coupe de Ville. And you know, if you had a nicer setup here, I prob'ly would've just dialed straight. But it looks to Frank and me like you might be in an early stage of your doctor career, if you don't mind me sayin' that."

"You're right," I said. "The business, well, the business is lagging. People're just so *damn* healthy."

"Is it lahhging, Hughie?" Frank said in a loud voice. He was using some kind of strange accent and refusing to meet my eyes. "Is business bahhd, Hughie?"

"Hush, Bubba," the girl said.

I sank down onto the couch. Was that what Mary-Ann's brother meant, that I talked like that? I didn't talk like that, not by a long shot. I crossed my legs, but since Frank now had his eyes on me, I quickly uncrossed them. As a matter of fact, I tried to sculpt my legs in exactly the same position that Frank's legs were crossed. I have a masculinity crisis sometimes—it comes from having a lunatic as my fraternal role model. I also have another thing I do that annoys me to no end. That is, I tend to imitate whoever it is I'm talking to at the time. If I'm around my brother, for example, I'll end up talking in whatever way my brother has chosen to talk that particular day. I had a feeling that in a matter of minutes I was going to end up talking in a Texas accent. *Don't do it*, I told myself sternly. *Control your vocal cords.*

Frank's head was hidden under a dirty tan hat, but when he reached to put his bottle on the table, I could see his features more plainly. He had a small, delicate face that in the strange caramel light of the candle looked capable of infinite cruelty. All things in his face ended up in narrow, triangular points. His nose was a flat, freckled bone and his chin looked whittled and his teeth were tiny white squares, like Chiclets. Those teeth looked as though they might be eligible, with the proper paperwork, for federal aid.

"Mom says to say hi," Mary-Ann said. "See, I promised I'd call her, tell her we made it up here all right." She hesitated. "We fired up one of your candles, 'kay? I wanted to surprise you, kinda like a late birthday surprise, and all this candlelight's sexy, ya know—"

"The lights are fine," I said, snapping on a switch for the first time in nearly a week. The glare almost brought me to my knees. "I really need a lot of light right now."

"Rahlly." This came from Frank across the room. "Rahlly, I need light right now. I come from Hahvahd, Massachusetts."

I ignored him. As I said, I don't talk like that. I don't even come close to talking like that. "Well," I said after a minute. I was having trouble making words that might. "You came up here on a bus, huh?"

"Bus, then a plane, then a bus." Frank got up out of the chair and started wandering around, touching things. In front of the bookcase he made a fist, just to see what it felt like. I saw a fat red ring on his little finger. He picked up a book, I couldn't see which one it was, and leafed through it, just to see what leafing felt like. Then he whirled around suddenly, flinging the book at me. "Catch," he said in a low, leisurely voice, several seconds later.

Of course I missed it. You don't have a chance when someone says "Catch" or "Think quick" after they've already hurled something at you. The book went sprawling.

"Behave, Bubba," Mary-Ann said.

"I thought you said his name was Frank," I said.

"It is. But I call him Bubba sometimes. Like when I used to do when we were kids. And he calls me Sissy for the same grounds. It's shorthand, you know. For brother and sister."

Bubba and Sissy, I thought. *Great.*

"Bus," Frank said, his eyes studying the ceiling. "Bus, then plane, then bus."

"Bus, plane, bus," I repeated, conversationally at sea.

"Some dink tried to pick me up at the bus station," Mary-Ann said. "This guy, he comes up to me, he goes, Hi, honey. Pull down your pants if you want a piece of candy. And I go, What kind of candy do you have there, mister? Right? And I'm goin' like, I'm not your honey. Not that I'd ever've done anything with him, I just wanted to know what brand he was offerin' by way of candy cause I'm like this chocolate fanatic, right? And I go, It'll take more than some Heath Bar to get me to take *my* things out. Then Frank comes back out from the boy's room and he"—here she made a hitchhiker's thumb at her brother—"comes over and about breaks the guy's wrist. It made this sound like steppin' on some branches in the woods." Mary-Ann giggled. "I go, Frank, all the guy's doin's talkin' to me."

Frank's face didn't move.

"Then," she went on, "at the bus station, *here* in NYC, this black guy, he goes, Can I get you a taxi? And I say to Frank, This is service, right? Let's splurge on a taxi, 'kay? So this black guy, he takes my bag and brings it over to this taxi that's just *waitin'* there *already*. I mean, it wasn't though there was any hailin' or *entrepreneur* stuff involved here. And then the black guy goes, That'll be five dollars. And Frank, he goes, You know, blow it out your ass, mister, that taxi was just parked there, steamin' up the street. So the guy, he pulls out a knife, right? And Frank goes, You're messin' with the wrong guy, my dark friend." Mary-Ann shook her head. "It was wild."

"So what happened?" I said.

"I kicked his butt," Frank said, "that's what happened."

I nodded sagely, as if I, myself, Hal, personally broke at least three wrists a day, two in the morning and one in the early afternoon. I didn't want to hear about Frank's revenge at the bus station—I don't like violence all that much, except when it's subtle and psychological and harrowing, dealt back and forth skillfully by an unhappy, perfect couple on their last legs. "And then you came up here to visit me," I said awkwardly.

"Then I just gave your door a little shove-in," Frank said. "We figured, didn't we, Mary-Ann, you were a doctor, you could fix it." He grinned through his disaster-area teeth. "So where's all your bowlin' balls and those fancy diplomas, huh?"

I laughed. "Right!" I said wildly.

Mary-Ann rubbed the back of her neck. "My neck *kills* from sittin' on that airplane. Oh, and I brought you up somethin' from Texas, Bob. To warm your house. So's you can make it into a home. And I've got some slides, too, so you can see my life, for what it's worth. We can do that later. At some point we'll rig a projector and run through 'em. I took 'em all myself, and some of 'em aren't half bad. Maybe we can flash 'em on the ceilin' so we can lie here on our backs and watch." She laughed at this outlandish notion of hers, then dug inside her small white purse and pulled out what looked to be a miniature furry rug, about ten inches long and just as wide. "Here, Bob." Mary-Ann handed it to me. "Here's your Texas mouse fur."

I took it from her with extreme distaste, turned it over and read in bright red stenciled letters TEXAS MOUSE FUR.

"It's a joke, Bob," Mary-Ann said. "You get it?" She peered into my face. "See, everything in Texas is supposed to be bigger than anyplace else. So this is supposed to make you think, God, those mice down there in Texas must be as big as about the biggest rats they got up there in NYC, right? It's a joke, Bob, so why ain't you laughin'?"

"I'm afraid it's far too subtle for me," I said.

"What are you, Bob, dumb?" Mary-Ann turned to her brother. "I *told* you he wouldn't get it." She waved her white-gloved hands in my face." *Texas*, Bob," Mary-Ann said very clearly. "The *state* of Texas, right? Things are much bigger down there? You know, like all the people and the cars and the highways? It's a joke, Bob. This fur says MOUSE PELT on it, but it's really not, because—"

"I get it," I said. "That's witty, all right."

"I gahht it," Frank said. "Yes, Hughie, I gahht it. It's vahrry wittah." He gave a single snort of laughter.

"Thank you both so much," I said, tossing the grotesque gift down on the coffee table. In the silence that followed, I decided I wanted to get something straight. "So where are you all staying?" I said casually.

"Well," Mary-Ann said, "there's that little room in the back. I saw it when we came in. Little room with all this garbage in it. I figured one of us could lay down in there and the other of us—hell, I don't know, Bob, you're the boss. You're the Port Authority here, right? Anyhow, I threw all my bags and junk in the back." She patted the couch. "This guy here pull out?"

"Wait a second," I said, terrified. "You can't stay here."

"We can't? Well, Bob, where else are we gonna stay? On a park bench someplace and get ourselves knifed in two? Why not stay here?"

"Because." I thought: Because you didn't knock. Because you're both legally insane and belong behind thick steel bars. Because I didn't invite you. Because I don't need this at the moment or at anytime in the indefinite future. Suddenly I couldn't think of a reason that didn't sound selfish. "Because," I said finally, "I live alone. And if you were here, then I wouldn't be living alone anymore. Then you'd be here, too, with me, and my aloneness would be . . . a parody of what we know as Alone, an untrue thing . . . See?"

This sounded reasonable enough as I said it, and it had the hidden advantage of being the truth. I wondered if I couldn't drag the landlord into it as well. I could always say that the lease specified that only one person was allowed to live here, but then I realized that I was living in the building illegally myself, that if I met the landlord in the lobby, I was supposed to pretend I was Bob's violinist-brother Coco, and that perhaps this wouldn't be a smart ploy, after all.

"Aw, shit, Bob," Mary-Ann said after a minute. "I mean, shit. You know you're the only person we know here in New York. You *invited* us, don't forget."

"I did *not* invite you," I said. Then I said it again.

"You said, Sure, Mary-Ann, come on up to New York, meet the stars and the models leanin' on the lampposts. You told me, and I quote, Come on up. I remember it 'cause it was like the diagonal opposite of *The Price is Right*. I remember I thought of Bob Barker and I would never've thought of Bob Barker otherwise. I mean, Bob Barker's not on my mind at all times or anythin'. It was come on *up*, not come on *down*."

"I was being breezy," I said. "I was joking. It was a joke. I'm not the sole representative of this city. I can't invite people here officially. I don't guard the gates. I don't possess the key to the city. I said it just in passing. Meaning, come up here and live here sometime, like when you grow up. Not here.

Somewhere else, I meant. I don't even know you, for chrissake. I was just being friendly."

"Well, we did come, Bob," Mary-Ann said. "Obviously. These are not our ghosts here you're talkin' to." She suddenly looked angry. "You know, your word's practically good as shit, you know that, Bob? It's worth zeros and maybe less. If the situation here was reversed and you came down to Patent anytime, I'd say to you, Go ahead and eat my food, sleep in my bed, here's a key, here's a sandwich, a toothbrush with the right head you like on it, you like a hard pillow or a soft one, welcome to Texas. My junk is like your junk, et cetera." By now Mary-Ann's breath was short and violent. "So where we supposed to go?"

Frank was standing in front of the window, rubbing a smear of white paint with his finger. "I figure if the doctor invited us up here," he said to one of the panes, "we should get to stay on. It was an oral thing. An oral . . . invite."

"Oral agreements are not honored in this state," I said, and noticed that a slight but definite Texas twang was beginning to creep into my voice. "Many times I've said I'll be at such and such a place at such and such a time, and I haven't done it. You know why? Because when I don't do it, I'm not breaking the law, I'm actually, in some ways, *honoring the non-law*."

"Don't be a jerk," Frank said mildly. "We do stuff different where I'm from. Like keep our words."

"Look," I said, "okay. You can both stay here tonight. I'm not saying you can't stay here tonight. I'm not going to kick you out. But you can't stay here your whole trip. You can stay a couple of days, that's it."

"Don't be such a jerk," Frank said again.

"After that," I said, "you have to leave. I don't have room here."

Frank turned around. "You are *such* a jerk, Bob. You gotta helluva lotta room here so far as I make out. Back room just sittin' back there, 'cept for all the crap on the floor."

"Bob, you did invite me," Mary-Ann said in a low voice. "Don't you say you didn't. Unless you're tryin' to make me feel like I'm some insane person, imaginin' totally crazy stuff—"

"That *crap* in the back room you mentioned," I said stiffly, "is my *work*. Those are my constructions."

"Don't be such a jerk, Bob," Frank said. "Now what do you construct, Hahvahhd Gahrbahge? Ahre you a gahrbahgemahn?" He laughed and turned to face Mary-Ann. "This guy does a lot of stuff, Mary-Ann, he's a doctor . . . and he's a bowlin'-ball expert . . . and he's a gahrbahgemahn—"

"I'm not a jerk," I said. "Stop saying that."

"I'm naaht a juhhk, Hughie," Frank repeated. "I'm too busy with my clahhsses at Hahhvahd Univahsity to be a juhhk."

Frank gave another of his one-snort laughs and started pacing the living room again, giving each wall a thud with the heel of his hand. Watching him made me dizzy. I felt as though the couch were spinning and Frank was standing completely still. Suddenly it was easy to imagine Frank breaking people's wrists, knifing them in two in their sleep, murdering their pets and children, chopping up the bodies and then burying them in abandoned lots.

"There's so much I wanna do here, Bob." Mary-Ann had reverted to her good mood. "NYC looks just like Texas from the air. You know, we got crops and all down there. Planted in straight lines. And from the airplane the buildings in NYC are in all the same rows. Evened out. So you see these crop after crop of lights." She stopped talking suddenly. "Whatsa matter with you, Cat? You look funny."

I was sitting there with my head buried in my hands. "Nothing."

"No, what?"

It had occurred to me that before anything else I had to get out of my first lie with a second one. "I have had to leave the dual worlds of medicine and bowling," I said in a choked voice. "I couldn't take the pressure anymore. The long hours. The suffering, the frames, the strikes, the spares, the sutures, the nurses, everything subcutaneous . . . nothing up front, aboveboard . . ."

I felt Mary-Ann sit down next to me, her hand on my shoulder.

"Mary-Ann?"

I felt Mary-Ann look up.

"C'mere," her brother said. "I got somethin' in my eye. Need a capable person like yourself to come over here and figure it all out."

"The doctor'd do it," Mary-Ann said. "Why don't you ask mean ole go-back-on-his-word Bob here?"

"Come on, Mary-Ann, get over here."

"Bob knows the map of the eyeball prob'ly better than anybody. Even if he is an Indian giver."

"I was actually a heart and stomach man in my prime," I said hastily. "And by the way, I also had to change my name. From Bob to Hal. As a symbol of my leaving the two professions that I loved the most, and as a mask for my disgrace."

"Hal?" Mary-Ann said. "I don't like that name at all. That's a stupid name. That's an egghead name. Why'd you choose Hal if you coulda had your pick? Like Montgomery or somethin' else good."

"Get your ass over here, Sissy."

Mary-Ann rose with a sigh. Frank took a seat in the armchair and Mary-Ann knelt in front of him with her white boots kicked back behind her. Frank leaned his head down. "Left eye. Feels like a weevil or somethin's floatin' around in there." He glanced over his sister's lowered head at me. "S'all this crap in the air . . ."

"I don't see anything," Mary-Ann said after a minute. "Looks clean to me."

"Then quit." Frank gently pushed her forehead away from his eye but not before kissing her once between the eyebrows. "It's gone," he announced, letting his head loll back. "Whatever it was, it's gone now."

Mary-Ann sat down next to me again, but this time she kept her hands in her lap. "I'm sorry you're givin' up things you love, Bob, I mean, Hal. All those years of schoolin' for nothin', I guess, huh? I guess I can't call you Doctor no more."

"I'm sorry too," I said, feeling terribly sorry I'd ever confessed dishonestly to being a doctor in the first place.

"And here I had all these *ailments* I wanted you to get outa my way. Plus Frank wanted to go bowlin' with you."

"A damn shame," I said. "A *goddamn* shame."

"I was just kiddin'." Mary-Ann beamed. "I'm pretty healthy."

There was a silence in the room then. Across the courtyard, I could see the pink and blue clothes fluttering in the evening breeze. I went into the kitchen and made myself a gin and tonic. When I came out again, Frank announced he was going to bed. "Mary-Ann, why don't you turn in yourself?" he said. "You, too, there, Bob."

I stood there with my drink, staring back at him. No one was going to tell me when to go to bed. After all, it was my apartment, or Bob's apartment, actually somebody whose camp I belonged to's apartment. I was saved by Mary-Ann.

"'Cause I'm not tired, Frank. I'm in New York now, NYC. What's that poster I saw? *La Ciudad que Nunca Duerme.* I saw that on the one of the bus boards. I liked that. Some ad for some bank. It means the city that never goes to sleep. Patent's like the city that's never woke up ever."

She was pouting now, for her brother. "It's our first night here and I wanna go out and *play*. I wanna go to Bloomin'dales and try stuff on. Don't you wanna go out dancin' or something, Frank? There any good dance and drink and act-foolish places 'round here, Bob? Hal, I mean? Is Bloomin'dales even open now?"

"It's one in the morning," I said.

"Yeah, but the bus thing said this is the *ciudad que nunca duerme.*"

"Well, Bloomingdales is *duerma*-ing," I noted viciously.

"Mary-Ann," Frank said, "you know I don't like goin' to bed when there's other people still up . . ."

"It's *only one o'clock*, Frank. It's like ten P.M. in Patent. I don't go to sleep at ten P.M. There's things *on* at ten."

"Well, tonight I think we all need some shut-eye."

Mary-Ann glanced at me. "Frank has this *thing*, Hal, he's always gotta be the last person to go to sleep in a place. It's like this *thing* with him."

"Put a lid on it, Mary-Ann. Put a lid."

"So where'm I gonna sleep? Where do *you* sleep, Hal?"

I pointed beyond the French doors. "Through there."

"I can't remember if I brought pajamas along or not. I was plannin' on a much bigger place, like I said. I thought I'd have a like this gracious view over all the old buildings and the water and everything. Then I could sleep in the naturale and kinda press myself up against the glass at the window. Make glass angels. That's all we got down in Texas, 'cause we never get snow 'cept once in a while. So we press up to whatever we can. Or whoever, right?" Mary-Ann laughed.

"I got pajamas," Frank said, "If you forgot yours. You ain't walkin' around here anywhere in the raw."

I followed Frank into the back room, hoping to get him, then his sister, settled in, and then, for myself, to forget they ever arrived in the first place. He glanced out the window down into the dark courtyard. "Pretty high up here, ain't it?"

"Sixth floor," I said, as though this were something of which I was very pleased and proud.

"Place needs a good coat a paint. I'll do it if you want. Gotta earn my keep somehow."

"That's okay," I said. *You won't be here long enough*, I thought. "The super paints the place every two years."

"Don't be a jerk, Bob. I made you the offer, all right?"

"Thanks." Then I said, "Your sister can sleep on the couch in the living room."

I was doing it again, and I hated myself for it. I hadn't said "living room," I'd said, "livin' ruhm." My Southwestern accent was becoming more and more pronounced. I knew it had something to do with being a man, or with not being a man. Why did I harbor the sneaking suspicion that Southwestern men were somehow better than I was? I felt like punching myself in the mouth but realized that this was something only a Southwesterner might do, and that I'd gone too far in this direction already. So I kept my hands pinned to my sides.

"Well, no, Mary-Ann can sleep right in here with me." Frank took off his hat to display short hair the color of a rusted oil drum. "Don't want to opportune the doctor and all."

I couldn't tell whether this was meant to be sarcastic or not. "It's no problem," I said, clearly and normally. "The bed pulls out."

"Well, then, I'll be sleepin' on it. Or Mary-Ann can just sleep in here with me." Frank laughed. "It ain't like she's never seen the old bod before—"

"Ain't it," I said, feeling nauseous. He kept laughing. After a while I joined in, without being altogether sure what I was laughing about. Within me, I realized, was a vast residue of false laughter.

I drifted back out to the living room, where Mary-Ann was standing in front of the dresser, playing with a little glass rhinoceros that Veebka had given me. This particular rhinoceros, Veebka had told me, resembled Kitty. The candles my guests had lit spattered in their dishes.

"Hey, this place isn't so bad," Mary-Ann said. "This room kinda makes me think of some beat-up old farmhouse . . ."

I went around the room, blowing out the candles.

"I like candles personally. They're like this cognac commercial, right? You know, make this night last in your memory or whatever." Mary-Ann squinted at me. "Where is it you sleep again?"

I pointed through the darkness. I had become my favorite ghost, the third in *A Christmas Carol*, the wordless one who goes around draped in a black tunic, pointing at things.

"Oh, that's right. I lost my sense of direction for a sec. I got the worst sense of direction of anybody in the history of people trying to get from one place to another. Tell me where a place is and I'll lose it for you. Hey, Hal," Mary-Ann urgently whispered, "y'ever get those poems I sent you?"

"No." I don't know why I lied. I was tired. I wanted to go to bed. I didn't want to stand around talking to an intruder.

"You *didn't*? *Shit.* I sent 'em nearly a week ago. I could sue that damn P.O. for that, you know?"

Briefly I entertained the idea of suing her and her dreadful brother, but rejected it since I didn't want to be tied up forever in court. "Well," I said finally, "If there's anything at all you need, just give—"

"Hey, Hal, I wrote you a poem on the plane comin' up here." Mary-Ann burrowed into her white bag and produced a folder. "Bus schedule . . . it was the only paper I had to write on and, awww, I still have this pen some nice fat man lent me. I would've brought a pen myself, but none of them we had back in Texas worked, anyway." She turned the stolen pen over and over. "He trusted me, right, and it didn't work out for him, it didn't pay off for the guy . . ."

"Read that to me in the morning," I said weakly.

"It'll just take one sec." Mary-Ann smoothed out the bus schedule. "It's entitled 'Bob My Pal'—"

I couldn't stand it anymore. "You mean, like *My Friend Flicka*?" I closed my eyes.

"Yeah, sort of . . . whatever that is, right? Oh, you got nice eyes, Hal. You look like you got a sparklin' drop of retsin in 'em even though you don't."

Mary-Ann recited her poem, which was just as bad as the others and maybe worse. She rhymed *boy* with *metal alloy*, and NYC with *Swell Guy, He.*

"Mary-Ann," I said, interrupting, "*please* let me go to bed now. I'm exhausted."

"In a sec, Cat! Now I can either read you the last two lines, which kinda sum up your whole entire life, or else I can show you my hands. Remember I told you how good my hands were? So you got a choice here: poem or hands. Which'll it be?" Mary-Ann took a few steps backward and smiled eagerly at me. "See, I'm like this singer here, right? With only five minutes left in her concert, and she goes, this singer goes, We've only got time for one more number, you, ya know, all you wonderful fans who came out here tonight in this drivin' rain pourin' down so hard. Right, Hal? See, it's rainin' durin' this concert, this singer's in an outdoor stadium and she's standing inside a cherry picker, she could be electrocuted any second, but she's brave 'cause she knows the fans got her where she is. Then she goes, So which is it gonna be, All You Fans? You know, you, the audience, decide. And if you were my audience, Hal, if there was like thirty thousand of you standin' here instead of just one of you, you could let me know which choice you liked better by tellin' me on the old applause meter, so—"

"What?" I said, horribly confused by all this.

"You decide, Hal. By your applause. It'll go on the old applause meter. It's like the peter meter, but it's clappin'. That's how we'll make the decision, 'kay?"

"What are my choices?"

"There's somethin' wrong with your brain, Hal. The choices here are, I told you before, I could finish the poem, which sums up your life, *or else* I could show off my hands. Those're your two choices."

I couldn't bear any more verse. "Hands," I said.

"No, you gotta choose. Do it like an audience does by clappin'. Pretend there's like this huge meter reader backstage, 'kay? Now, *poem?*"

I just stood there.

"Well, clap!"

I clapped my hands four times.

"No, Hal. Clap in proportion. To which one you prefer. You're not all that sharp, you know that?" Mary-Ann peered into my eyes. "You might wanna have your motor controls checked out by a professional moron-checkin' outfit real soon, 'fore your slow uptake gets you in a jam. I mean, I'm sure there's somethin' in the yellow pages about that . . ."

I didn't answer.

"Just kiddin', Hal. I didn't offend you, did I?"

I was beyond offense. First Lisa and Beck, now Mary-Ann and Frank. At this point in the evening nobody could offend me. "Of course not," I murmured.

"All *right.* Now, *hands* . . ."

I clapped a little harder, but not by much.

"Hands it is, Cat!" Mary-Ann sounded delighted. She dropped her purse onto the rug and started pinching at the tucked lace of her right-hand glove.

"Mary-Ann . . ."

I looked up to see Frank standing in the hallway. He wasn't wearing anything except for his little black bikini briefs, no more than a slash of black across his abdomen, and his ludicrous hat. His stomach was flat, with hard ridges, as though he were storing charcoal in his gut.

"Time to hit it, Mary-Ann," Frank said without looking at me.

"Well, I gotta go to bed now," Mary-Ann said brightly. She patted the sleeve of her glove. "We'll do that other thing tomorrow, 'kay? Night, Hal, thanks for puttin' up with us here . . ."

She kissed her gloved palm and blew me the imprint of her lips, which landed somewhere in my hair, where the grease from the rickshaw ride killed it instantly, but she made no move toward her brother.

"Let's go, Mary-Ann," her brother said.

I stood there, uncertain. "Well, you all sleep wherever you want to."

Frank looked at me for the first time. "You goin' to sleep now yourself?"

"If it's any business of yours," I said, then added suddenly, "and hey! wow! It's not, is it? And I don't *know* what I'm going to do right now! Maybe I'll *read!* Maybe I'll play with the *dog!* Maybe I'll vacuum all the floors in this apartment *very loudly!*"

"Well, then I ain't goin' to bed, either."

"Frank, come on . . ."

Frank just stared at me. He was still staring at me when a minute later I went into my bedroom and closed the French doors behind me. Soon, when I looked up, I saw Frank's mean little face peering at me through the white curtain that shielded the bedroom from the living room. Then he made a sleep gesture at me, two hands swooning together, sloping next to his ear as if in prayer, on which his head tipped and, for a moment, rested. I didn't believe in ghosts, except my own, and I knew it was Frank there at the door, but a shiver trickled down my back, anyway. By the time I finally turned out the light, Frank had vanished.

I slept badly. It was a loud, hot night in the city that never goes to sleep. Salsa music played, the rooster across the courtyard wailed in the casual, dingy rain. Someone shouted, "Manuel, Manuel." I heard guns going off, or firecrackers, or tires blowing out, or assassinations, one of those ambiguous, emphatic urban bangs.

The apartment was empty when I got up the next morning. I took BB for a walk, fed her, then had a shower and made myself some coffee. I was tiptoeing around in case Mary-Ann and her brother were still sleeping in the back room. Then it occurred to me that I was acting like a guest in my own abode, so I began stomping and mewing loudly.

In the bright gray morning my situation seemed ridiculous, that two Texans, dreaming of becoming national treasures, had dropped into my life and into Bob's back room. I blamed myself partly. If I hadn't told Mary-Ann that I was the famous bowler, then none of this ever would have happened. I knew that it was a mistake to have kept her on the phone so long, but I never expected she'd actually come to New York and, what's more, to make it out of the bus station without getting killed, or pressed into prostitution. New York had failed me! The pimps and the leeches had fallen asleep on the job!

I noticed a note pinned to one of the couch pillows.

> Hal, have gone to check out the modeling agencies, also Bloomingdale's! Left the door open, so hope no one cuts you up while you sleep just kiding! There is no good lock, anyhow, so what is the point, who cares! We will all die someday except for me! Have a nice day.
> Mary-Ann.
> P.S. Frank caught a she-bat last night and strangled it (we'll find a trash thing on the street if they have them here). One for the good guys, right? (Us!) (Me!)
> M-A.

Fortunately they didn't return until around four that afternoon. "Hey, Cat," Mary-Ann said vaguely, "whatcha doin'?"

I was working on a new construction, in fact, so I glared at both of them. The box in front of me contained a photograph of me at age fifteen, and several others of stocky Lithuanian peasants that I'd cut out of a stack of *Russian Life* magazines. I'd just finished gluing an empty white bottle of Kero lotion to the back of the box and was sitting back on my heels, surveying my work, a little red screwdriver in my mouth, when the Terrible Two from Texas waltzed in.

Frank remained in the doorway, frozen in a slouch. Mary-Ann was wearing tight black jeans and silver earrings so large they looked like discuses. She crouched down and peered inside the box. "Oh. That's nice . . . nice, Hal. This somethin' you do like in your spare time, glue stuff in boxes?"

"Yes," I hissed. "This is *exactly* what I do in my spare time."

She straightened her back. "Hal, you in kind of a bad mood today over somethin'?"

"No!" I yelled. "I'm in a rare mood!"

"Well, that's good, 'cause we had this really excellent day too. Frank and me did, that is. I went to this modelin' agency in the mornin' to see this friend of my mother's cousin's sister's friend that gave her the name of the guy who's some big modelin' deal here and who's the guy behind the Face of the Decade thing, so I dropped off my pictures with the assistant to his secretary—"

"You go right to the top, don't you?" I said, almost chiding myself for being so mean to this girl.

"Well, yes, Hal," Mary-Ann said uncertainly. "See, they're tryin' to find the Face of the Decade. The girl who wins gets a contract, and then they'll fly her 'round places, first-class, too, so she has tons of legroom, and free everything. And after that, you know, it's movies, TV, cuttin' ribbons, the whole whirlwind-fame thing . . ."

Mary-Ann's face was flushed just talking about it. "I left this number, if that's kosher by you, I hope. They call if they want to see you again. Anyways, I go the assistant to this secretary, Don't you want me to sing something? Show you what I can do? It was really embarrassin', 'cause I guess I just assumed it'd be like one of those pageant things you see on TV, you know, with a talent part of the evenin' and everything. I had a song ready, a dance, too, if they wanted me to strut my stuff. But this lady, she was kinda mean, she said not to wear myself out—"

"What's your song?" I said. "'Tomorrow'? 'Don't Cry Out Loud'? Something insanely up-with-people like that?"

"Nooo. It's country. A country song I wrote myself. Well, Amy Stardust helped out at the end . . . the last verse 'n' all—"

"I *hate* country music." I snarled. "It's so relentlessly whiny."

"Well, different strokes, whatever," Mary-Ann said, tossing her hair. "Oh, and Hal, I never saw so many beautiful women before—not just hangin' around the agency, either, but just walkin' down the street. I was just goin' along myself doin' some errands and so forth and everyone's dressed up *so* nicely. Like they've all just come from this one big nice party. They don't look all that healthy in the face, not their bodies so much, either, they're kinda pale, but they're dressed totally like glamour girls. And look . . ."

Mary-Ann pulled a small envelope from her purse and waved it around like a winning ticket. "Gold, Cat! I brought home some gold dust! Little flakes of gold dust! Or diamonds, whatever, it's somethin' valuable. Why didn't you tell me that ever, Hal? No wonder there's so many rich people here in NYC, they can just run around sweepin' up gold dust on the sidewalks all day. You don't even need a Geiger counter, it's sittin' right out there, anybody can just reach down, stick it in their pockets. And if you got yourself a soldering thing, you could make gold rings for people's weddings and sell 'em on the street."

"That's broken glass," I said tiredly, "not gold dust."

"Yeah, sure, Hal. You're sayin' it's glass just 'cause you're jealous you didn't think up the weddin' ring idea yourself. Just 'cause you want all the gold dust for yourself."

"That's glass," I said loudly. "That's glass from people jumping out of apartment building windows and committing suicide because they've failed at what they set out to do. That's glass from the windowpanes of failed actors, failed drummers, failed playwrights, failed everyone. That's glass from two hundred years of Manhattan failures. And you're not the first person to be suckered into thinking it's gold, and you won't be the last. In fact, I'm sure a thousand million people have had this same *conversation* about the fact that it's not gold. And I really don't want to talk about it anymore, it's *boring*."

"Hal, you *are* in kind of a cranky mood, you know? I was in a bad mood, too, last week. But it passed, 'kay? I thought everybody was out to get me. Then I had this nasty little business with Eldridge and I just felt totally gone." Mary-Ann sighed loudly. "But then I pulled up my shoulders straight back into the air, and I said to myself, Mary-Ann, you go lose that long face—"

"Yeah, sure." I beamed. "Smile though your heart is breaking, let a smile be your umbrella, the tears of a clown—"

"*Right!* Go get that long face lost! Wrap your troubles up in dreams, that's a best one. And I told myself I had to be good to me, you know, *me*, Mary-Ann, go pamper myself a little. So I made myself my favorite food, then I took this long bubble bath and afterward I felt about two million bucks better. Really I did. And I had about a bottle and a half of Ol' Grand-Dad all to myself too. That helped out lots. In fact—"

She pulled a bottle out of her purse. I recognized the caramel label, with the swirling script, the syrup color of the whiskey. This particular Ol' Grand-Dad was about half gone already. Mary-Ann beamed. "In fact, Frank and I sort of helped ourselves on the way back home. How's that song go, I'm always getting high when I get low, right?"

She brandished the bottle at me. "Here, Hal, have a nip, it'll cheer you up. And I got some Gummi Worms too. You wanna Gummi Worm?"

"*I* wanna Gummi Worm," Frank said, "*I* paid for 'em."

I took the whiskey and wiped off the lip of the bottle. Mary-Ann split open the packet of Gummi Worms with her left fang and shook four yellow and green worms onto Frank's palm.

"Oh, Mr. Hygiene from Hahvahhd," Frank said in a high, effete voice. "Scared of a little spit on his bottle top."

I took a couple of swallows and handed the bottle up to Frank, who was reaching for it. He wiped the top with his T-shirt, absently, like a mechanic wiping a windshield. "I'm vahrry concerned about gehrms, Hughie," he drawled. "Vahrry, vahrry."

"I don't talk like that," I snarled.

"Honestly, I rahlly don't talk like that. No, rahlly, rahlly, Hughie, I don't—"

"Hush, Frank." Mary-Ann turned her attention back to me. "I got Frank and me tickets for the boat next week. The Circle the Line deal. They point out stuff of interest, you know, all the sights 'n' all. I think it'll be a major blast. Maybe you want to come along?"

"I'm busy that day," I said. Though she hadn't specified the day, I was sure I could manage to be busy. "You probably won't even be here by then," I went on.

There was a long silence, which I finally broke by hurling the screwdriver into the corner.

"Well," Mary-Ann finally said, "our plans, Frank's and mine, are kinda up in the air now, they're not really all that final . . ."

"Is that so?" I said.

"Mary-Ann, here. Open." Frank jetted a Gummi Worm in the direction of Mary-Ann's mouth, which landed on her collarbone.

"Aww, come on, Hal, I bet you never seen NYC from the water. I bet you're just like me. Livin' in Patent all my life but never once been down to the Diablo Salt Mines."

"The Diablo Salt Mines? How could you have resisted?" I said with as much sarcasm as I could manage without contorting my face into a horror mask.

Mary-Ann passed me the Ol' Grand-Dad again, but this time I was careful not to wipe the top. "I don't know," she said. "I don't know why. Guess I thought they'd always be there, so I never bothered myself with goin' down. I mean, y'ever been to the Battery?"

"No."

"How 'bout Wall Street?"

"No."

"How 'bout the mayoral mansion?"

"No." It's true—I never did anything.

"You just sorta sit around here in the dark, right? Like some bat-channel boy? In your same bat-apartment? With all those fences coverin' up your windows? Ooohh, that she-bat last night was so disgustin'. She flew straight into my face and flapped me with her wings. Did you hear me protestin'? I protested so loud I thought I'd wake the whole city up. Then Frank took care of it. He snapped her—"

Up until that point I had imagined Frank opening the window and letting the she-bat fly off to her nest, calling after her, "Be free, Little One," but I realized this was something of a long shot. More likely Frank had squeezed the she-bat to death in his fist. "I don't want to hear about it," I interrupted. "What if that animal was my own pet? What if I just happened to raise she-bats for a living? Did that ever occur to either of you? What the hell is a she-bat, anyway?"

For several very good reasons, I was in a bad mood that day. For one thing, I had called the gallery in the morning, and just by accident Maude had answered the phone instead of making her assistant do it. "Hal, I'll call you *right* back," Maude said, and hung up. I waited around Bob's apartment for hours, but she never called me back. Later her assistant called to say that Maude had had to leave the office abruptly—"An emergency," she explained, without going into details—and that she wouldn't be back until Christmas. I took this to mean that Maude was too embarrassed to speak to me.

Then, at noon, the Great William called. I was surprised to hear from my father, actually, and was even more surprised that he knew where I was living. After asking me about the opening, the Great William asked if I'd ever considered opening up my own gallery.

"Thanks a bunch," I said, wanting to hang up on him. "That's the single most insulting thing you've ever said to me." My father was always telling me, or more often an intermediary, that I should get a normal job, something less dependent upon whimsical inspirations, a job that offers, at year's end, a proper W-2 tax form and not merely a shoe box full of ragged receipts. The construction I'd built for him as a peace offering was used by the Great William as a box in which to store dripping paint cans.

At the end of our conversation, almost in passing, he mentioned that he'd asked his lawyers to alter the terms of my trust.

I panicked. "What do you mean?"

"The terms," the Great William said. I could hear his crazy, tricolor budgies screaming in the background. In my paranoia it sounded like they were saying, *Kill, Kill.* "We decided to *up* the age proviso, that is, when the capital becomes yours, is turned over to you. Given the past performances of . . . your brother's, well, various careers—and your own. . ."

He left it dangling. "So how have you altered the proviso?" I said uneasily.

"As I say, we've *upped* the age, so that the capital will become yours when you're rather more able to, uh, *responsibly* handle the money."

"So what age did you and the lawyers come up with?" *Don't panic*, my rational mind screamed silently. *Perhaps he wants to give it all to you now.*

"Would sixty-five be fair?"

"Sixty-five years old?" I shouted. "No, that would not be fair! I was *counting* on that money! Next year I was counting on it!"

"Son, you have to admit you're hardly making a good case for yourself, the way you've hardly managed to hold on to the money that you've already been given. Your brother tells me that very few of those crates of yours were purchased last night . . . by the way, I'm sorry I couldn't be there myself. I'm getting a little too old and stuffy for New York, plus your mother—"

"It's early on!" I yelled. "The fact that I haven't sold anything *yet* doesn't mean a goddamn thing! The exhibit goes on for another *two weeks*, Father. What's the use of getting money when I'm sixty-five? My career will be ruined by then! I'll be in a *hospital* cot, sipping liquids from a crazy straw! I'll be working as a temp in a travel agency in some Florida *mall!* I'll be working in a secondhand bookstore, customers will ask why I got into this work in the first place, and I'll tell them I've been working on some science-fiction book for *seventeen* years that you know *will never be published!*"

"Well, I hope you'll have Blue Cross/Blue Shield," my father said. "You don't have any coverage now, do you? That's what I gather at least. . ." The

Great William paused. "I had hoped you would understand my . . . our position. But at any rate, your mother wants to speak—"

I slammed down the phone. Everything had gone wrong for me, every last thing—pets, apartments, siblings, trust funds. Maybe I could cash in one of my pink dividend checks for seven dollars and two cents and buy six boxes of Wheat Thins. Six boxes of Wheat Thins to see me through the next thirty-six years!

You are a genius, I repeated over and over to myself as I strolled around Central Park after my father's phone call, *and it is imperative that you act like one.* Winning a genius award was now an urgent financial and romantic necessity. It was the only possible means I saw of winning Veebka back from her commodities broker, as well as for supporting myself until I turned sixty-five. Sadly, based on what I'd read, the judges for the genius awards remained largely anonymous. Any given person on the street, or walking his mutt, or shuffling around the subways, could be one, cleverly disguised. The blond woman sitting on the bandshell with the live mink on her shoulder could be a judge. So could the punks on the hillside playing their radio too loudly. As could the tanned prep-school girls wearing rumpled boys' oxford shirts, strumming their guitars on the Great Lawn. My mind reeled at all the possible judgeships right under my nose.

The day was warm and bright, and everybody in the city seemed to be outdoors. Men and women in tight, gleaming bicycle pants jogged past me. Many of the joggers held baby carriages out in front of them, and whenever the wheels struck roots in the dirt, the babies' heads bobbed up and down, their gums thumping softly together. At the boat pond, where Veebka and I had dragged the lamb and the duck, I glanced down at my genius's outfit, vaguely discomfited by what I saw—a pair of stunning black pumps, an aquamarine skirt printed with moons and stars, fishnet stockings and, dangling from one hand, a Macy's bag filled with chocolate bars. On my head I wore an orange sombrero with real fruit on it, and a chic black wig that tied in pigtails.

Where are all the goddamn children? I thought desperately. Remembering Einstein and his tenderness with the young, I'd come to the park intending to pass out chocolate bars to urban children in the hopes that some genius judge would spot me, reflect upon my outfit and my beneficent manner, stop on his heels and award me a fat check right there. He would recall seeing a picture of Albert performing similar acts of charity, and something in his mind would click. It was a long shot, of course, but I didn't know where else to begin, and the odds were in my favor that one person out of the crowd of weekend pedestrians was a judge, or at least knew where one was hiding.

Unfortunately, whenever I brandished my bag at a child—on the swings or toddling around the lawns—the child's nurse would scream and she would snatch her young charge away before I even had a chance to give the child a compliment, or muss its hair, or tell it a joke or anything. In retrospect, these nurses saw only a poorly made-up transvestite, not a genius, even though it's the rare transvestite who's capable of muttering scientific equations under his breath, or complex logarithms or the odd foreign word or idiom. And whenever I noticed someone looking in my direction, I began muttering as though there were no tomorrow, since of course, if I failed to score one of these genius awards, there wasn't.

By early afternoon my heels were giving me blisters and I was hungry and frustrated. Spotting a collection of benches, I wobbled over and knelt in front of a tot. "Care for a chocolate bar, kid?" I muttered.

"Get away from us, you freak!" the tot's Caribbean nurse shrieked, gazing in horror at my outfit.

"Keep your powder dry," I commanded, and made up a haiku on the spot, on the off chance that this harpy was in fact a genius judge disguised as a nurse.

> *Little tot*
> *Mean Caribbean woman, Genius stands tall before her*
> *But she's blind!*
> *Fog cherry blossom fog fog*

"Stay away from us!" the nurse shrieked again. Panicked, I attempted another:

> *Chocolate bar*
> *Take it, dammit! Eat it! Me, Genius!*
> *Fog, fog, fog, buoy, fog*

"Oh, won't you *please* take one!" I begged. I emptied all the chocolate bars onto the cement. There were Mars Bars, Twix Bars, Hershey Bars, Reese's Peanut Butter Cups; all my favorites. "Here, *please!*" I went on frantically, as a genius judge disguised as a mounted cop ambled toward me. "*Hurry!*"

After my failure in the park, I'd changed clothes, swapped high heels for sneakers, and taken the subway uptown to the public library, hoping to check out some books on Einstein; I needed to study how he had handled his own failure and poverty. It turned out the Einstein section of the library was enormous. There were scholarly dissertations of his work, biographies, volumes on relativity and a lot of oversize picture books written by his venal relatives. These showed Albert in a medley of casual poses—eating hamburgers, walking along the streets of New Jersey, imitating Mae West in a variety show. In almost all of the photographs Albert's expression was meek and kindly. In his face there was not even the slightest hint of mania.

I took all the picture books down off the shelves, the better to pore over Einstein's mild, sane expression. I wasn't much interested in reading the scholarly stuff, since photo captions were about all I could handle in the way of reading.

I carried the stack of picture books up to the front desk. The main floor of the library was stifling. Old people were slumped in chairs pulled up in front of the large glass windows, and even though a couple of fans were turning aimlessly, they couldn't penetrate the heat. Outside, men were drilling holes in Fifth Avenue and a host of construction workers were sprawled across the front steps of the building, eating lunch and drinking sodas between the massive and protective-looking stone lions. Everybody on the sidewalk was scurrying against the heat of the day.

Seven dollars and two cents a year, I thought gloomily, elated to discover that what they said was true, that anger turns quickly to depression. All right, so maybe the pink checks came three times a year, depending on the stock market—all right, then, *twenty-one* dollars a year. *Fifteen* boxes of Wheat Thins as opposed to only six! I felt hungry just thinking about the trim yellow boxes, how I'd have to parcel out the crackers one by one, breaking them in fourths and chewing calmly and slowly, one every few hours, to make them last.

The librarian was young, pleasant and dark-haired. She asked whether I had a library card and I said no, I didn't. I didn't think this would pose any problem, but immediately I learned that *no one* could take any books from the library without a card. She dug inside a desk drawer and pulled out an application form. "It takes about three weeks."

"Well, then, in the interim, can I borrow these on loan? Until I get my card? Just for a few days?"

The librarian's lips were moving as though she were memorizing formulas. She attached a thin strip of brown paper to the spine of a book in front of her and glanced up without interest. "I'm afraid not."

"What's that?" I said.

"Tape."

"For what?"

"So no one will steal our books. Nape tape, we call it."

"Nape?"

"For the nape. The nape of the neck of the book."

"Ah." I stood in front of her desk a little while longer until I realized that she was waiting for me to say something else. "About that card," I started to say.

"Well, are you a resident of the city?"

"Yes."

"To get a card, then, we need two forms of identification. Some proof that you live here, that you're a resident. We take driver's licenses and something else. Either a copy of your lease or a phone bill. Anything with your name and home address on it. So, if you have your license here with you, we can begin to process—"

"I don't drive here that much," I said. Even though Fishie had turned Son over to me, I kept the car parked in her driveway up in New Hampshire. My license was inside Son's glove compartment, buried under three inches of bird seed.

"Well, as I said, a lease or phone bill will be fine—"

"I didn't bring my phone bill," I said, slamming my hand hard against my forehead as if to suggest I usually carried it with me but that today, for odd personal reasons, I'd left it at home.

"Well," the librarian said, "you'll just have to come back another day." She pressed a new strip of tape against a book's spine, then threw the book into a low white hamper behind her. "We're open from ten to four, Mondays and Fridays, ten to two on Saturdays."

The librarian's reply angered me, though, I don't know why. Usually I have a pretty long fuse, but when she started giving me the runaround, something uncoiled inside me. *Sixty-five years old*, I thought angrily. A *mower of lawns, a duffer at a skating rink, a travel agent in a mall* . . . Nobody had bought any of my constructions, or even expressed a flicker of interest in them, and my attempts to lure genius judges in the park, while perhaps poorly executed, had failed beyond my wildest dreams. I didn't have a girlfriend anymore. And there were two obscenely ambitious Texans in my apartment and I didn't have the faintest idea how to get rid of them.

To steady myself I placed my hands on the librarian's desk. "Go ahead," I said testily, "ask me something about New York City. To prove that I live here. Go on. Anything. Ask me anything. A trivia question that only a full-time resident would know the answer to. Please."

The librarian shook her head and smiled softly. "I'm sorry, sir—"

"Go ahead." I raised my voice. "Don't be shy. Just ask away. Teams, ask me a question about the teams. The New York teams. Let's see . . . the teams are the Yankees, the Knicks, the Rangers, the Mets . . . the old *Dodgers*. Remember the good old Dodgers?"

The librarian glanced nervously behind her.

"Look," I said, "have you by any chance noticed how tense and beaten-down I look?" I lifted up my knee and held my sneaker with two hands. "Look at my sneaker! Look, see how scuffed this sneaker is! The bottoms of my sneakers are completely ruined—they're trashed! I've only had this pair for a couple of months and already they're completely destroyed! City sneakers, right? I mean, they *must* be. If I lived out in the country, these sneakers would last me at least two years! The soles would be perfect!"

"Sir," the librarian said, "I can't help you today. But if you—"

"Look!" I snapped, letting my leg drop heavily, "if I lived out in the *Hamptons* or the *Berkshires*, I wouldn't be this tense, would I? If I lived in *Connecticut*, I wouldn't even be standing here, right? I'd be dozing in some sleepy little county library staffed by blue-haired ladies, wouldn't I? I'd be *hugely* relaxed! I'd say, Well, that's fine, they need your lease, I'll just come back another day, with a lease, with my phone bill, tomorrow's another day, la la la, what's the big rush and so forth. But I'm not *from* there, I'm not *from* the goddamn country! I mean, maybe I was once, but I'm not anymore! And I want these books now! Would a person from the country say that? Would a person from the country ever be *remotely* so demanding? Would a person from the country even *care* if he got his books today or tomorrow?"

The librarian was now refusing even to look at me. She made a motion as if to get out of her seat.

"People who live in the country wouldn't be making this scene!" I screamed. "They'd say, We live in the country! We're a peaceful lot! We plant basil and parsley! Bulbs! And arugula! Tulips! Look at my skin, goddamn you! It's gray, *my skin is gray!* It's pale! It's pale skin! This is not the skin of someone who lives out of town!" I grabbed my skin and tried to stretch it out, but it would give only a little. "This is the skin of someone who stays indoors all day eating Wheat Thins! Caged! There are circles under my eyes! I'm a raccoon! If I lived out in the goddamn country, I wouldn't even *have* circles under my eyes! I'd go to bed early! Like seven-thirty! Eight! No later! I'm a resident here, goddammit!"

I was escorted out by a giant, unsmiling guard who told me not to pass again beneath the eyes of the stone lions.

A couple of nights later I planned to ask Mary-Ann and Frank, sweetly, whether they had found other accommodations, or whether they'd even attempted to look for some.

I was more than slightly concerned. Their second day at my apartment they had proceeded to set up house. Mary-Ann hung up her shirts and skirts on hangers in the back room and along the shower rod, and Frank moved out into the living room, sleeping under a single gray sheet on the couch. Obviously he didn't trust me anywhere near his sister. The night before, for example, when I was stumbling back from the bathroom at three in the morning, I was startled to see Frank's naked figure standing in the hallway when I opened the door. "Whatcha doin'?" he said.

"I just took a leak," I said, "if that's all right."

In the dark Frank nodded. "Hell, yes. But keep it movin' . . ."

"*Keep it movin'*?" I said. "What are you, a guard at a Bon Jovi concert?" When I didn't move immediately, he added, "You're back over that way, case you forgot."

"Look," I said, "this is *my* apartment, quit ordering me around." *Or I'll offer Satan a Milk Bone to maul and kill you,* I thought.

"Just makin' sure you don't go hasslin' Mary-Ann, that's all."

"I wouldn't touch your damn sister," I said, "with a ten-foot barge pole." Then I stormed off to my bedroom, slapping the French doors hard behind me. "Hey," he called behind me. "Don't you talk about Mary-Ann that way." A minute later a candle flared up, and soon the living room was filled with faint yellow light. Frank was reading, if that was the word or the act, and wouldn't blow out his candle until my own went out.

Two nights later Mary-Ann was at the kitchen table, bent down over a tablet. She'd spent the day at Bloomingdale's, picking out a bathing suit, and now she was writing a letter to her friend Amy Stardust. Mister Softee music drifted in nightmarishly through the windows. "Amy told me I just had to go to Bloomin'dale's A-sap," Mary-Ann said. "She wanted me to take pictures of all the clothes and send 'em on home."

It was then that I heard a click in the living room. It came from Frank's direction, from underneath his jacket. My first thought was that Frank was not Texan at all but one of those Africans who make a *tuch* noise in their throats whenever they speak. Then Frank calmly brought out a small tape recorder from under his shirt and flipped over the cassette.

"What *is* that?" I said.

When Frank didn't answer, I repeated the question.

"What's thaahhtt . . ." Frank repeated in a high, languorous voice. "Hey, Mary-Ann, Hughie wants to know what thaahhtt is."

"Were you taping me?" I said.

Mary-Ann glanced up from her letter. "Frank, were you tapin' us?"

"Nobody'd believe the way this guy talks." Frank turned the machine back on. "Would you like to say something to the machine, Hughie? Maybe tell us something about your clahhsses at Hahrvahdd?" He turned to Mary-Ann. "Would you like to read Hughie some poetrayyy?"

"You taped me? The other night?"

"Oh, Hal," Frank said, "lemme show you my hands, they're so mahhvelous. My hands ah so mahhvelous to me. I wanna be your lovebird, dahhling . . ."

"Gimme that tape recorder." I snarled.

"Don't be such a jerk," he replied.

I held out my hend.

"What are you gonna do, Hughie? Fight me for it?"

He slipped the tape recorder underneath his shirt. "I got a excellent idea, why don't we tape the two of us, get a master tape of the two of us, mixin' it up right here? To bring home?"

"Frank, give 'im the *tape*."

"It's my tape, it ain't his tape."

"Bubba, give Hal the *tape*, 'kay?"

Frank stood up, tossed the tape recorder on the couch and put up his hands in a boxing position. "Come on, mister, you wanna fight me? You wanna fight me for the tape?"

Beck often wanted to box me, but usually while we were talking on the phone. "*Chicken*," he'd yelp when I'd declined, and presently I would hear him shuffling lightly around the kitchen floor, and the soft thumps his fist made as it grazed repeatedly against the receiver—"*gotcha, gotcha, gotcha*." After several minutes of this unequal match he'd say, "Had enough, Hal? Or you want a little more?"

"I warn you," Frank said, "you're messin' with the wrong guy here. . ."

"That seems to be your line," I said after a second had passed.

"What's that, Hughie?"

"You said that at the bus station too. It's boring and it's repetitive and I don't know how you can live with yourself. Saying the same things over and over again is an embarrassment."

Frank looked confused. "Come on," he said, raising his fists. "I gotta warn you 'bout somethin', though, I don't play by any Marcy Queenshead rules." He laughed loudly.

"Okay," I said. "Out of this apartment. Out."

"Don't be such a jerk," he repeated, but something deep in his voice weakened.

"Bubba, if you don't hand him that tape, I'll call Mom up and she'll crucify your *butt*."

"Yeah? What's Mom gonna do, Mary-Ann, sprout some wings and fly up here and take your side? Take botha your sides? So it's me against you three? Gee, I'm just tremblin' all over . . . I mean, don't confuse me with someone who gives a shit or anything—"

"If you don't give me that tape," I said coldly, "I will get a court order to evict you from this apartment. I will rain lawyers on you."

"Don't be such a jerk, Hughie," Frank said, now almost sleepily. He was fingering the insides of his jacket.

"You will be out on the streets," I continued, "alone and timid and stupid."

"Frank, give Hal the *tape*."

"You'll be sent packing to Riker's Island," I went on. "And I have to warn you of something, that the boys know you're coming. And the boys don't care for people from Texas all that much—not at all, in fact."

"Whatsa matter with people from Texas?" Mary-Ann interrupted. "Texas's only the best state in the whole country."

"And I wouldn't hop in the shower at Riker's Island if I were you," I said. "Those Riker's boys can get pretty nasty when they're soaped up and pissed off."

"Frank, if you don't give Hal that tape, I'll scream. I'll scream rape and fire and mur—"

"Oh, Mary-Ann, I wouldn't want you to scream, honey," Frank said in a high voice. "You might wreck that beautiful singin' voice." He picked up the tape recorder and stared at it for a minute. Then, whistling through his teeth, he pulled the lid open, took out the cassette and threw it across the room. He was aiming for the window, but he missed and the cassette clattered behind the radiator. "Hughie's gotta get me a new cassette, though," Frank announced. "That's a one-twenty-minute job, too. . ."

"I'll get you a new tape," I said, thinking of something along the lines of *Christy Lane: One Faith, Twelve Songs* or *The Best of Mister Softee*.

Thirty minutes later, when Frank was out buying beer, I turned on the television.

"Ooh, can we watch *Dynasty?*" Mary-Ann said. "What's tonight? Is this Tuesday? What night's *Dynasty* on? Now I can't even remember what night it is, and—"

"No," I said, flipping back and forth through the channels. "We're watching a swim meet."

"Swim meet? What in the world for? Don'tcha wanna watch *Dynasty?* "Crystal's—"

"My sister," I said, "she's racing."

Mary-Ann's eyes got wide. "She's on TV? Your sister is?"

"Right," I said.

"Well, so who is she?"

I cleared my throat. "She's a swimmer."

"Is she famous? I mean, is she like in the magazines and stuff?"

I didn't know. Maybe Fishie was famous. Then again, I was never sure whether her fame extended beyond her narrow sport into the general world as we know it.

"Would I've heard of her?" Mary-Ann looked like she was ready to climb up into my lap.

"I don't know," I said. "I don't know which people you've heard of."

"What's her name?"

"Lily," I said, wanting to give my sister full dignity.

"Lily Moore," Mary-Ann murmured. "Lily Moore. . ."

"Lily Andrews," I murmured back.

"She married to someone?"

"No. She . . . she just likes the name Andrews. She won two gold medals. In the Olympics. And one bronze. Which she doesn't like to discuss. She won't discuss it at all. You bring it up, she leaves the room. She calls it the Brown One. Have you ever seen the ads for Coke? My sister's the one who swims the entire length of the pool, and when she comes up for air, she's holding a Coke in one hand and she says, I just drank this Coke underwater and I feel just *great!* Then she glances at the timer and says, Hey, my best time ever!" I looked over at Mary-Ann tiredly. "As though this Coke had anything to do with her time. That ad makes no sense, no sense at all. The viewer thinks he's going crazy."

"I love Coke," Mary-Ann mumbled. "Coke's excellent."

I found the station, and on the screen the announcer, Ahmaad Jones, was interviewing the Dutch promoter.

"But she's kind of a liar," I went on. "My sister is. She hates Coke. She says it's too sweet."

"Well, I love Coke," Mary-Ann said weakly. "I mean, Coke's like my favorite drink. Cheery Cherry Diet Coke. Does your sister do commercials for cheery Cherry Diet Coke too?"

"No—look, there she is." Fishie strode up to the interviewer's table, wearing some kind of silken purple boxer's bathrobe. Her hair had grown in slightly, and a faint sheeting of light black dust now covered her scalp. *Not very attractive*, I thought.

"What happened to all her hair? She's not dyin', is she?"

"Marlene swims very well under pressure, of course," Fishie was saying, "and she always has. But that's one of the great differences between our two countries, isn't it? The Western swimmers have a certain freedom that the Eastern Bloc athletes don't . . . or perhaps aren't permitted, or encouraged, to have. It's not a job for those of us in the West, it's more a way of life."

I sat back on Bob's moldy couch, yawning at the new heights of boring-the-audience that my sister was reaching for.

"And Amsterdam," she blathered on, "is an extremely hospitable place— the people, the friendliness, the children. It's the children I believe I'll remember the best . . . their whimsical folk dances, the flowers in their hair, the way they chanted my name at the airport, the beautiful floral tribute they presented me at my hotel, their tiny clogs—"

"Oh, come on," I barked at the television. Fishie despises children and always has.

"Well, congratulations to you again," Ahmaad Jones said.

"She won," I said, practically to myself. "And I missed the whole goddamn thing." I glanced at Mary-Ann in irritation. If I hadn't been arguing with her insane brother, I wouldn't have missed the race.

"And we understand you have a new look here," Ahmaad said.

"What? Where?"

"Your hair. We understand you've cut your hair. . ."

I didn't know why this idiot had bothered to phrase it so delicately. There, standing in front of him, was Fishie, looking like a chihuahua. "Oh, right, that," my sister said. "Yes, obviously, Ahmaad. Well, I chopped it all off about a month ago—which reminds me . . ." Fishie faced the TV camera head-on. "Hal, if you're watching, *quit bitching* about Bob's apartment! You're lucky to be living there in the first place. For chrissakes, you're there rent-*free*, I mean, what's—"

"That's you, Hal!" Mary-Ann squealed. "She's talking to you!"

The station cut away to a commercial, and when they came back, Fishie was nowhere to be seen.

"Fishie's losing her mind," I said, feeling horribly depressed. "Way to go, Fishie."

"You said her name was Lily," Mary-Ann noted.

"It is. Fishie's a nickname. It's a family thing."

"What'd she win?"

"The *race*. She won the race."

"You didn't even tell me you had a famous sister swimmer?"

"It's slightly embarrassing," I said. "It's embarrassing when your sister makes not even the slightest attempt to conceal the fact that she doesn't use any of the products that she endorses so gaily."

"Oh, I don't believe that."

"What?"

"I don't believe your sister doesn't not drink Coca-Cola. Or whatever else it is you said she didn't do. I mean, she's on TV! You prob'ly must never seen her when she's drinkin' Coca-Cola, that's all."

This wasn't a winnable point. "Well, she just doesn't use any of those products. My sister—" I stopped myself. I was accidentally telling a complete stranger part of my life story, my family's life story.

"So this Fishie person won two gold medallions, huh? What'd she end up doin' with 'em?"

It was strange, hearing Mary-Ann refer to my sister as "this Fishie person." It sounded uncomfortable on her tongue, and I wasn't sure I liked it.

"*We* call her that," I said pointlessly. "And she threw the medals in a box."

"You mean, Fishie doesn't keep 'em around where everybody can see 'em?"

"No," I said, wishing again that Mary-Ann were less familiar in her address. "She never did. She just brought them home and threw 'em in a box. And she didn't even keep the Brown One. A couple of years ago she tried to melt down the gold, but no one—no gold jewelers, I mean— would do it for her. They said it was like burning the American flag, even though the gold part of a gold medal's only about ten percent—"

"Once I won somethin', Hal. A contest. When I was seven. Fifty bucks. I wrote an essay and sent it and I won. It was this Why I Love the USA contest. They printed it in the paper and—"

"What paper was that?" I said, already falling asleep and dreaming a tiresome but awful dream.

"The Patent *Sunrise*."

"Oh, really?" I said. "That's very *prestigious*."

Mary-Ann sat back, lit a cigarette and beamed.

"No, it is," I said, feeling quite bad. "It's good." I waved my hand. I heard Frank burst through the front door and slam it shut, and the rustle of beers in his bag. "And what else? What else did you ever win?"

She was still beaming. "That's it."

Animal Kingdom

T hat night the two of them fought. The fight, for what it was, took place during dinner, after Fishie's stirring victory. We were eating pizza in .... the living room, surrounded by candles. Mary-Ann and I were sprawled out on the floor and Frank was sitting on the couch, his fingers tucked under the waistband of his pants. The huge white pizza-box cover was raised like a nun's cornette. WORLD FAMOUS, the box blurted. BEST PIZZA IN TOWN. Since every other shop in the city claimed the same thing, I didn't really know whether or not to believe this particular pizza joint. It was impossible to believe any of them, when you came right down to it.

Around ten Frank belched and stretched. "Time to hit it, Sissy . . ."

"What?" Mary-Ann asked through a full mouth.

"Time for beddy-bye and dreams." Frank nodded at me, then turned back to his sister. "You can bring your pizza piece in with you."

"I don't wanna go to bed yet."

"Well, that's fine, then." Frank sat back down on the couch. "I'll just postpone my own personal bedtime till you're both good and ready."

He sat there with a dim smile on his thin lips. He loosened the collar on his shirt and flopped his head around in circles. I was beginning to get accustomed to Frank's wardrobe. He seemed to own only that one pair of tight, rancid jeans, over which each morning he threw on a different Western-type shirt, each one uglier than the next. Tonight Frank was wearing a watermelon-green shirt with a long, pointy collar, and fringe dripped off the elbows like seaweed on an anchor. He looked like someone had dredged him from the bottom of the ocean.

Mary-Ann threw her crust into the empty pizza box. "If you think him and me"—she made a stiff thumb in my direction—"are goin' off someplace to get all hot and heavy, you're flat wrong."

I stared at her, amazed.

"Mary-Ann," Frank said, "don't talk that way, it's ugly when you talk that—"

"I'll talk whichever way I want, Frank. I'm in New York, for God's sake, and you can just quit orderin' me *around*. I paid for your ticket here, it's my money, remember? He didn't have *any* money, I mean, zero, nothin'," Mary-Ann said to me. "He blows it all on this cheap Chatty Cathy number with a cantaloupe butt on her who goes 'round pretendin' she's pretty or sexy or whatever. And now that he's here in NYC, he doesn't want to do *anything*."

This much was true. Frank spent most of his days lazing around in the back room, wearing only his black underwear, drinking Irish coffee and forgetting to shave. Occasionally he left the apartment, and when he returned, it was merely to bring back bottles of liquor and packages of slender brown cigars. Mary-Ann, on the other hand, was gone most of the day. Most mornings she went off sight-seeing alone, and in the afternoons she repaired with her autograph book to her favorite hiding spot in the bushes of Central Park, where she waited patiently for exercising movie stars to run or bicycle past, bodyguards in tow. Rushing out into the park road, she'd ambush them, and then badger them for their signatures. "That's a pretty dangerous approach," I told her. "Bodyguards are wound up fairly tightly. They're just waiting for a little pest like you."

"Oh, those bodyguards know it's just me," Mary-Ann replied dreamily. "I wouldn't hurt a fly, they know that."

Now Mary-Ann glared at her brother. "I *paid* for you to be here, Frank. Which mean I got a whole lot less money to buy all the things *I* desire personally. How the hell'm I gonna ever make it as an actress or model if all I got's one stupid evenin' gown? I mean, I *work* for a livin', Frank, in case you hadn't noticed. Versus some other people I could mention but won't since my manners are too developed. I don't hang out all day playin' pool at Hooter's and writin' suck jokes in pen on the wall and throwin' up pitchers of beer in people's laps."

Quietly Frank said, "Mary-Ann, I told you I'd pay you back."

"Yeah, well, like when? What're you gonna do for it, Frank? Have a bake sale? Bake yourself and sell it? Section out these little squares and triangles and stick candles in 'em and then light 'em up? And by the bye, buddy, if I wanted to sleep my way to the top, Hal here would hardly be on my ladder. He would not be one of *my* rungs, Frank." Mary-Ann glanced over at me. "No offense, Hal, but you're not what I'd call like some show-business *legend*, you know, known to all the models and the stars. You're not like this big industry *heavy*."

"I'll go out right now," Frank said, "and get you your money, Sissy. If it's such a big damn deal."

"Yeah, what you gone do—marry some rich lady, then throw her out the window?"

Frank tore out of the room and Mary-Ann stared after him. I shut the pizza lid because it reminded me of church, and I hadn't been to church in years. Soon I heard the black police lock fall heavily to the floor, and the front door slamming.

"Pouter pigeon!" Mary-Ann screamed. "Pouter pigeon!"

Meaninglessly I said, "Why is it that you have to go to bed when your brother does?"

"Pouter pigeon! Pouter pigeon! Pouter pigeon!" she screamed.

"Why?" I said. "Why is that?"

Mary-Ann lit a cigarette and inhaled and exhaled deeply and quickly, then stubbed it out. " 'Cause he's weird. Frank's weird. My brother's *too* weird. I seen inside Frank's head and there's nothin' there but weirdness. I was born with a weirdo for a brother. You know why Frank hates me sometimes? 'Cause he's older than I am but I'm better. That *kills* him. And 'cause he'll always be two years and thirty-seven days older than me and still won't be as good, and that's forever and ever. He can't do a damn thing about it. And he doesn't want it as bad as I do, either. He's happy just livin' the life of this ruined person. Frank'll turn older and he'll be one of those people you feel sorry for."

"So where's he going?" I didn't really care all that much. Frank made me extremely uncomfortable, and my own Texas accent was getting way out of control; I'd forgotten what my normal Eastern vowels sounded like.

"Don't ask me, Cat. I don't know. But he'll get the money. Is that bad of me? My brother leaves and all I think about is me havin' some money to buy some new clothes."

"How do you know he'll get the money?"

"Because Bubba usually gets what it is he wants. He's like Lola that way." Mary-Ann leaned back on her gloved hands. "Hey, Hal, I'm sorry about that sleepin-my-way-to-the-top comment. I wouldn't do that, anyway. And you're kind of a babe. I mean, you're not as good-lookin' as I thought you'd be, but you're not like this collie-lookin' person or anythin', either." She giggled. " 'Cept you dress funny."

"What do you mean?"

"Things you wear, they're all these *baggy* things. You need to get somethin' tight on, you know? Show off your body some more. You got any jeans? I mean, you even own a pair of jeans?"

"Of course I do," I said, annoyed.

"Well, you should wear 'em night 'n' day." Mary-Ann lit another cigarette. "As I was sayin', if you were in a position to help me along in the modelin' world, we might just get ourselves together, but that wouldn't be 'cause you could advance my personal star in any way, or—"

"Ah, thanks," I said. "That means a lot to me."

"I haven't had many people in my love life, anyhow. Eldridge, Eldridge and Tommy. The Eldridges are two different people. And Duane. So that's four. And who else? Oh, hold on to your seat 'cause I fooled around once with a girl, but we were both pretty messed up. And the Duane thing doesn't really count. I drank too much that night too. I don't even remember the half of it. I call him up at work the next day, he does roofs for people, I go, Hey, Duane, what exactly did we get up to? And he just hangs up, says he can't talk. So I figure I musta done somethin' either great or else it was plain awful for everybody." Mary-Ann looked confused. "No one's ever told what I did . . . I guess it's one of those little mysteries of life. But it's good for a person to have mysteries, right?"

As I watched, she started scribbling something on a napkin.

"What are you doing?"

"Makin' a list. A list of all the people I've slept with. It'll drive me nuts if I don't remember who's who, you know? Who'd I say—Eldridge, Eldridge, Tommy, Duane . . . oh! I know! *Jessie.* Jessie's number five." She beamed at me. "I like makin' who-you've-slept-with lists. That's what I doodle like when I'm talking on the phone. Once Mom came in and I was makin' one out and she goes, Honey, what's that? and I go, Mom! It's for this party I'm givin'! And then I had to throw this dumb party so Mom wouldn't get all suspicious, but I didn't invite the list. I don't like bein' in a room where I've slept with more than one guy. I get paranoid they're comparin' notes—about my body, or what I *do*, or somethin'. Anyhow . . ." She bent her head over the napkin, in which the names were stacked on top of the other, like kindling. "So who do we got? Eldridge, Eldridge, Tommy, Duane, but Duane only counts for a half. Jessie, like I said. Wait, I know. I know who six is. This Italian guy. Gianni or somethin'."

"Gianni?"

"Some Italian guy, kinda good-lookin'. His whole body turned red when I touched it. It was like I had this power to turn boys into lobsters this one night. I touched him on his chest, it went lobster. I touched his neck, it goes the same way. The color, I mean. I had the lobster touch that night. Then I turned him over on his stomach and he was all lobster there too. I mean, his back was like this Q.T. tannin' lotion orange-pink color like he'd been boilin' for about two days. He was a total lobster boy." Mary-Ann grinned. "Any-ways, Gianni makes six. That's so far. And I'm only twenty-five, twenty-six practically. So I guess that's like the national average, isn't it?"

"May I see?" I said.

"Nope." Mary-Ann crumpled up the napkin and tore it into small bits. "You can't. 'Cause I rank 'em all too. Based on eagerness and niceness."

"What did Eldridge get?" I said.

"Which Eldridge?"

"The one you're going out with now."

"*Was* goin' out with. We're not goin' out anymore. That dead person threw a beer in my face last week, then stomped off someplace. My hair felt like wet rope afterward—"

"Why'd he throw beer at you?"

"'Cause." Mary-Ann's voice got slightly prim. "'Cause I told him I was comin' up here to be with another guy."

"Well," I said, "it's not as though we're goin' out." *Going out*, I said to myself sternly. *Going, with a G at the end*. It's not as though we're *going* out.

"I know," Mary-Ann said. "Yeah, I know that." She lit another cigarette and stared at me. "But you see how it could look to dirty-minded folks. I wonder," she said after a minute, "whether that *is* like, the national average. Six guys. Or five and a half. Or whether I'm not sleeping with enough people. Amy's up to fourteen and she says she feels *real bad.*"

"So what did you give Eldridge?"

"Oh, he got an A minus slash B plus."

"I thought you hated him."

"You bet I do. But he's got a few things goin' for him. Well, one thing. Whatever, right? Just kiddin'. Mary-Ann, you're gettin' so *crude.*"

She stood up and walked toward the window. She leaned over to look at the candle on the bookshelf and, only inches away from the flame, her face looked strange and elongated. It was all shadows and hollows, like a face you see in a rock you've been staring at for a long time. "So how's your own personal love life, Hal?" she said casually.

"It's amazing." I hardly felt like going into it with Mary-Ann.

"I thought you said you were goin' out with somebody. On the phone you said that."

"Well, I was."

"You mean, you're not anymore?"

"No."

"I woulda killed her, anyway." Mary-Ann brandished her cigarette like a piece of chalk. "Ever smelled a burnin' iris, honey? No, just kiddin'." She tapped her ash onto an uneaten slice of pizza. "I mean, this place hasn't exactly been overrun with girls since I been here."

* * *

Frank didn't come back to Bob's apartment the next day, or the day after. He seemed to have vanished into the streets of lower Manhattan, which did not upset me in the least. When he hadn't come back after a week and a half, Mary-Ann moved out of the back room and onto the living-room couch. The back room got too cold at night, she said, and the loud snorting noises she claimed she heard behind the walls at four in the morning frightened her.

She didn't, however, seem all that concerned about Frank. "He's so provincial, he's prob'ly gone back to Texas. He didn't stand a chance of makin' it here."

"What," I asked, "was he planning on doing here, anyway?"

"Oh, he wanted to be a model, just like me."

"He did?" I couldn't imagine this specimen modeling anything, unless it was bowie knives or some company's new *Menace* line. "He doesn't really seem the type."

"Sure. Bubba'd never admit it, though. I was the one who went to modelin' camp while he stayed around goin' to bars. Plus, he's only in it for the money, plus he thinks he'll meet a lot of girls that way, you know, his fellow models. I mean, Bubba doesn't really have the modelin' desire that's *pure*, you know?"

By this time Mary-Ann had been there for almost two weeks, and I didn't really have the heart to ask her to leave. When, on numerous occasions, I'd tried to bring up the subject, Mary-Ann always grew quiet, and sometimes her eyes would moisten. "I don't have much money left, Hal," she invariably would say, lighting a cigarette as she did whenever eviction loomed. "I think I'd be kinda scared movin' out into a place of my own, some kinda Barbizon joint, you know, plus I really like it here with you, Hal. I mean, you're a real good host and everything, and you got so much hot water here, it'd be a waste . . ." I noticed that always after these too-light discussions she'd busy herself around the apartment—cooking, walking the depressing dog, sewing buttons back onto my shirts, vacuuming the filthy rugs. She was gone quite often, too, either lying in wait in the park or else, of late, standing patiently in front of the Russian Tea Room, hoping to pry autographs from celebrity diners. Some nights she would come home and flip open her autograph book. "I got Kirk Douglas today," she'd report happily, or "Look, I got Dustin Hoffman's agent's sister!"

"His agent's sister?"

"Dustin didn't want to sign. He kind looked as though he felt sorry for me or somethin'." Mary-Ann shrugged. "I don't care. Guess he's shy or somethin'. Or else he thinks he doesn't need the fans. I was set to bawl him out, but I didn't, too intimidated to, I guess. Anyhow, his agent was there, and so was this agent's sister, who I suppose came along 'cause she wanted to meet Dustin too. I mean, who wouldn't want to meet ol' Dusty, right? So she signed his name and her name both."

Mary-Ann showed me the autographs, an illegible name and, below that,

Dustin Hoffman's forged signature. "My, that's certainly one to treasure," I said in my most touched, dignified voice.

One Thursday afternoon in late August, I was standing at the stove cooking when Mary-Ann came into the room. She had her arms crossed even though she was wearing a sweater. "This apartment's freezin', Hal. Brr."

She came closer. "What's that horrible smell?"

"I'm making you dinner," I said, stirring the rabbit-skin pellets.

"Smells like dead animals to me."

"It is." I explained to her that you mixed up dried rabbit-skin pellets with water and heated them until the pellets dissolved. "It makes a jelly. You freeze it and then you slap it on your canvas as a kind of backing."

"You're really gettin' into this art stuff, aren't you?"

"Well, yes," I said. Mary-Ann was still under the impression that I was merely a former bowler/intern.

"It smells gross. Maybe that's what attractin' all the birds."

"Birds?" I said. I followed her into the living room, where five blue pigeons sat blinking and burbling on the windowsill, the hazy lights of the courtyard glowing behind them. The window was closed except for one inch, a crack into which the pigeons had managed to wedge their claws. I rapped at the window, but they held their ground and beadily eyed the living room, which in the late-afternoon light looked elderly and diminished.

"Maybe I could sleep somewhere else tonight, Hal. Wherever," Mary-Ann added, glancing over at me. "I just don't want those birds starin' me up and down all night. Wherever," she said again.

"You could pull the shade—"

"Yeah, but I'd still know they were Peepin' Tommin' in on me. I don't want any weird old birds seein' me naked."

"Well, you sleep wherever you want to sleep," I said, and went back into the kitchen to sauté my pellets.

She followed right behind. "You mean that? Anyplace I want?"

"Within reason," I said. Reason meant: *Not with me.* I was still at a point where I felt that even paying attention to another girl would amount to disloyalty toward Veebka. I knew how ludicrous this was, and it didn't even make much sense—I hadn't heard a peep from Veebka since she had come to collect her clothes. As far as I knew, she was still up in Maine with Mark, and at any rate, it was doubtful Veebka was counting off the seconds until she could see me again.

"Did any agencies or anything call for me today?"

The phone hadn't rung all morning. "Maybe today's an agency holiday," I suggested.

"Yeah, people're takin' a holiday from me's more like it. I called the Face of the Decade guy yesterday a coupla times, but his bitchy secretary wouldn't put me through. She said the guy's in a meetin' all day, or'd wandered off from his desk, or he had somebody in there with him, et cetera. I think I shoulda heard by now, don't you? Whether the guy liked my pictures and all? I thought this would happen faster, you know?"

"What?"

"Me makin' it. Me gettin' to be famous. Gettin' a bunch of jobs. I was readin' *Vogue* the other day, and they showed this model hangin' out in Africa with all these animals behind her. She was doin' a shoot. *I* was prettier than she was, Hal, 'least in my opinion. I don't see why that girl gets to go to Africa and I don't. I think the prettiest person should get to go. That's like a rule: The prettiest person should always get to go. Maybe I got to hang out on the streets a little more, where they'd spot me. You think that'd ever happen?"

I didn't know what to say. *I doubt it*, was the only answer, but I couldn't give it. I poured my rabbit-pellet mixture into an old black-and-yellow coffee can.

I said, "You can't expect to be plucked out of nowhere and jetted to Africa. Nobody even looks at anybody else here. Do you know how hard it is just to get someone to look at you cross-eyed in New York?"

"Nope, I surely don't."

"Well . . . it's very hard," I said, turning back to my pan.

"You know of any luncheonettes where people who hire people like me go? People who matter? I'd prob'ly just get fat there, though, waitin' around and eatin' carbos. Oh, I wanted to ask you: Do you think my voice is all wrong? Does my voice sound funny to you? My speakin' voice, I mean? Maybe I should take pronouncin' lessons—"

That night Mary-Ann came in when I was getting ready for bed. She was holding out a package. "Here, Hal, here's a present for you. I've had it for a coupla days, but I was just waitin' for the right time to give it over . . ."

At that moment the phone rang and I ran into the kitchen to answer it.

"Hal," I heard. "Greetings . . ."

It was my brother. Now what? I thought uneasily.

He immediately started in. "Hal, do you remember how we once went to Washington when we were kids? We saw all the monuments. It was so hot, we stood in lines a lot, for that one day our collective childhood experience was *one of lines*, and our aunt, she kept saying, Isn't that impressive, Beck, isn't that impressive? and I kept saying, Why, yes, it certainly is, that one, too, you're absolutely right. And then I fainted, I fell down right in that heat?"

I had a vague recollection. "Yeah," I said.

"Where was that place? Where I fainted?"

"I can't really recall," I said. "That was a long time—"

"Hal," my brother shrieked, "you've *got* to remember!"

"Why?" I said. "Are you and Lisa going to Washington? Is Lisa planning to march against the homeless?"

"I'm here right now. In Washington. I had to leave Greenwich, you see, I got *scared*, Hal. About the baby coming."

"What's so frightening about that?" I said. "Besides, the baby's not even due for another six months."

"I know, I know. But Lisa wants me to *be* there. For the actual *birth*. To watch, to help, to assist . . . to take all these night classes with her and the other parents . . . so that the baby can be born in our house and not in a hospital. And in the classes they show these *films*." My brother moaned. "These terrible films of babies being *born*. I saw one the other night—*The Miracle of It All*—and at the end everybody else in the class stood up and burst into . . . spontaneous applause, and I had to raise my hand and excuse myself. I was in the bathroom for an *hour*, Hal. What's the matter with everybody? Why can't they show *good* films? What about *Old Yeller, Mary Poppins?* Or even *Lady and the Tramp?* What's the matter with the old days when films were clean and wholesome? None of this sex and violence and gore? Oh, Hal, it sickens me. Whatever happened to the days when the husband was paged from the racquetball court and then someone stuck a big cigar in his mouth and said, It's a boy! or, It's a girl!"

Or, I thought, in your case and Lisa's, *It's a jackal!* "Don't be so immature about this," I said. "All husbands help out nowadays. It's something most men *want* to do."

"But that's in these modern times!" my brother cried. "What about yesterday? *Ou sont les neiges d'antan?*"

"They melted, ha ha," I said, trying to keep the conversation from becoming too serious or Lisa-like in its language of choice.

"Oh, that's true, isn't it? This film, Hal, it was like this woman, she was at *war*. She wasn't an actress, either, she was an actual woman. And she was the star too. Whatever happened to the *old* stars? The old star system? More stars than there were in the sky? What about Garbo, Dietrich, Gable—"

"Beck," I said, "go home. Go back to Lisa and go back to your Lamaze classes or whatever they are. If Lisa's going off to war, she needs your support. Face it like a man, not a moth."

"But the shoe, Hal," my brother said quietly, grimly.

"What shoe?"

"The shoe. The role that the shoe plays in marriage—"

It seemed that several weeks earlier Beck had gotten up at dawn one morning in Greenwich. While he was collecting the morning paper he'd noticed an old pink slipper, discarded in the dew of his front lawn. The pink slipper had put my brother in mind of the many lost-shoe situations in marriage ("Honey, have you seen my shoe?" "Check under the bed, honey."

"I see it, honey, but can't reach it; could I borrow your long arm?"), and this had had a profound effect on him.

"I have much better things to do than search for Lisa's pumps," Beck said now, sounding almost huffy. "Is marriage . . . is marriage supposed to be this banal?"

"Look," I said, "you leave Washington this minute. I don't think Washington's having all that good of an effect on you. You go back to Lisa and I'll go back to what I was doing when you called. And if you want to go to the dump with me sometime, we'll do it. You just let me know when."

My brother was silent for a minute. "Wanna box?" he finally murmured.

"If it would make you feel better," I said politely.

We phone-boxed for a minute; rather, Beck put on his gloves and I stood there in the kitchen, three hundred miles away from him, listening to the blows rain lightly into the receiver, dumbly taking it like a man. "How about that last combination, boy?" he said presently, out of breath.

"You're just too tough," I said. "I give up, Champ." I hung up and went back into the bedroom.

Mary-Ann was standing where I'd left her, still holding her package. "I didn't think you were comin' back," she said softly. "Who was that, some girl? You fallin' in love with someone? Here, I got this present for you and everything—"

"I'm sorry, that was my brother . . ." I took the package from her. "You shouldn't have," I added mindlessly, realizing I should probably wait to see what I was getting before saying anything. I opened the package and pulled out a pair of jeans.

"They're real Rider Jeans, Hal. Straight-leg stingers. They're kinda made originally for people who wear boots, but you can get away with wearin' 'em with just about anythin'."

I held them up against my legs. "They might be a little small . . ."

"Uh-uh. No-way no-how no-good dogs. Small only versus what you're used to wearin', Hal. What you think of as small for you is totally normal for everybody else. Go on, try 'em on. Go ahead."

"This minute?"

"Yup. I wanna see if they fit. Come on, I've seen boys in their underwear before."

I sat down on the bed and slid my pants down and started pulling on the blue jeans. I got them halfway up my thighs, then my arms gave out. "I can't do it."

"Sure you can. Just pull. Pull up."

I pulled. I got the pants halfway up my hips. The snap didn't come close to touching the hole for it.

"You gotta breathe in, Hal. Breathe in deep. Then, with your elbows close up to your sides against your ribs, you tighten your butt, make firm your pelvis as you move in, then across. In, then across. So it's A, breathe in deeply; B, tighten your butt; C, make firm your pelvis; D, elbows up, in, then across. Now we'll do it on a count of five."

Mary-Ann counted off, and at one I did what she said, jerking the button under the slit and up and in.

"There," she said. "Perfect fit. Now turn around."

I sat down, and even when I was sitting, I felt like I was standing at attention. The waist dug into my skin.

"Woo woo!" Mary-Ann clapped, as though I'd just done eight somersaults in a row.

"I can't tolerate this," I moaned. "They *hurt*."

"It hurts so good, you mean, Hal. Those pants'll warm you up if nothing does. Keep 'em on for a while, you'll get hot before you know it. Speakin' of hot, you don't have a sweatshirt or somethin' I could put on?"

I pointed her toward the closet. A moment later she pulled down a green sweater that Veebka had made me for my birthday a year ago. Since it was homemade, there was no label. I could never tell which side was the front and which was the back. One day I had noticed two inches of loose yarn on one side of the neck, and from then on the side with the loose yarn was the official back of the sweater.

I didn't want Mary-Ann wearing anything that Veebka had given me. For some reason it seemed faithless. "Not that one," I said.

"It's pretty." she held one of the sleeves up to her cheek. "Did someone you like make this for you?"

I nodded, ashamed.

"Who?"

"No one," I said quickly. "It sprang to life fully knitted."

"Some girl?"

"Nope."

"Can't I wear it, *please?*"

I knew I was being too fastidious, but this recognition merely made me press the point. "No," I said. "It may look warm, but it's actually quite an icy sweater. And there are insects in it. Lice. Little coughing birds. And it leaks too. The wind goes right through it and freezes your bones." I held out my hand. "Here, I'll wear it."

Two days later, something sickening happened.

I hadn't seen much of Bob's dog since moving into the apartment, and this arrangement seemed to suit both of us. I walked her, of course, rapidly, once in the morning and again at night—skipping the mid-afternoon session—and

I also laid her food out several times a day, but otherwise I seldom actually saw her. I never, for example, actually watched BB in the act of eating. A few hours after filling her bowl I'd look down under the card table and it had been emptied until it glistened like the top of Fishie's head.

One Sunday in early September I dragged BB out to the park by the river for her first walk of the day, with Mary-Ann trailing behind me. It was a hot, still morning and the park was practically empty. Elderly men and women were stationing themselves under arches and on benches, lips murmuring mutely, newspapers spread under their bottoms or open across their laps. The rusty swing sets were damp and strangely cold from the rain early that morning. Unused, they looked like primitive ruins, gleaming, untranslatable. When I looked down a second later, BB was lying on her side.

"Let's go," I said. "Let's move it."

I told Mary-Ann to give the mutt a prod, but she only stared down at her. "Hal, I think maybe she's fallen asleep on you."

"She's been sleeping all night," I said, tugging at the leash.

"Maybe she's pooped—"

"From what—sleeping? Sleeping doesn't wear a dog out that much. Come on," I commanded again, and pulled at the red leash. BB didn't move. Her face and nose were pressed against the pavement.

"She looks about like she's dead."

"Oh, sure," I said, "instead of being the normal depressed zombie dog she usually is."

"No, really."

I turned around. "She's not dead—"

"No, Hal, I'm *not kiddin'*. Her stomach's not even movin'."

I knelt down and touched my hand to her furry heart. Neither hand nor heart moved. Then I pressed my finger against her throat, not knowing whether dogs had pulses in their necks or not. I cupped her head with both hands and saw a spray of beady pebbles clinging to her thick purple lips. There was no expression in her dark yellow eyes. *What was I expecting, tiny Xs?*

I stood up. "I've killed her. I've walked her to death."

I stared down in horror at my hands. I was a murderer, there was no way around it. As far as household animals were concerned, I had a black thumb. I let the leash fall through my fingers and staggered over to one of the benches. My first thought was, What will Bob the Bowler say?

"It's not your fault, Hal." Mary-Ann was down on the ground now, stroking BB's head. "She was like twenty years old or somethin'."

"I killed her," I moaned. "First I killed Kitty—"

"You didn't kill your cat, Hal. She killed herself. You told me, she fell out the window before there's anything anybody could do about it."

The minute we got back to the apartment I called up my sister in Paris, where she was swimming her third and final challenge match with Marlene Bauke. I'd carried BB's corpse all the way home.

Lamar answered the phone after sixteen rings. "I killed the dog!" I howled.

"What? Who is this?"

"Bob's dog!" I shouted. "Dead! And my fault!"

I pleaded with Lamar to put my sister on the phone, but he explained that Fishie was on a tour of Parisian cemeteries, making rubbings of the gravestones of great French thinkers and essayists. "I'll have her call you the second she gets back," Lamar said tiredly. *Great*, I thought, hanging up, *now I can look forward to another lecture on national TV with half the world listening in.*

That night, after Fishie's victory, a French interviewer approached her by the side of the pool. "For our French viewers—"

My sister went into her usual postrace stupor. "It was a wonderful event," she droned. "Marlene looked pretty unbeatable out there, but this was my day, I suppose, and I'm grateful for the opportunity . . . to have triumphed over such a first-rate competitor, in a country so rich in tradition and excellence as France. Everybody here has been so generous: the promoters, the fans who came to watch, but mostly the children. Their small, oval faces, their . . ." Fishie paused to smile at the interviewer. "Would you mind if I said hello to someone back in the States?"

"Of course not."

"Hal!" Fishie yelled to twenty-eight countries, "I cannot believe you killed that old animal! How could you? I left you *instructions*, Hal. On the fridge, remember? Did you even bother to look at—"

The station cut to a commercial, but by then I was already up out of my chair, yanking at the wall cord. I just can't stand being yelled at.

When I went to take a shower the next morning, I found Mary-Ann kneeling down in front of the bathtub, rubbing the drain with a gray tangle of steel wool. She was dressed in a T-shirt that read, CLASS OF 1980, LUCIAN BEEBE HIGH SCHOOL, LAKE HELENE, TEXAS. Underneath, there were about two hundred names spelled out in black, in alphabetical order, from Anita Acton to Greg Wyszinski, Jr. Mary-Ann Beavers was circled in faded red Magic Marker.

"I'm settin' your life back together, Hal. You've let your life slide into kind of an obvious disorder here."

I stood in the doorway of the bathroom with only a blue towel wrapped around my waist; I felt like a frazzled health-spa attendant. A dewy can of Diet Cherry Coke sat on the toilet seat, Mary-Ann's beverage of choice from the time she got up in the morning. Coffee, she said, was too hot. "It's okay," I said. "You don't have to do that."

"I *know* I don't have to. But it's what your life's cryin' out for." Plastic baggies covered her hands, and as she scrubbed, she kept her fingers extended so she wouldn't snap off any of her nails. I realized that I'd never seen anyone who was as careful with her hands.

After a while she stopped scrubbing and turned on both tub faucets. Brown water moved the bubbles, and the fragments of bright white-blue Comet circled toward the drain. "It's my *opinion*," Mary-Ann said stiffly, "that you need some good orderly direction in your life. And you know what that stands for, don't you?"

"Stands for?" I'm not all that sharp in the morning.

"Good orderly direction. G-O-D. I know you M.D. people don't believe in that 'cause *you* think you *are* God. You putter around the hospital in your little golf carts thinkin' just 'cause you're all dressed all in white you must be . . ."

I stood uncertainly in the doorway. Then I said, "I'm not a doctor."

"What are you sayin'?"

"I'm not a doctor," I said. "Or a bowler. I never was. And my name was never Bob. It was always Hal. I just said that on the phone because I didn't think it mattered what I said. I was just diverting myself. I didn't think I'd meet you ever."

"Oh, I knew that." Mary-Ann started scrubbing a turtle-shaped stain. "I'm not *that* stupid, I was just playin' along with you too . . ."

"Well, how'd you know that?"

The steel wool moved deftly back and forth over the turtle. "I just did. One thing, you never go to any hospitals. And you don't have any diplomas hangin' around here, either. Or prescription pads. The second night we were here, Frank turned this place upside down lookin' for a pad. He wanted to fake your name and get some Demerol somewhere. Oh, and you never once been bowlin' since we been here. And when I asked you who one of the bowlers was hangin' on your bedroom wall, you said it was Mike some-Italian-name when it's actually Earl Anthony. I reckoned a real bowler woulda known who Earl Anthony was. And, Frank, well, I shouldn't tell you this, you'll get mad—"

"What?"

"Well, when Frank was goin' through your closets that night lookin' for pads, he said none of the clothes hangin' there were doctorlike. He couldn't find white anythin', no coats or shirts or anythin'. So then he told me you were full of it. And I go, What diff 'rence does it make, he's lettin' us stay here, anyway, ain't he? It doesn't really matter to me all that much. Oh, and then I looked in your wallet and saw your real—"

"You looked in my wallet?"

"Don't get mad. I wanted a picture to remember you by, Hal. Supposin' I get hit by a truck tomorrow? And your last name's Andrews, by the way, prob'ly always has been."

"Yes," I said. "I know it's Andrews. I'm sorry." My embarrassment overcame my outrage that Bubba had picked through my closet and Sissy had gone sniffing through my wallet. "I don't know why I made all that up."

Mary-Ann bit her lip. "And . . . and there's one other thing. Don't get mad at me, Hal, just hear me out." She hesitated. "Just that Frank, the same night he was goin' through your closet, he found all this women's clothing. Like, in your size too. Giant pumps and all." Mary-Ann stared at me imploringly. "Hal, if there's a woman in your man's body who's strugglin' to get out, *free her.* Don't suffer it in silence anymore or you'll go *nuts.* 'Cept I hafta admit it'd be kinda weird talkin' to you woman-to-woman all of a sudden, I mean, what if we liked the same guy? *That* might get a little—"

"Don't worry," I said, "those are only my—" *What were they?* "Those are my genius clothes," and I proceeded to explain the events of the last month. When I finished, Mary-Ann said, "Oh, honey. Honey, that's terrible. *I* think you're a genius, Hal. No, *really* I do. I mean, you prob'ly don't think my opinion counts for that much but"—she paused—"no, I *do* think you're a genius. You're a real Einstein. And you're younger than he is, too, so you got a real head start."

"Well, Einstein is dead," I said. "But thank you, anyway. And as I said, I'm sorry I made all that stuff up about being a doctor."

"Prob'ly you did 'cause doctors know how to take care of 'emselves and you don't. You're like this born patient, Hal, you need round-the-clock constant care. Anyway, I was sayin', long as you got good orderly direction in your life, you'll be fine, if you ask me."

"Any word today from your psychotic brother?" I don't even know why I was asking, especially after what she'd just told me.

"Nope." Mary-Ann blew at a meringue of bubbles that fluttered before disintegrating into the drain. "Which means there's an extra ticket for you to go on that boat today. That Circle-the-Line deal."

"No thanks," I said, too vulnerable after BB's demise to feel up to going out, especially amidst hordes of Spanish-speaking natives and other truly spectacular tourists.

"Well, I don't much like things goin' to waste like that. Tickets and all the rest. You know, you had all this stuff in your fridge goin' bad, and on all your shelves too. I was cleanin' up in there this mornin'. So I whipped you up somethin' out of all the stuff you only had a little bit left of. Hush puppies. Y'ever had hush puppies?"

I shook my head.

"Well, they're these little balls of flour 'n' grease. Kind of like a corn bread. Like this quasi corn-bread stuff. They're Southern. They got their name 'cause some cook with a lot of puppies in his kitchen was playin' around with some grease this one time. And these puppies, they'd just been born, they were still kinda pink, and they were screamin' and yappin' while this cook was fryin', and the cook, he got so disgusted he threw some fried grease balls onto the floor and said, Hush, puppies, hush now, goddamn your hides. In this soothin' voice. And these dogs hushed right up, 'cause they couldn't eat and squeal at the same time. Long as the cook kept pitchin' grease balls at 'em, they stayed still. At least that's the version I know."

"They sound delicious," I lied.

"Anyhow, I cooked you up a couple a trayfuls. Not to make you shut up—I don't think you say half enough in the first place—but just 'cause they're good. They're coolin' on top of the fridge now. You woulda thrown away that grease in the coffee can, but I did somethin' constructive with it. *Before* you had a chance to throw it away. My mom, she says, It's a lot easier to be *de*structive, Mary-Ann, than it is to do somethin' *con*structive."

She turned on the hot water faucet. "You're pretty American, you know, Hal, in that respect. Wasteful, I mean. You waste a ton of things. You prob'ly order up huge amounts of food at restaurants and then you don't eat it an' you end up throwin' half of it away and then—"

"That was my rabbit-pellet mixture," I mumbled.

"What's that, mumble-puss?"

"My rabbit-pellet mixture. In the coffee can." I cleared my throat. "You use it as a painting surface."

"Well, you weren't *usin'* it, Hal, it was just sittin' up there, *anyhow.*"

"And what do you mean, I'm American?" I said loudly. "I'm American and you're not? You sum up everything sad I've ever *heard* about this country."

Mary-Ann turned off the hot water. "Well, Hal, that's your opinion. You know, diff'rent strokes 'n' all. My mom says there's somethin' extremely European about certain aspects of me. The way I think, for example. The way I form my thoughts. She says the roads of my mind make her think of some picture she saw once of them little cobbled streets over in France. Some town that got bombed. Somethin' Italian or French, German maybe. Prob'ly got that from my father's side—"

"Texas is a very European place," I said sarcastically. "Houston, with all those old churches and basilicas, the *châteaux* of El Paso, the Dallas vine-yards. And that huge clock in Fort Worth, Big Benji—"

"Don't make fun. I don't like it when people make fun of Texas. My dad, see, he was some kind of European personality. Prob'ly an antiques dealer someplace."

"I don't think you mean that exactly," I said.

"What do you mean?"

"Well, was he?"

"I don't know. I mean, I'm here, right? On earth, right? I made it here, didn't I?"

"You certainly did." I was starting to feel foolish having a conversation in a towel.

"Mom says, The thing is, you get into the movie, not who pays for your ticket, and the same goes for bein' born. Mom says she doesn't even know. She thinks she knows who the guy was, just from a feelin' she has, but she won't tell me. It coulda been one of several guys, actually. Coulda been the candlemaker. Coulda been Elvis Presley. Old Elvis sure got around."

Mary-Ann stood up and stared down at the bathtub. The drain was clogged and the dirty bubbles were just sitting there. "Elvis once gave Mom one of his scarves. Mom was at this concert of his in Greensboro, North Carolina, she and a coupla girlfriends of hers. Did you know Elvis had a man whose only purpose on earth it was to hand Elvis his scarves? It was like, Here, Elvis, have a scarf. What? You want another scarf, Elvis? Sure thing, Big E, here's another. Anyhow, that particular night this scarf man had run out for some reason. He hadn't thought ahead. Mom was sittin' in the front row and she thought Elvis looked kinda warm, so she handed him up her red scarf. And Elvis wiped his forehead and his mouth with it, then he handed it back down to her. Mom said she nearly vomited. I mean, she nearly lost it right there. See, what she meant was for Elvis to *keep* the scarf, but instead he ended up ruinin' it with all the glop he had pourin' out of his forehead. Mom gave the thing away, she didn't even want to touch it. I mean, she liked Elvis plenty, just not in that . . . body-fluid way, you know? I mean, there was hundreds of crazy women wrestlin' her for it, and Mom had to give the scarf away to the strongest lady. Then about fifteen minutes later there was this giant blackout. The whole auditorium blacked out for twenty minutes. Elvis got all pissed off, you know, over that blackout, he was kind of a control freak—"

"So what does that have to do with anything?"

"So my point is they coulda done it then. Mom and Elvis. In the dark. Mom coulda overcome her disgust. Elvis coulda gotten over bein' mad that his show was wrecked. And so maybe I'm the glorious result!" Mary-Ann threw up her arms triumphantly. "Hey, maybe I can sue Elvis's estate for some money! Maybe Mom can write some love poems and pretend old Elvis wrote 'em for—"

"Maybe . . ." I went into the kitchen. The stove and the kitchen floor were immaculate. All the windows were cruelly clean, even the outsides. The hush puppies were sitting on a cookie sheet on top of the refrigerator, rows of stiff brown nuggets, each in an individual puddle of rabbit-pellet grease. I sniffed the disgusting smell, not unlike blood.

Mary-Ann brushed past me and reached into the fridge for a large black bottle. "See, I even got us champagne. To celebrate your new good orderly direction. I got the cheapie stuff 'cause I ran outa money."

She started untwisting the muzzle, then she gave up and handed the bottle to me. "I can't do this with gloves on, plus I don't wanna break a nail. You like champagne, don't you?"

She saw me glance at my watch. "My mom's boyfriend, Lorne, he says, It's always cocktail hour someplace in the world. Everytime's Schlitz time, so long's you know what it is you're doin'. All you gotta do is pretend you're in like Borneo or Greece or someplace like that where it's later on in the day and they're already gettin' crocked . . ."

Drinking champagne at eleven in the morning is a decision that cancels out all others, at least for the next, say, ten hours. After the first swig all my plans for the day lay in tatters. From then on I knew there were certain things that, if asked, I wouldn't be able to perform. What, for example, would happen if someone requested me to deliver a speech in front of an assembly of sheet-metal manufacturers? He's drunk, people would murmur after a few minutes of my incoherent rambling, something is horribly wrong with our speaker. The champagne hit my empty stomach and softened, and soon the daylight grew disorienting and harsh.

"I wanna take a tour 'round New York," Mary-Ann said after we'd drunk most of the bottle. "All the places *you* like to go to, Hal. I want to see, like, Hal's New York."

"No, you really don't want to do that," I said.

"Oh yes I do. You can tell lots about a person that way. Besides, I don't wanna sit around here all day, it's too pretty out. I don't wanna wait around for that agency guy to call me. How 'bout you and me go visit some celebs? I think that'd be, like, *excellent*. There's like this celebrity smell in the air today, like this odor in my nose I smell—"

"That's baked rabbit pellets," I slurred.

Mary-Ann shook her head. "Nope. It ain't that, it's somethin' else. I smelled whatever it was right when I got up this mornin'. I opened up the window and it came straight in, straight to my lungs. Betcha if we went downstairs I'd see a celeb right now. Like just standin' there at the magazine stand. Leanin' against a lamppost. Someone good, too, not just some stupid extra in a crowd scene or somethin'. Buyin' gum so whoever it is can keep up star breath and so on . . ."

By the time we left the apartment, just before noon, I was very drunk, and so was Mary-Ann. She brought along her camera, as well as another bottle of cheap champagne, which she kept concealed under her coat, and held on to my arm as we stumbled forward.

Mary-Ann was sniffing the air. "Celebrity . . . I smell celebrity, Hal. I smell rock stars. I smell all the soap-opera people. I smell people who're in the news. People who *make* the news . . ."

She nattered on in this vein as we drunkenly made our way north. Mary-Ann insisted on walking only on sidewalks that lay in direct sunlight. This, she explained, was because she was from the South. I didn't mind walking on sunny sidewalks, except that the sun at that time of day shone exclusively on certain blocks and not at all on others; just about every other block was under shadow. Walking ten blocks took us about an hour. She was extremely difficult to keep up with, too—it was like tracking Squanto the Indian.

At Twenty-third Street Mary-Ann suddenly reined herself in on her white pony heels. "Oh, my God, it's Liza Minnelli!"

"Where?" I said.

"There. Right over there. That little thing goin' in the door. Look, *there*, Hal, over there in front. Aww, *shit*, I knew, didn't I say I knew? There's like this *odor.*" Mary-Ann heavily sniffed the air again.

I couldn't detect anything but truck exhaust. "I still don't see her."

Mary-Ann pointed. "Look, Hal . . . she's right *there.*"

I stared beyond her manicured fingernail. There was Liza Minnelli, standing behind a dumpy man in front of Richie's supermarket. We watched as they breezed through the supermarket doors, Liza's head resting on the man's shoulder.

"See, Liza's tryin' to disguise herself," Mary-Ann said, staring at the doors. "Nice try, Liza. Try and fool us all, why don'tcha? These celebs, Hal, they put on all these idiotic diguises that any dumb person could see right through—dark glasses, wigs, weird beards and mustaches, gas masks, baseball caps, and stupid knee socks and baggy things if they're women. No make up ever. Like Madonna, right? I saw Madonna joggin' in the park last week, wearin' these little granny glasses. And this little golf visor. And I jumped out in front of her, I went, Madonna, *please.* Give us all a break. It's so obvious it's you, why even bother tryin' to fool me? Just come clean and give me that autograph. All it does is call more attention to the *fact* of 'em—the disguises, I mean."

She kept staring at the supermarket, then she yanked at my arm. "Come on, Hal."

"Where are we going?"

"We're gonna follow Liza around for a while. Track her like a little red fox."

"Oh no we're not," I said. "I refuse. That's sick. That's pathetic and sick."

Mary-Ann didn't seem to have heard me. "I don't think that's Liza's man, either. Liza's real man's much bigger than him. Liza's like this little dot compared to her real guy. Sculptor and downtown personality Mark Gero. I think maybe that's Liza's half brother with her, Joey. He's real publicity-shy for some reason. Judy's son by the producer Sid Luft," Mary-Ann added importantly. "And Lorna's brother. Lorna's shy little brother. You know Lorna just had a kid? Seven pounds eight ounces, wait, was she? I get her confused with Farrah's kid. Farrah Fawcett. By actor-boxer Ryan O'Neal. You know that guy knocked out his own kid's front teeth? I couldn't *believe* that. . . ."

Mary-Ann pulled me toward the door. "Get a move on, Hal. I need somethin', anyway. For my throat. I'm from the South, remember? I get parched real easily. If I don't get a Cherry Diet Coke A-sap, I'm about to choke on my own lips."

I allowed Mary-Ann to drag me through the wheezing doors even though this mission was insane. Inside, Mary-Ann stopped in front of a row of silvery carts all stuck together. She pulled one out and kicked its front wheels to aim in the right direction. "Now, where's that soda-pop section, I wonder," Mary-Ann said softly.

"This is really *psycho*," I hissed.

"Shut up, Hal," Mary-Ann whispered. "Liza hears you and she'll bolt like a rabbit."

I followed along reluctantly as she pushed her cart past the milk and the half-and-half. I walked very lightly, as though any moment I might be forced to make a run for it. I was trying to pretend that I didn't know this person, that I was in the supermarket for my own good reasons. While Mary-Ann was looking at Italian specialties I studied the spices—oregano, thyme, cracked peppercorns. When Mary-Ann pushed her basket in front of a shelf of sour cream and cottage cheese, I began examining napkins, squeezing them for firmness the way people did on television. Ahead of us, I glimpsed Liza and the dumpy man huddling in front of the tall stacks of egg cartons.

"I wonder whether Liza'll buy brown or regular," Mary-Ann said thoughtfully.

"I don't give a shit," I said in a drunken voice louder than my own.

Liza looked up when she heard my voice. I pretended to look at oven cleaners: did I want Easy-Off or the generic brand? Liza resumed opening up cartons, checking for cracks in the shells. The man picked up a carton and studied the small print along the top. I suppose he was looking for the expiration date. Liza pointed to a particular carton and the man tucked it under his arm. "Brown," Mary-Ann whispered dramatically. "Now, that's interestin' that Liza prefers the brown to the white . . . wonder why that is, you know, how that particular thing of hers, how it took shape and all. Maybe Liza had a bad experience one time with the white eggs. Maybe they make her think of Easter, blowin' out eggs and shit, Judy out on tour, and film director Vincente Minnelli off on some shoot, and Liza there at the house all alone. And see, now that Liza's all grown-up, she can't do kid things like that anymore . . ."

Liza glanced in our direction again, and Mary-Ann smiled back at her brightly. Liza muttered something to the man and put another carton of eggs into her cart. "Yes, Liza, yes . . ." I heard Mary-Ann whisper. "Two cartons're better than one. Two mints, two mints, *two mints* in one. Maybe Liza's havin' a big brunch tomorrow, Hal, you know, like this gala celebrity fest. I didn't really know celebs liked eggs all that much, though. I thought they just ate pâté and caviar all the time. Oh, wait, *I* know," she said, turning to me, "those eggs're for Joey. The brunch's called off. Those're Joey's eggs. Forget what I said about the brunch."

"How the hell do you know that?" I snapped. I wanted to be anywhere but here, in Richie's supermarket, following Liza Minnelli around.

"Because I know these things," Mary-Ann said, pushing her cart up to the eggs. "Eggs're like psychic conductors. The yolk, see, it engages my ESP, right?"

Mary-Ann did exactly what Liza had done. She picked up several cartons from the back of the shelf and opened their lids, checking for cracked eggs. Then she placed two cartons in her cart and pushed down the aisle.

Ahead of us, Liza pulled a chunk of cream cheese from the shelf and brought it up under her nose.

"Liza's checkin' the dates here," Mary-Ann whispered. "She's interested in the shelf life of things. Liza prob'ly got burned by some cream cheese gone bad in the past. It was prob'ly spoiled, all green or somethin' that night, and Liza's never forgotten that lesson a life." Mary-Ann wagged her finger, trying to sound wise. "See, Hal, psychology. But maybe this time. Hey, maybe this time, right? The song? Maybe this time Liza'll be lucky! Maybe this time the cream cheese won't go bad so quick! Maybe this time, for the first time, the cream cheese won't hurry away! So, Hal, you think Liza's goin' ahead with that Sunday brunch idea or not?"

"I don't really care what Liza's weekend plans are," I said sharply.

Mary-Ann tossed her hair back. "You're just jealous, Hal. Jealous of Liza 'cause she has people clappin' for her and you don't. Nobody claps for you, Hal. You have like this zero amount of applause in your life." She pushed up to where Liza's cart had just been and took down three bars of cream cheese and put them in the basket. "It just so happens that I have a need for some appetizers myself," she murmured.

"What the hell are you doing?" I said.

"I'm attemptin' to get inside Liza's *mind-set*, Hal," Mary-Ann said angrily. "If you don't *mind*, Hal. I don't really see where it concerns you much, *Hal*. It frankly doesn't have anything to do with you, *Hal*."

She was mad at me, I could tell. I wasn't acting the way I was supposed to in front of Liza. Having had very little experience with celebrities in supermarkets, though, I didn't really know how you were supposed to act when you found yourself trapped in an aisle with one. We followed Liza and the man down past the detergent and dishwashing sections and over to the meat counter. Every now and then Liza would rest her black booted toe on the shopping cart's rubber wheel and whisper something into the man's ear. Whenever she did, I could see Mary-Ann straining to eavesdrop. "Liza sings so damn loud," she whispered furiously, "so why isn't she that loud when she's talkin' normally?"

"Maybe she's resting her diaphragm," I suggested.

"Look," Mary-Ann whispered. "Liza's gettin' that man's opinion on those artichoke hearts. Who *is* that guy, anyway? Look how careful she's bein' with the items she's selectin'. I think Liza prob'ly comes from the you-break-it-you-buy-it school of shoppin'. Judy prob'ly taught her to be gentle with merchandise she hadn't paid for yet. I mean, she could buy up this whole damn dump nine hundred times over if she wanted to, but she's still careful."

I looked down inside Mary-Ann's cart, which was identical to Liza's. By now they each had two cartons of brown eggs, vanilla ice cream, cream cheese, Doritos and onion dip, seltzer water, lemons and walnuts. The only difference was that Mary-Ann had added copies of *The Weekly World News* and *The Star.*

"I think this is weird," I said. "Really weird."

Mary-Ann answered in a hoarse, angry burst. "Do *not* embarrass me in front of Liza, Hal, or I will kill you. I *mean* that too."

Liza was flipping her fingers through some avocados.

"What a pretty ring Liza's wearin'," Mary-Ann commented, staring. "I wonder if it's real at all—they mostly keep their real stuff hidden at home, you know? Like the ring that's worth a million dollars, she's got one of those. Betcha this is just a fake ring she wears on the streets so she won't get ripped off by a—"

"Oh, yes, I'm sure you're right," I interrupted. I was getting the impression that Mary-Ann, for whatever reason, had begun to turn against Liza; I had no idea why, since Liza had done no harm to either of us. I'd noticed this mood swing back in the nut section. Liza was looking at walnuts, taking down can after can and then replacing them on the shelf. Mary-Ann had stared impatiently at the back of her head. "Get a move on, damn you," she muttered. "Jesus, just take that one right in front of you. Walnuts are walnuts, they're just dressed up different. Even if you are a major song stylist." Mary-Ann was shaking her head. "Liza doesn't even know I'm here in the store. I mean, I'm in the same *store* as her, for God's sake. Why doesn't she *do* somethin', for God's sake?"

"Like what?"

"Like cast me in somethin', that's what . . . like gimme a part in some-thin'."

Now, in front of the potato and onion sacks, Mary-Ann had halted her cart. "I wonder—"

"What?"

"I wonder—no, I just don't have balls enough. No, I was just wonderin' to myself whether I could just march on up to that basket of avocados over there and pretend to be, you know, just another shopper. And get Liza goin' in a conversation, kind of shopper to shopper. I wonder if she'd know it was me, or whether she'd think it was just some girl. Some girl in the supermarket. But—"

Mary-Ann sounded sad all of a sudden. Everything seemed to go limp at the same time. When Liza moved past the avocados to the netted sacks of red and green grapes, Mary-Ann didn't bother to follow.

"Well, Hal . . . I don't feel so much like doin' this anymore."

I gestured at her groceries. "What about all this crap?"

Mary-Ann pushed the cart away, and it coasted down the aisle about ten feet before butting into a cardboard raisin stand. When she spoke again, her voice had the dull control of people who are about to start crying. "I wasn't gonna buy any of that shit, anyway. I just did it. I just wanted to feel what it was like. Bein' Liza for twenty minutes. But to hell with that, right? I'm not even thirsty anymore. I'm not even drunk. Plus, I don't like New York. New York's stupid. It's *stupid* here."

Outside the store, Mary-Ann uncorked wordlessly the second bottle of champagne and took a swig. We sat down in a small park, filled with men and women who already had passed out. "I'm pissed off, Hal," Mary-Ann said. "Liza has pissed me off *royally*. She coulda put me in somethin' back there, you know? Some show. Some stupid TV movie, even. I mean, what does a person have to do? She caught my eye a coupla times, too, it's not like she didn't know I existed, that I wasn't in the same store as her . . ." Mary-Ann took another long sip. Some of the champagne dripped down her chin, and she swiped at it with her elbow before handing the bottle to me. "I can't believe Liza just stood there and ignored me. She musta thought . . . she musta just thought—"

"I don't think she thought anything, Mary-Ann," I said. "At least nothing against you personally."

"She musta thought I was just some *girl*. Some creepy *fan*. I mean, she had no idea—"

"Maybe she didn't have a good enough look at you," I said gently.

"Aww, come on, Hal. Liza coulda just said, Hey! I want that girl in my next movie! She has what it takes. I know from what it takes. That girl Mary-Ann would be perfect for such-and-such role. She'd be just perfect for the role of Callie the blind girl, you know, who gets her sight restored at the end. It would be a tour-de-force role for her. Liza coulda marched right up to me and said, Say! I'm lookin' for a sensitive newcomer, and Mary-Ann Beavers, you are *it!*" Mary-Ann looked at me imploringly. "But she didn't. And you know why she didn't? 'Cause Liza knows damn well what a tour-de-force Callie would be for me, and she'd want those kudos for her own self. That's *just* what Liza was doin'."

I was confused. "Who's this blind girl?"

"Oh, some part I made up. Some tour-de-force part. Either in a movie or a show. See, 'cause Callie's blind, the actress playin' her has this amazin' opportunity to show off her different facets. I just made her up. It's a made-up part, there's prob'ly no part like that. Aww . . ." She sighed. "I didn't do so good for myself, you know?"

"Liza was shopping." I was trying to sound soothing, but handing her back the champagne bottle, I felt instead like a wino. "Maybe when Liza shops, all her theatrical instincts lie dormant . . ."

Mary-Ann lit a cigarette. "You know," she said, shaking out the match, "when I was a kid, I used to think there were casting agents in my own town. In Patent. Like when I walked down the street, you know? I used to think they were just sittin' around in Meredith's Coffee Shop, waitin' to spot new talent. I mean, I think of it now, I go, What the hell would any of those guys be doin' down in Patent? The only people down in Patent are people like my mom and Lorne. The ladies at the drugstore. The ladies at the church. The ladies at the supermarket. Did I ever tell you that's how Lorne and Mom met? In a supermarket? That's how I know good things happen in supermarkets, least most of the time they do . . ."

The Circle Line was waiting at Forty-fourth Street. It was a large, pristine-looking ship with red railings running along the top deck and, below, the large protected area filled with benches and chairs, for tourists who didn't want to get spray in their faces.

Mary-Ann and I had finished off the second bottle of champagne and were working on a newly purchased third. At this point I could barely mew, much less speak—my lips were as numb as seat cushions. Mary-Ann gave the attendant our tickets and we lurched onto the top deck, passing by a white sign that read, NO ALCOHOLIC BEVERAGES, NO SPITTING. Mary-Ann kept the third bottle under her jacket as she leaned over the railing. "My head feels like it's *thumpin'*," she said as we watched the other passengers boarding. "'F I fall, Hal, promise you'll catch me, 'kay? Will you promise?"

"Sure," I said.

She grabbed my arm. "Say it. I promise you, Mary-Ann . . ."

I repeated it, as I would have repeated anything anybody wanted me to repeat. I hadn't been so drunk in a long time. As I stood there watching the water wash up against the heavy white hull, I loved the world. I loved the summer I'd just come out of, which is not to say I didn't love spring, winter and fall every bit as much. All things, I realized, would take care of themselves. My mind drifted around, dully sorting things out. From where I was standing, the view of New York seemed as vivid and magical as it would for someone in love, and there seemed to be a heightened keenness in the early autumn air, an urgency and regret that I associated with a change of season, and perhaps a change of heart.

"To BB," I said, brandishing the black champagne bottle. "To a verra special pup . . ."

"To BB," Mary-Ann repeated solemnly.

"To Lisa Lyman, the most sincere . . . kid . . . on this earth."

"Who's'at?"

I remembered how enchanted New York had seemed when I fell in love with Veebka. Every street seemed inexplicably bewitched, since each one held the possibility that she'd walked down it, stood there chatting with someone on the sidewalk. Her physical presence made me ache, made the area behind my eyes ache, made every single building in the city ache. Away from her for the weekend, I would rent only movies that took place in New York. I would listen only to music played and sung by New York bands. I felt the same way I had as a kid, alone in the dark at night, listening to *The Make-Believe Ballroom*, a radio program that played only the old jazz tunes of another generation, and the only New York station my pitiful bedside radio could pick up, live scratchy-sounding performances from clubs like the Mad Hatter and the Hotel Pennsylvania, places long since razed and turned into office space. It was that same radio show, with its promises of elegance and glittering lights, that made me want to come to New York in the first place.

From the top deck of the boat New York looked oddly serene, perfectly clear, unimpressed by its own sprawl. People were always complaining about how noisy and terrible the city was. They were shocked that murders and horrors occurred there, but I was amazed there weren't greater horrors, that there weren't five hundred murders a minute! The fact that we weren't constantly at one another's throats filled with me gratitude and something resembling love.

I noticed I had practically gone numb. As I stood there the children of the other passengers played with parts of my lower torso, but I barely noticed them. Whenever I felt my sneaker lace being untied, or my fly being pulled down, I would merely glance down fondly and mutter something like, "Hey, come on, guys." Sensation had vanished in the lower regions of my body, along with my usual unrest. Perhaps my foot will have to be amputated, I thought, but this notion gave me no displeasure—people would come visit me in the hospital and tell me how brave I was, that I was a role model, a genius of pain! The president of the United States would call me, and I would listen to his trifling platitudes with a little smirk, holding the phone out slightly from my ear. Then I would hang up on him, and laugh, laugh, laugh, until they gave me another shot.

Above my head, lipstick-colored life preservers hung in delinquent rows, like the surprised, open mouths of dancers in a cancan line. Beside the railing, a mother was bent down, singing to her children in French. A Frenchwoman! What an opportunity! Ever since the Singing Nun had killed herself I'd wanted to discuss this unfortunate event with an actual French-woman. How could that rhyming sister have killed herself when there were beautiful early-autumn days like this left to live? I opened up the newspaper that had miraculously appeared in my hand and scrutinized the diagram in the Tots of the World section—of a poor, sad tot stuck halfway down a Phoenix well like a bean in a windpipe. And I vowed that if that tot wasn't rescued in a day that I would fly to Arizona myself with a giant eye dropper over my shoulder. "Let me through," I would say as I elbowed aside the various digging teams. "What is this, amateur night?" I would insert my numb, lanky form into the gaping well-hole and squeeze myself down to the tot who—grateful, cranky and bemused—would adhere to the end of the eye dropper with a satisfying slurp, whereupon, releasing the rubber bulb, I would yank the Well-Tot up to safety.

Mary-Ann was still depressed about Liza's Minnelli's snub, but drinking a quantity of champagne had given her a version of events that wouldn't keep her up nights. She seemed to cheer up once the boat pushed off, honking, from its berth. "She saw me, I know she did. There was some kinda electric-eel charge that wiggled between our eyes, some kinda recognition. It was like she's this established person now, but when she saw me, she saw a kinda miniature picture of herself when she was little . . . the same drive, the same eat-the-whole-audience thing—you know, excel, excel, and who cares what anybody says?"

"When I get famous, Hal," she went on, "I won't give *anybody* access to my person. I'll· be livin' off in a castle someplace. Like in Italy or Ireland. Then I'll have a regular phone for like two months, and then quick, without any warnin', I'll go get myself an unlisted phone number and I'll only give out the unlisted phone number to people who've survived the second cut. Then I'll buy myself a phone-answerin' service. You know, where the lady answers and just gives the last four numbers. Then I'll say, when I meet folks, So here's my number. Call up, and if you pass the screenin', then they'll connect you to my electric phone-answerin' *machine*. And then after that, one of my domos might get back to you. See, Hal, I'll have domos by then, majors and all the others. But one of Mary-Ann's people prob'ly won't get back to you 'cause Mary-Ann's so busy. Mary-Ann Beavers is an extremely busy model slash actress—"

"—slash National Treasure," I slurred.

"Right! And I won't give anybody the right number in the first place unless they're cute. Or unless they have a lotta money and power. And no girls. Just cute boys. Or, yeah, powerful girls with a lotta money. So that every time the phone rings, I can say, That's that cute boy callin', or, That's that rich, powerful lady. Everybody'll think I'm psychic. I mean, I *am* psychic, but people'll know I'm like, *constantly* psychic."

I went into the boat bathroom, and when I got back outside, Mary-Ann was standing against the railing, posing. A Japanese man was standing six feet away from her, preparing to take her picture.

"Just press that little red dot," Mary-Ann said loudly. "You should know what a little red dot is. I don't mean you *are* one, just that you Japanese have all that technology—all this techno stuff you guys got. I mean, aren't you takin' over the world or somethin', didn't I read? No, in fact, you're taller than most Japanese I met. Not that I met all that many of you all—I mean, you just don't come across all that many Japanese people in my parta the world . . ."

The man didn't appear to understand much English, I realized gratefully. He took the picture and Mary-Ann retrieved her camera.

"Thanks a lot. Now, you get over there and sit on that life-preserver box, next to Hal there. Hal's the guy over there who's drunk. He's a friend of mine. The guy with the bloodshot eyes."

The man looked startled, but he came over and stood next to me, anyway. "Hal," I said, shaking hands with him lifelessly.

"Hal, you look *stupid*," Mary-Ann called out. "Smile. Let a smile be your umbrella. Now, both you guys, now say cheese when I count to three . . ."

Since neither the Japanese man nor I was about to say cheese, Mary-Ann did, and then she snapped the picture. A minute later a tall black man happened to pass by, and she asked whether he'd take of picture of her, the Japanese man and me. He took the camera and the three of us lined up against the railing, with the sky and the water behind us. Mary-Ann removed her floppy hat and held it up against her stomach with the hollow part facing out. When he'd taken the picture, Mary-Ann said she also wanted a picture of the Japanese man, the tall black man, me and her, but the picture had to be taken the exact same moment the Circle Line passed by the Statue of Liberty of else its meaning would be lost. "You know, 'cause we're all in this country together, right? And look at us, we're all so different, but now look, here we all are, 'kay? That's what makes the USA numero uno, right?"

This, I could tell, could go on forever, and both of the recruits looked unhappy and uncomfortable, so I took the camera away from Mary-Ann and wandered over to sit on a white hamper that held the backup bilge pump. I saw Mary-Ann talking in a low voice to the black man. After a while I noticed he was staring at her in disbelief, and then he put his face close up to hers and said something. Then he shook his head for a long time before disappearing into one of the passenger cabins.

Mary-Ann swished over to where I was sitting. "What's that guy's problem? I can't believe it."

"What happened?"

"Nothin', I told him how much I like black women singers—that's it and all and the end of it. I said, At this very minute there's this cassette of Aretha Franklin—you know, the *Who's Zoomin' Who* album?—in my Walkman back home, 'kay? What a coincidence, right? 'Cause both you and her are black, right? And the guy, he gets all *offended* all of a sudden. Here I was just tryin' to pay him a compliment, and he goes, It's a shame, young lady, that you have to say 'black woman singer' instead of just plain 'singer.' And I go, Well, I think black women singers are *better*—see, here I am, I'm payin' you this gigantic compliment here, so what's your problem? I go, You know, black people've made like this *contribution* to music. Then I go, Are there any white singers *you* like? Sort of in the interests of the U.N. and world peace and all—and the Statue of Liberty and all—but the guy, he just walks off in a huff . . ." Mary-Ann shrugged. "I just wanted him to feel . . . sorta more global, 'kay? I mean, what exactly did I do that was so bad?"

I just shook my head.

"He said it was a racist thing to've said. Was it—was that a racist thing of me to say that? I was just tryin' to pay a compliment . . ."

The boat moved smoothly down the Hudson, trailing a churning, white, wishboning wake. Outside the lap of the city, the water seemed clean and green. Gulls flew, falling and feinting behind our wake, adjusting themselves to certain higher and lower heights, as though trying to create an ideal binocular sharpness to their altitudes. I was watching the sky and the city moving away from me behind the boat when Mary-Ann sighed loudly. "I wish I was gonna live forever, but that ain't gonna happen . . ."

"Do you have something wrong with you? I mean, are you sick?" Suddenly I felt sick to my stomach myself.

"No." Mary-Ann held out her hand, palm up. "See, I got this life line that's about an inch and a half long, that's all. I'm prob'ly gonna get it in the face with a machine gun when I'm about thirty. Here's the life line." She traced the line, sitting tentatively next to me. "It stops right about here. And there's this weak little stringie here connectin' it to another line like a cat's cradle string. That's the IV cord. That's one of the things the M.D.s are gonna do in order to keep me alive. I s'pose I'll have to hire some teenager to come in an' read to me. Maybe I'll be one of those guys on a life machine who paints these landscapes with a paintbrush between their toes. Or who plays like, a guitar with like just their eyelashes. People who're in jail get really jacked-up prices for their crummy landscapes—the cons do, I mean. I prob'ly could, too, if I was on a lifeline.

Mary-Ann snapped her middle finger and the rest folded up under her thumb on her palm. "Let's see yours, Hal."

I held out a hand.

"Wrong one. Your Gypsy hand. Right one's the only one that counts for palm readin'."

She took my right hand loosely. I don't know what it was, the champagne, the cool wind, the fact that I hadn't been touched by a girl for a long time, but when she touched my hand and traced her fingernail across my palm, I got shivers on the back of my neck and down my back. I even felt them behind my ears.

Mary-Ann wasn't aware of any of this. "Oh, you gotta nice life line, Hal.

It's real long." Her eyebrows *boing*ed up and down. "It's endless, in point of fact, it goes right into your wrist and just disappears. You're gonna live forever an' a day." She peered down closer. "It's pretty shallow, though."

Great, I thought. *A long, insubstantial life.*

Her hair was blocking my palm, and she bent down over my fingers like a microsurgeon. The shivers on the back of my neck got sharper, and I felt as dully excited as the champagne allowed. "Nope, it just means you'll be on the go-go-go all the time or somethin'. Mom tol' me what everything means. And you got all these little stars 'n' hexagrams between your life line and your career line. That means you'll be totally successful in your chosen field . . ."

She rubbed a nail down my life line as the Circle Line tour guide said, "Testing, testing, one-two-three-four, hello." Since my hand felt so good, I was hardly listening. When Mary-Ann lifted her head, I was planning to kiss her, violently, on the lips. The thought of this was strangely exciting. I wasn't listening to a word she was saying, all I was thinking about was that first good kiss. I shut my eyes and the world spun warmly around.

"Eldridge tried to get a readin' but I wouldn't. I looked at *his* hand and it had all the signs of mental derangement in it. Mom has like this palm-readin' manual at home, it says, When you come across a palm that has all the signs, you should make up a polite excuse as to why you can't deliver. But you gotta be real polite, 'cause the person might be packin' a gun, right? There's three things the book says you can say. There's, Oh, but you don't actually want me to read your palm tonight, do you? Then there's, Haven't we had enough palm readin' for tonight? Why don't we go out dancin' at X—and then the book leaves this little space for whatever, your fav'rite dance and act-foolish place, 'kay? In Patent that'd the the Eleventh Hole. Then there's . . ."

I wasn't listening anymore. Mary-Ann stopped talking, and instead of tracing my palm, she was now kissing the tops of my fingers, one by one, and then slipping them inside her mouth. The little finger she kept in her mouth, and about thirty seconds later I slid it out.

"The World Trade Center, on the starboard, or right, side of the boat, is a hive of international business, and it also houses the Manhattan office of the Governor of New York. Not only is it the tallest . . ."

I waved my finger into the wind, trying to dry it off. Then I stood up dizzily.

"Hey, Hal" came Mary-Ann's sleepy-sounding voice, "I ain't done with you yet . . ."

The voice of the boat announcer was plain, flat and female. It stuttered over the word *building*. It said its little *huh* at the end of *York*, even though it was trying to conceal this lapse. It was a voice I knew. Now it was going on and on about the World Trade Center and the Battery. I was pretty sure it was the same voice, the same mouth and lips and tongue, and I started toward it as if it were early one adolescent morning and I was blurring in and out of a waking dream.

"Hey, Hal," Mary-Ann called behind me. "I'm not finished yet! Or you can say to that mentally deranged person, My, what excitement I see in these here lines—these lines here certainly show a life led on the high wire. Why don't you tell me about your safaris in Africa . . ." Mary-Ann's mouth was set tight, and her bottom lip looked glazed from having sucked my little finger.

"Yeah?" I said, having already forgot the first good kiss. What kiss? "I gotta go downstairs for a sec . . ."

I took the steps slowly, holding hard on to the banister—realizing midway down there wasn't one—until I reached the bottom. The deck was so white it made me blind. It seemed to have been polished with something extraordinary, something that could make you slip and fall, something much stronger than the grip of my own sneakers. Since I didn't trust walking across it without help, I stayed close to the side of the cabin so I could grab hold of its wall as soon as I felt the shining floor begin to move beneath me.

I couldn't figure out where the voice was coming from; the microphone gave every word both a shadow and an echo. I glanced wildly around the benches, filled with families chattering away in strange languages. Then I glimpsed Veebka, seated in a wide chair, a sheet of orange cloth behind her shoulders. She was wearing a blue sweater under a bright yellow slicker, and her hair was tucked up under a cap that read CIRCLE LINE on its brim.

I stood behind an empty bench for what seemed like an eternity, until Veebka glanced up from her text.

"Veebka . . ." I waved, even though I was standing only six feet away from her chair.

She shook her head rapidly. "No," her lips said. "No."

"Many of you," she went on, "saw the Statue of Liberty during the Bicentennial Celebration . . ." The microphone Veebka was holding was huge and grotesque, a deformed and earth-blackened pinecone. Her hands made small shooing motions at me, and her miked voice was agitated. This amplified agitation seemed to lend to my presence, and to the sheer loneliness of my past month, a divine sense of urgency. "A gift from the French government originally, she was last year renovated completely. Funds for the statue's reconstruction were made possible by public donation, and by grants from private corporations. To our right is Ellis Island, the former embarkation point for many of our ancestors . . ."

"Not my ancestors . . . Veebka-I-have-to-talk-to-you . . ."

It is terrible not to realize how drunk one is, and then to fail to proceed to act in an accordingly discreet way. When the beaming floor began to slip under my sneakers, I realized that I was walking toward Veebka and that she was wielding her enormous microphone like a nightstick. As I stumbled past a corner, the sunlight touched the back of my neck like a warm hand. "Veebka," I mumbled. "Sweetheart . . ."

"—buildings are part of the great financial nexus known to the world as Wall Street. From there the vision of the Lady—"

Now here was an expression I loathed. The Lady. In retrospect, maybe the Circle Line management had forced Veebka to use that expression. Maybe if she *hadn't* referred to the Statue of Liberty as the Lady, she would be out of a job. Once, though, we had insulted that expression together.

"Veebka," I called out again, and I was surprised to hear the echo of my voice enter the microphone, go forth and multiply. My voice now had the ringing enormity of Veebka's, and it made me feel vaguely like a minor, tremulous god. Several people sitting on the benches said "Sshhh" and "Quiet Down," and I hissed right back at them.

"We've gotta talk, Veebka," I yelled across the deck. "We gotta talk right now. We gotta talk. I love you. I miss you so much." At that moment I felt as if I had relinquished all the control I had spent so many years building up, and that I no longer even cared.

I was now only a foot away. "Hal, get away from here," Veebka whispered furiously. My fingers touched the base of the microphone, and she yanked it away. "The Dow Jones is a leading—"

I grabbed it from her. "The Dow Jones is a big stupid nothing," I slurred. "The economy's a mess, who cares about the Dow Jones? We're all gonna lose our money and end up in the gutter—but some of us're looking at the stars . . ."

"Hal, you're make me lose my job" came Veebka's tight whisper. "You're drunk!"

"The Lady," I slurred. "Don't call that the Lady. Don't you remember? We *hate* that expression. We hate it *together*. She's just . . . some old dame."

Sober, I don't think I would ever have used the word *dame* about anybody. It was not 1940, and I was not a gangster, or a bettor on horses or greyhounds. By now people were beginning to stare, and several tourists positioned themselves to take snapshots. I smiled winningly and obliged them, holding my hand to my forehead in a salute. I threw my arm around Veebka's shoulder so the tourists could bring home with them a bright and enduring image of Hal Andrews and the girl he loved. We would be flashed onto walls and screens from Tokyo to Cornwall; our fame would be international. Unfortunately, just as the shutters were going off, Veebka escaped me, yanking the microphone cord with her.

We struggled briefly for the microphone. "Hal," Veebka said angrily, "you're *smashed*." She held her hand over the microphone, but I yelled right through her fingers and the ring she was wearing.

"J'I jove jou." It came out "J'I jerf joe." "Jalk jo je!"

I was possessed. I was possessed even by her fingers which were now trying to wrench the microphone away from my grasp. We were grappling, and my face ended up in Veebka's hair, so I took the opportunity to inhale deeply this smell that was as familiar as breath. Veebka didn't smell like anybody else I had ever met. I now remembered that Mary of Munich had said this about men, and I gave her belated credit for having said at least one creditable thing during the course of her short, stoned life.

The tourists were getting shots of a more candid nature: me with my hair falling into my face, me drooling accidentally, me being shoved by Veebka, me falling heavily onto the deck and climbing slowly back to my feet. Then, when I finally held the microphone cord in my hand and Veebka had stopped grabbing for the cord—she just stood there, in front of her chair, looking helpless, furious and lovely—I lost all energy. And I lost all desire for Veebka. I stared at her as if she were someone I no longer knew, or had ever known. The cord hung limply from my fingers. Everyone was staring at me, waiting patiently but expectantly for my message.

How could I disappoint the International Community? I decided on the spur of the moment to sing a Peggy Lee song I remembered from my childhood; I'd lately read somewhere that it was an existential classic. But then Peggy Lee was always howling existential classics. I began somewhere in the middle of the song. "My old flame," I sang into the mike. "Can't even think of her name . . ."

By this point a Circle Line official had arrived and was whispering something to Veebka. "Yes," I heard her say hysterically, "unfortunately I do." Then the official attempted to grab my wrists, but in drunkenness my hands felt preternaturally fast, arrogant, stunning. I assumed a boxing position which, since I never learned how to box—except for boxing over the phone— was slightly stupid.

The Circle Line bouncer hit me in the mouth. Someone had taught *him* how to box—he hadn't led the same long, insubstantial life. I felt my lip slice open on a tooth, but the tooth stayed in place. *What marvelous teeth I have*, I thought. *What good genes.*

Then he hit me in the stomach, a punch I wasn't prepared for, since I was too busy admiring the excellence and maturity of my teeth. The absurd microphone clattered on the desk a couple of seconds before I did. It picked up the commotion of my head hitting the white deck, and then shouted the crack-sound back up to a sky that looked—as my brother had said in his most recent Christmas letter—just like boards.

The men on the Coast Guard boat that puttered me into the South Street Seaport were quite understanding. They confiscated my wallet, promising me that I could pick it up at their offices anytime convenient the next day. I sat in the stern of the boat, my tongue throbbing around my mouth; my bottom lip felt like a huge, fattened goose liver. Miles away from me now, the Circle Line cruise passed Grant's Tomb and hooked beyond the George Washington Bridge to the placid Hudson River Valley beyond.

When I was finally escorted to the captain's cabin, I had mumbled something about having a friend on board with me. The first mate had announced: "Will anyone who knows Hal Andrews please report to the First Cabin . . ." as though I were a dropped handbag or a child lost in a large department store or zoo. I explained that my friend's name was Mary-Ann Beavers. "Will a Miss Mary-Ann Beavers please report to the First Cabin," I heard the P.A. proclaim. I waited there on the couch for Mary-Ann to come and get me. The announcement was repeated twice, three times. I lost count, but I kept asking them to keep at it—until someone came down. When no one came after thirty minutes, the captain radioed the Coast Guard.

I was dropped off at a pier that was actually a phony complex of shops and attractions. There were vendors, fruit stands, and bars, from whose windows piano music flew like swallows or moths. The place was teeming with stockbrokers, drinking beers, holding their glasses to their ribs like awards they were sick of carrying; a couple were vomiting on the sidewalk behind the Paine Webber building. Stockbrokering women in white sneakers chatted in groups of three, their black alligator office pumps sticking out of canvas bags. A Hispanic man with wild eyes was pushing around a cart of stuffed orange ducks with yellow bills; he must've had a hundred of them, lined up in neat rows, their stiff orange flippers overlapping uncannily. "Baby ducks," he called out. "Twenty bucks for one baby duck, two baby ducks for thirty. Get your baby ducks . . ."

I stumbled the twenty or so blocks back uptown and east. Someone had painted tiny, sodden purple footsteps on the sidewalks and I walked along their path. I'd heard this was the work of a lunatic environmental group, their goal the destruction of all industry and, less ambitiously, the annoyance of all inhabitants of New York. To the left the sunset appeared, a soft red rock between unyielding buildings. A slight snapping breeze carried in from industrial New Jersey, cleaning my head, forcing me to walk faster. The buildings on either side seemed to be rocking, mesmerized, like switches. My stomach ached from the bouncer's dull punch. In the early-evening air there was a strange, burning smell, and salt pushing in from the river, and the rot of many green garbage bags, slumped, their plastic twist ties slowly pulling apart, tick by tick. On lower Broadway an old man was standing in front of a Porsche showroom—one minute leaning on his cane, looking in the windows, wishing he had a couple of Porsches at his disposal—and the next thing I knew, a sudden sour gust of wind blew him backward, as he'd neglected to bend his knees. He fell down hard on the sidewalk, and his cane trickled away from him.

I tried to help him up. "Get away from me!" he screamed, terrified.

* * *

I slunk back to Bob's apartment. At the corner of Eldridge Street, salsa music blared from open windows, and in front of my building the fat white Mister Softee truck was parked and tinkling away. I wasn't thinking at all about Mary-Ann—I assumed she could make her own way back. I had other things on my mind: my chin, my stomach, Veebka.

Upstairs, exhausted, on the sixth-floor landing, I pushed in my door, and there in the hallway stood Frank. He was holding my long black police lock like a baseball bat.

"Oh, it's just you . . ." he murmured.

I glared. Did he think I was running a residence hotel? Did he think he could come and go like a transient?

"That's right." I pushed past him. "Just me, the guy who lives here, remember? And look, *I* decide whether I have visitors in this apartment."

"Don't be a jerk, you fake-Bob," Frank said pleasantly.

I heard a scuttling sound in the living room. Something large and powerful ran up against the living-room wall, butting it, flicking a long, hairless tail.

Behind me, Frank laughed his one-note laugh. "I tol' you there was prob'ly some things behind your walls, mister. You prob'ly thought it was just mice in there. Well, welcome to your mice. I caught 'em, trapped 'em for you."

"What exactly did you trap?" I said as the dirty, shelled figure belted the wall again, then streaked blindly across the rug and disappeared under my mattress. "What the hell *is* that?"

He came up behind me. "Where's my sister? Where's Mary-Ann?"

I was still staring at where I thought I'd just seen a large animal. "I don't know where your sister is. . . . What is that?" I said again.

"Don't be such a jerk, son. It's an armadillo. You never seen one, I bet, but I nailed him, all right. And he's got a coupla little kids 'round here someplace too." Frank leered at me. "That wasn't the only thing come crawlin' out your walls. Big gash in your closet, they just burst on through. Coupla deer, but I let 'em run off. And a big mama pig, too, nipped at me. I sold mama pig to one of the spic guys downstairs, sake a bacon . . ."

"Then give me the money." Even in my dazed confusion I tried proudly to keep my priorities straight.

"Forget it. And there's a coupla death-breath prairie dogs climbin' all over each other too. Got rid of them too. Told 'em to take a walk. What are you runnin' here, anyway, mister, a wild animal farm?"

Frank made me sick. I detested him. He seemed at that moment in the hallway to sum up everything that unnerved me about other men, and about certain American lives I had no desire to know anything about. Staring back at him, I was overcome by his quiet potential for violence, a violence I'd always suspected lay beneath the smiling and amiable faces of the Mid— and Southwest—hot black nights, cars, beers, grins, piety, but after eight, nothing to do and nowhere to go. These were the kinds of girls and boys who were conversant with court orders, leather straps and grave robbery, boys and girls who, on a school night, strangled their best friends, or their stepparents, and then went on to testify they'd done it in God's name. Frank was probably no different—a churchgoing time bomb.

There was a new meanness in Frank's face. He hadn't shaved in several days and his beard had grown in red and ugly. His clothes, though, were different and I stared at them with surprise—a light blue polo shirt and a pair of pleated beige pants, attached to his waist with a black rubber belt.

"Fox, pig, armadillo, deer . . ." I repeated, dazed and terrified that this was my life, and the nature of my squalor. "Prairie dogs . . . bacon . . . pigs, deer . . ." It was true, I thought, as the Mister Softee melody, childish and nagging, wafted through the open kitchen window: Bob's building was as decrepit, dangerous and unsanitary as I'd always suspected. This was much, much worse than merely having mice, rats and the occasional roving horsefly in the apartment—there were actual wildebeests behind the walls.

"Prairie dogs I turned loose . . ." Frank went on. "They're 'round here someplace. I named 'em. Ed 'n' Red. You should call up a zoo, mister, get yourself a little tax write-off—"

"Just get out of my face," I spat.

I went into the kitchen to make some coffee. I needed to sober up, and even though coffee didn't really do the trick, it would at least create the illusion.

In a minute Frank appeared in the kitchen doorway. "So when's Mary-Ann comin' back?" His voice was casual. "Got some news, somethin' she might be real interested in . . ."

I didn't even want to look at him. "I don't *know* when she'll be comin' back." *Coming* back! I yelled at myself.

"Don't be such a jerk, fake-Bob. An' you better not've touched her, mister."

"Touched her? You mean, moved her emotionally? By playing a patriotic piano concerto that reminded her of her goddamn youth?"

"You know what I mean."

"Gee, I'm quivering with fear," I said. "See the blood leave my face? Quiver, quiver, quiver—"

"If you did anything to her, then that's it for you, boy. I'll tell you that much."

What I said was, "I wouldn't touch your crummy sister if you paid me." But where did these adolescent taunts come from? In moments I knew: Beck. What would I come out with next? *Fake-out, fake-out? Copycat?*

"Don't talk 'bout Mary-Ann like that." Frank took a step forward, still carrying the oily black police lock. I was holding the coffeepot, and Frank looked as though he thought it were in the strike zone.

"I don't want to see your vicious little face," I said. "Get it out of this apartment!"

"*You're* tellin' *me* to get outa here?"

"Yes." I was armed with boiling coffee, black and strong, made of the finest Colombian beans. If he made a move, I'd splash him to death. I pushed past him into the hallway and went into the living room. Under my bed the armadillo snorted. Its chewed black-whip tail moved back and forth, and when I shut my eyes and opened them again, I couldn't tell the difference between the armadillo's tail and the black line that ran from the lamp, or the television cord. I didn't know whether or not armadillos assaulted people, but I wasn't taking any chances. If this armadillo attacked me, then it would get splashed to death as well. The same rules applied to nocturnal mammals as they did to churchgoing time bombs.

"See, I've had a coupla weird weeks," Frank said as he walked in and sat down, before I could, on the couch.

"We've missed you terribly," I said. "It's been *traumatic* here without you."

Frank ignored this weak, adolescent sarcasm. "Spent a coupla nights out in the park, gettin' hungry. Got myself a job, though."

"What?" I said. "Head of sanitation? Rat catcher for the entire five-borough area?"

"These people, they want me to sell their cigarettes . . ."

"What people?"

"Flash—the Flash Modelin' Agency. Y'ever heard of the Flash Modelin' Agency?"

"No," I said slowly, keeping an eye on my bedspread. "What do you mean, they want you to sell their cigarettes?"

"What I said. They want me to sell cigarettes. They like the way I ride. They say I got the look, you know?" Frank sounded pleased with himself. "You know, I *like* New York. I *like* it here. There's good people here. I think I might just stick around a little while—"

"Not here," I said. "Anyway, what do you mean, they like the way you ride?"

"Up at that park," Frank said, "there's a carousel there—right in the middle of the town, but in that park. So I got on one of them horses, rode it around for a while . . ." He shook his head. "Anyway, there's a lady there, she's with her kids, three of 'em. She says to me, Mister, if you look that good on a horse, then you could be the man for me. I says, What? And she goes, If you look that good on a horse, meanin' a real one, then we'd like to see you again. So I ask what she means—who this we is—and this lady says Marlboros. I want you to sell Marlboros. We're looking for a new guy for some Marlboro account or somethin'. She wants an address, and I says, I don't got a real address here. So she gives me this fancy card with the address on it and says if I need a place, I can crash with her. I been takin' her up on it, too, that's what I'm doin' back here, pickin' up my gear." He tossed a card that landed at my feet.

It's not fair, I thought after this had sunk in. Mary-Ann wanted to be the famous one, not her brother. She was the one who'd waited outside the Russian Tea Room, clutching her autograph pad. She was the one. . . It didn't matter, none of it was remotely fair. My mind went blank yet still managed to make room for the unhappy revelation that I had more in common with Mary-Ann than I'd ever thought. *It's not fair,* I thought again.

"Well, when she shows up, you give her that. Tell her to come on over—it's huge, the place this lady has, not like this fuckin' animal reservation."

"She liked the way you ride," I said dumbly. *Poor Mary-Ann,* I thought. *Poor me.*

"Hey, the phone called for you. 'Bout twenty minutes ago . . . some girl."

"Who?"

"Polack-soundin' girl. Some crazy name I didn't catch."

"Veebka?" I said instantly.

"Somethin' weird like that."

"Was it Veebka?"

"Don't recall. Sounds kinda like it, though."

"What did she say?"

"Nothin'. Wanted to know how you were." Suddenly Frank grinned at me. "So how the hell ahre you, Hughie?"

A couple of hours later I heard the front door open, and then I heard the door to the back room slamming shut. It woke me up. I'd fallen asleep once Frank left, his suitcase under his arm. The coffee had done me no good at all. I'd hustled the armadillo into the bathroom, using a variety of kitchen implements—a broom, a dustpan, a paint-specked drop cloth—and slammed the door behind it. It took over an hour, and the armadillo was still banging its body against the wood, but the door was holding firm.

I remembered everything and reflexively hugged the bed, as if mattresses and pillows and sheets have ever had the power to alter anything. I said to myself, *You had better start packing.*

Soon the door to the back room opened and I heard footsteps in the kitchen. The refrigerator door squeaked open, then thudded shut. I heard the sound of the phone being dialed and, a minute later, the receiver being slammed down.

"Shit!" Mary-Ann yelled. I think she was trying to make as much of a racket as possible. Through the paint-spotted French doors I saw her eyes glancing across the living room to see if I was in my bedroom.

I called her name from my bed.

Mary-Ann was holding a Diet Cherry Coke in two hands. She kept at least two six-packs in the fridge at all times, which together blocked out the small, pale refrigerator light. "What do *you* want?" she screamed across the living room.

I couldn't stand just lying there in bed, saying nothing. "So I'm sorry," I called.

"Sorry about *what?*" she said nastily.

"You know." Then I said, "I'm sorry about what I did. And about just leaving you. I didn't know she'd be there. Veebka. I didn't know . . ."

"I just want to know the particulars of what you're sorry for. Since there's so goddamn *much*, you know?"

"All right. I didn't mean to strand you on the boat. I didn't mean to make a scene. What else didn't I mean—"

"Oh, did you *strand* me? Is that what you did, Hal? I wasn't aware of anybody strandin' me on any boat. One minute you were just sittin' there, I was readin' your hand, we were getting *kinda* close if I may say so, and the next minute you're screamin' and yellin' and embarrassin' the hell outa me. You know, you got like *zero* sense of proportion, Hal. Who taught you the ways of life, some wolverines?"

She caught her breath. "I think *you got the worst manners* of anybody I ever met. All of a sudden you act like I'm nothin', like I'm some dim-witted cracker that doesn't know Northern ways. Who doesn't know my ass from my own mouth. Well, I'm *not* nothin'. In fact, I'm far from it." Mary-Ann was practically strangling her Diet Cherry Coke. "I'm gettin' outa New York too. Nobody calls me back, and they're all as bad-mannered as you are—rude as *anything*. They act like you're nothing at all. In Patent, people *answer* your phone calls. . . ."

"Well," I said, "good-bye, then. . . ."

In the moment of silence I imagined Mary-Ann was either making up her mind about something or preparing to hurl herself out the window. "Thing is, I gotta borrow some money off you first. Or off someone. Since I spent all my money gettin' treated so good up here. NYC right? I need three hundred, maybe even more."

"I'm sorry, Mary-Ann, I just don't have it right now," I said. *But would you like a Wheat Thin?* I felt like saying.

"So, then I'll *walk* back home. I'll *hitch*. Somebody'll prob'ly kill me . . ."

"Go ahead," I said. "I didn't even want you here in the first place."

A moment later I heard things breaking in the kitchen, things being hurled against the walls and floors all over the apartment. I got out of bed and watched from the doorway as Mary-Ann threw one of my boxes against the wall. Veebka's box was now in splinters; the knife had slipped out and was lying gleaming underneath the table, surrounded by lamb hair and girl hair. Matthieu had returned all my boxes a couple of days earlier, with a note saying, "Sorry things didn't work out better," and enclosing a four-color catalogue of Perry's latest broken television set extravaganza.

I didn't mind all that much to discover my career was over or, at the very least, on hold. Geniuses often suffered hopelessness in the middle of their lives. They lost faith. They pitched their work onto smoking grates and outgoing tides. They died undiscovered, and later on their lazy, ungrateful heirs lived off the proceeds of their accomplishments. I picked up a wad of wool and held it up against the wall, just to see how this aged lamb's white wool would look against a whiter background. "Feel better?" I said presently.

"*Yes.*" Mary-Ann snarled. She glanced around the floor for something else to throw.

"You're actually doing me a huge favor," I said, "though I hate to say that."

"Then I won't do it anymore." Mary-Ann kicked a box frame, which rolled clumsily, turning over and over, before coming to a stop next to the knife. "I'll *quit.*"

"Look," I said, "I can take you to wherever you want to go. I'll take you home. Patent, I mean. I do have Son at my disposal, after all."

She stared at me suspiciously. "What's that? You married or somethin'? I mean, what *else* haven't you tol' me 'bout yourself?"

"Son. Family car. My car." I had never referred to Son this way before. *My car.* I liked the unambivalent sound.

"Son?"

"Right," I said, positively relishing the name. "That's what we always call it. My family."

"That's *pathetic*, Hal. That's a loser name. Why don't you just get married, have yourself a kid? I know, 'cause you're scared it'd be a little girl, right? And you want a little boy that grows up just as bad-mannered as you—"

"What does that have to do with a car?"

"A car for your son, Hal, that sounds real pathetic."

"It's not that way," I said. "It's not a surrogate anything. I don't pour any hopes, dreams or wishes into—"

"Well, what is it, then? Like, Here comes the Sun? The Sonna God? Isn't that kinda blasphemous? *I* think it is. Jesus wasn't a *car.* Jesus didn't have wheels an' an engine, four on the floor or whatever—"

"It was my sister's," I said. "Fishie's car. Remember Fishie? She doesn't have any children, so she named it Son. It's not mine. I mean, it's my car now, but I wasn't the namer of it . . ."

Mary-Ann seemed to be quieting down. She walked into the kitchen, then glanced at the kettle on the stove. "What else can I throw?" she said mildly. "So who was that girl, anyway?"

"That was my old girlfriend."

"You still like her?"

"Yeah," I said. "I did."

"She's pretty, I guess. In kind of a slick way." Mary-Ann shrugged. "I guess she has nice hair . . ."

"Yup," I said. For some reason women were always noticing each other's hair, first thing. Thinking about Veebka, however, made me silent and stupid, and I slumped against the refrigerator door.

Mary-Ann leaned against the sink. "You have any idea what I did after you dumped me on that boat? After you *ditched* me? I went to the movies. I went to this movie theater that was showin' about twenty-five movies all at once. It was like this twenty-five-plex. Each theater's 'bout as wide as a single-wide trailer, real long and skinny. So I bought a ticket and went into some kid's movie and cried for an hour. Somethin' about a boy who swallows serum or somethin' and turns into an NYC pigeon. Everybody was tellin' me to shut up, quit cryin'." Just talking about this made Mary-Ann look like she was going to fall apart again. "I told 'em to go to hell, every last one of 'em. Then someone bitched to the usher, and he tol' me if I didn't quit, he'd boot me out. I felt like kickin' him in the balls. I coulda beaten *hell* outa that guy."

I was positive she could have. Listening to Mary-Ann rant on made me feel strangely peaceful.

"Then I go outside and there's this tiny guy with a beard out there with a camera. I'm thinkin', Well, here I am at my lowest point on earth, lookin' like total shit, you know, and finally somebody from this modelin' agency's all set to take my picture. So I act real cool, walkin' past the guy like a dignified person, but he keeps goin', Excuse me, excuse me. So I go, *What?* What do *you* want? 'Cause they like haughty models, they like it when a girl gives 'em shit. And I'm thinkin', this bearded guy's gonna send me to Africa, right? 'Cause he's got a bushy beard, I start thinkin' of the bush—you know, psychology, right? The way the mind works an' all? And then he hands me this card that says he's the Inquirin' Photographer."

I nodded. I had seen the Inquiring Photographer section of the newspaper. It always came a couple of pages before Tots in the News. The Inquiring Photographer was a one-man poll on issues like "How would you rate the president's performance?" or "Should New York City build a new, superior zoo?" For ten dollars you got a picture of your head, reduced, in the newspaper, and your answer in full, even if it completely skirted the topic.

"So this bearded guy goes, Miss, where would you go if you didn't live in New York? And I go, *Anywhere.* Patent, Texas. New York's horrible. It's cold and horrible. I wouldn't live here if you paid me a million dollars. So the guy gives me ten bucks and says I'm in the paper next week, prob'ly Thursday. And I figure, so much for that. The question here is, should I wait and see everything, or should I just say, Good-bye, New York, catch ya later . . ."

"I'd say good-bye," I said.

"But I haven't *done* anything yet."

"Well, neither have I," I said, thinking fleetingly of the genius award I was bound never to win, an image soon supplanted by one consisting of rows and rows of Wheat Thins. "You can always come back," I went on, thinking that I would probably not be around myself if she returned. "New York's not likely to close, you know. It doesn't keep—"

"*La ciudad que nunca duerme* . . . right?" Mary-Ann walked over and slid her hand across the refrigerator door. Her voice was sound. "Listen to that sound it makes. Your fingers squeak when you do that."

"Right." Suddenly I was feeling very sad.

Mary-Ann dragged her fingers across the fridge a couple of more times, and then her eyes were challenging mine. "So whaddaya make of my hands, Hal?"

Her fingers were startlingly white, her nails long and pale. I felt as though these were the hands of someone a lot older, or just somehow different from Mary-Ann. I looked into her face and then back down at her hand, the white fingers and the girl who'd invaded my apartment.

"They're quite . . . beautiful," I finally said.

"Look." Mary-Ann waved her fingers, fluttered them, then held them out as a child would. "See, there's not a bit anywhere on 'em. Not a single mark. They're like my proudest possessions on earth. You can touch 'em if you want to."

I did. I rubbed my index finger across her palm, which was small and dry. "They're wonderful," I said.

"Well, have you had your fill," she said after a minute, "or are you all eyes still?"

"They're beautiful," I said. "Really."

"You can touch 'em if you want to."

This time I touched the fingers. "Turn 'em over," I commanded softly, and she did. The back of her hand was as smooth and clear as the skin of a baby. I brushed each knuckle once, with my index finger.

"That's all you get, Big Guy," Mary-Ann said after a minute. "Say good-bye. So, now what do you do—about sayin' good-bye? I mean, how do you go about doin' that?"

"You just do it. Nobody notices anybody coming or going here." Mary-Ann looked slightly offended, so I added, "Look, nobody'd notice if *I* went, either. You just go. You can do it in broad daylight, in front of a thousand people, and not one'll ever notice. Even if you're carrying seven suitcases and a guitar."

"What'sat noise?" Mary-Ann said as the armadillo, which had been silent for ten minutes, loudly butted the bathroom door.

"Mice," I said. "Old building."

"So you'd really drive me back home?"

"Sure," I said. I had no place to go myself. "This is nearly the end of the line."

"What about Frank?"

"Frank wants to stay on a little longer, I think," I said diplomatically.

"You saw him? You saw Frank? When?"

"He was here when I got back." I decided not to mention it. Frank's triumph might upset her; he could tell her about it himself.

When I heard the front door open, I froze up. But when I looked up, it was only Fishie, shrieking victorious hellos, followed by Bob the Bowler, who refused to meet my eyes, obviously still upset about his dead dog.

Measured Miles

*M*ary-Ann was singing "My Guy" along with the radio. Her gleaming
lips barely moved as she sang, and her eyes were half closed, trem-
. . . . .bling at the edges. The station was exactly ninety-eight, but at
ninety-seven point seven a sex talk show was elbowing in as we left behind the
monuments and hot, autumn rain of Washington, D.C.

She wasn't really singing, and the noises coming out of her mouth weren't
words, just syllables chipped out of her throat. Mary-Ann's arms were extended limply, one out Son's half-open window and the other across the
buttons of my shirt, her white-gloved fingers unable to snap properly. The
country slid past us like a handrail, darkly greased and steamy.

"Nuh-ya-say-ca-tay-mah-way-from-mah-gah," she sang. "Nuh-yah-doo-
may-mah-u'tru-ta-mah-gah . . ."

When Mary-Ann wasn't singing half syllables, she was doing something
equally annoying, and I had a cold, I didn't need annoyances. A song would
come on the radio—for example, "Help," by the Beatles—and she'd look at
me imploringly. "Hal, there's somethin' I been meanin' to say to you, and that
is, *Hey,* I *need* somebody—"

"I need somebody," the Beatles would sing on the radio.   231

Mary-Ann would stare into Son's glove compartment, pretending to look thoughtful. "Hey, Hal, if I was like given an option here, well, *hey*, I think I, well, *gee*, I'd take *anybody*—"

"I'll take anybody," the Beatles sang.

"You know, Hal . . . how can I put it? Just that back when I was young"— her moody voice would wander—"aww, heck, Hal, you know, so much younger than today . . ."

"When I was young, oh, so much younger than today," the Beatles sang.

"Oh, shut up, mew, mew," I would mutter to the steering wheel. "Mew, mew, shut up . . ."

At any rate, "My Guy" was buried by the voice of a girl complaining that the phone lines had been busy all night. It was Laura, from Binghamton, New York. "Is this Dr. Baransky?" Laura wanted to know.

"Indeed it is," Dr. Baransky replied, "and I *care*."

"Oh, good," Mary-Ann said. "People with sex problems."

Laura told everyone on the road, the cigarette lighter, the road signs enmeshed with fog, the simple rest stops, the measured miles, that she was twenty-two years old and married to a man named Shep. Laura's voice was shrill, even though it was midnight on a Monday and I was somewhere on a highway dyed green on the glove-compartment map, stoned on cherry Nyquil and driving Mary-Ann back home to Texas.

"Where's Shep tonight?" I said conversationally to a road sign.

"Ssshhh . . ."

I found out that Shep worked nights and never had time for Laura anymore.

"It is because you are shrill . . . and unbearably stupid," I remarked to the radio.

"*Hal*, hush up!"

Laura had taken on a lover, a chain-saw juggler from a depressed mill town in upstate New York.

"My, that's dangerous work," Dr. Baransky commented, then she blurted, "Laura, can't Shep *juggle* you and his work better? Without the *chain saw* of indifference coming between you two?"

Dr. Baransky liked making puns using key words from her callers' lives. She also made it a point to address her callers exclusively by their first names whenever it was her turn to speak. This I recognized as an old journalistic trick—the victims actually believed the journalist was sufficiently concerned to listen to their dreary stories!

"Laura . . . does Shep satisfy you?" the doctor demanded.

In the dark Mary-Ann snorted. "My Guy" was a thin, distant melody by now, a cry for compassion from the fair side of the radio woods.

"What do you mean?" Laura sounded confused by Dr. Baransky's bizarre sense of wordplay, and also frightened by the word *satisfy*.

"Sexsationally speaking," Dr. Baransky said, "can you bring yourself to an orgasm manually, Laura?"

"Wait . . . how do you mean?" Laura answered in terror.

"Manually," the doctor snarled. "Using your digits."

"I *think* so."

"That's *sexsational!*" Dr. Baransky cried, then took this opportunity to address her scattered radio audience. "It's so important . . . the discovery of one's own sexuality, in private, behind a shut door. The most important thing to remember, Laura, is that nothing is *dirty*. Nothing is sexcemped from our own self-discovery. There is enormous joy to be had in our bodies, and it is up to us, as human concerns, to discover and refine that joy. And remember, Laura: Anything that occurs between two consenting adults is A-okay with Dr. Baransky, provided that neither of the two partners is physically hurt or crushed . . ."

Needing to study the map, I pulled over to the breakdown lane and missed Laura's response. Son whined to a halt. I could feel the Nyquil squeaking around inside my stomach, coating it in red. I was altogether wary about stopping Son on the highway, since the last time I'd braked suddenly, oustide Trenton, a hundred crickets had poured out of his front grill, dragging their black, weighted bodies across the windshield. For five minutes I couldn't see anything ahead of me except for wriggling cricket bodies, moving silently and clumsily up the windshield glass. Most of them dived off Son's roof into the milky puddles of water in the breakdown lane, but about a hundred diehards remained, holding stiff against the exhaust from other cars and the copying flight of the others. Son was a child of the country if nothing else—the automative equivalent of a pig farmer. It made sense that his insides would be infested with low-level country life.

I must say, I loved driving that car. The mythology of the automobile was something that had always been denied me—"that whole deluded, terrific USA thing," as my sister liked to say." A guy named Hal and his car, a guy Hal and his girlfriend Sal and his car, a guy Hal and his dog Butch and his girlfriend Sal and his car, a little Ry Cooder on the radio . . ." And Nyquil at large in your stomach, I wanted to add. So many times I had rehearsed climbing inside Son, shoving the seat forward in case Beck had driven him last, and pulling out into the apocalyptic heat of the summer highways. So far Son was behaving obediently except for the constant heat issuing like the hot breath of a mob from the rag-stuffed vents.

My sister had been understanding when I said I was finally taking Son away, emptying her driveway. The night before, we went out to a celebration dinner: Fishie, me, Bob the bowler and Mary-Ann. I explained to Bob about his dog, and by the end of the evening he was actually talking to me, in his slow, deeply repetitive tones. Meanwhile Mary-Ann talked to Fishie about the Coca-Cola Bottling Company.

Later, on the street, Fishie took me aside. "Hal, surely you're joshing your old sister." She began bowing her head. "This is a joke girl you hired for the evening, perhaps? Tell me I'm right. And I thought you didn't have any money, Hal, but no, you certainly had enough to hire a joke girl!"

"She's for real," I said.

"You're kidding."

"No," I said. "But—"

My sister had already pulled a wad of bills out of her pocket and begun counting off fifties. The heat that night was amazing—twisting clouds of steam rose up from the manhole covers, in streets empty of anyone, clumps of garbage festered along the sidewalks and in the gutters. *You're right to leave this place,* I said to myself.

"Fishie," I said, "you don't have to pay me anything. I'm hardly going out with this girl, so there's no need for you to ante up."

She took several steps backward and ran a hand through her brittle blond stubble. "Ah, Hal," she said quietly, menacingly—whenever Fishie starts counseling Beck or me, she sounds like a veteran gangster on the day of her daughter's wedding. "You insult me, Hal, you show me no respect . . ."

"Please—knock off the Cosa Nostra stuff," I pleaded.

"As I've said many times, I am *not* your enemy, Hal, I am your *friend.* And I see the way this joke girl looks at you across the table." My sister looked away—she was making up her mind. "Twenty-five thousand, Hal. I think you're making a big mistake driving her back . . . the guaranteed awkwardness of the sleeping arrangements I can already foresee, not to mention the dreadful states and precincts you must pass through . . ."

"Fishie," I said, "we're not going *out* or anything."

"*Please,* Hal, I'm not *that* stupid." She held up a nail-bitten, water-wrinkled hand and proceeded into her disagreeable money spiel. "That's twenty-five K, a third on signing the agreement, another third on dumping her . . . on a roadside somewhere, the final third—let me see, that would be eight thousand three hundred and thirty-three—all yours on returning alone—that's by *yourself*—from parts unknown."

"But I'm not—"

"I don't care. She *likes* you. A girl can see that about a girl. It's worth the peace of mind . . ."

A check for eight thousand three hundred and thirty-three dollars lay in the glove compartment, since my sister didn't have that much in cash. I had accepted it in a daze. In retrospect I don't really know the reason why—insurance money for the highway, I suppose. Fishie had even lent me her gas card, which I felt stiff in my shirt pocket. Leaving New York, I hadn't known which way to go, what highway to take, but Fishie was an old hand at cross-country travel and had presented me with a pile of marked-up maps. Texas was eight or nine states away from New York, but even with all these maps plastering the front seat, I didn't have the slightest idea how to get there. New York City seemed to insure that you could never leave, since you would never figure out how. Highways surrounded its corridors wherever you looked, and the elderly, sinister bridges made an elaborate maze over its rivers. But it turned out that all you really needed was the desire to leave and a faithful car—there were roads built expressly for this purpose, not to mention exit signs and tollbooths that made you feel like a child approaching them and, afterward, when you'd made it through and were out the other side, like some kind of adult.

Laura and Shep and the chain-saw juggler, whose name was Willy-Boy, accompanied us for fifteen more miles.

"Eat the dust of my son!" I cawed over my shoulder, to a cavalcade of slow-moving trucks.

"Get counseling, Laura! Both you and Shep!" Dr. Baransky finally barked.

"That doctor *always* says that," Mary-Ann complained. "That's not any answer to give."

"Give 'em some Nyquil," I slurred to the yellow stripes below me and to the left, which Son, as he sped along, seemed to be eating. I had a suspicion that if I ever got out to examine the underside of Son's chassis, I would find a million road stripes inside a small gray safe, piled one on top of the other.

"How's your cold, anyhow, Hal?"

"She's great," I slurred. "No problems here . . . with the cold. I can feel her being lifted . . . already . . ."

Just before leaving New York, I'd stopped at a drugstore and bought nine bottles of Nyqil Nighttime Cough Medicine, in both the cherry and the spearmint flavors. I loved Nyquil. It was a love without reservations, I noted proudly, like the love you feel for a child. Each bottle contained twenty-five percent alcohol, more than two beers' worth, and the containers even came with an attractive and useful plastic cap that both resembled and served as a jigger. When I called up Beck to say good-bye, I mentioned that I'd laid in a store.

"Hey, welcome aboard, sailor!" my brother had crowed from Greenwich. "Welcome to the most exclusive goddamn club on earth! That's stuff's superior, really amazing! Try it with a splash of bitters . . . some club soda to speed its energy to the source . . . of the heart. Slip into the Robe, too, Hal, the Robitussin!"

"Hal, you're drinkin' too much." Mary-Ann stared at the tiny direction printed in black on the back of the bottle. "It says here, take one cupful every six hours. And that's for adults too . . ."

"Or when needed!" I shouted unclearly. "When needed! That's a very important point! Do not skip over those lass two words!"

"You've had like a quart in the last ten minutes."

People are so slow, I thought with Nyquil glumness. Even though it was none of her business, I explained to Mary-Ann that the servings evened out. You drank two cupfuls at a time and then skipped the next six-hour feeding. You waited until twelve hours had passed! Or you drank a whole bottle at once and then waited until the next day before replenishing your veins.

"Do not ingest while operating heavy machinery," she recited like an exorcist.

"This car," I said dreamily, "This li'l car's *light*. Son is *light* machinery. Son is a *feathery* V.W., for chrissake."

"Call me later, Laura, when you've grown up enough to realize what a mess you've made out of your life." Dr. Baransky had grown tired and said, "And remember, Laura, I *care*." Whenever the doctor uttered those two words, her voice deepened electronically: I C-A-A-A-R-R-R-E-E-E. It scared me.

"Have a li'l Nyquil, Laura," I slurred again.

Erroll was calling Dr. Baransky from Provo, Utah.

"*Provo.*" Mary-Ann snorted. "That's where the *Osmond Brothers* come from. Yuckerama. You know it's a fact you can't even drink a Coca-Cola in the whole *state*, it's against the religion or somethin' . . ."

"May I ask you something, Erroll?" Dr. Baransky intoned. "Are you a member of the Church of Latter-Day Saints?"

"Yes, I am," Erroll said.

"I knew it," Mary-Ann said. "I just knew he was a Mormon. He sounds like a real tightass—"

"Sex knows no religion, Erroll," the sex doctor said confidently. "It can be just as sexciting if you're Mormon, Jew, Christian, Black, American Indian, Korean, orange or purple."

"Baransky, shut up!" I screamed at the radio. I hated any liberal racial sequence that ended with the word *purple*.

As I drove, Mary-Ann stared at the radio as though it were a darkened television set. Erroll was a shy man. He used words like *thingie* for *penis* and for *vagina*, until Doctor Baransky said, with astonishing curtness, "Erroll, what you're doing now is infantile and regressive. Grow up, Erroll, for God's sake!"

"Aww, poor Erroll," Mary-Ann said.

"Give 'im some Nyquil," I suggested, by now drowsy and unreceptive to any sympathy offered to strangers in radioland.

Erroll's problem, it turned out, was that his new wife wanted him to "talk dirty." However, he was too embarrassed to repeat the words his wife wanted him to say.

Mary-Ann turned the volume down slightly. "Hal, you like bein' talked dirty to?"

"You mean when I'm driving?" I think I said.

"No, like when you got somebody in the old sackeroonie with you . . ."

I turned onto Exit 27. Son's breath was a stuffy lapping against my leg, and the pant leg was sticking to the tingling bone in my left knee. My mind was blanking out—cherry Nyquil and lack of sleep. It's easy to forget you've been driving at all when you've been out on the road for thirteen hours. It's easy to forget you even have a body.

"Hal . . ."

"What?" I sprang back to dazed attention.

"You like it . . . when people start talkin' to you when you're tryin' to be all solemn and holdin' it all together? Say stuff like love throttle and things like that?"

Luckily this had only happened to me a couple of times. I'd once been forced to tell the woman I was with, "Will you please be quiet," and then, "I'm afraid I am really going to have to ask you to keep your voice down, please," and then, when both these responses failed, "SHUT UP! GET OUT OF HERE NOW! LEAVE IMMEDIATELY, I'LL SEND YOU YOUR CLOTHES!"

Dirty talk filled me with chagrin and sorrow. You went to bed with someone to rest your voice, not to start up a whole new conversation.

"Guys, they like it sometimes if you say dirty stuff. They make you say, like, Oh, I'm enjoyin' this so much, you know, when I'm really not at all, like you weigh seven hundred pounds or something' an' I'm bored outa my mind—gee, what a nice ceilin' you got, you know, you got great beams 'n 'all. But since I'm an actress, I can even make 'em believe it, I can put it over. And the boys never even notice the difference."

This, finally, was something we agreed on, but I wasn't about to talk sex with Mary-Ann, even though this was one of her few topics. Once Fishie told me, with her usual *omerta* affect, that whenever a woman—usually a woman over thirty—brought up this topic, it meant she was interested in you. "With few exceptions," she said, smiling her opaque smile before jumping off the diving board and vanishing under innocent blue water. "Otherwise," Fishie resumed, coming up for air after what seemed like an hour, "the woman, she'll smile politely, obliquely enough to make you want to smash her, and she'll change the subject, Hal, to, oh, dominoes or incense or books you haven't read, and wouldn't be likely to have read, either."

"That's the most disgusting thing I ever heard!" Dr. Baransky screamed. "Counseling would have no effect on a mind such as yours, Erroll! Zero!" She hung up on him.

"What did Erroll say?" Mary-Ann said. She jiggled my shoulder. "You hear what it was he said?"

"Hello, Walter from New Orleans," Dr Baransky resumed.

I shook my head, too busy plotting out our trip to answer. It would take three or four days to reach Texas: that is, if nothing evil or remarkable befell Son, Mary-Ann or me. Patent lay in the upper right-hand corner of the panhandle, nearer to Oklahoma than to the perfumed heart of the Lone Star State. I concluded from the maps that eight to ten hours on the road a day would take us to Patent before the week was out. We were taking a strange route, too, away from the interstates, so I could see the countryside at the same time.

Mary-Ann kept urging me to take a third route, the picturesque; she wanted to drive along dirt roads, stop at carnivals, ride the Spider, buy Pronto-Pups and Dilly-Bars and Karmel Korn and such like. Several times she mentioned a tour of Graceland.

"No," I mumbled. "No to Graceland, no way. I don't even *like* Elvis, uh, Elvis, uh . . . Elvis *Presley.*"

"But, Hal, he was my *dad,*" she whined. "I could sue his estate for millions and millions, Lisa Marie and me could be, like, step—"

"Look," I said, "we've been through this before and he was *not* your goddamn father."

"But he might still be alive! There's been sightin's of him all over the place! Like in supermarkets, I think it was in Michigan they kept seein' him. I mean, he's supposedly gone an' grown this beard and muttonchop sides an'—"

"No," I interrupted. "No more on this tired topic. And besides, Graceland's *overdone.* As a symbol and a fashion statement it's become meaningless—it's vulgar, sad and empty." I told Mary-Ann, if we took the picturesque route down to Graceland, this drive was liable to take several years. I didn't explain that these backwater towns of the South frightened me witless. I imagined nightmarish scenarios in which I was tortured by two giggling rednecks named Mitch and Ollie and forced to play the banjo while Mary-Ann danced Scottish reels and played the Jew's harp.

Outside of New York, I didn't even know how to act. "How should I dress?" I asked Mary-Ann before we left. I didn't want to stand out in America by wearing the wrong style of pants or an unacceptable shirt. I wanted, I *needed,* to blend into the angry hoards of shoppers grazing the malls and parking lots.

She recommended against anything baggy, or else people would think I was a professional clown, that I worked the circuses for a living. "Wear what Frank wears—no one's ever made funna him for the way he dresses. You know, nothin' all that formal, no ties or nothin', no coats . . . I mean, you can wear a jean jacket but that's about it . . ."

I neglected to tell her that no one made fun of her brother because they knew he'd squeeze the blood out of them in his tight little fist.

Outside Mount Nebo, Virginia, I asked Mary-Ann to get my other pair of glasses. She hauled my bag into the front seat and stared down in horror at my clothes.

"You wear these guys?" Mary-Ann held up a pair of light blue boxers. "These little ol' guy C.P.A. things?"

"Well, yes," I said, "I do."

"Awww, don't wear *these*, Hal. You forgot everythin' I said? This is like coverin' your body with a big pup tent or somethin'. Amy Stardust and me when we were like thirteen, we'd get high and put on her daddy's boxers, then stick flashlights down there and walk around like we were boys. They was just like these ones. Why don't you get somethin' a little sexier? You brought along those jeans I got you, didn't you?"

That particular pair, I thought gratefully, were in the back of Bob's bedroom closet, where I'd hurled them in a frenzy. "May I have my glasses, please?" I said.

She handed them to me. "When I get rich someday, I'm gonna send you like three cases of *real* underwear, Hal. To go under your new jeans. That's what boys wear . . ."

I wished, and not for the first time, that Mary-Ann wouldn't use the word *boy* all the time. She said it the way elderly homosexuals and battered Southern women did—yearningly, romantically, as though the idea of *boy* was something uncorruptible: a lean, blond, thistlelike figure tipped against a barn, or a Greek cornice, after finishing his chores, or his degradations.

"Ellie, turn your radio down! In your room, Ellie! Now, Ellie!" Dr. Baransky shrieked.

Mary-Ann tossed my bag into the backseat. Son's old, black, skin-tattooing vinyl squealed underneath her elbow like something newborn. "Where we gonna spend the night?"

That part, at least, I had planned. "Kentucky . . ."

"You know any folk there?"

Folk, I thought gently. Sometimes Mary-Ann used words that endeared me to her, and *folk* was one of them. "No," I said.

She was quiet. "Where we gonna stay, then?"

"I really don't know."

"You know any good places?"

I gargled with another capful of cherry Nyquil before responding, "Nope, but I wish I did."

Mary-Ann cleared her throat as Dr. Baransky, overcome by feedback, disconnected Ellie. "I don't have that much money on me, Cat," she said solemnly. "I sure as hell hope you do."

Even in my stupor I saw where this could be a problem, but I didn't say anything. I like to pretend I'm a big spender, a high roller, even when I'm combing through rugs and couches for dimes and nickels. I had three hundred and fifty dollars in my wallet, not to mention Fishie's gas card, and her uncashed check, and that was the extent of my riches. My American Express Card had been revoked several weeks before, when their man had called at seven in the morning and woken me up and then, while I was still groggy, demanded that I work out a payment schedule. I told him I didn't feel like it. In fact, I wanted to start afresh, just as the first settlers to this country had begun sowing fresh fields when the old ones eroded and blew away in the wind. "Haven't you ever heard of tabula rasa," I said to the man. "Why don't you and I, working closely together, usher in the dawn of a new era, an era in which we honor our ancestors instead of just *criticizing?*" He'd become very angry, threatening me with legal action and the promise I'd be hearing from him again soon. *Damn* American Express, I thought after hanging up. Their cards were cheap-looking, anyway, especially the gold model, which looked like a urine patch in the snow. Besides, I'd been happy in the arms of a splendid dream before he called.

"We can borrow *lots* from my mom when we get home," Mary-Ann said. "Mom's always glad to help people out of a jam—who's this on the radio, Artie Shaw or somebody?"

We had lost Dr. Baransky just before the Virginia border, in a locality known as Bob White. Now a local rock-nostalgia station was playing "Moon-dance," the antique Van Morrison song.

"Artie Shaw?" I repeated.

We spent that first night at the Thrifty Scot Motor Lodge, just off the interstate in Miss Lucie, Kentucky. We got a small, squalid room with two beds separated by a low table, and a dirty white rug that smelled of creosote and old cigarettes, and then I ran across the interstate to Tina's Nipa Hut for a pizza we ate in the room. The box read, WORLD FAMOUS and YOU'VE TRIED THE REST, NOW TRY THE BEST. What could you do? Call the Better Business Bureau, maybe, or sue someone? Unless all the pizza shops and barns in the land were under the same management, they were all compulsive liars who no longer even bothered to cover their tracks.

While Mary-Ann was taking a shower I stared out the windows onto the interstate. In that part of the world nothing looked familiar. It would've been reassuring to see the jagged borders, the *shapes*, of the states as you passed through them, the way you saw them drawn on maps, but once you were lost inside a state, its borders were distant and invisible. Once you left New York City, everything was the same: all the towns had sidewalks, dirt, sky, lawns, graveyards, and these sidewalks of Kentucky looked just like the sidewalks of Illinois or Pennsylvania. Only the green road signs told you where you were, in Dixon, Guthrie, Goshen, Horse Cave, Wink Hollow or wherever.

Mary-Ann went straight to sleep, but I stayed up late, juggling the pizza crusts. At one point I had four crusts going in the air at once. Soon, though, I tired of my brilliance, but television's the same all over, too, and there was nothing to read but the Bible, so I read the part about Adam and Eve. Unfortunately I already knew what happened—snake—so after a while I closed my eyes and tried to sleep while the trucks kept passing through the Kentucky night.

When I woke up at around seven the next morning, Mary-Ann wasn't there. I found her eating breakfast at the coffee shop in the back of the motor lodge. On the way in I noticed a huge black Lab who was leaping hysterically and uselessly at a row of gray shingles that composed one side of the motel. Once she was satisfied with her grip, she wrenched the shingle off and trotted over to the edge of the parking lot, where a large pile of chewed wood was already stacked. There, holding the shingle down with one thick black front paw, she ripped it into strips before loping back to the hotel for more.

I joined Mary-Ann at a table from which I could see a TraveLodge, a Koala Inn and a cluster of small, beaten-up houses stretching down the road, and then the road itself disappearing behind the start of a measured mile. The sky above resembled an enormous pool of spoiled milk. Ten yards beyond the Thrifty Scot parking lot, past a dirt driveway, nailed to a tree beside a rain-bearded mailbox, someone had hung an outsize, upright wooden hand. I looked closer and read in the fleshless palm: BILL AND SALLY DENHAM. WELCOME. WHAT'S OURS IS YOURS.

"Now that's pretty sad," I remarked after I'd ordered breakfast.

"What's that?"

"That little house . . ." I gestured weakly at the Denham's driveway, the wooden greeting. "That little house, buried in the middle of nowhere."

"This is Miss Lucie, Kentucky," Mary Ann reminded me.

"I know. I know it's Miss Lucie, but where the hell's that?"

"Right here." Tattoos of Kentucky adorned both our place mats, and Mary-Ann was pointing to a green, grinning star that was captioned YOU ARE HERE.

"No. I know it's Miss Lucie. But it's also nowhere. Miss Lucie's lost in the middle of the country. Which makes the Denhams, Bill and Sally, doubly, triply, quadruply, *lost*."

"So what's so sad about that? I don't get what you're sayin'."

"Oh, nothing." I didn't really know what I meant. "It's just—" I stopped. "It's just this little house in the middle of nowhere in particular, and that upsets my sense of . . ." Again I couldn't finish. What was I trying to say?

"This is Miss Lucie. *Kentucky*, Hal. This is the breadbasket of the nation— the dark and bloody ground, for heaven's sake." Mary-Ann was reading these phrases off her place mat, which showed places of interest—cannons, racetracks, battleyards and golf courses—all around the state. "Dan'l Boone's from here. So's the Kentucky Derby, and juleps. There's Mammoth Cave, there's a bunch a whiskey distilleries . . . a lotta little horses and all. Isn't the Black Stallion from here? That book horse? And Misty? Misty outa Chincoteague?"

"The Black Stallion is dead," I said cruelly, "and so is Misty. What I suppose I mean to say," I went on in a lower voice, almost a whisper, "is just that here are the poor Denhams, Bill and Sally, one of ninety million Denhams here in this country, and they're *buried* down here in their little house . . . with their wall-to-wall carpet, their Andy Williams and New Christy Minstrel Singers albums, their length of green hose hanging off a hook on the basement wall. And Mr. Denham—Bill—he won a bowling trophy last year, but it was only for being the best bowler in this *county*. It wasn't even statewide! And then in the winters here, dust starts floating up from their brown carpet, and Bill and Sally both start sneezing as though they'll never stop and—"

"Don't be so patronizin' of people, Hal. You're always—"

"Okay," I said, "It's not so sad. I said it was because I can't think of another word . . . sad for lack of a better word."

"Well, you better think up another, 'cause Bill an' Sally're prob'ly happier than you'll ever be in a hundred—"

"Listen," I said, "are you gettin' a little defensive? You who's always criticizing these dirtball towns for being, and I quote, *stupid? Dumptown*, I believe, is how you characterized your place of birth . . ."

In the dull stillness that followed, I imagined my own—the schools and universities, clubs and pastimes, the rehab clinics and doughnut joints, the broken cookie factory, the tennis courts, public and private. Outside the coffee shop, the black Lab wrenched off a splinter of windowsill. Already she had bitten through to the insulation, and fluffy pink clouds clung to her lips. That dog is eating this motor lodge, I thought mildly.

"So you remember what I said," Mary-Ann said, sounding pleased.

I was still hunched forward. *"You're* the one who wanted to come to New York, because you said, no place else was quote-unquote *big enough."*

"New York's *disgustin'*, Hal. Too noisy an' too big and too filled with garbage from people. There's no *life* there. You don't get any sense of what folks are all about, there's just like these boxes all over the—"

"You mean, my boxes?"

"Nope. Just plain boxes. You go out to dinner in one, you go to the movies in one, you work in one all day long. Then you come home to your own box. Then you go, like, what box'll I go visit tomorrow? Maybe the grocery-store one or the dry-cleaner's one or the—"

"Where's our waitress?" I interrupted. "That dog's going crazy! I'm hungry! Maybe that's *her* dog!"

"I don't know if she'll come over *here*," Mary-Ann said cooly, "you were so patronizin' . . ."

"You're the one," I said, "who's always putting these people down for not being sophisticated . . ."

"Now, what people, Hal?" she said innocently.

"The so-called 'little people,'" I answered.

"I never said anything bad about them. You must've got me confused with that ol' Voodoogirl, Verplank, or whatever her name was . . ."

I watched as Mary-Ann unpeeled the paper from her straw and squeezed it between her thumb and index finger, until it was an inch in length. Putting it aside for a moment, she dipped her straw into my water glass. Then, pressing one finger over the top, as a kind of stopper, she trapped a half inch of water inside the straw and held it over the pulverized straw paper. She released her finger and a drop of water fell heavily. The wet straw paper sprang to life, softly jerking, unfolding like a snakeskin.

"Jesus," I said softly.

"Look, it's growin'," Mary-Ann said. "Like my *love* for you, Hal." Seeing the look on my face, she added, "Just kiddin'. Actually I don't like you one bit. I think you're kind of a box yourself . . ."

We left Miss Lucie at eleven, an hour before checkout time, and headed toward Tennessee. Even though the sun was still bright, I was already thinking about money. I'd attempted to pay the motel bill with my American Express Card, just to see what would happen, but my card number was already listed in a floppy gray catalogue containing the names of delinquent customers. Three months in arrears and I was already listed in the Hall of Shame! I was forced to pay eighty dollars cash instead, not to mention the money I'd already spent on food.

Mary-Ann had stared down at my rejected green card. "Why don'tcha get one of those gray ones, Hal?"

"Gray?"

"Yeah, there's the green 'Merican Express, then kind of a yellow, and up on the top there's this gray one."

"Platinum," I said. "Why don't I get a *platinum*? Because it's possible to go . . . too *far*."

"How's that, Mr. Bowler-Doctor?"

"Well, there's very few people—people with any money—who carry the gray, the *platinum*, ones. Really rich people insist on green and—"

"That don't make much sense, does it, Hal? Are you *really* rich or somethin'?"

"No, but even if I were, I wouldn't. They give you this enormous line of credit but—"

"Then why's your sister got one?"

Fishie had paid for dinner with hers. "Because," I explained, "she swims a lot in the Third World, and they're very impressed by that color over there. Plus, she's always forgetting her wallet—her cash, I mean. She does it over and over, she's practically the ideal candidate for platinum. It's the combination . . ."

I then explained, painstakingly, that we'd have to sleep the next night, at least, in Son himself.

"No way, Jose! I'm not sleepin' in this car. I don't even *like* this car!"

"Don't insult Son!" I roared, for the Nyquil was again beginning to take effect in my limbs. "Be thankful you even have a goddamn *ride*. I have better things to do than to ferry a little ingrate cross-coun—"

"*Brother!*" Mary-Ann whistled. "Brother, Hal . . . this car's gonna keel over an' die any second now, and you expect *me*—I can't believe you!"

Something, in fact, was wrong with Son. Ever since we'd left the Thrifty Scot, he'd been driving erratically; a joint within the steering mechanism must've slipped, since it took two or three turns of the enormous black wheel to execute a right or a left turn. Only massive doses of Nyquil—the spearmint flavor, for I'd already built up a somewhat unattractive tolerance to cherry— softened the edges of this mechanical fret. Moreover, Mary-Ann had been acting distracted all day, playing with Son's knobs, teasing him, smoking up the glass with her breath. She stuck her bare feet out the window and pointed at other drivers with her big toe. She repeatedly pushed in the cigarette lighter, and after pulling it out, she'd fence with flies on the inside of the windshield. "I got the four-walls-and-one-dirty-window blues," she started humming outside Macedonia. "You know what I'm gonna do to you, Hal?" Without waiting for me to answer, she said, "I'm gonna cut your throat and drink your blood like wine. Then you know what I'm gonna do? I'm gonna take your dead head, Hal, and *throw it out the damn window.*"

I just ignored her. Most of the time I didn't even know what Mary-Ann was talking about, and too many other things occupied my mind—my rising paranoia, for example. Thus far I'd determined that my own country was a violent, sinister place, and I couldn't shake this idea no matter how much Nyquil I slugged back. In Tennessee we drove past miniature armies of boys and girls clustered around false mall fountains, or else slumped outside in the parking lots. Both sexes wore military fatigues, and their black T-shirts wore names—Anthrax, Whitesnake, Metallica, Iron Maiden, Megadeth—and bottles of poison silhouetted frenziedly over the stomachs. The presence of these quiet, bellicose suburban tribes gave the harmless towns we drove through an aura of suppressed menace. Some burgs seemed to trade exclusively in religion and guns: their church boards read, THE WAGES OF SIN IS DEATH and SUFFER LITLE CHILDREN, and that sounded to me like a threat. Bumpers read, INSURED BY SMITH & WESSON and DON'T SHOOT, I'M CHANGING LANES or DON'T LAUGH, WE HAVE YOUR DAUGHTER IN HERE. I kept Son over in the right lane most of the time. He couldn't possibly keep speed with the other cars, and I wanted to protect him as long as I possibly could from the recklessness of the left and center lanes.

That night we parked at a rest area outside McMinimum. Mary-Ann stretched herself out in the front seat and tortured the radio dial to a country station, then she reached around and locked all the doors. "I'm scared of these guys, you know, one arm comin' 'round, and they got like these rusty hooks for left hands they drag across the roof. Then they kill the boy, an' when he's dead 'n' gone, they do horrible things to the girl—with the hook, I mean . . ."

In the back I scrunched up my duffel bag under my head and waited for sleep. Once again this night, Son was a banana republic, sultry and tropical—lying there I wanted to chatter in Spanish—and even once the engine was cold, a hot and mysterious air continued to pour in through the vents. "I hope you don't sleepwalk," I muttered.

"Uh-uh. I sure don't." Mary-Ann propped herself up on top of the front seat, and I realized then that she'd been waiting for me to start a conversation. She ran an improbably gloved hand across the black leather. "Used to have a cat that did, though."

"Yeah, yeah, sure you did." Ever since Kitty had flown out the window, I'd felt zero interest in kitties, or kitty-related themes and imagery.

"She did. I swear. Ask my mom when you meet her. Ask anybody I know. This cat went out like a light 'round six P.M. We'd all be in the kitchen havin' whatever meal we were havin', and we'd look up to see Marie—that's her name—and she'd be makin' this slow, kinda crafty beeline toward the table. She looked like this fuckin' zombie, you know?"

"I'm sure she'd just woken up," I said stiffly, remembering the many stoned, unpleasant glances that Kitty had thrown my way, "from her nap."

"Nope, she sure hadn't. She was sleepwalkin'—don't look at me like that, Hal. Her lids were flickin' 'round, just like someone who's dreamin, and that tail stuck straight out like a ramrod. So we led her back real careful to where she liked sleepin', 'cause wakin' up a sleepwalkin' animal does heavy damage to their insides—I read someplace it actually makes 'em mentally deranged. Anyhow, we got these pictures showin' Marie doin' it, just ask my mom."

I certainly didn't want to meet Mrs. Mary-Ann, whom I pictured as an enormous woman with camel hips and a beehive haircut that reached for the stars. My plan was to drop Mary-Ann off at the first Patent exit and let her walk the rest of the way.

Mary-Ann curled herself up across the front seat. " 'Night," she said presently. "Those crickets are pretty noisy, aren't they?"

I nodded, and the vinyl under my head squeaked yes, no, maybe. Nyquil settled over my body like darkness, and when I shut my eyes, I saw the armadillo again. Right before dining with my sister and Bob, I'd called up Emergency Services who, when they arrived, shot the armadillo in the ribs with a muscle relaxant. When it was out cold, they threw a large blue net over its calm form and carried it downstairs to their truck. The armadillo had looked coldly beautiful laid out on Bob's floor—I almost wanted to keep it, to train it to serve me."

"Hey, Hal! Don'tcha wanna go to Graceland?"

"Nooo," I slurred, the vision of the armadillo replaced by one of the horribly still, bloated corpse of BB.

"Don'tcha even like that one song? That Paul Simon one? I mean, maybe if we did, your cold'd get better."

"I don't follow you," I mumbled. "Graceland isn't a fucking *spa*. It has no holy healing waters, and besides, I have my Nyquil . . ."

"I think you're abusin' that stuff there, Hal . . ."

"Every patient is different," I choked. "Every cold patient has his, or her, or its, own private tolerance level to medicine. Plus, my cough's at least a hundred percent better by now. Sleep yourself well, honeybunch, don't let the bugs bite . . ."

The next morning I woke up with the distinct impression that someone was dripping water from a washcloth onto my face. I burrowed more deeply into Son's plastic seat and put one sweating hand over my forehead and eyes. Then I moved my pant leg slightly and felt the fabric grip my calf like a warm, wet vise.

It was still raining, and all of a sudden I remembered that I'd left a window open. Fishie had always warned me—the proud next owner—about this obvious pratfall, and now here I was with sour, tobacco-smelling juice pouring onto my face, arms, legs and neck.

At first I was still. I listened for crickets but could hear only the soggy descent of the dawn rain into the pines. Probably all the local wildlife had drowned. The rain ticked down in heavy, dark beads onto my bag and the synthetic black seat, drenching even the seat belts. I sat up and looked over the front seat at Mary-Ann, who was still sleeping idiotically.

"Mary-Ann," I whispered, "let's get up."

She didn't move. *Maybe she died during the night,* I thought. *Maybe I killed her accidentally in my slumbers.* I'd always thought that when Veebka slept late in the morning that during the night she had tried to draw a breath and had a bit of pillowcase caught between her lips and suffocated. I would then proceed to her funeral, wearing extremely dark glasses, and attempt to read something at the service, but midway through I wouldn't be able to continue. People would point and say, in hushed voices, "That was the boyfriend. *Christ,* he was good to her, she was happy for the first time in her life . . . If it hadn't been for Hal, she would've died accidentally, sordidly, *a whole lot sooner.*" At one time or another I had killed off all my girlfriends in this very way.

Mary-Ann had the initial of the car lock tattooed on her cheek, a dented, reddish acorn. "Shit!" she yelled. "Shit, I'm soppin' wet!"

"Uh, your window's open too," I mumbled. It was six in the morning and the sky was beginning to lighten with the most depressed-looking clouds I'd ever seen.

I extracted myself from this calamity and stood in the warm rain that flowed down my collar, wondering what to do next. Behind, me, Mary-Ann slid out wearing only white underpants and a red T-shirt. Now, with his front door open, his frame and windows beaded with rain, Son looked like an ancient and disappointing shipwreck. "Shit!" Mary-Ann barked. "I've gotta go to the bathroom."

"Well, go ahead," I barked back.

She disappeared beyond some disordered wooden picnic tables into the woods off the rest area, while I began mopping up Son's insides with a shirt that I liked the least of all the ones I'd brought along on this awful road trip. This swabbing method was so useless that I wanted almost to switch over to the free *Star Wars* cup we'd been given when I filled Son up with fully leaded gas outside Cornelia. Obviously the pump jockeys of America never thought they'd ever have to give away anything, since most cars these days took unleaded, so everybody offered lots of cheap, free merchandise if you filled up with the old lead-ridden gas. This was a crucial mistake on their parts, because Mary-Ann and I had made out like bandits at every station we'd pulled into, and Son was now loaded down with all kinds of worthless trinkets and plastic baubles: cups, caps, gift certificates for hand lotion and hamburgers, and about fifteen different car deodorizers.

Anyway, the upholstery smelled rotten, bothered, the rain and the smells of a night's sleep making the old black vinyl raw and spongy—almost like leather—soaking even the straw stuffing inside the seats. I was still swabbing the backseat when I noticed that Mary-Ann's white purse had spilled over in the front, and that loose items had fallen out. Now, I hated this low-rent purse—it was flabby and ridged, and it made me think of dead cows and, farther along, the abattoir. I stuffed her makeup back into the pockets, the lipsticks, mascara, eyeliner and rouge, a small gold bottle of something called Seduction, and I stared down at what remained on the black seat.

Mary-Ann had saved everything. The tall, stiff folder her plane ticket to New York was encased by, the dated stub from Greyhound, the stub from the Circle Line tour, a torn movie ticket, white price tags from Bloomingdale's and two mood rings and a space decoder we'd picked up at a gas station outside our nation's capital. There was an open pack of Gummi Worms, a jar of red Tiger Balm and four pre-rolled joints wrapped inside a silver gum foil. She'd saved an envelope filled with shattered glass from New York sidewalks, and inside a Band-Aid box I found a rubber diaphragm wrapped in dry white tissue. The last thing I picked up was a small red notebook.

Normally I'm not a nosy person, but if a strange notebook falls into your lap, when the author has vanished into the woods, it's tempting to look at it, or at least to casually glance through its contents. Besides, I told myself sneakily, *she* looked through *your* wallet. The notebook had Mary-Ann's name written and underlined on the top left-hand corner, and I tossed it into the seat. What Mary-Ann had written was none of my business, and would I like someone reading my five-volume *Kitty Journals*, in which I traced my pet's every hesitation and exaltation from infancy to final flight? A couple of minutes later, though, when Mary-Ann still hadn't returned, I opened up the note-book and started leafing through it.

There were poems, a grocery list I guessed she'd written before coming to New York and a page that said, in ten different scripts, "I want to die, ha, ha! I want to die, ha, ha!" I skipped past Dustin Hoffman's forged signature and the genuine autograph of his agent's sister. Many spreads were empty, but I kept turning until I found some writing. The final page, marked "Memory Things," had two separate columns; the first labeled "Things I have to do: Professional": and underneath a list including "Call Mom's friend's friend. Use conditioner *two* times after shampoo. Drink tons of water. Keep pelvis forward at all times. Move like a dancer. Keep toes *out*. Learn more about customs of Africa."

Alongside was a second, longer column labeled "Things I have to do: Personal." This list looked as if it had been abandoned midway through. "Learn more about the world of medicine. Bowl more. Learn about parakeets and gerbils. Learn history of Olympics (Hal's sister) so you can give dates, cities, etc. Read books, see movies Hal has read and seen, so you can have *long discussions* about them. Learn how to make rabbit-pellet mix, H. likes it. Get H. to talk about Kitty, since this was a sad thing for him. Act *sexier*. Negligees, perfume in little hole in neck, etc. Remember: Mind is erogenous zone supposedly, not just ass, tits, etc. *Do not forget this!!!!!*"

Colored with guilt for having picked up the notebook in the first place, I couldn't read any more. I was also—I'm loath to admit—flattered. Before laying the notebook down on the front seat, I did reread that passage about me two or three more times.

When Mary-Ann came back to the car, she knelt down on Son's front seat and started brushing out her hair in the rearview mirror. She didn't seem to notice that her purse had been moved. "I wish I was a boy," she complained. "Oh, and this is my mother's underwear, you know, I'd never wear borin' old stuff like this . . ."

We drove around the top of Missouri for a while, lost as you can get, and Mary-Ann had the road map spread across her dark, bare knees.

"Find me seventy-nine," I murmured.

She traced her nail up and down red strings struggling across the sheet, where the numbers of the highways bubbled like blood clots in a vein. "Here's Minnetonka," Mary-Ann said, almost to herself. "Wayzata. Saint Bonifacious up here—but we're in this blue part now . . ."

"Seventy-nine," I said, "*please*. Before this intersection." I glanced down into Mary-Ann's lap, where instead of Missouri I saw Minnesota. "Damm it!"

I yelled. "You're way north! *Missouri!* For God's sake, that's where we're supposed to be! *Down* three states!"

Directly in front us us, gray roads split off, one pushing out straight, another forking, a third looping around the intersection and disappearing. On the right a sign read, SLOWER TRAFFIC, KEEP RIGHT. I didn't want to be identified with that crowd, so I repaired to the middle of the highway, somewhere between dissolution and safety. There were no other cars on the road, here where decisions are always momentous times, and this was a moment of truth.

"Mary-Ann," I said gently, after a minute. "Seventy-nine."

"Hal, I'm *lookin'*. Here's forty-one. And here's four. No, make that four-A. This one goes all the way to Tupelo or someplace. So maybe you don't want that one. But they got Dad's birthplace there, and some kinda little museum with all his gold records stuffed along the walls. And a bunch a karate stuff, and his guns—"

"Gimme that fucking map," I snapped, grabbing at it while Mary-Ann held tight to the corner, and the sheet promptly ripped in two.

"Sorry," she murmued, looking at me guiltily. "I was just kiddin' around, Hal."

I slowed down to about two miles an hour and then pulled over to the side of the road. I studied the road map while the brake lights lit the bushes red behind the rasping exhaust pipe. Son felt like he was about to explode. I could hear Mary-Ann breathing seriously next to me, and the low, wet click of her lips. She sniffled once, then brought some of her back hair around for inspection. For her, every time the car stopped was an occasion for vanity. She'd turn on the overhead light and gaze down at her fingernails or start pulling at her bangs or else take out her makeup kit and start grooming her eyes.

Seventy-nine ran through the center of Memphis, so that's where I headed. In a couple of hours we were on the outskirts, and twenty minutes later we turned down a long commercial road. As I drove past various stores and restaurants Mary-Ann read off the names under her breath. "Mingo's Hamburgers, White Castle, Chi-Chi's . . . Jingle Bell Poultry . . . Family of God Lutheran Church. There's Sergei's Bowlatron . . . the Rabbit Hole . . . Welcome International Federation of Meat Packers . . ."

It was a worn, airless night. You could see the humidity even in the darkness, like a stalled white wind. McDonald's arches towered over the highway like a stalk of prize-winning corn. Up high, moths fluttered under the beams of the street lamps. This was more Mary-Ann's part of the world than mine: the farther we got away from New York, the more relaxed she became and the tenser I got. She knew the names of things—the stores, supermarkets and towns—whereas I didn't, and without names I felt at a terrible disadvantage.

We drove through Memphis's business district, where the streetlights seemed like floodlights. Kids were sitting on benches, smoking, bored stupid as the glow reflected off their caps and long hair. There was no one else at large.

"Let's see what those babes are up to," Mary-Ann said as we drove past.

"No thank you," I said, "let's not."

"If you see a drugstore of any kind," she said, "I wonder if you'd do me the favor of pullin' over . . ."

When I asked what she needed, Mary-Ann didn't answer. "Huh?" I said.

"Some feminist items," she said primly.

I spotted a pharmacy on Mud Island Avenue and followed Mary-Ann inside, mainly because I needed directions to Arkansas; moreover, I'd run out of my favorite nighttime cold medicine. Even though my cold had improved dramatically, I thought it might be wise to keep drinking Nyquil—to prevent myself from ever getting a cold again! A maintenance dose, as it were.

The drugstore was just closing for the night. Its corridors smelled of clean plastic products, chain-made and retailed by trucks from all over the country; you could've closed your eyes and been anywhere in America. Behind the counter was a very fat woman, and beside her a fat little girl in a red shirt and tight pink pants. The girl was about five years old, with blond hair parted down the middle.

I followed Mary-Ann up to the counter, but she suddenly turned around. "Hal," she said, "why don't you go browse around in the men's section? I'll only be a quarter sec . . ."

Though I couldn't bring myself to explain that drugstores didn't really have men's sections, I wandered up and down the various aisles, anyway. The closest thing to a men's section was the athletic-injury aisle—mostly yellowing jockstraps hanging off peg hooks, knee supports, Ace bandages and cushioned insoles for your sneakers. I fingered the stretchy bands of a jockstrap, just for something to do, then I went over to a far corner and stood looking at alarm clocks and brown and black combs.

After a while I joined Mary-Ann at the check-out stand, just in time to see the fat woman stuffing a box of Tampons into a shiny brown paper bag. Mary-Ann was looking the other way and, at the same time, trying to block what the clerk was bagging up.

"Excuse me," I said to the fat woman. "Do you know where I could get onto Route Seventy-nine? To Arkansas?"

"Where you two tryin' to get to?" the woman said.

"Texas," I said, "ultimately."

"Well, you're in Tennessee now, right? Oh, I think I maybe overcharged you for them Tampaxes. Don't wanna be cheatin' your wife. Now, you, Sir, can cheat on her all you like, but that's your own very personal business. I always say, you can goose the goose, but then the goose can go screw the gander." She cackled. "My business is tryin' to keep the day's receipts straight and narrow. Dinah," she said to the little fat girl, "be a lamb chop and go check the price on these Tampaxes, fourth aisle down beside the home pregnancy tests."

Dinah ducked under the counter but didn't duck low enough and almost decapitated herself. I was about to complain about the wife business, but then, I thought, Who cares? Mary-Ann's face was still averted, and she was picking through the top of the display rack, her fingers going from green Trident gum to pink and to red and cinnamon, then bouncing down to the Reese's Peanut Butter Cups.

Dinah returned, head and all. "Four ninety-five," she said. Her high, prissy voice made me wonder if she'd been sucking on a helium hose all night. She crawled underneath the countertop on all fours, like a farm animal petrified of thunder.

"Thanks, darlin' . . . You want some of that Bubblicious too?" the woman said to Mary-Ann. "Or wild strawberry, maybe? The orange's awful good, that's Dinah's personal favorite."

"So any ideas you might have about how to get out of Memphis," I said moodily, "would be really welcome."

"Hal," Mary-Ann said, laughing, "you sound like Dorothy and her red shoes."

"Where you two be hailing from?" the fat woman said.

"New York City," I answered.

"The Big Apple," Dinah mewed in her distorted voice. She was standing next to her mother, peeling the label off a bottle of generic barbituates, her fat little arms resting on the counter.

"The Big Apple." I chortled in the manner of a Rotarian or an Elk. Rotarians lived peaceful lives consisting of slapping smaller men on the back and wasting entire days at the lodge, and the Elks, well, the Elks just drank a lot.

"If this town's the Big Apple," Dinah sang, "then let me take a bite . . ." With her fat hands she pushed back from the counter, then she looked up shyly at me. "Michael Jackson."

Her mother rang up the Tampons for the second time. "Must be nice to be outa that hellhole. I was up there once, all I remember's pictures of monkeys screamin' from lab experiments. On every street pole, pictures of monkeys in agony. Their jaws all wired up, little electric box lunches in their heads, their eyes crazy from—"

"Does seventy-nine maybe pass through this part of the world?" I asked, interrupting.

"You know, we got a lot goin' on *here*, too. Good newspaper, passable symphony—"

"I just don't know," I mused nonsensically.

"Say, you been to Graceland yet?"

"No," Mary-Ann said, glancing at me quickly. "But we want to."

"It's big business mostly," the woman said. "Yessir, I bet Elvis'd roll over right there in his grave. That is, if he's *in* his grave. You know, *Elvis* is an anagram for *lives?*"

"It's also," I noted impolitely, "an anagram for *vesil*. And *seliv*."

The dull white numerals spun to a stop behind the filthy, olive-colored glass of the cash register. Meanwhile Dinah sang "If they say, Why? Why? Tell them that it's human nature . . ."

"Whaddaya think?" the fat woman said, fixing Mary-Ann and me with a suspicious, appraising look. "You think she has what it takes? She's memorized that whole *Thriller* by heart."

"Takes for what?" I said, appalled as Dinah plowed into the next song, gazing straight ahead of her into the rows of toe clippers and mirrored sunglasses.

"She's doin' Adelaide now, from *Guys and Dolls.*" The clerk had to raise her voice to be heard over Dinah's racket. "I swear, she has the presence for it already—for her age, I mean—the whole thing, even the talk they do between songs. Sometimes I go into her room without knockin', and there she is in front of the mirror, holding a bottle of deodorant for a mike—you know, a *microphone*. It's the cutest thing you ever seen in your life, second cutest be those panda bears in China, but I hear those two don't even like each other."

She looked at me earnestly. "You don't know anyone in New York City who works with little ones? Who'd cut Dinah a deal a some kind?"

By now I was backing up. "Well, no," I said, "I don't."

"That's all right; even so." The woman suddenly laughed. "You don't happen to know Michael Jackson personally, do you?"

"No," I said—too tired, sore and lost to pretend Michael was my dearest friend on earth.

The woman flashed me a brief, hard smile. "It was a long shot, anyways." She handed Mary-Ann back her change, coin by coin. "I got Dinah a tape of that *Thriller* album, one with just the behind music, no singer. But the same musicians—so she could sing along, not havin' to duet with somebody she never met before. This November we go to Nashville and—"

"About that Route Seventy-nine," I blurted. "That Arkansas road we were looking for?"

"A poyson," Dinah sang, "could develop a cold—"

The fat woman cupped her ear. "Can't hear you so good . . ."

"Look," I said wildly, "can't you tell Dinah to take a break?"

"Dinah, darlin'," she said, "pipe down a sec. The man's tryin' to say somethin'. . . . In answer to your question, I don't know where this Seventy-nine is. All I know is where my own house is at, the motor vehicle, Dinah's little school." She peered down at her daughter.

"I don't care," Dinah sang passionately, "what they may think of me. I'm happy go lucky, they say that I'm plucky. Contented and—"

Loudly, over Dinah's shrill voice, her mother said, "I know where Dinah's father's at. I *do* know where the best swimmin' lake is. Penscot—twenty miles away but worth the extra gas." She scrunched up her face. "I don't go out on the highways much 'cause they scare me, eight, nine lanes, right lane, fast lane, breakdown—"

Briefly I gave up on people, sick to death of agreeing with strangers about nothing at all. If you said you were from New York, everybody thought you were a talent agent; everyone unburdened themselves onto your helpless head. What I needed was a dose of my favorite nighttime cold medicine. "We'd also like four bottles of Nyquil," I said.

"You mean, the cough stuff?"

"Hal," Mary-Ann started to say, "I do think—"

"The cherry," I said immediately preferring cherry to spearmint, which obviously tasted too medicinal. "Four containers, if you can manage."

"*Four?*" The woman shook her head. "You must really got a helluva cough goin'—"

"I cough," I snarled, "about all the time."

When I had paid for the Nyquil, I was in no mood to be charming. Behind the counter, Dinah waved good-bye and attempted to manipulate her body into a split but instead crashed up against some pill canisters, scattering them. When we were nearly out the door, I heard her mother say, "They can't help, sweetie. But there's all the time in the world."

Back inside Son, Mary-Ann bunched up her shoulders and looked out the window. "You got a real problem with that Nyquil, Hal."

I uncapped a fresh bottle and took a swig. Almost immediately I could feel the cherry-red river washing away all my irritations. I held out the bottle to Mary-Ann. "Want some?"

"I don't *have* a cold," she said. "And, anyways, if I did—"

"Neither do I," I snapped, slugging back another mouthful.

We drove down an abandoned strip of the commerce district. All the stores were closed except for the bars, whose parking lots were crowded with cars and trucks. By then I was exhausted and still had no idea where we were going; the map lay on the floor, wadded up under my feet. I had given up trying to find the magic Seventy-nine, which I'd begun to assume was just a misprint. My new plan was to drive and drive until someplace looked final.

While I was figuring out which road to take, Mary-Ann was babbling about the drugstore woman. "Did you see how fat that lady was? I mean, don't people *care*? I mean, do they get married and then there's like this one moment where their eyes like, meet, and all eyes, all four of 'em, they let out this giant sigh of relief, like *Wheww*, let's gorge! Finally we can gorge! And if that fat kid wanted to go on a diet or somethin', right, that fat mom wouldn't give her any help. She'd just hand her a Twinkie and say, Eat *that*, little piglet. My mom, she got married, but she keeps in shape still. Got a butt on her you wouldn't believe."

In the blackness the only colors we saw were yellow, lime, red—which someone a long time ago had chosen for everything at night. We were in the suburbs now, and there was a leaden and concave beauty to the houses, darkened except for the violent, stabbing, respiratory flashings of a thousand televisions. At the end of the street we finally drove past a house with a single light ringing out from a second-story window.

"Look at that . . ." Mary-Ann sounded thoughtful. "One little pasty-faced teenage boy up there jerkin' off. Thinkin' of somebody, some girl from ages ago. Everybody else dead asleep, dead, dead, and that one little critter's stayin' up so's to be sexy with himself . . ."

The dark lawns outside the houses were quiet except for the *thwick-thwick-thwick* of the sprinklers turning in a threatening circle. I could see the side of one house drenched as the sprinkler water splatted it, then it was left alone to drip as the water turned toward the street, spraying water over thatched edges. Then I remembered that a lot of people in the Armed Forces came from the Midwest, and it made sense that they kept their lawns as crew-cutted as their heads.

"Wanna go pay that little kid a surprise visit?"

"Not particularly," I said.

"Why not, Hal? He's *lonesome!*"

"Because we don't know him," I said. "And I refuse to knock down the door of someone I don't know. Anyway, it might be someone sick or old, not your teenager. Someone crippled. Probably an old woman sitting up watching *The 700 Club*—worship for shut-ins—"

"I think it's a lonesome boy, Hal, and I know how he's feelin'. This *ain't* a sexy town, period. This town has like zero sensuality in it." Mary-Ann rolled down her window an inch. "Wake up, Memphis!" she bawled. "Everybody wake the hell *up! Do* somethin' for once in your whole lives . . ."

She gazed back at me. "It's only ten-thirty, Hal, so why the hell d'you s'pose there's no lights on anyplace?"

"Will you please be quiet?" I said, reaching over to roll up her window, but Mary-Ann caught my hand.

"I want somethin' to *happen*, Hal," she whined. "Anythin' at all. You be at all interested in doin' somethin'? And, aww damn . . ." She paused. "I gotta go to the damn john again."

"You went," I reminded her. "You went earlier."

"It's not a onetime thing, Hal. It's not like Expo 67, where they just do it for a while then tear all the rides down . . . You gotta keep doin' it over and over again. Plus, my throat's parched, and I think I got a little fever. Here, feel my head."

Mary-Ann grabbed my fingers from the wheel and pressed them to her forehead. "Feel."

"It feels like the wing of a sculptured ice goose." Cherry Nyquil tended to make me grandiose, I expect. "Not like the hot breath of a slavering pack of wolverines—"

"Well, that's bad, ain't it? Like, it's extremes, right? Beware of extremes, that's what my mom says. When you got the extremes, start worryin'. It's fever either way. It's chills prob'ly, but it could maybe be TB or AIDS or somethin'. Do I look like I have anythin'?"

"Nope." Mary-Ann's face, half in shadow, the roots of her bottom teeth showing, her lips gleaming, looked fine to me.

"Why'nt'choo ever look over here, Cat? Where I'm sittin'? You think you're drivin' here all by yourself? I'm sittin' here lookin' as good as I ever have, and you're just starin' at the dumb road . . ."

I kept my glazed eyes on the pointless, narrow, empty road.

"Ah, don't you wanna go to some better city, Hal?" she said softly a moment later. "Where people always cook oysters for each other and drink champagne all the time? Where you wake up and immediately set to doin' a buncha sexy things?"

"Because we happen to find ourselves in America's *breadbasket*," I shouted, "thanks to your lousy sense of direction! Where would you rather go—Reno? Las Vegas? Lake Tahoe? We left one sexy city already, remember?"

"Not my fault, Hal. If the people was nicer, I just might've honored 'em with my presence a little while longer. But all I want now is to go to the leak-oir—hey, look, there's a river . . . I wonder what that one is . . ."

I turned on her. "What river do you *think* it is? The Tigris and the fucking *Euphrates*? That's the Mississippi, for chrissake."

Now, from the highway, Mary-Ann saw something she actually recognized. "Hey, there's a Target. They got bathrooms, 'least the ones I been to did, and they're open real late too . . ."

Target, as Mary-Ann explained in riveting detail, was a department-store chain that covered the South and the Midwest, selling just about anything ever manufactured. Their ambition was to knock out every other little store for miles around; you could do all your shopping in a Target and never have to go anywhere else. "There's almost too much junk in 'em," she finally said. "It's a little bit overkillin', ya know?" This particular Target took up about four acres of Tennessee soil and was flanked by an enormous parking lot filled with arrows and arc lights, trash cans and yellow paint bleeding into the pavement.

I'd never heard of Targets, but since it was seemingly the only place open at that hour, I parked Son and we got out and started walking toward the bright automatic doors. Just in front, on the sidewalk, a boy in a wheelchair was waiting patiently outside a brown van, while a lift attached to the rear slowly lowered to the pavement.

Mary-Ann stared without saying a word. "Poor little thing. I got an uncle in one of those chairs, fell off a horse named Calvin and smashed himself up. But everybody's handicapped these days, ain't that right, Hal? I read that someplace."

I sort of shrugged my shoulders.

"We're all of us handicapped in some ways," she said, "aren't we? I mean, like the detective says to the hooker, We're all prostitutes, Sister, when you come right down to it? They always say that at the end of those TV crime shows . . ."

"I have no idea." I didn't feel much like talking.

"Well, Hal, all I'm askin' for's a little agreement once every few years, for chrissake! I mean—"

"Yes, we're all handicapped," I snapped. "And we're all prostitutes. We're all handicapped prostitutes! Does that make you feel less loathsome?"

Above the bank of automatic doors, an enormous, blood-red bull's-eye was painted on the wall, a theme repeated inside the stitching of the brown rubber floor mats. Bathed in yellow fluorescence, I felt like a captive within an enormous, prosperous country; the other end of the store seemed as far away as my hometown. As I walked along I kept passing groups of young blond girls, no older than seventeen, many of them carrying babies who wore tiny T-shirts sporting Iron Maiden and Anthrax and Twisted Sister logos. These babies, evidently, were rehearsing to be members of the mall platoon, and the few girls without babies smiled brightly at me. "Hi," they said, "how you doin' tonight?" Shocked, I said hello back. It had been a long time since anyone had greeted me in a department store, and certainly never in New York. Actually it had been a long time since anyone had greeted me under any circumstances whatsoever.

When Mary-Ann came out of the bathroom, she dragged me over to the fishing section where green-and-white coolers were stacked like bricks on the top shelves, and rods hung down over the bright white floors like green nylon whips; small plastic packets of crawdads, shagbugs, grubs, jib heads, bug bodies, leech rigs; not to mention the collections of bagged tackle, spinner-baits, fish-'n'-filet knives, rod racks.

Next to Fishing was Glassware, which took up the entire fifth aisle. Meanwhile country music was playing gently over the concealed store speakers. "Been down at Pete's," Mary-Ann wailed, "been shootin' some pool. Bartend's mixin' drinks, he's talkin' outa school."

"Stop it." I snarled.

"Why should I stop what, Hal?"

"Because I hate country music, like I told you. It's whiny—"

"It is *not* whiny."

"It *is*," I said. "Sentimental and whiny. And repetitive: verse, verse, chorus, verse, verse, chorus, chorus, fade out, end of song, boredom, inertia, stupor, coma. You've heard one, you've heard 'em all."

"Well, I love it. It's good music. And it's not even *country*, it's just good music. Country just means the whole country listens to it. It ain't called city music, Hal, you might have just noticed. That's where we beg to differ. 'Sides, it's what I grew up with. It makes me feel like I'm in a truck goin' down some road alone . . ."

I wandered past stacks of snowy cups and wineglasses, and Mary-Ann followed behind. "Randy Travis would just *loathe* you," she said in a low voice. "He'd think you were just another Yankee with his head up his ass, or else he'd spit hard at you. That's what Randy'd do—he'd use your face for a gutter. Merle Haggard an' Vern Gosdin'd just laugh in your face, knowin' right off who's the better man. And Emmylou'd just say, Oh, yeah, I know Hal. Not my type."

Mary-Ann started pulling things off the shelf. She opened a package of wineglasses, unbuckling the cardboard wings, and ran a finger up and down the stem. Each glass had a garland of pink flowers around its bottom. She held one up. "You like this?"

I didn't answer.

"I didn't mean that. About Randy spittin' hard on you."

I pretended to be looking at plates, and what ugly plates they were. An offer underneath the display announced that you could superimpose a picture of your dog or your family or your new baby onto the plate and then laminate the image. *Great,* I thought, *eat right off your loved one's face.*

"Hal, I didn't mean what I said. You're a fine example of someone who's a good man. I meant, you don't care about all that rigmarole, and that's a good thing. It don't matter if you're wearin' boots or not. Emmylou'd like you a lot, I know she would. She'd never in a million years kick you out of the sack. For eatin' popcorn or anythin'. Anyhow, who cares what Emmylou thinks?" Mary-Ann hesitated. "I like you lots."

"Okay," I said briefly.

"Hal?" Mary-Ann stood in front of me and waved. "Hello?"

"Yeah, hi," I said. "Hi, hi, hi."

"So you didn't answer my question, about what you think of these glasses."

I said, "I like plain ones," even though there were none in sight. Every single glass was decorated, some with cartoon characters, or fleshy babies without sexual organs, but others with various animals, alive and dead, and automobiles of every sort.

Mary-Ann looked at me apologetically and started repacking the glasses. Her shoes slurred softly against the aisle floor as she turned around. "I reckoned you would. I knew that already partways." She paused. "I got the worst taste in most things, I can't help that. It's nothin' to get all snobby about.

My mom's the same way. Show either of us two things, one's white, the other's purple, and that purple gets the nod every time. The good white stuff goes right over my head. You're either born with taste in things or you don't get it. I know the glasses without crap on 'em are better, but I just like the ones with petals and clowns and shit. They seem fancier. Oh, hold on to your seat, 'cause I know they're *not*, really. Simplicity is like, the hallmark of elegance, right? But I end up pickin' the flower ones, anyway."

"Let's get out of here," I said.

"Now, why should somethin' without flower petals be in better taste?" she went on. "I don't get that. I think they should change that."

"Because," I said, "that's the way taste works."

"So what's not in food taste?

"Lots of things." I began babbling. "Those glasses you just picked up. Lake Tahoe. Most of California. An excessive interest in . . . your family gen-ealogy. Plastic slipcovers on furniture. Rubber outdoor pools. Homilies mac-raméd on pillows. The expression 'apple crisp.' People named Mark." I looked around wildly. "Most of the things in this store—lots of things . . ."

"Well, like what?"

"Mount *Rushmore*, for instance. Mount *Rushmore's* in bad taste—"

"Well, why?"

I stood there, uncertain. "You just know."

"So what else?"

"Well, there's a blank check—*giving* someone a blank check. Or getting a wedding invitation that says, In lieu of gifts the bride and groom would prefer huge cash gifts. Or dressing your dog up in a little plaid sweater, that's in bad taste . . ."

Mary-Ann was silent. Then she said, "Well, I like all those things. Nothin' wrong with a blank check you can write anythin' on. Make yourself an instant milionaire, it don't count! And I think dogs in sweaters're adorable, maybe if you'd put BB in a sweater she'd still be kickin' . . . So what else is in lousy taste?"

"Graceland," I said. "Makeup. Lots of makeup on a girl . . ."

"I wear lotsa makeup and I'm a girl."

"I know that," I said. "That's what I'm talking about."

"So what you're sayin' is I don't have good taste? I still don't get why Mount Rushmore isn't in good taste. I think Mount Rushmore's kinda cool, if you want my humble opinion. I never been there, but I seen pictures that make it look pretty cool. And Graceland's *huge*. Elvis even had a waterfall put in right there in the livin' room—"

"The only reason to go to Graceland," I said, "is to laugh at the sheer . . . excess and . . . terribleness of it all."

"Hal, that's not nice."

"Well, whatever," I said. "Let's get out of here."

"So why's makeup in such bad taste?"

"Because it looks *cheap*, it looks like a little smudge of *Graceland* on your cheeks."

"Now you think I'm cheap?"

"No," I said desperately. "I think lots of *makeup* is cheap. On a woman. And I don't want to talk about this anymore. Let's go."

"We don't have much gas, remember? Why don't we just stay here tonight?"

"Where?"

"Here." Mary-Ann stamped her foot. "Target. Right where you're standin'. I can't take another evenin' in that car. Hal. I wrecked all my clothes last night, everythin' smells like the rain. And people aren't curved to sleep out in cars. Well, girls are more than boys, maybe, but not really. Except for some times but they're just for a little while. At least I don't—"

"How do you propose we spend the night here in this *department* store?"

"Easy. Cinchy. We just hang out in the stockroom till it shuts up, and then we come out."

"What if we get caught?"

"Then we say we didn't know shoppin' hours ended already. Cinchy. You got me with you. People are nice to boys with girls. It's the natural way, you see. Like there's this group of boys late at night on some dark street, and you think, Uh-oh, they're gonna mug me an' kill me an' rape me, and then you make out two girls with 'em and you go, Brother! Whew, was that ever close! Like they're not this pack of weird people if they got some girls along. Girls *tenderize* situations. They're like steak sauce that way. And I'll be your tenderizin' girl. I'll be your A-1 sauce. Your A-number-one sauce . . ."

I had to admit, the idea of spending another night inside Son didn't exactly thrill me, either.

"Come on, Hal. It'll be fine."

"Well." I dragged my sneaker toe around in a circle, like a humble, careful man.

"And there's tons to eat. You said you were hungry, didn't you?"

We had to wait until eleven, when the Target officially closed. At ten forty-five I followed Mary-Ann through a door at the rear of the store that read, EMPLOYEES ONLY, and hid in the back of the stockroom behind two washing machines still in their cardboard crates. Fortunately no one was working the graveyard shift there, and only a couple of janitors passed through as we were lying on the floor. Only one big redneck boy came close, a pile of flesh with tiny red eyes whose job it was to push boxes, grunting, into customers' cars. A greasy curl of hair was rounded up by a green rubber band at the back of his head, and the brown tag on his jeans read, HUSKY. We listened to him thumping around inside the shadowy pantry beside the stockroom door. Twenty minutes later the door shut behind him. It was twelve-thirty.

"What if we're locked in here?" I whispered to Mary-Ann. "What if Husky Boy's standing guard out there?"

"Who cares, Hal?" Mary-Ann shifted her body like an iguana rearranging its scales on a rock. "I mean, big deal. I mean, the worst that can happen is there'll be some misunderstandin'. Like me sayin' like, I got this boyfriend who's easily confused an' all—"

"I'm not your boyfriend," I said.

"That's just a figure of speech, Hal," she said primly. "*Brother.* I meant boy-who's-a-friend. I don't know why you're this official grammar person all of a sudden . . ." Presently she sat up. "The big lights've gone out. That crack under the door's all black."

We waited in the stockroom for ten more minutes, then started toward the door. When Mary-Ann touched the knob, it made a loud click. I sat back, listening for Husky Boy noises—the grunts and sudden exhalations for which they're justly famous. Then she slowly turned the knob and drifted off into the vast darkness of the store. In a minute or so she called my name.

"It's like the big sky country at night," Mary-Ann shouted hoarsely. "We got the whole joint to ourselves . . ."

I joined her at the doorway. Where an hour earlier there had been yellow fluorescence, now all was black gel. The shelves rose in the darkness as still as the hills of a garbage dump at night. I shut my eyes, then opened them again. It seemed lighter behind my eyes than in the store. The only exceptions were the exit signs, red scars that shone dully over the doorways.

Mary-Ann disappeared down one of the aisles. I stood my ground, occasionally tapping my foot to remind myself I was real. Mary-Ann was gone for only a short time before I heard her voice call my name from the other side of the store. A dim light rose up in the back aisles near the bathrooms, and when I reached the end of the telephones corridor, I saw that this was the lamp section and that Mary-Ann had turned on several hideous sale items.

Mary-Ann leapt out at me suddenly, from behind an aisle, and sprayed something in my face. At first I thought it was mace.

"Aaagghh!" she screamed, holding a can in her hand. The air was filled with a sweet, pungent aroma. "Now you're a *sandalwood* face, Hal! I like that smell on a person. Sweat's like my all-time favorite smell on a boy, but sandalwood's at least number two . . ."

I was wiping the sandalwood off my face with my shirtfront. "Dammit!" I yelled. "Don't rush out at someone like that! And don't spray that goddamn crap on me!"

Mary-Ann acted as if I hadn't said a thing. "That's what they do to you in Bloomin'dale's. You're just kinda walking' along, and every time you go 'round corners, 'nother person blasts you in the face. It's kinda like runnin' a marathon and havin' people hose you down every other mile. I just wanted to make you feel at home, Hal. I mean, if you're missin' NYC at all, Bloomin'dale's, et cetera. There's English Leather too. Here—" Mary-Ann held out her wrist. "See if you like this. It's called WomanFire. You like that smell on me?"

"I can't tell," I said, still wiping myself. "I have all this other crap on me."

"My mom used to have a boyfriend who liked his English Leather, all right. You know, that stuff's about fifty percent bourbon or somethin'. She'd go, Daniel, what *is* that thing you're wearin' that's drivin' me so crazy with sexual desire? And after a while Mom figured out he didn't have it back behind his ears or anythin' but on his breath. He drank it, Daniel did, when there was nothin' else handy. He says to us this time, All her men drink English Leather, and he's pointin' to my mom when he says that . . ."

I noticed Mary-Ann was holding a beer in her other hand. The label read, DAMM'S BEER. "Where'd you get that?"

"Oh, someplace over there. They're on special. They're pretty warm 'cause they're out, but they still got their bubbles."

"You mean, you just took it?"

"Sure I did, Hal, don't be lookin' so mad and anguished. I left some money, two bucks. All I had on me, just about. That's more than it ever cost them. They're makin' out on this, our bein' here, they get everythin' whole-sale, anyhow. I mean, beer's two-fifty for a six, and tax an' all, but here I'm payin' the wholesale price. I think that's fair enough."

"I don't think we should turn on all these lights," I said.

"I put 'em on 'cause I wanted to feel homey. Mom always puts on all the lights even if it's just me and her at home. She says, People'll think you and I're havin' a party just among ourselves. Mom's always doin' things like that. Anyhow, there's a lot of good stuff over there, Hal, if you're still hungry. They got this special on Pringles potato chips. Those are the chips that touch each other, you know, in a roll. So pull up a chair, pull up a glass, eat up, for God's sake . . ."

"We can't just eat whatever we like," I said.

"Why? Anyhow, drinks are on me, so drink up, Hal, drink it all on up. Or as Mom used to say, All the drunks are on me. I think we should have like a little party . . ." Mary-Ann gave me a huge, gleaming smile. "I'm in kind of a let-loose kind of mood tonight."

I said, "I'm going to bed."

"Yeah, where you plannin' on sleepin'?"

"I don't know," I said. "I'll find some dusty crawlspace somewhere." Actually, and obviously, I hadn't thought about this at all. I could sleep over in Legware. Legware, I seemed to recall, took up two aisles, and in one of those aisles was a huge white hamper filled with soft stockings, and this would be comfortable enough.

"I can try another perfume," Mary-Ann said presently, "that is, if you really dislike this—"

"All I can smell is sandalwood, anyway, so don't bother."

"I put lots on you, I know it. Sorry."

"I know," I said. "I know you did."

Mary-Ann was silent. "Fine," she said finally. "You just go to bed." I couldn't hear what she muttered under her breath.

I wandered off and soon found myself in Sporting Goods, looking down on one of those huge children's floats for swimming pools. The float was in the shape of a large pink grapefruit, with huge triangular sections stitched out from the center. There were down sleeping bags stacked on the shelves, and I brought one down for my bedding. I decided not to work out before I slept—they say it makes your heart gallop. That night I wanted my heart to lie particularly still. I lay down on the grapefruit float and stared up at the black ceiling. Thirty feet away from me I heard the crunch of potato chips being eaten. Soon another light came on, a glow that rose up like a stretch over the aisles, expanding until the ceiling was washed with a pale silver glow. I heard Ed McMahon's voice, and his loud, appreciative laugh. I heard *The Tonight Show* orchestra playing their collective heart out, Doc Severinsen whipping them higher and louder and louder.

I got up after a while and made my way over to the Home Entertainment Center. I couldn't sleep with all that racket going on, nor could I sleep with sandalwood all over my body. I couldn't sleep, period. Turning the corner, I saw that Mary-Ann had at least twenty sets going at once. The televisions were arranged in descending sizes, from big to little, on the shelves. Mary-Ann was sprawled out on the floor in a funnel of blue-white TV light, drinking a beer, not watching any set in particular but instead gazing vaguely and determinedly at all of them. There was a row of empty Damm's bottles between her thighs. She was using one as an ashtray, but the butt at the bottom wasn't extinguished, and a frail, shaky fog wobbled up from the bottle's mouth.

When Mary-Ann wasn't gazing at the multiple televisions, she was leafing through a pile of color photographs, the yellow sleeves shucked onto the floor next to the empties. Above her head, twenty Johnny Carsons tossed their pencils into the air, and all twenty pencils dropped behind the flat brown desk. Roars of applause issued from all twenty TVs.

"Could you please turn at least one of those down?" I shouted.

Mary-Ann lolled her head back, eyes shut. "Turn it down yourself, Hal, I ain't movin', I'm comfortable. I found these photos. Over there in the personal pho-toe section. Of all these families from 'round here, these

Memphis families . . ." Mary-Ann flashed me one of the pictures. "Look at this ugly fish this fat guy caught, Hal. What is it, a slime trout? A sea shit?"

This was extremely annoying. I systematically turned off each of the TV sets, surprising myself by wrenching the knob off number eight. I threw it over my shoulder into the dark, where I heard the plastic carom over the empty linoleum. I could feel Mary-Ann's eyes steering into my back.

"There's some naked people in these photos, too, woo woo," she said. "Brother, if I was takin' naked pictures of somebody, I'd never send 'em off to a Target to get 'em developed. I'd do 'em myself. I'd make a darkroom some-where and do all the printin' on my own, 'stead of havin' to walk over to the photo counter and get that I-seen-you-naked-and-now-I-want-more-a-that look. You know the look I mean . . ." She gazed down at the picture in her hand. "This lady looks sad, don't she, Hal? But she's cute. Betcha she can—"

"Put those away" is what I said. What I thought was, *You're going to end up like Great-aunt Loreen.*

"You wanna brewski, Hal? Halski?"

By now I had worked my way up to the top shelf, turning and twisting and extinguishing the light. The volume in the store was getting more bearable, but I still had about seven sets left.

"If you wanna watchski somethin' elseski, you may have the useski of that big color Sonyski over thereski. Johnny Huckleberry Head's havin' an anni-versary show. I can't believe Johnny's been on for so long, you know?"

"Thanks a whole lot," I said, "but I think I'll decline." I was standing in front of the Sony, trying to find its knob. A moment later I gave up and yanked its plug out from the wall.

"That's my favorite TV of all of 'em. The one you're in front of, it's the best set on the whole floor. The sharpest picture. And it's got a little box thingie so you can see two channels at once, one big one and one little one inside a cube. And its re-mote control looks like a pistol, that's why I'm givin' it up to you, Hal. 'Cause it's my personal favorite. So you can be Pistol-Hal instead of just plain ol' Hal. *Brother,* I'm such a nice guy I can't stand it. It must be totally hard bein' me . . ."

The only set still playing in the dark store was another big-screen monitor.

"Hal, you think I'll ever make it to *The Tonight Show?*"

"No," I said as cruelly as I could, then added, "Only as a representative of some *zoo* somewhere."

"Bet you my brother could get me on. He could kidnap Johnny and say, You let Mary-Ann on your long-runnin' show to show off her wares, or else your days're numbered, you got that, Johnny?"

This was the first time I'd thought of Frank in a few hours. Every time I pulled into a town I expected to see his rotten face staring down at me from a billboard. "I don't want to talk about your brother."

"That's 'cause you're so jealous. You pretend you aren't, but you sure are, Hal, and I bet you thought I didn't know that. It's like this internal fire inside you, that jealousy, or these termites eatin' you up . . . Damn, it's hot in here. I think they turned off the AC, those dumb bunnies." Mary-Ann replaced the home-porn pictures inside their yellow packet and opened another sleeve. "Hey, look, here's a weddin'. Somebody's weddin' pictures. How old's this girl, do you think? She looks like she's about six, six an' a half, and she's gettin' married already. Here's a fat girl playin' the harp—that's real romantic. Angels play harps. Why don't you ever play the harp for me, Hal? Look at all that food. I can't make out all the food they got. They must be rich. I bet you they have lots of those gray American Express cards. Maybe they got a fan department here—oh, and hold on to your seat 'cause I got us an alarm clock, by the bye. It's one of those ones that turns off if you yell at it. It rings and rings, you say, Shut the fuck up, li'l clock, and the li'l clock does it just like that. It's sonar or ESP or somethin'."

"Mary-Ann," I said, "did it ever occur to you that some of these items are rigged with sirens? That you pull something out from one of the walls and this whole store will start howling?"

"This ain't New York, Hal. People down here trust you. They *like* each other. It's not like New York where the clerks follow you 'round the store and keep askin' you if they can help, even though all they're doin' is keepin' a sharp eye out. Boy, am I ever glad to be outa that dump . . ."

I started walking uncertainly in the direction of the bathroom. There was more light in the front of the store, since floodlights hung from outside the revolving doors, cocked out toward the parking lot and trickling a ghostly light back inside the store, illuminating the exhibits of the front aisles; in one aisle I saw eight different women's legs coming out of the wall, bent like the Rockettes', a different-colored nylon on each. Inside the bathroom, I washed as much of the sandlewood scent off myself as I could, then stared at myself in the mirror for a long time. I looked different. My face showed low, winged lines where my cheeks met my mouth. *You're looking old*, I said to myself. I washed my face again as though soap could remove the oldness. How had my face gotten old so quickly?

Back in Home Entertainment, Mary-Ann had switched channels. Now she was watching an old black-and-white movie with Olivia de Havilland as twins, one mad and judgmental and the other sweet and good. She'd taken off her clothes and changed into a pair of silky green boys' gym pants and a little pink bra that made her breasts look stiffly triangular.

"So what do you think a my new outfit?" she said. A white price tag hung below one of the bra straps. "Sexy, right? Shouldn't I maybe have a whip? I'm like this kitten with a whip, 'kay? Y'ever seen that movie, *Kitten With a Whip?* Ann-Margret or someone?"

"Where'd you get that?" I said wearily, knowing the answer.

Mary-Ann put her hands on her hips. "Lingerie, where do you think?" She tossed me a plastic-wrapped package. "Hey, and I got you some underwear too. Skimpy little things."

"I don't wear 'little' underwear," I said.

"Well, you should. Take it from a girl in the know. Take it from a girl who's fast on the uptake. Hey, you know what's a sexy thing?"

"Good health?" I said sarcastically.

"Nope. It's a boy who's leanin' down from the back so you can just see the rubber snap, the white snap, of his underwear. I go Woo-Woo to that. Now *that's* sexy, an' it's even better sometimes if he's wearin' the colored stuff . . ."

I said, "You can't keep ripping off this store."

I noticed that Mary-Ann had opened up another bottle of Damm's beer, about her seventh. I sniffed. "Are you smoking a joint in here?"

"Sure. Why, you want some?"

"Listen," I said. "This place is probably rigged with smoke alarms, and when they all go off at once, I'm warning you, I'm going to say I don't know you, I've never met you, I don't *want* to meet you and—"

"I don't give an effin' eff. I don't know you, either. Never even met you, sure I wouldn't like you one bit if I did . . ."

I gazed at Mary-Ann and she gazed back at me. "I'm kinda bored out here," she finally said, breaking her gaze. "Drinkin' all this beer just makes me unhappy. Unhappy with my own destiny." Suddenly she looked miserable.

"We have to get up by six tomorrow," I said. By the time the store opened, I wanted to be deep into Arkansas, and nearly to Patent by nightfall.

"Aww, Hal, don't you wanna stay up an' play tonight?"

"How do you mean?"

"Oh, I dunno. Dance or somethin'. We got all these major compact disc things all over the place. I won't put on any country. We could put on the city stuff. All the stuff *you* like and—"

"Nope," I said. "I'm going to bed."

I left her there, a puddle of Southwestern girl sprawled in darkness, with only a beam of colored light from the Olivia de Havilland good twin–bad twin movie to light her path to bed. I crawled back to my grapefruit float and lay there for a a while, my knees raised. I still stank of sandlewood, and I took off all my clothes trying to get rid of the smell. I broke open the package of underwear that Mary-Ann had thrown at me, just so I was wearing something. The underwear was even tighter than the jeans she'd given me. After a while it got so cold, I put my pants on again.

When I woke, a shape in the darkness was moving toward me on tiptoes. "Hal? Are you 'round here someplace? Are you sleepin'?" She crashed into a display and something tumbled to the floor. "Aw, *shit.* Come on, Hal, where are ya?"

"Right here," I said.

"Where?" Mary-Ann was so close that her ankle was almost in my face, and I smelled the sweet reek of marijuana and beer.

"If you move any closer," I said, "your foot will enter and widen my lungs."

"Jesus, there you are!" She knelt down beside me. "Maybe there's another float up there I could sleep on? We could be like campin' buddies, 'kay?"

When I told Mary-Ann there were plenty of floats on the wall and all she had to do was reach up and grab one, she sighed and her knees cracked and then I heard the sound of something heavy being dragged down off the shelf. "I'm gonna let a little air outa this one," she said. "This is kind of a princess-and-the-pea deal here . . ."

Mary-Ann got settled and I heard the slow, rich gasp of air from the compressed raft. "Hey, now I feel like a millionaire," Mary-Ann announced. "I even got a place to put my beer. I could get 'faced and read a magazine at the same time. Hey, butler," she called out through the empty lanes of the store. "My butler ain't comin' 'round tonight," she said a moment later, sounding disappointed.

"You left the television on," I said after a while.

"Oh, I kinda like keeping TV on, Hal. It's the voices, you know? I like it when the voices are goin'. It gives you two best things. Like if it's the middle of the night and you're in bed or somethin', you got two best things goin' at once, voices and you all by yourself. You have voices, but you don't have people standin' in front of your bed starin' at you, you know? I remember when Mom used to have parties, I'd be upstairs in bed and I could hear the voices, but I was all alone too. It used to make me incredibly happy . . ."

"Well," I said finally, "good night."

"You remember how in that store that fat lady thought we were married?"

"Well, she was wrong."

"I hate it when I get my period, which is now. If you were my husband, though, I'd announce that sort of as a matter of course. I wouldn't feel embarrassed, plus it would involve you, anyhow. I wouldn't sneak around buyin' tampons while your back wasn't lookin'. That's why I'm feelin' so mean today, my PMS—actually, it's not even P anymore, just MS. But if you was my husband, you'd accept that and go, So Mary-Ann's havin' her period, my, what a fact of life that is, that's just so unweird . . ."

Then she said, anxiously, "Hal, would you mind if you just put your arm 'round me? My shoulder? I'm not sayin' we have to do anythin' more. More than that. Just your arm. You can even make pretend if you want to. You can pretend we're like two married people like on the last legs of their marriage. Married folks go in for cross-country trips so they can argue about where to stop an' end up not likin' each other anymore. We could act like them . . ."

I did. I placed my arm around her neck so my fingers were touching the small bones beside her throat. Mary-Ann touched my fingers with the tips of hers. "You smell like VapoRub," I said.

"It's Tiger Balm. See, whenever I smoke a jay-bow, I smear it on the corners of my forehead. And right under my nose. Sometimes other places too. There's two kinds, white and red, but I always get the red, it makes you feel like your face's on fire. It feels weird. You want to try some on you?"

"Thank you, no," I said with great nobility.

For a minute Target was quiet. Then Mary-Ann said, "You know, Hal, I think you an' I'd have these great-lookin' children. I think they'd be like these total stars . . ."

"I thought you didn't want children," I murmured.

"What I said was I didn't want to be this unhappy person with children. What I said was I didn't want to *do* children and have 'em be like my only immortal thing of my life." Mary-Ann was silent. "Hey, so how's that new underwear?"

"It's all right," I said.

"Are you really wearin' 'em?"

In the blackness I nodded and made a sound that meant yes.

"Lemme see if you're tellin' the truth."

She pushed my pants down an inch, until her fingers were touching the black waistband. She lifted it, snapped it back, did it again. "Woo-Woo," she said softly, keeping her fingers where they were.

"Hey," Mary-Ann said suddenly. "You wanna pretend we're married? Like that Prince song? Let's pretend we are. Yoo hoo, honey, are the lights all out?"

"No," I said. Mary-Ann's voice had the vapid sweetness of television mothers, and I didn't want a pretend marriage with someone who talked like that.

"Honey, have you locked the doors?"

"No, I crave intruders," I said, turning over onto my ear.

"Honey, where's little Bobby?"

"Still in the drug rehab." I snarled.

"Come on, Hal, play right." Mary-Ann started in again. "Yoo hoo, honey, where's baby Alexis? She was here a just a minute ago—"

"I sold her down a foamy river," I hissed.

"Where's our sheepdog? Where's Lad? Is that that dog's name?"

"Our dog," I said, "is in the oven. With an apple in her mouth." I turned over, but Mary-Ann maintained her grip on the band of my underpants.

"Y'ever read that book, Hal? *Lad: A Dog?*"

"Nope," I said.

"Y'ever read *Mittens: A Kitten?*"

I didn't answer.

After a while I heard sniffling, so I turned toward her in the dark. Mary-

Ann immediately twisted so her back was to me. By now her shoulders were heaving. "Why've you always been so mean to me, Hal? I thought when you offered to drive me back, maybe there was somethin' goin' on, you know? I really *did* think that. But it doesn't mean that—it doesn't mean it isn't—it doesn't mean anythin' at all. Nothin' means anythin' at all to you, Hal. So what's the point?"

I wondered why it was that when I thought about people making love, it was always from an aerial position. Maybe it was because it seemed from that angle a sadder thing to do. Even when I *was* one of the people, I always imagined myself and the woman being watched from the ceiling and sighed at. In his horrible moment I imagined a huge camera on the ceiling of the Target, concealed in that darkness, and that the ceiling camera fed to a bigger camera, and through the distant prism the tumbled flesh below got smaller, paler, less stately, farther away.

I rolled out of my grapefruit float and into Mary-Ann's lemon version. "Don't worry about anything," I said, putting my hand on her shoulder, the words and gestures of hundreds upon thousands of stunted, helpless men through the ages. "Ssshhh, don't worry . . ."

The alarm clock rang at six, and I tested it. "*Shut up!*" I yelled, and *voilà*, the beeping stopped. I looked around for Mary-Ann but the huge rubber float was empty. I got to my feet and stretched and did the first of five genius exercises I had developed—a painful back stretch designed to give me an Einstein-like stoop. It had rained all night—I had listened to the rain batter the roof of the Target for a long time before I fell asleep. Now a bluish glare filtered through the windows up in front, and a figure in a bicycle came pedaling down one of the pharmaceutical aisles. It was Mary-Ann, panting heavily.

"Mornin'!" she said gleefully. "Just doin' my exercise here."

The bicycle had thick black wheels like a beach buggy, a tiny brass horn, and orange flames on the frame and wheel rims. Mary-Ann's skin was pink. "It's prob'ly about a mile 'round here. I already done five or six laps or somethin' already. That's five, six miles maybe. Brother, all that pedalin' beats me up!" She pushed her wet hair back. "*Woo-Woo*, I'm in a totally great mood this mornin' . . ."

There was beer in her sweat and I could smell it. This is a terrible smell to wake up to—you never know what time it is. I'm never very friendly in the morning, so I just muttered a few soft mews and a brief, rattling purr, and kept walking toward the bathroom. Mary-Ann pedaled behind me, softly. "One bad thing about this place, Hal, there's no showers. And they got this little specky blue soap in the bathrooms. Come on into the snack bar after you're done an' I'll make a little surprise for you. Oh, and Hal?"

I turned around.

Mary-Ann stood up on her pedals and kissed me on the lips. "Mornin'!" She pedaled away.

In the bathroom, I showered in the sink, using the gritty soap and the hard brown paper towels. I sort of sat in the sink, scrubbing parts of myself; I ducked my head under the faucet, then lathered it, then stuck it under the faucet again, then toweled off with stiff brown paper.

"I wanted to make you a real country breakfast," Mary-Ann said. I was sitting on a stool in the Target snack bar, drying my hair with a couple of napkins, and Mary-Ann was standing behind the counter, holding an enormous spatula in her right hand. She was wearing a red hunting cap with the Target bull's-eye logo. Probably she had stolen it from the Fish and Game section. "But all they got here's these frozen burritos. And freeze-dried bacon—all this astronaut-type food. But there's coffee. And there's those little orange Sanka packets if you want to go that sleep-away-the-day route."

She wandered over in front of the griddles. "Here, Hal, I'll be your good-mornin'-sunshine-waitress. I wanna show you what a good actress I can be. You never saw me at that before, and I'm *very, very* good." Mary-Ann looked away, then quickly turned around to face me.

"Mornin', sir. Quite a hot spell we're havin'. What'll it be this mornin'? Are you from these parts? My, what a lovely, talented wife you have! Is she a model slash actress by any chance? It's her beauty makes me think that! Why, with those looks of hers, what else could she possibly be?"

Mary-Ann dropped the waitress voice. "That's referrin' to me, of course. The woman with all the good looks." She picked out a frozen burrito from a pile in the refrigerator. "Say, Hal, you ever see the movie about the guy who meets this waitress in a hick joint, but then there's this hitchhiker with a kinda crazed face who keeps followin' the guy 'round in his car? Frank took me to see that movie about six times or somethin'. This guy, he really likes this waitress a lot, but then this crazed hitchhiker ties her up between the bumpers of a couple of semis and snarls the whole deal into reverse. This waitress comes right apart like a bad knot. She just unties. The girl who played the waitress's the same one whose father got his head sliced off with a copter blade in real life. Vic, who's the same guy who—"

"Why do you care?"

"'Cause that girl was a star," she said simply. "That girl was a star, and so was Vic."

I'd just about had it with stars. "Who you think of as stars," I said loudly, "what these people who you seem to be on this intimate first-name basis with, are nothing but a bunch of cheap dumb-ass lucky people from small, ridiculous towns. They're nothing, do you understand me? Do you have any idea what they buy with all their easy, mediocre money? Do you? They buy the worst possible cars in the world, Porsches or BMWs or Jaguars, *small-man's cars*, they give big, vulgarian tips of two hundred dollars to waiters who are nothing special, they buy fake Tudor houses in the pathetic hope that it'll bring them some mock-antiquity dignity. That's what it means for them to make it—to buy what they've seen people winning on game shows! Have you any idea what they have hanging in their bathrooms? *Framed* Playbill *covers*. They have *framed covers* of all the fourth-rate shows they've ever been in hanging on their *bathroom walls*." I stopped, suddenly exhausted, and then concluded in a lower voice. "If you want to know what bad taste is, there it is. People who want to be *famous* are in bad taste." Is that true? I wondered immediately.

Mary-Ann ducked under and through the counter. "Would you like your frozen burrito now, sir?" she said coolly.

I wasn't really listening. Instead I was wandering around the snack bar, ready to punch out the walls.

"They're not half bad, sir. I've already had about eight myself so far."

"I'm not hungry," I snapped.

At seven-fifteen the overhead lights came on automatically. The Casio Music-makers in the Electronics department started playing at the same time, and from the back of the store the children's organs began their rhythmic, anonymous drumbeat. I had already decided that we should hide out in the back until the store opened, in order to avoid Husky Boy and all the rest. We chose the Record and Tape Department, kneeling behind a giant cardboard cutout of Whitney Houston's head and shoulders and ringlets.

Mary-Ann put her hand on my shoulder. "You didn't really kiss me good mornin'," she whispered. "Not in the right way . . ."

I kissed her and she didn't move her lips away. "Let's do it again," she said.

"Be quiet," I said, just as the front doors opened and the first unfamiliar voices I had heard in a day rang through the long white aisles, and customers began filing into the store. There was a sale day in the Telephone and Gym Equipment sections; the Princess Slim-Lines were discounted fifteen percent, and you could buy eight barbells for the price of four.

"Oh, Whitney-Cat, you're gettin' so bony," Mary-Ann whispered.

We crouched there for another half hour, and then I strolled out of the store with Mary-Ann trailing right behind me, looking like anybody else in Memphis who'd gotten up early to take advantage of these new bargains but who hadn't found anything she liked.

As soon as we'd climbed into Son, I noticed a cop walking toward us, and I immediately thought the worst. The cop knew we'd spent the night inside the

Target, and had been waiting around all night for us to come out so he could throw us in jail. *Your redneck nightmare is finally coming true*, I thought. I'd finally done something illegal, and now I would be made to go canoeing in white water with a family of sex-deprived hillbillies. "Row faster, Elgin," one of the hillbillies would say. "We gotta get this boy out onto the middle of the lake so no one'll hear him scream."

Mary-Ann didn't notice the cop until he'd almost reached the car, and immediately she wet her lips and stared ahead.

"Mornin' to you." He was a small, plump and mournful cop who looked as though he'd been on duty all night. "You have handicapped plates with you?"

I was so relieved I almost vomited. "I wasn't aware, sir," I said, "that this *was* a handicapped space."

The cop pointed down at the drained yellow circle on the pavement. I leaned out of the window so I could nod my head hysterically, but since the window only went down halfway, I could only get my bangs and half my brain out. I silently cursed the worthless Son.

"Mornin', officer," Mary-Ann called across the seat. "How're things with you this fine Memphis mornin'?"

The cop nodded. "Young lady . . ." He took out his pad and bit the top off a black pen. "I'm afraid I'm gonna have to write you people out a summons. There's fines in this state for people who park in unauthorized zones. I see you're both not from here, but in the end, you see, what you're doin' is takin' space away from folks who really are—"

"Well, see, Officer, we're not really breakin' a law here . . ."

I stared at Mary-Ann.

The cop stopped writing. "Say what?"

"I say, we're not really breakin' any laws here . . . 'cause there's this plate involved here."

"May I see it, please?"

"Oh, I wish I could show it, Officer. I wish I could just whip it out and show you, but I can't."

"Where is this plate, then, young lady?"

"The plate? You mean the license plate? You're talkin' about the handicapped peoples' license plate?" Mary-Ann got out of the car and leaned over Son's roof, so she and the cop were having a conversation directly above my head. "You mean the one with the little chair thing on it? Well, there's a little problem there. You can't really see it, that's the thing . . . See, we'd have to kill Hal here to get at it—this is Hal, by the way—and this plate we're talkin' about, it's in Hal's *mind*. His *heart*, I mean. It's kinda like this *inner license plate*—like he swallowed the plate, kind of, and now it protects his heart, 'kay? See what I mean? It's an *emotionally* handicapped thing we're talkin' about here now. See, Hal here has this fear of commitment you *would not believe.* Anytime some poor girl tries gettin' up close to him, he just blows her off. I mean, if you want the plate number it's like, B-A-S-T-A-R-D, you can radio that in to headquarters if you want to . . ."

I smiled anxiously up at the cop, who looked confused.

"See, that's why we gotta park up so close to the damn Target," Mary-Ann continued in a melancholy voice. "Hal, here, he can't even commit to spendin' more than five minutes in one place. Can you believe that, Officer? I barely can myself, but Hal, he needs to have his getaway vehicle up close to the doors, he's gotta have some way of escapin' from people and places, you know, general escape clause and all . . ."

The cop stared at me through Son's clouded, half-open window. "Is there any truth to this, son?"

"Uh, well," I said. "I sort of, not really."

"Oh, it's true, all right, Officer," Mary-Ann said. "The more you show you like Hal, the worse off it is for a person."

The cop bent down to the window. I could smell the coffee on his breath as he peered in. "Well, I don't know if what the young lady says is true, but I hope it's not true, for your sake."

I shook my head. On the one hand I didn't want to get a ticket, but on the other I didn't want to agree with Mary-Ann. Finally I whispered, "Okay, there might be a little . . . shred of truth to that."

The cop was still leaning down to face me through the window. "There is nothin' so fine," he said, "as the love between a man and a woman. Now abideth, faith, hope, love, those three things, but the greatest of these is love."

"You said a mouthful there, Officer," Mary-Ann said. "I'm with you all the way on that one. Love suffereth long and is kind. Love vaunteth not itself and is not puffed up. Except sometimes. I mean, you hope. Not to be a filth-monger or anythin'. You're a good man, officer, you want me to say a little prayer for you?"

"Thank you, young lady, no," said the cop, still staring at me. "What I do want is to extract several promises from this young man. Do you have any wee ones at home?"

"No, we don't . . . not yet," Mary-Ann said, "but we're sure workin' on it. I think family's real important. I mean, what else is there, right?"

"I agree with you on that," the cop said. "But you wouldn't want the wee ones growin' up in an atmosphere of an emotional *trial*, would you?"

"No, sir. See, children know, they pick up—"

"Exactly," the cop said. "Children know. Now, we don't know what it is they know, but we do know they know it."

"Ain't that the truth."

"Son," the officer said, and I almost didn't look up at first, thinking he was referring to the car. "What is it with you? You really got a plate buried in your heart?"

"How do you mean?" I said, by now deeply embarrassed.

"I want you to get out of the car right now and come 'round here, give your young lady a hug."

"Noooo," I crooned into Son's wheel. *Save me, Big Wheel,* I thought.

"I think that's a very good punishment, Officer. You have a real fine sense of what's right and wrong. And tell Hal you'll arrest him if ⸮e's not better to me. Tell Hal it's my birthday and he has to be a good guy to me . . ."

This was the first I'd heard of Mary-Ann's birthday, but at that point I was so angry that I immediately disregarded this information. I got out of the car sullenly and stood there on the pavement, blinking and scowling.

"Young lady, you come over here too."

Mary-Ann came over and stood in front of the cop and me, putting her arms out like a windup doll's.

"All right, son," the cop said. "I order you to hug this wonderful young lady."

Mary-Ann waited with her arms extended, and after a minute I bashed into her. She hugged me hard and laid her head on my shoulder. I tried to pull away but she held on. The cop was beaming. "See how easy it is, son, lettin' go?"

"Yes," I said in a choked voice.

"Let go and let God come, that's my own personal philosophy. Let there be no more spaces between you two people—"

"Like Sting says," came Mary-Ann's muffled voice. "Take the space between us and Fill it up! Fill it up!"

"You won't get a medal in heaven for keepin' love outa your heart, people away from you . . . There is nothin' so fine," the cop repeated, "as the love between a man and a woman. Will you repeat somethin' after me, son?"

"What?" This was turning into a nightmare.

"When I was a child, I spake as a child . . ."

"When I was a child, I spake as a child . . ." I mumbled.

"But when I became a man, I put away childish things . . ."

"But when I became a man, I put away childish things . . ."

"As our most famous and most generous resident, Mr. Elvis Presley once put it so fine: Like a river flows/Surely to the sea. Come on, son . . ."

"Like a river flows," I repeated, gritting my teeth. "Surely to the sea . . ."

"Darlin', so it goes/Some things . . . were meant to be . . ."

I repeated this final couplet.

"We sure miss him here," the cop said. "Elvis . . ."

"He was the greatest," Mary-Ann said. "Totally excellent legend guy . . ."

"Good luck to the both of you," he said.

I managed to extract myself from Mary-Ann as the cop walked off. Furious, I got into Son and glowered for about ten minutes. I almost told Mary-Ann that I was turning around to drive back to New York by myself, that she could get out and walk the rest of the way. She climbed into the passenger seat and sat there, looking ahead, pleased.

"Thank you very much for embarrassing me," I said finally, starting the engine.

"Oh, don't mention it. Anytime. No, but see, Hal, I *did* save us gettin' arrested."

Mary-Ann looked different for some reason, and I realized why. "Aren't you going to slobber up your face with makeup? You're running the risk of looking halfway normal."

"Oh, I don't like makeup. I read someplace it blocks the lungs in your cheeks. Your *pores*."

"Yeah, where'd you read that?"

"I read it a couple a years ago in *Vogue* or someplace. My mom's got *Vogues* all around her store . . ."

"Then why have you worn makeup ever since I've known you?"

" 'Cause it took that long to absorb that piece of information, 'kay?"

We drove down the turnpike, following green signs that directed us all around this sprawling mess of a city. "I hadn't realized you knew the Bible so well," I commented stiffly.

"Oh, that. Yeah, well, I'm a pretty religious girl, and I like that part of the Bible the best: Corinthians thirteen. That was Elvis's favorite chapter too. When I get married, I want the minister guy to read that part to everybody."

"You and about two million other people . . ."

"Well, then it must be good, right?"

"One of the pivotal differences between us," I said, "is that you think if a million people like something it must be great, it must be a work of art. I, on the other hand, believe that if a million people like something, then it's probably terrible, no better than garbage."

"Well, that's a real difference, then, isn't it? It doesn't mean we can't like each other."

I wasn't certain on this point, so I kept my mouth shut.

"Hal, can't we go to Graceland?"

"No," I said. "I'll eat dirt first."

"But I'll prob'ly never get to Memphis again in my life. C'mon, Hal, it'll be fun to laugh at it. Just think, *Graceland*."

Surprised, I glanced over at her.

"Really, Hal. I hear that place is totally ridiculous—all pink mirrors and shit—and I just wanted to go see those people who like, worship him, 'cause their own lives're so, whatever, they're so pathetic, they got nothin' at all goin' on in their lives. That's why I've always wanted to go . . ."

"Is today really your birthday?" I said.

"Yup."

I cleared my throat. "May I see some identification?"

"What kind?"

"Something with a date of birth on it. And a picture. Some proof."

"No, Hal, the picture of me on my license's too bad."

I held out my hand, as though I were the dish dryer.

"No way, Hal. It don't look good. I don't want you lookin' at me when I look like that, you'll just think I look dumb."

"I go to church," a woman on the radio was complaining, "and I pray three to seven times a day . . . so I ask you, why doesn't God give me what I deserve?"

The Christian broadcaster took less than a second to answer. "If God gave any of us what we deserve," he hissed, "we'd all be in Hell!"

"If we go by Graceland," I said finally, "we're not staying long."

"I tol' you, Hal, I don't wanna stay that long there. I just wanna get a fast laugh outa the place—you know, ol' Fatso Hound Dog . . ."

Mary-Ann said these last three words in a wound-up, mocking voice, but when I glanced over, her features were blank.

"Hmmm," I said. "Well, well, well . . ."

I was skeptical about this change of temperament and opinion, but for the first time I became strangely excited about seeing where Elvis Presley had lived. "We can see the multi loci of the King's spectacular drug taking," I intoned. "His red-leather bedchamber, the Leopard Room, his hobbled living-room waterfall, the racquetball court he never once set foot on. We can hear the tour guides gild his life—"

"Yeah," Mary-Ann said with a deep sigh. "They got lotsa TVs there too. Mom tol' me they're all 'round the house 'stead 'a flowers, 'cause Elvis liked to sit at home and watch for hours on end."

The huge black gates of Graceland, decorated with oversize notes and clefs, were wide open and lashed to double stone posts. Up a long, curling driveway was the actual house, giant, remote and white-pillared, resembling the president's mansion at a Southern women's college. I parked Son across the street from the gates, behind a cluster of gift shops, and from the parking lot I could hear thin strains of an Elvis ballad blurting over loudspeakers—the same Elvis ballad coincidentally, that I used to like to sing to Kitty, gripping her aristocratic jaw in one hand and crooning the wise lyrics straight into her mouth while Kitty screamed out the chorus.

We got out of the car and walked in the direction of the gift shops, past a low, bloated pink Cadillac with a plywood board stamped over its backseat, littered with crushed coffee cups and damp pine buds. Enclosed within a high-walled cage to our left were a wide-bodied DC-10 and a Cessna eight-seater, standing there mute in the fog like father and son.

Mary-Ann stared longingly at the DC-10. "S'pose that was Elvis's peanut-butter jet? You know, that time Elvis flew to Denver at like four in the mornin' for peanut butter and jelly sandwiches . . ."

As we approached the shuttle-bus stand I heard a tour guide in a brown uniform tell a group of listeners, "Elvis's great-aunt, Delta-Mae Biggs, still lives up in the main house, the result of an agreement between her and the Presley estate . . ."

"Old Delta-Mae," I whispered to Mary-Ann, "probably pads out about two in the morning, dazed, stumbling over trip wires and red-eyed beams, setting off the burglar alarms . . ."

When she smiled weakly, I gave her enough money to buy tickets for the complete Graceland tour, which included the house, the grounds, the meditation garden, the museum, the trophy room and the half-hour memorial movie. Since the shuttle bus to the main house didn't leave for another twenty minutes, we sailed into one of the gift shops to browse. I saw at once that the mall was constructed in such a way as to funnel all visitors invariably through one of the gift shops. Very clever, I thought, making my way over to the Keep Time With Elvis Counter of the store—Elvis wristwatches and clocks—while Mary-Ann positioned herself in front of the record and cassette bins. As she riffled through the entire Elvis Presley discography I wandered around the back of the store, playing with key chains and place mats and shower curtains tattooed with Elvis's young, handsome, pink face.

Presently I sidled over to her. "Here is your mission: Find the most appalling object here and I will reward you, I shall make you queen . . ."

She produced an Elvis ashtray with a dreamy diagram of Elvis's house in its middle.

"Theah's a contendah, young lady," I said, pointing to a Graceland coffee cup that read MARIANNE.

"They spelt my name wrong," Mary-Ann murmured.

"Those bastards." Delicately I cleared my throat. "Those damnable bastards."

"It's *Mary-Ann* with a little thing between the two words. A little slash." She smiled shyly. "Like actress-slash-model."

"Elvis's personal motto, Takin' Care of Business in a Flash, or TCB, with a lighnin' bolt through it," I overheard the tour guide say, "is imprinted on both the tail of Elvis's private airplane, the *Lisa Marie*, and throughout the mansion itself . . ."

"Taking care of business in a flash," I whispered to Mary-Ann, "so you can go home and shoot out television sets and eat drugs."

She smiled weakly again. She was staring at a photograph of a big, sweaty, red Elvis in his last years, reprinted on the front page of the local newspaper the day he died. "Elvis looks so *sick* in this picture, Hal. God, it just makes you want to *cry*."

"Look," I said, bypassing the stack of newspapers, "we can buy a Presley family cookbook—mashed potatoes and banana sandwiches, all smushed and lathered together. Just add two Demerol, a Valium for that chunky effect, and *mange*, baby, *mange.*"

I didn't know why I was saying these things, but I couldn't stop myself.

"Elvis expired of natural causes on August 16, 1977," the tour guide said. "There is a long history of heart disease in the Presley family. . ."

"Natural causes?" I whispered into Mary-Ann's ear. "Natural causes *in the music business?* Don't you love it?"

In the back of the shop a large cashier with gum in her cheeks steered a little girl in Osh-Kosh B'Gosh overalls over to a brightly flickering jukebox. "Here, honey, press one. Pick your fav'rite, now, and we'll all listen to it—your mom and me and everybody else. And love it. Go on, just reach out your finger and press. . ."

I'm not sure what it was exactly—whether it was the men and women, weary from the humidity, clustered around the tour guide; whether it was the pink-boarded Cadillac raised on cinder blocks in the parking lot; whether it was the familiar music hanging over my head; or seeing a tour guide rush into the gift shop and grab an Elvis record and, while it was being wrapped, call out, "I must be goin' crazy! I *work* here, I hear Elvis all day long, and here I am buyin' a record!" and laugh, dash back out of the store and into the driver's seat of the shuttle bus—but I felt suddenly duly ashamed of myself, as though I'd broken into a chapel with a can of spray paint in my hand and desecration on my mind. All of a suddenly I hated myself.

I went outside and stared across the street at the large, empty white house. A low girdle of fog pushed out from the bushes along Elvis Presley Boulevard, obscuring the trees and road signs. A crowded shuttle bus, ours, crept ticking down the hill from the house. The grounds seemed abandoned, deadened, and when it began to rain, I turned back inside the gift shop and searched my pockets for Son's keys. I felt weak from hating myself.

What was the matter with owning a pink Cadillac? Or crystal chandeliers, or mirrors in your living room, or gold-leaf trim inside your bathroom sink? I recalled Fishie's stern advice when I turned sixteen: "There are four cars available to you as a member of this family, Hal. You may purchase a battered Volvo, a BMW of a certain vintage that BMW no longer offers—but keep in mind that in thieves' parlance BMW means Break My Window. Anyway, there's also the old station wagon or some other sickly car for the beach, which you are only allowed to buy from a relative for a symbolic, gentlemanly amount, say, a dollar, or you may, of course, wait and drive Son. . ."

I went over to Mary-Ann, who was holding up a bright blue Elvis T-shirt to her breasts. When she saw me, she tossed it back onto the pile. "I was jes' holdin' it up to see if I've grown any in NYC. Can you jes' imagine the kinds of people who'd buy somethin' like this?"

I stared at her. And then I chickened out. "Listen," I said. "I'd like to go now. This place is just too . . . too *much* for me. I can't take it anymore. . ."

"But Hal, we got the tickets and everything!"

"We can resell them."

"But you *said* we could."

"It's too much for me," I said. "Whole thing is. I can't deal with it. I'm sorry. . ."

She was trying not to look disappointed. "Maybe we can resell 'em to somebody real pathetic," she finally said. "Maybe we can goose 'em a little, like that lady in the—"

"Whatever," I said, cutting her off. Everything Mary-Ann said made me feel even more disgusted with myself.

"Aww, I wanted to go see all the crumminess up at the house and everything."

"No," I said softly, "it's just too awful, I'm afraid. I think you'd only feel let down." Briefly, staring at her, I struggled against saying something else.

"Wait, Hal, first I wanna check that big magazine store they got over there. Maybe get a copy of the *Daily News*, since it's Thursday an' all. Maybe my thing, my picture's, in there—you know, the Inquirin' Person. . ."

Mary-Ann slumped back a minute later. "They say they get 'em sometimes but not this week, somethin' about the distributor. . ." She brightened then. "They musta had a mega-run on 'em up in ol' NYC. . ."

Leaving Memphis, I realized I hadn't gotten Mary-Ann anything for her birthday. I'm afraid I wouldn't even have thought about it if she hadn't kept reminding me whenever I asked her to do anything, like change the radio station or drive. "I *can't* drive, Hal," she kept saying. "It's my *birthday* today and people do things *for* you on your birthday. Plus, there's too much meat on the street. . ."

It was true: Mary-Ann had spent several hours counting off dead animals on the side of the road. She wanted to break a personal record: forty-one animals on one highway outside of Dentyne, Texas, when she was seventeen. "If you ever wanna stop, Hal," Mary-Ann said at one point, "you jes' gimme the word. . ." Soon she grew bored with road corpses and began playing tic-tac-toe on the inside of the windshield.

I was seeing signs for Texarkana. We were in Pine Bluff, Arkansas, now, passing oil rigs on both sides of the highway, huge black mantises sucking and jolting in the earth, a constant lone prayer, like flies on cheese.

Son had begun to rattle whenever I went over forty, so I couldn't drive as fast as I wanted to. His insides smelled clammy and sweet. Something had gone runny in Mary-Ann's cow purse, and a strawberry smell was stinking up the front seat. In Smackover, Arkansas, the HOT light lit up red on the dashboard like a pint of bright blood. Son, despite his ancient age, still spoke in sullen, babyish monosyllables. The whole inside of him was written out in one-word blurtings. LIGHTS it read under one knob, ASH RAY under another, since Beck had torn off the *T* one time when he was embarking on a weight-lifting program, and glued it to the back of his Nautilus set as an example of a manly, well-defined physique.

I pulled into the first gas station I could find, a Gaseteria outside Smackover, on the road to Pecan Hollow. I got out and opened up the back, where Son's huge, dirty engine sat, and I searched around the parking lot for something that looked like an official water pitcher. I should explain that city boys like me aren't very good with cars. In fact, I don't know the first thing about them. I especially didn't know the first thing about Son, whose eight-hundred-number Parts Hotline had been disconnected twenty years earlier. All I knew about Son was that for some reason the engine was in the rear and the trunk was up front.

I groped around the engine area, looking for the radiator, until finally I wrapped my hand around a knob that looked like a rare black flower. I nearly burned my fingers off.

I went around to Mary-Ann's window and knocked on the glass. She continued to stare off in the other direction, so I went around to the driver's side and opened the door. I said coolly, still clutching my inflamed fingers, "You wouldn't happen to know where the radiator is, would you?"

"Why, yes, I would."

"Well," I said, shuffling in place like a circus act, "might you be persuaded to help me out here a little?"

Wordlessly Mary-Ann drifted out of Son and came around to the back, where she noticed my suffering. "The radiator's there," she said, pointing. "An' it's extremely hot, Hal. That means if you touch it, it'll burn your fingers. It's not really so hard a concept to figure out." Her voice was bored. "Wait, I'm wearin' gloves, lemme—"

"I'll do it," I said. "All I want you to do is point."

"All righty." Mary-Ann stared at me, and without saying anything more, she reached down and turned the radiator cap clockwise. "Sometimes," she said in a low voice, "you're stupid, Hal. Really the king a dumb. Sometimes you jes' say the wrong things to people."

Mary-Ann loosened the radiator cap, and a hard, silent whistle of gray steam spat out as she kept turning. Dark water dribbled out, then another jet of steam, as though Son were Tommy the Tugboat and not a car at all. "Now we gotta have some water," she said slowly. "I shouldn't have to tell any *man* that."

I wandered back into the small, dingy garage. By accident I stepped on the hose, and a bell cried out in the afternoon air. Loitering in the back was a teenager with a pencil in his teeth. When I asked for water, he pointed me toward a water fountain with an antique silver bowl. The boy was even younger than Son was. "For the car," I said. "I'm not thirsty."

The boy went into a closet and brought out a plastic pitcher that looked as though it were used to water azaleas. I followed him outside to where Son was parked.

"Hey, honey," Mary-Ann said to the boy.

The boy's eyes trailed her as she bent over the front of the car, her shirt slipping out from the back of her pants. Then Mary-Ann turned away from Son and lifted up her arms, her eyes half closed, as if to stretch. Her fortune-cookie breasts rose up under her white shirt. The boy's eyes glued themselves there.

"Just pour the water, kid," I snarled. "And get the generator B-40 suspension coils aligned, check the jackscrews—"

"What?" the boy said.

I'm sometimes good at turning situations in which I know nothing to my own advantage, and here I rose up to my full height. "The *carburetor*," I said. "It needs the ninety-eight-point-six-degree spin screws in the torque of the axle; the forward clutch needs abrasion tactic number LC twenty-nine; the digital idle stabilizer's cooked—"

"What are you talkin' about?" the boy said to me.

"Look," I yelled, "do you work here or not? I'm talking about *engine seepage!* The zircon tail ends need refastening! So does the crankshaft flange and the f-glow plug relay! Because otherwise the axial wheel cylinder bearings tilt! The steam piston ends need some force . . . and lube! Lube of the brake of the shift of the power overdrive!"

"Hey," the boy said, "wait."

"Wait?" I raged. "Right on, I'll wait! And have my car fall apart while you stand here figuring out the lessons of first-year mechanic's school!"

"Oh, boy, I'm so sleepy," Mary-Ann announced loudly. "I'd like to just go take a nap somewhere, curl up someplace cozy an' warm."

"There's a couch in the station," the boy said eagerly, obviously delighted that I'd stopped talking.

"You got a key for the little girl's room for a little girl who's gotta go?"

"There ain't no rest rooms here," the boy said slowly, as if this were just dawning on him. "I got, though . . ." He hesitated. "I got a place in the station. Ain't supposed to let customers in there, though."

Mary-Ann came over in front of him and stretched again. "Oh, pleeeze. Pretty please. Please with a cherry on top. With a cherry *and* a banana on top. I'll give you a present if you let me."

"Water!" I yelled at the boy, who was still holding the empty pitcher. "Radiator! The diverter value linings readumbrated at once! Use the B-nine hundred Vatka Cloaca screws! And a Fulcrum Hammerhead so you won't disengage the bindings!"

"The radiator needs water," Mary-Ann told him.

"Oh, right, sure enough." The boy filled the pitcher and began to pour. Then he wrestled a key out of his jeans pocket and handed it to Mary-Ann.

"Aww, you're a sweetheart." She started walking toward the station, her hips swinging as though she were pitching aside soil with them. I'd never seen Mary-Ann walk that way before. At the entrance to the garage she bobbled the key, dropped it, and bent over to look for it on the warm tar. It took her about two minutes to find it, even though I could see the key gleaming on the sidewalk from twenty feet away.

The boy filled up the radiator, then had me start Son's engine. The HOT light flickered, dimmed, then finally disappeared into the general gloom of the dashboard. I told him I also wanted to buy two big red cans worth of gas. This time I bought unleaded and put it on Fishie's gas card. When he returned with the cans, I loaded them onto the backseat, next to my duffel bag. Then Mary-Ann came back out of the bathroom and handed the boy his key.

He stood grinning idiotically in the hot sunlight. "So what's my prize?"

"A big, wet kiss," Mary-Ann said, reaching up on her pony heels and pulling his face down to her. She kissed him long on the lips, and then once, sneakily, on the neck, then she cut him loose. " 'Cause you know so much about cars an' things."

Mary-Ann clambered back inside Son and gazed away from me. She smelled of fresh perfume, and her skin appeared to be glowing. Without makeup she was very pretty. "Where we goin' now?" she said enthusiastically.

We pulled back onto the highway. By this time I was sick of anything resembling a road. We pased by the Pecan Hollow signs, and as we passed another gas station I remembered something. "Oh," I told her, "I got you a birthday present."

"You did? Liar, I thought you said you didn't have any money."

"I don't. I charged it." I pointed behind me.

"What is it?" Mary-Ann leaned over the seat. "Jewelry? Clothes, maybe? I like jewelry an' clothes an'—"

"It's in those two red barrels," I said.

I could hear a slash of breath as she decided whether to touch the barrels or not.

"It's gas," I said. "Two weeks' supply."

"Oh," Mary-Ann said, slumping heavily into the seat. "Thanks."

"I would've got you something else," I said, "If I had any money on me. But all I have is the gas card. And I thought maybe you'd like it because you're such a media glutton. People win prizes like this all the time on game shows. A thousand gallons of gas, for example. Only this is a slightly lesser amount."

"No, it's really nice. Thanks, Hal. No, really, that's fine. Gas is nice . . ." Mary-Ann sounded more disappointed than I'd ever heard her sound before, even in New York. "Maybe I can wear my gas to a party. You know, a gallon over each shoulder like a milkmaid—only it'd be gas and not milk, after all."

"Look," I said, "I'm sorry. But I wanted to get you—"

"Well, Hal, even if you bought me a Cherry Coke, it'd be more personal than a coupla gallons of unleaded, for chrissake."

"So why didn't you ask that pimply adolescent back there for a Coke?"

"At least he knew the first thing about cars. And he was a nice piece of talent, that boy. Woo-Woo."

"Don't talk like that." I realized I sounded like Frank as soon as I said it.

"Why *can't* I talk that way? I can talk any way I goddamn want. Janis Joplin talked that way, an' she was from Texas just like me. She used to say so-and-so was a nice piece of talent, and I'm from Texas, too, so I can talk whichever way I goddamn want to talk."

"Janis Joplin is dead, I'm afraid."

"Hal, all you do's tell me people and things're dead. The Black Stallion, Janis Joplin, Misty a Chincateague, Elvis—*all* my things I like. It's like you got this *death* obsession, and if you're tryin' to make me face reality or somethin', well, just *don't. Don't.* I'm fine just the way I am. And that major piece of talent back there liked me a lot, I could tell."

"That boy back there would like anything remotely resembling a woman!" I yelled. "He'd flirt with a snowmobile if it had hips!"

"You're just jealous 'cause he liked me."

"Fine," I said. "Why don't you let me drop you off here and you can walk back to the station and get married to that little teenage know-nothing delinquent, and in later life, whenever your mobile home is broken, he'll always know what to do. Not to mention the annual auto conventions and trips tv..ce a year to Graceland to lay Quaalude-shaped wreaths. Really, you'll make a nice squalid couple, may you live in peace and harmony forever—"

"Hal, you don't understand a thing. I was just—aw, nothin'." Mary-Ann put out her fists as if to hit me, then pushed them under her thighs. "Nothing."

I drove all night and all day, without stopping for lunch, and entered Texas at dusk the next day.

Mary-Ann started noticing things she knew. In Clinton, about thirty miles into Texas, she pointed out what looked like a small college. "Over there's where we spent a summer once: Swansea Modelin' Camp. Amy Stardust and I went over together. I won a certificate for Most Endearin' Camper. You know, the camper with the best heart. That's basically 'cause I couldn't do anythin' else right . . ."

Now we were passing enormous fields of brown, linted with sheep. Black trees came up out of the soil like horns, and on Country Music KLIP a woman was singing about how she'd recently redecorated her house to look like a bar and grill, just so her husband would stay at home.

By this time I was halfway liking country music, but now I twisted the dial to another station. Life was not a country-western song, no matter how you looked at it, but every station I turned to played another lick about little sisters, about miners coughing blood onto the snow, about drinking and drinking and not being able to forget the girl who chose Bobby or Jimmy or Joe over you. And though I kept searching out Son's windows for local color, there really wasn't any. The whole trip, in fact, had been as study in gray highways. Fishie's guidebooks had lied. The only interesting place in the guidebooks was the National Softball Hall of Fame in Oklahoma City, and the line was too long to wait in. I hadn't seen any *country* at all. All I'd seen was one long road after another, as gray and monotonous as the suits of New Yorkers rushing off to work.

"You smell the air at all?" Mary-Ann said when we came within thirty miles of Dallas. "It's dustier but a lot cleaner. Here, Hal, turn in here!"

I took the exit, past a sign listing the names of ten cities. Patent was one of them, the fourth up from the bottom. I opened my window and breathed deep. I could smell soil in the air, dust, and something sweet like lavender. The wind was blowing across the beaten fields and around the hallowed barns, and the few low, lone houses set back shy in the fields.

"Where are we?" I said.

"Lake Helene. Darcy's the other direction. Kind of a nothin' town. Patent's not so far from here." Mary-Ann dug down in her seat. "It'll be good seein' Mom. See my room again. My stuffed animals. See Eldridge, maybe. Amy. Lorne, even though Lorne's kind of a jerk. I wonder what Mom's got me for my birthday."

"Maybe she'll give you back your old job."

"Yeah, maybe." Now she sounded truly depressed. "So you changed your watch back yet?"

My watch was still on Eastern time—I preferred it that way.

"Wonder what I'm gonna do with all this gas," Mary-Ann said presently.

"Arson, for a start," I suggested.

"Frank set a school on fire once. His fifth-grade classroom. He—"

"I don't ever want to talk about Frank . . ."

"Wait, hold on now. Just slow it down, 'kay?"

I reined Son into ten miles an hour.

"Tuck your shirt in," Mary-Ann said. "And button up your second button—you look like a slob. Don't you have a comb or anythin'? 'Cause you're in Patent, that's why. I want you to look good for my mom . . ." She took a comb out of her purse, reached over and combed my hair. I let her, though I was accelerating all the while.

"So what do you s'pose my fate is gonna be, Hal?" she suddenly asked.

"I just don't know." I didn't know, to tell the truth.

"I'm not some nine-to-fiver, you know. I can't see workin' them hours anyplace."

"Maybe you could try eight to four. Or ten to six."

"No, you know what I mean, Hal. It's just that I can't see myself locked up in an office all day. Gettin' coffee for my boss. Havin' to file a suit against him for molestation and stuff. Not bein' the boss myself. If I was the boss, maybe it'd be all right, but what am I gonna be the boss of? See, I got a lot of talent, I know that, but I just don't know what to do with it yet. You know?"

I knew this for certain. "Yup."

"I didn't mean to get so weird about famous people and all up in NYC. I mean, it's just that I wanna be famous too. That's all I ever wanted, to be a famous person . . ."

It seemed to me we were moving into another country, a country within a country. The sky seemed bigger and darker and more threatening. I felt diminished, and Son must have felt like a speck, bait for a diving bird. The towns flying by had sand on their sidewalks, and sand roads turning off larger tar roads; they smelled like oil, gasoline, rain, cow manure, frying food. We passed shirtless boys outside beer and pool halls, and a group of Mexicans walking along the side of the road, hitchhiking halfheartedly. Train tracks ran alongside the road, dry stalks and grass blades pushing up through the rails, binding the tracks to the earth until the next accident. "Texas is kinda beat these days," Mary-Ann said, noticing my look. "What with oil an' all. The bottom flat dropped out. But it's still a really nice place to live . . . Over there, Hal, is where I used to work. Big-Cat Hamburgers. They made me wear a button that read, MARY-ANN, HOT AND JUICY MEAT. It was so humiliatin', Hal, servin' the public. After I quit, I used to get revenge on 'em by pullin' up in the take-out lane and disguisin' my voice and' orderin' like twenty-five burgers and a hundred boxes of fries, and they'd say, That'll be seventy bucks, come 'round to window one. But then I'd just speed off, hang fire. Real mature, right?"

The sky over Son was suddenly full and white, free of plains and clouds. The only obstructions were the TV aerials on the rooftops, enormous metal nests that might've been built by unimaginably large birds. I switched off the radio, and minutes later I saw the turnoff for Patent.

"Here it is." Mary-Ann sounded deflated.

"Here we are," I said. "This is it. This is what it is. You are here."

"Hope somebody's home," she remarked a minute later. "I tried callin' Mom again but there's no answer. She didn't even have the machine on."

"I didn't think people in little towns had machines. I thought phone machines were city—"

"Mom had to go to Dallas to get it. See, she needs it for people settin' up appointments and rinses and so on." Then Mary-Ann said, "You don't have to go back anytime soon, do you, Hal? I mean, you put us up, Frank and me, in NYC. We'd kinda like to return the favor."

"Don't worry about it," I said.

"Can't you at least spend the night? I know Mom'd want you to. Or longer. I mean, you can stay here as long as you want. I'd surely like that if you did." She put her l and on my knee and kept it there.

We rumbled into Patent at about twenty miles an hour, on a road that was half blond sand, half melted black tar. Meanwhile Mary-Ann pointed out the window at things. "Over there in that seed shop's where the guy who has the weird disease works. The one where you shout things that're dirty without even meanin' to. You go up to this guy for some of those seeds and he goes, Breasts, breasts! Or you're askin' him to repot somethin' for you and he starts screamin', Fuck! Shit! It's that disease that has some French name." She pointed to a house down a dirty lane. "Over there's where I lost my virginity. The window with the shade pulled. To Eldridge. The first Eldridge. He left me there, too, said he had to go fix somebody's ceiling, and I said, Can I go along with you? 'Cause I'd just had this really great time, right? But he said no, and he kinda tossed me a key, tol' me to let myself out after washin' up . . ." Mary-Ann was silent. "So I just sat there in his house cryin' for about seven hours."

We passed Desert Pest Control, Jake's Saddlery, and a bar called the Bike Stop. "That's where all the Mexicans hang out. I think it's maybe a whorehouse too. After a certain hour, that is. Frank told me. They got a cola machine there with five things to push but only one's ever lit, so you get Orange Crush like it or not, which makes me sick it's so sweet in your mouth. See, Patent's gas station even got a sign that turns 'round an' 'round. It flips 'round in the air like it wants to hypnotize you or somethin'.

"That supermarket's where Mom and Lorne met up the first time. At the booze counter. That's one thing I missed about stores here, they sell booze right out in the supermarkets, so you can charge it along with your tomatoes or whatever. Anyway, it wasn't really by accident they met, it was their singles night, 'cause grocery stores are s'posed to be these really great places to meet people. You can make all these comments on what the person you're attracted to's buyin'. Mom read Ann Landers, and she said if you want to meet a good man, join a church group, and Mom said, Later for that. So she waited 'round for singles night at the Grand Union and it worked out."

Three quarters of Patent was dark this Sunday night. Patent had shut up early, or maybe Patent was always partially closed. Driving through Mary-Ann's hometown made me extremely thirsty, since the air and the roads seemed to lack even the promise of water. A coat of dust hung down over everything. Even the neon signs in the bar windows looked as if they were coated with gray. Mary-Ann chattered away. "I feel like I haven't been here in like five hundred years or somethin'. Look, that's Mom's shop over there!"

She pointed out a dark figure of a building, and I slowed down, even though it was difficult to go much slower. "You can't see the sign, but it says THE SNIPPERY. Mom thought that name up. Isn't that a good name for a hairdresser's? It looks good from the road here, too, don't it? Here, you go left here . . ."

I nosed Son onto a narrow street past the beauty parlor. His light swiped across the frames and lawns of the small, shabby houses, only a few of them lit. Son illuminated the wheelbarrows in their yards, silent clotheslines pinned to trees with the draped ghosts of clothes falling limp from them, drying out. In front of another house Son's lone beam swept over a red truck that had been jacked up and abandoned for the night if not forever.

"It's this one," Mary-Ann said, leaning forward in her seat as I pulled up in front of a cinder-block house, the third from the corner. The yellow crisscrossed transom on the porch was shattered, and garbage and bottles were sprawled across the sidewalks. I could at least see the start of a lawn, the low-hedged path leading up to the pale, peeling columns of the porch. The house was as dark as night.

"Aww, hell, doesn't look like anybody's around . . ." Mary-Ann slid out of Son but left the door open. "Usually Lorne's up till all hours screwin' 'round, doin' his accounts. Screamin' at Mom for somethin' or other he thinks she's done wrong when it's usually *him*. Up there's my bedroom." She pointed toward a dark corner of the house. "That window. That little one."

I got out and walked across the lawn until I was on the stone pathway, where I kicked at the low, dead hedge.

"I used to try 'n' walk that walkway so that one foot would land in each square, you know, goin' up to the house. But my legs were never long enough, so at about the fourth square I'd hafta jump with both feet. It used to really make me frustrated. Then my legs got longer, and then I could do it, not easy but I could do it, but by then it wasn't somethin' I wanted to do anymore, right?"

"So where is everybody?"

Mary-Ann stopped and waved me toward her. "Come on. Come on in and meet the people. Here, take my arm. I want Mom to see me bein' escorted . . ."

She tried the front door, but it was locked. "Shit." Then she crossed over the lawn to the side of the house and knelt down by a rusted drainpipe that ran underneath an electric meter. I could hear the meter ticking from where I stood. Mary-Ann started groping around behind the bushes. "I got Mom one of those fake rock thingies, the kind that holds your spares and slides open. It looks just like a real rock too. I got her that and one of those safes that looks like a head a cabbage. Not that Mom ever keeps the house locked or anythin'. Nothin' to steal, anyhow."

Mary-Ann began pitching rocks across the lawn. I could hear the *tump-*

tump-tump as the rocks struck the grass and rolled a few inches. She rose and smeared her hands on her jeans. "I jes' don't know. That dumb rock's usually there. Mom says she uses it all the time, but maybe she's just tryin' to make me feel she didn't hate my present or somethin'."

"Anyone else around here have a key?"

"The Thompsons did. They live over there, but then Junior Thompson, he's my age, he had a party in our house one time when Mom was away, so she made him give it back. It was just 'cause she wasn't invited, that's why she got so royally pissed off." Mary-Ann paused. "I mean, it not like she could *be* anyplace."

"Is there another door?"

"Mom had Lorne seal it up last Christmas. Said the house was gettin' too blowy."

"Maybe they're asleep."

"Yeah, but it's only nine o'clock, right?"

"Well, bang on the door, anyway."

She touched the door with her hand and rapped lightly. I could hear the metal of her leaded-gas mood ring mixed up with her knuckles.

"Harder," I said. "*Knock,* don't tap." Even though the air was warm, I found myself shivering.

She rapped harder. She rang the doorbell only once but held her hand near the buzzer. The single bell echoed through the house. No one came to the door, and no lights flew on.

Mary-Ann started trudging back across the lawn, as though through deep snow. "Well, why don't we just wait here a while till they get back . . ."

I sat all night with Mary-Ann inside Son, outside the door of her house, reclining against the locked driver's-side door with my knees raised over the stick shift. The lights in Tucky's Grill windows blinked, then shadowed, blinked then shadowed, until finally, at three in the morning—Eastern Time, that is—they went off. This wasn't because the place was closed, Mary-Ann told me, but because Tucky wanted to save on electricity. He knew that everybody would know he was open, even when his front lights went dark. Now the whole block was quiet, inked over. A cat screamed from under the bushes somewhere, and scruffy moths skimmed the windshield as if they were toasting us.

The middle of the night was cool, and soon it began to rain. I turned Son's engine on and shuffled the wipers across the dirty glass. Out of all the gas stations we had pulled into, not one had offered to clean the windshield, not once. I made a note to call someone about that, some official bureau that handed out awards for great moments in American sloppiness. I finally pulled the rags out from Son's heat holes, exposing dusty black gills and a series of small lemon-colored wires. Now the heat blew out at the wires, which trembled as the warmth pulled past them into our necks and faces. I had heat coming up my pant legs. Soon it would be winter again, and I knew exactly what to do with those rags—I'd observed both Fishie and my brother in the same predicament. The rags would get balled up and stuffed in the glove compartment until the weather turned warm again. *Where will I be when the weather turns cold?* I wondered. *What will I do for money?* Then I remembered, with dull surprise, Fishie's Dump-the-Joke-Girl check in the glove compartment, with two payments still to come, and I stared bleakly out the window.

Mary-Ann gazed at me through wide eyes that looked serene and magnificent, as though they themselves had been rained into. "So you goin' back, Hal?" She sighed. "What're you gonna do?"

"I will be going back North," I said. It sounded noble when I said it that way, as though it were two hundred years earlier and I was taking a trip of great, ferocious import. "If Son holds up." This time, I thought to myself, I would take an alternate route. I would attempt to see some of my country. I would go southeast, through New Orleans, and up past the small saturated islands off the Carolinas, then back up to a town in the Northeast. Then— and here my imagination hesitated—I would have to live in a city again. Cities, I realized, were the best places to meet people, especially girls. The odds were low that I would ever meet the woman of my dreams over a Cheetos rack in a backwoods grocery store.

How did people decide where they were going to live? The answer was, they stayed in the places necessity had already created, or had recently formed. They stayed deep inside their hometowns, their college towns, the towns where the people that had married lived, towns where their friends were still living, towns where their children could grow up innocent and unbothered. They moved to where work was, and then they forgot their reasons for moving or not moving, and they stayed on in that one place forever.

"Be like Mr. Northeast again, right? You know, Mom was real excited when I called from New York. Both for the modelin' and also 'cause she's always said doctors made the best husbands. That's when I thought you was a doctor. Jeez. Mom's always said, Mary-Ann, Go marry yourself a good doctor from the Northeast sector of the U.S., not some guy makin' boxes."

"I'm sorry," I said, again feeling extremely guilty for some reason. *Put your hand on my knee,* I started thinking. *Please, my knee, it's just sitting there.*

"You don't wanna spend some time down here with me? You wanna start spendin' nights in this car again, do you?"

I didn't answer her at once. It was also dawn, and the lighter air was beginning to define the dull, shabby paint on the sides of the little houses, columned to look nobler than they were. Phone wires sagged along the treetops like broken strings on a guitar. The earth was sweet-smelling and the colors of the ground were far more vivid than the soil and drained green hillsides up north. A stuffy purple color was dragging across the huge sky, distinguishing the houses that had blended together in the dark. Two houses away a truck was parked; a soggy, blue, wide-eyed teddy bear was lashed to the front bumper. Birds were grinding up their hearts to sing, and Son was a cave and the heat breathing onto my lap was as warm and comforting as a moss.

"Hey, it's sunrise," Mary-Ann said, pointing. "Look. Over there, comin' up over Mindy Raype's house . . ."

We must've been looking at two different sunrises. From where I was sitting, all I saw was gray, and muted, blubbery, purple streaks.

"Kind of a pathetic sunrise," I murmured, "if you ask me."

"I like it, Hal. It's like a real movie moment we're havin' here, you 'n' me. I like it here when no one's up, when it's real, real early. It's nice 'round here, the birds an' all. You can have a dog, and if the UPS comes 'round, your next-door neighbor takes it in for you. Everybody knows everybody. So why don't you just stay down here a little? *Please?* I'll make you a bed. That's only if you want. I've told Mom about you already. I tol' her so much, Mom goes, Mary-Ann, why are you tellin' me all this stuff? And I go, 'Cause I like him tons, Mom, that's why."

Son was crouching, purring on the cool pavement, still dark with rain. To save the motor I turned him off, turned everything off but the heat and the radio. There I was, within a perfect construction: girl, boy, "fun" car, but no buyers.

"I wonder if I could land a job out in LA. LA's like the home of the stars, right? They all have these houses on stilts. That's where Sylvester lives. I mean, just to take a name out of the air. And Madonna's out there. And Merv. I think it'd be fun to hang out with them two. Go joggin' with her, whatever, maybe she could teach us Italian, Merv could teach us how to spin the Wheel of Fortune wheel. I mean literally too."

"Maybe you could," I said. "Get a job there, I mean."

"Maybe Amy'd come along. And Mom. We could leave Lorne behind. And we could all live in Beverly Hills. Or Malibu. Hobnob with the celebs. You could come out and live with us. Lounge around in our big Olympic-size swimmin' pool. Hey, your sister can come, too, if she wants. Give us all swim lessons."

"Yeah," I said, "all that could happen."

"Do you love me any, Hal? A little bit?"

"You really want to know that?" I said.

"Yeah. That's what I wanna know."

I didn't say anything. "Look—" I started to say.

"The reason I wanna know's that if you do . . . whatever me a little, then you won't say much about me later on. You won't be able to describe me to anybody. Mom says the people you like the most you can't describe, really. You end up havin' to say stuff like, You'll just hafta meet 'em to find out what I'm talkin' about. The people you like less, you take 'em right apart. So the reason I'm askin' ain't personal. It's general as hell. I'm just generally askin'."

I thought for a long time. Son purred, hanging low over the damp, silent cement. The pathetic sunrise rose up over the flatland houses, blooming into different hues of gray and purple. I shut my eyes and tried to think of how I would describe Mary-Ann to anyone I knew. How would I describe her to Fishie, or Beck, or my parents? How would I describe Fishie or Beck to other people, for that matter? I couldn't imagine how I might. I simply wouldn't know what to say. I kept my eyes shut. A minute later Mary-Ann tried to peel them open, but I clenched my lids tight. Blinded—like Homer, like a genius—I couldn't even think what Mary-Ann was like, even though I'd just been looking at her just a millisecond earlier.

"So I wonder what LA'd be like," I said.

17 December

Dear————.

Greetings from the gloomy woods of Greenwich, Connecticut, where I am spending the holidays again in virtual seclusion. It has been two years since my last Christmas letter, and that bicentennial has been filled with many amazing and troubling events. Outside, it's snowing, huge flabby flakes destined not to last long, falling within an entirely confusing afternoon, when the other half of the sky is a mild bluefish color, the high tips of the branches bathed in a despairing orange afternoon light, the faces of the Irish merchants and the Metro North conductors with the set, freckled look of gravestone . . .

It has been a difficult two years, hot with funerals—Lisa's foremost among them. The main reason I did not write last year was, of course, Lisa's freakish, unlucky death . . . untimely as all get out. As most of you know—read no further if this is "old" news—Lisa was "killed" last year in the very basement of our house, Egret's Nook, or as my late wife stubbornly insisted on calling it, the Big House (even though I pointed out to her at least a thousand times that there are no other houses anywhere near it), "killed" while attempting to rearrange some very heavy boxes stacked on shelves about our aged, white, chubby, hum-

ming freezer . . . these junk-laden boxes, twenty-six of them in
all, fell onto my wife's head and shoulders, burying her under a
glimmering mud slide of good silver, ice buckets, serving trays,
old musical instruments (including my Stratocaster, which
snapped its—expensive—neck in the fall), and the coup d'état,
Father's ancient windup gramophone, with its pegs and nails for
needles, turntable cover like a downy putting green (they don't
make 'em like that anymore, I'll tell you that much!) Fortunately
this deadly, monogrammed rain shower killed Liza instantly . . .
she had no idea what had befallen her . . . or what had "fallen
on her" (English: a fun, sometimes dopey language!) . . . Also
killed in torrential, silvery avalanche was our old maid, Fresca
. . . sad to say, the agency that sent that old woman to us has
vowed never to send another my way ever again . . . am still
quite "pissed" about agency's sheer contrariness.

Lisa's funeral was tedious. Outside, it rained. I never realized
my wife had so few friends . . . service rivaled Eleanor Rigby's
for sheer number of no-shows . . . Later I rented a helicopter
and scattered Lisa's ashes over the varsity hockey field lawn at
Miss Porter's School, where Lisa kept attentive, almost per-
cussive ritual at the mouth of the field-hockey goal—during the
best years of her life . . .

Assorted Family News: My brother Hal is living in LA with
new wife and kitten . . . married last year in a brutally simple
ceremony in Texas . . . we all like Mary-Ann very much,
though of course she took some getting used to at first . . . she is
perhaps too "unpretentious" for the East Coast, so the West, the
steaming, sinister city where they are living, the dull, unreflec-
tive pleasures of its daily suns, seems right for them both . . .
Hal had three concurrent shows last summer, and in October
was commissioned by three shifty Arab businessmen to "wrap"
the Gaza Strip with cheesecloth. Too, Fishie convinced Father
to let Hal have his share of the kitty, as it were, pointing out
Hal's marriage as a benchmark of something or other . . . Fishie
now spokesman for Diet 7-Up, a drink she actually enjoys, or so
she says . . .

Baby is excellent as well . . . a brilliant boy, complex and
multilingual. . . . As many of you already know, the baby was
christened Garon, thanks to Lisa's unseemly, almost Midwestern
Anglophilia . . . but now that Lisa's gone, I've renamed the
child Spot, a good name, I think, arrived at by group consensus,
in memory of wonderful dog I loved as a child . . . Fishie, Hal,

his wife and I plan to raise him together, so he will get the best of all of us. Lucky boy!

As George Eliot said, "Our lives will have nothing in them like the beginning," and the first time this strikes me as perhaps not so uniquely bad an arrangement . . . A very merry Christmas to everyone . . . a wonderful year to you all up ahead . . . this may well be the last of these letters since I foresee Spot taking up more and more time . . . but I will keep you all in mind in years upcoming . . . I hope you, too, keep me in mind . . . and especíally in mind the powers of family, and of love.

Beck Lorin Andrews
Greenwich, Connecticut